PRAISE FOR BLACK STREAM

"*Black Stream*'s feverish prose will transport you to a realm of psychic synesthesia that is at once fantastical but also a mirror of our own world: full of dark secrets and emotional phenomena. [Balstrup's] characters are deeply developed, her world so tangible you can taste the sacrificial blood, and her narrative set on an arc of spiritually epic proportions. This is fantasy of transcendental scope and exquisite execution."

— JOSEPH SALE, AUTHOR OF THE BOOK OF
THRICE DEAD & VIRTUE'S END

BLACK STREAM

VELSPAR - ELEGIES
BOOK 2

SARAH K. BALSTRUP

First published in 2025 by Burning Mirror Press, ACT, Australia.

ISBN Paperback 978-0-6454747-2-5

ISBN E-book 978-0-6454747-3-2

ELSHENDER
GRISLET
LADAIN
BRAEDAL
ASKIER
AVISHAE
BRIVIA
LINDESAL
SELTSLAND
NOTHELM
VAELMYR
MAGLORE

A SHORT HISTORY OF
VELSPAR

The Visions of Skalen Karasek: When Time Began

In the beginning, there was no Velspar. Only clans at war and endless, senseless, savagery.

Skalen, of the Karasek clan, lived in cursed times when the blood of battle ran hot, and babes withered in their mother's wombs.

The clans came swarming over the peaks and crags of Jokvour, all intent on claiming these lands for their own. Normally, Skalen anticipated the enemy through portents and dreams, and yet he had not foreseen this. The Battle of Jokvour raged both night and day, with heavy losses on all sides.

Wandering among the battle-dead, Skalen was overcome by unutterable despair. Covered in blood, he fell to his knees, seeing all about him the vacant eyes of his kin, the brutalised flesh of those who had rushed the mount. When would it end?

He wept the tears of the forsaken and lay down. His clanfolk, all injured and destitute, gathered around him and watched as he fell into a fever. In the heat of his suffering, Skalen dreamed.

He saw the battlefield and the bodies that lay around him, just as they had been when his eyes were open. And yet it seemed that light arose from them, escaping into the sky. A powerful sense of grief redoubled in him and for a moment, the light paused its journey, waiting, as if called.

To his wonder, a great bird came down, one he recognised from life. The kshidol gathered the escaping dust and swallowed it. As he watched, the kshidol's belly swelled with light that coalesced, forming the shape of a child. Like a great black egg, the kshidol's belly cracked and a boy child was born. On soft winds he fell as the kshidol gazed upon the water. There, Skalen noticed the light of spirit trickling from the battlefield, recalled to the sea. Beneath the waters, a colossal siatka opened her mouth and swallowed the light, as the kshidol had done. The girl child she bore rose upon the waves to greet her brother.

And then he knew: to these beings we must return.

Seeing the smile upon his lips, Skalen's people stroked his forehead and tried to rouse him but he was taken by a second vision, one so powerful it made his body tremble.

Light swarmed like fire, gushing from the earth's heart. It sparked in snaking streams, ensnaring the forms of the living world. Where the light found no purchase, it returned to its source. In some, the light lingered. Skalen recognised himself in this holy substance. Though his heart pounded with terror, he felt the word arise within: VELSPAR. The name, the breath of life, the spiritual blood that flowed and flowed like a Great Stream.

When Skalen awoke, his face was transformed. His eyes were clear and he spoke with holy purpose. All who lay in twilight there upon the mountain harkened to him. He spoke, and his words were like a spell that only the bright ones could hear.

The clans who fought and lost in Skalen's lifetime were forgotten to history, leaving only those who praised his name. These are the Seven Clans, their rulers gaining the title of Skalen as demonstration of their new faith:

The Braedals of	Nothelm
The Ladains of	Vaelnyr
The Askier of	Seltsland
The Hirvola of	Lindesal
The Esrene of	Maglore
The Karaseks of	Brivia
The Elshenders of	Avishae

The Rise of the Intercessors:
An Age Without War
(The Beginning - Mid-500s)

Skalen lived and died, and it seemed every year the children of Velspar were suffused with greater holy light. They dreamed in vision and could heal the sicknesses of the soul.

Those attuned to the spirit became Velspar's intermediaries. They developed secret rites to test and strengthen their arts, and only those able to pass through the Seven Gates of Wisdom could bear the title of Intercessor.

First	sympathy
Second	to know a vision's source
Third	to instil a vision
Fourth	to administer blood rites
Fifth	to know the nature of evil
Sixth	to draw out redness
Seventh	to cause evil's dissipation

Through sympathy, observation, and the laying of hands, the Intercessors learned to manipulate spirit according to their will. Under the Intercessors' watchful gaze, no passion was left to blossom into violence. They had ended the age of war and in doing so, gained insurmountable power, becoming the healers, judges, and executioners of the Seven Lands.

The Skalens managed trade, providing shelter and sustenance as clan leaders of the past had always done. Having little need for a standing army, the Skalens' Guard came to serve the Intercessors in maintaining order. When men fought in the streets, it was the Guard who dragged them to the Temple dungeons. Once the Intercessors had leeched them of their redness, they found no reason to fight and were returned to their families.

The Guard were sworn to a code of dispassion where none may take a lover, and where violence must arise, not out of personal conviction, but as an expression of the Skalens' will.

Working with the Intercessors, the Guard developed their own spiritual discipline. In order to remain impervious to redness, they sought to maintain a state of emotional equanimity known as Hiatus.

By contrast, the Skalens had no training in the sympathetic or visionary arts, having delegated their power to the Intercessors and the Guard. They held symbolic supremacy as representatives of the Seven, their principal area of responsibility to maintain the Tally, ensuring the fair distribution of resources across the Seven Lands. The Council of Skalens passed decrees but often they merely formalised the Intercessors' practices.

Rites of the Temple

The Seven Temples of Velspar were built of white marble, each circular level representing one of the Gates of Wisdom. There, the Intercessors presided over rites of birth and death, acting as the sole conduit between a person's spirit and the totality of Velspar. It was they alone who communed with the Holy Ones and who determined a spirit's ability to be reborn.

Blood Rites

The spirit flows as blood does flow. It is life-heat, and consciousness, and yet to know even this much is forbidden to the uninitiated. The Intercessor works with spiritual blood, rousing and calming it as need requires. The Intercessors' early experiments revealed that by consuming a drop of blood, a person's spirit could be discerned, touched, or even controlled. This knowledge was concealed in the rite of Blood Call.

Blood speaks the name of a spirit and when a child is born, this name must be communicated to the Holy Ones.

Each year, on the anniversary of their birth, the people of Velspar dedicate a small amount of blood to the Intercessor's offering bowl where it is prepared with meat paste and Alma. Those who share the same birthday are called Blood Kin and every year they perform this rite together, breathing of the Alma and taking pilgrimage to the sea and sky altars. At Blood Call, the Intercessors use Alma smoke to draw down the kshidol. To bring the siatka to shore, they pour Alma wine into the sea. As the blood offerings are consumed, the Intercessors perform the sacred chants to the beating of drums. Thus, the Holy Ones are reacquainted with the spiritual scent of the faithful, so they might be recognised in death and returned to Velspar.

Sea and Sky Burial: Rebirth
For the dead to be reborn, the Intercessors dedicate the spirit: to Mother Siatka if they are to return as a girl child, or to Father Kshidol if they are to be reborn as a boy. The Intercessors begin the rite by bleeding the body. They divide the flesh into seven pieces, wrapping them in linens soaked in holy Alma oil. The pieces are left to decay and collected blood is mixed with meat paste and Alma leaves.

Sky burial takes place at the mountain altar where the kshidol come down to consume the meat paste and the flesh parcels. Sea burial takes place at the sea altar where the parts are similarly dedicated to the siatka. Burial is witnessed by the whole community who recognise that Velspar has accepted the spirit.

Execution: Cleansing of the Stream
When redness contaminates a spirit beyond the remedy of Intercession, that spirit must be destroyed to prevent the contamination of the Stream. First, the person is stripped of redness. While the spirit is in this state of shock and disconnection, their throat is slit and they are set to bleed out in the Temple blood-troughs. The spirit seeks its centre and cannot find it, the spirit flowing down the drains, partly retained in the corpse, and in spiritual residue within the Intercessor's own body. The Intercessor must cleanse themselves to be rid of this taint.

   The condemnation of the spirit must be witnessed, just as holy burial is witnessed: by the whole community. The public annihilation of the spirit is performed by burning the corpse at the stake.

The Maglorean Heresy: Mid-500s

The Skalens Esrene of Maglore had long coveted the power of the Intercessors. Such was the arrogance of the High Intercessors in that period that they came to refer to Skalen Karasek as the "First Diviner," implying that he was merely the first and by no means the last. Sensing that they might soon contend with a "Second Diviner" from the priesthood of Intercessors, the Esrene sought to unlock the powers of Intercession. Based on their suspicion that Intercessors were those born with multiple souls in a single body, they sought to imbibe the spirits of others, taking them into their own flesh.

If, in burial rites, the spirit could be dedicated to the Holy Ones, then it could be dedicated in other ways. Taking this idea to its natural conclusion, the Esrene consumed the blood, and in time, the flesh of their people. They wanted power and through their acts they grew feverish with redness, corrupting a large portion of the Maglorean Guard.

The Council of Skalens bickered, speaking of the First Diviner's attitude to war. They could not simply execute one of the Seven.

The Intercessors would have to solve this, they agreed, and yet the Intercessors were not numerous enough to do so alone.

Fearing that no one would come to their rescue, the Greslet family of Maglore gathered together a people's army and stormed the Skalens' House. The Esrene and their guardsmen drove the Greslets back into the forest. Eventually, the Greslets defeated the Esrene in the catastrophic battle of Marain.

The Council of Skalens accepted the Greslets and blessed their clan with the rite of hereditary rulership over Maglore. Knowing that Skalens must be defended by guardsmen impervious to Intercession, the Greslets took a number of original guardsmen into their ranks along with the fiercest fighters from the Battle of Marain. This dark chapter contributed to the unorthodox nature of the Maglorean Guard's training regimen that some believe has lost its spiritual focus.

*The Purge of the Intercessors:
Preceding Events*

Skalen Reyan Ladain of Vaelnyr: Early Life

In the lands of Vaelnyr, young Temple adept, Reyan Terech, had commenced the rites of initiation. In attempting the Fifth Gate he had been prepared to stare into the darkness and know the nature of evil. Though he called upon his faith, he could not withstand the truths he witnessed.

The Fifth Gate of Wisdom

The small part of the rite that he relayed to his father, Galen, whitened the man's face. According to Reyan, the Intercessors had reached the Fifth Gate and had invited the darkness in, but they had never mastered it. They used their arts to hide their true purpose, to use Intercession as a means of feeding the animal within.

Determined to protect his son, Galen removed Reyan from the Temple and took him to start a new life among the Skalens' Guard. Galen trained his son in the ways of Hiatus and yet Reyan's fear and hatred for the Intercessors never left him.

Training in Hiatus

Working in the Skalens' House grounds, Reyan caught the attentions of Vivienne Ladain, the Skalens' heir. Galen had taken his Guardsman's Oath but bid his son to delay, knowing a better life awaited him.

When they were of age, Reyan and Vivienne married and soon ascended their position as the Skalens of Vaelnyr. They had two daughters: Lucinda and Sybilla. From the first, Reyan saw that Sybilla bore the Intercessor's gift and kept her at a distance. He put her training in his father's charge where Sybilla learnt the rudiments of Hiatus. And yet there was nothing Reyan could do to hide his psychic scars from his youngest daughter. Though she did not understand their nature, she took on his fears and carried her father's pain.

Marriage to Skalen Vivienne, Children: Lucinda and Sybilla

Now that he was in a position of power, Skalen Reyan sought to rid the Seven Lands of Intercession. Carefully, he began gathering allies. Following the illness and death of Skalen Jagoda Hirvola of Lindesal, Reyan tried to obtain the support of her widower, Skalen Cerek, with little success. Reyan then set his sights on the Greslets. Young Domhnall Greslet would soon inherit power in Maglore and Reyan knew that the Greslets had long suffered feelings of inferiority among the Seven. After a few secret meetings, Domhnall had sworn Maglore to Reyan's plan.

Reyan's Plot Against the Intercessors

Maglore Allies with Vaelnyr

Skalens Damek and Lenna Braedal of Nothelm were the

Nothelm Allies with Vaelnyr

next to ally with Vaelnyr. Damek had run afoul of the Intercessors on numerous occasions. They claimed that Damek's interests in seafaring and star reading were heretical. *Velspar returns to its centre*, they reminded him, *to move outward is an act of dissipation that weakens Velspar.*

Edict Against Sea Faring and Star Reading

Damek agreed with Reyan that it was time for the Skalens to assert their supremacy. Reyan appealed to him with the religious argument that Skalen Karasek had but one vision: that of a united Velspar. The vision of the siatka and kshidol was an ancient heresy that must at last be stamped out. "The First Heresy," Reyan called it. The siatka were reeking sea serpents and the kshidol, filthy carrion birds. They existed before Skalen Karasek knew the name of Velspar. They were animals, and to elevate them was anathema.

The First Heresy

The Holy Ones as Animals

There were many in Velspar who had felt a shiver of disgust during burial rites, and none more strongly than Damek Braedal, who was a man of intellect and who had long viewed the Intercessors' rites as empty pageantry. He liked Reyan's notion of "The First Heresy," how neatly it disposed of all that bothered him, whilst retaining the doctrine of Velspar's unity. Without the Intercessors and their grotesque rites, the people could once more look to their Skalens as the true source of holy wisdom. In his mind's eye, Damek envisaged the coast of Nothelm cleared of the siatka and gladly joined Reyan's cause.

Damek's Wish to Rid the Sea of Siatka

Meanwhile, in Brivia, the elderly Skalens, Emryl and Medard Karasek, had enjoined High Intercessor Waldemar to commence their secret initiation. Already, they had passed the First and Second Gates of Wisdom, with Emryl's intuitions sharpening by the day. It was she who first intuited Reyan's plot and who sent Waldemar to deal with the situation. Using Intercession, Waldemar mesmerised one of the Attendants of the Skalens' House in Vaelnyr, who locked the Ladain family in their chambers and set the place on fire. Skalens Reyan and Vivienne, and their daughter Lucinda, all perished in the fire.

Karasek Skalens' Secret Initiation by H. Int. Waldemar

Karasek Counter-Plot

H. Int. Waldemar Murders the Skalens Ladain

The Fire of Vaelnyr

Only Sybilla escaped with the assistance of Head Guardsman Peran, her late father's best friend and confidant. Fleeing to Maglore, Sybilla called upon the other Skalens to seek justice against those who had murdered her family. Unable to know for certain who it had been, Sybilla

Sybilla Ladain's Escape with H. G. Peran

let herself be taken up by her father's fears. With Guardsman Peran confirming the rightness of her plan, they set in motion the Purge of the Intercessors.

The Council of Vaelnyr: The Year 700

Following the Fire of Vaelnyr that killed her family, Sybilla brought together the Council of Skalens and presented them with an ultimatum. Using her father's words, Sybilla claimed that Skalen Karasek only had one vision: that of Velspar's unity. The deification of the siatka and kshidol was a heresy devised by the first Intercessors, whose modern counterparts now sought to overthrow the Skalens. The Fire of Vaelnyr proved that all Skalens were at risk. With the Greslets and Braedals her sure allies, Sybilla presented the Skalens with two flakes that they must swallow made of the flesh of the Holy Ones. In doing so, they demonstrated their allegiance to the Skalens and their rejection of "The First Heresy." To the Council it was clear that the Guard had already chosen their side by slaying the siatka and kshidol in preparation of these ghastly tokens.

Skalens Emryl and Medard Karasek of Brivia, and Skalen Cerek of Lindesal were the first to give their lives in allegiance to the Intercessors. The remaining Skalens swore themselves to Sybilla's cause: the Greslets of Maglore, the Braedals of Nothelm, the Askier of Seltsland, and the Elshenders of Avishae.

Carrying out the Skalens' execution order against the Intercessors, the Guard were prepared for the worst. And yet, when they arrived at the Seven Temples, the Intercessors held out their palms and smiled. "The Eighth Gate is opened," they murmured, as the Guard took them one by one to the blood trough. By the thousand, Intercessors were slaughtered and burned. Every citizen who wished to live was required to give their oath to the Skalens, taking the dried flesh of the Holy Ones upon their tongue. Many of those who remained faithful to the Intercessors perished at this time through mass suicides, especially in Brivia, the homeland of the First Diviner.

In all the Seven Lands, only three Intercessors resisted the pull of the Eighth Gate. High Intercessor Waldemar of Brivia, Intercessor Maeryn Rosemond of Vaelnyr, and Intercessor Amand Angenet of Seltsland.

Years of solitary wandering eventually led these survivors to meet, and in the Mountains of Jokvour they shared their grief, finding that the flame of Intercession had not gone out.

The Meridian Decree: The Year 707

The Meridian

Haunted by the Purge, Sybilla turned to a device known as the Meridian to cool the redness of her conscience. The Meridian includes three flat, circular fragments of blinding stone placed at the forehead, crown, and nape, held in place by leather straps.

Blinding Stone

Blinding stone, when properly mined, can attune to the spirit, having a soothing effect on the emotions.

Use Among the Intercessors

Intercessors traditionally used the Meridian after working with redness, as a part of their recuperation. Intercession involves the interflowing of psychic energies, requiring the practitioner to become porous and open. The Meridian seals the mind, generating feelings of calmness and seclusion. Sybilla, in fearing the consequences of the Purge, sought to calm the populace by institution of the Meridian Decree. From the Year 707, citizens of Velspar were to wear their Meridian on pain of death.

The Alma: Uses and Effects

During Sybilla's reign, use of the sacred Alma plant was repressed but was not entirely outlawed. The Alma, when inhaled as smoke, imbibed as oil, or mixed with wine, brings about a state of openness and trust, with increased doses having anaesthetic and visionary properties. Excessive concentrations bring about temporary paralysis and a sensation of spiritual liquidity.

Festival Original Form

Once a year, the people of Velspar would gather around Alma bonfires to celebrate Festival. There, joyful redness could be released through dance and revelry, the event presided over by the Intercessors. Following the Purge, Sybilla restricted Alma use to meetings of the Skalens' Council. In exchange for her agreement to sign the Meridian Decree in 707, Skalen Rebekah Elshender of Avishae asked that a new version of Festival be instated, one where the Alma could still burn.

Festival Reform

When Festival returned, it became a sombre rite where redness was released through silent confession, the guilt and wrongdoings of the year symbolically burned away when

Effigies

the person's effigy turned to ash in the bonfire's flames.

The Southland Rebellion

When Skalen Rebekah Elshender and her husband Ulric signed Sybilla's decree to execute the Intercessors, Rebekah was pregnant. Fearing for her young children, Zohar and Ambrose, she agreed to act against her conscience. Prior to the events of the Purge, High Intercessor Camis of Avishae had come to her speaking of the prophecy of the Eighth Gate. He claimed that the Intercessors were about to undergo a great spiritual transformation, and that if a situation arose that would destroy their bodies, she was not to intervene to protect them. He spoke of a new age of enlightenment where the spirits of the Intercessors would *flood the many wombs* so that all children born would possess the gift.

Reluctantly, Skalens Rebekah and Ulric did as Intercessor Camis bid them but this created a rift between Rebekah and her father Landyn Raeburn. As patriarch of the Raeburn family, he set up a gated community in Baden forest where no mainland reforms would be implemented. Whilst rejected by her family, Skalen Rebekah protected the Raeburn camp, allowing use of the Alma and freedom from the Meridian. Years later, Rebekah sent Zohar and Ambrose there to learn of their religious heritage in the hope that one day things would return to the ways of old.

Secret Allies of the South:
Avishae, Brivia, and Lindesal

As an island community, Avishae relied on Brivia for resources. Through trade communication, the Skalens Elshender became acquainted with the Regents of Brivia, Olinda and Jemryn Greslet, and their son Illiam.

Following the execution of the Brivian Skalens at the commencement of the Purge, their eldest son, Andrin Karasek, began his short reign by rallying his people to suicide as proof of their faith. Andrin's younger brother Sidney, thirty-nine years old at the time, tried to stop the bloodshed but Andrin had worked the populace into a frenzy that only subsided when he took his own life.

When the Council of Skalens sought to pass leadership to Sidney, he fled into the wilds of Thrale Forest. To restore order, the Council installed Regents Olinda and Jemryn Greslet to rule in Brivia, calling for Sidney's swift execution.

Olinda insisted that Sidney had taken his oath of allegiance to the Skalens with the flakes upon his tongue. When her objection was taken to Council, a majority decision could not be reached and the matter was delayed indefinitely.

Heartened by Olinda's bold refusal to execute Sidney Karasek, Rebekah Elshender held out hope that she might find others in the South who resisted the new order. Over the years, Rebekah and Olinda revealed their true convictions to one another, sharing a commitment to return to the ways of Intercession. At this time, Olinda revealed that the Regents of Lindesal share common cause and that Voirrey Braedal of Nothelm was a fierce proponent of Intercession. Together, these allies kept their heads low, rallying their people but swearing them to secrecy.

The Voyant Stone
Ambrose and his elder sister Zohar grew up in a world full of ghosts. At the age of eleven, Ambrose was sent to his grandfather, Landyn Raeburn, to learn the ways of Intercession. He soon discovered the limits of his grandfather's knowledge and began walking his own path. Ambrose's intuitions led him to a

hidden cave where he discovered an unusual stone. Feeling the stone's uncanny power, he came to believe that this was the Voyant Stone that Intercessor Janek had written about in his book of Visions some two hundred years earlier. With no living Intercessors to learn from, Ambrose clung to the scraps of knowledge his grandfather had shown him from the Temple books. Glimmers of knowledge that he must follow wherever they led. Using the stone to deepen his visions, Ambrose endured waves of elation and revelatory torment. After swallowing a fragment of the stone, his spiritual awakening quickly turned sour as his meagre training faltered in the face of the stone's overwhelming power. He died there on the hill surrounded by the spectral forms of the kshidol.

Illiam Greslet was visiting as an emissary from Brivia when Zohar discovered her brother's body lying under an oak tree. Her grief and terror was magnified by the power of the stone, which seemed to reach out to Zohar and Illiam, merging their spirits together. In a stroke of insight, she ordered her brother be covered with blinding stone.

The population of Avishae laid their Meridians upon his body, quieting the restless Voyant Stone.

Ambrose's Cairn

Sensing the power of the stone, Landyn stole among the crowd, slipping away with one of the three fragments in his pocket. In his hut, he had prepared a ritual using Sybilla's blood with the intention of killing her. Before he could use the stone to amplify the spell, Rebekah, Zohar, and a company of guards burst in. Still under the stone's thrall, Zohar reached for the blood-tie, feeling she must protect it from her grandfather. After she swallowed it, Zohar felt afraid and confused. Rebekah took the stone into her possession and forbade her father from seeking it out, knowing its corrupting power.

Sybilla's Blood Tie

Zohar Swallows Sybilla's Blood Tie

In the wake of Ambrose's death, the whole of Avishae sank into grief. The Skalens Elshender placed their son's cairn under constant guard, building what they called the "public cairn" where the people could pray without coming too near the dangerous stone fragment still trapped in Ambrose's belly.

The Public Cairn

Skalen Sybilla Ladain of Vaelnyr

In the days of the Purge, Sybilla's rage seemed limitless. But in the aftermath, all was hollowness and uncertainty. The only person she allowed near was Guardsman Gavril, who eventually won her heart. It was a transgression of Gavril's vows to take a lover, and for that lover to be a Skalen spoke of the Guard's true ambitions. She tried not to think on it. Life was suffering and Gavril was her one safe harbour. She clung to him, and let Peran take command.

Sybilla and G. Gavril

Still, the Southland rebels gave her pause. Trusting no one but Gavril, Sybilla took him on a secret mission to murder Sidney Karasek and end the rebel threat. They found Sidney but before they could kill him, a group of guardsmen attacked, slaying Gavril. These guards were working for the rebels but one was a spy sent by Peran to ensure Sybilla's protection. Peran's man dispatched the remaining guards and arranged Sybilla's escape. Aboard a boat headed for Nothelm, Sybilla realised that she was pregnant with Gavril's child. Sybilla spent her convalescence under the Braedal's protection. Voirrey Braedal cared for her, using her

Mission to Kill Sidney Karasek

Gavril's Death

Sybilla's Rescue

skills in midwifery to bring baby Davina into the world. Though Voirrey was heir to Nothelm, she resented her birthright and was secretly allied with the rebels. To Voirrey, Sybilla was both the instigator of the Purge, and a new mother. This presented a moral dilemma for Voirrey who knew that Sybilla deserved execution, but if Velspar had blessed her with a child, did she have the right to judge her? Knowing the delicacy of the situation, Voirrey sought guidance from her friend Intercessor Amand.

Following Davina's birth, Voirrey took Sybilla to face her judgement in the mountains of Jokvour. Sybilla sensed the inevitability of this moment and offered no resistance. Answering Voirrey's call, Amand brought with him Waldemar and Maeryn. The Intercessors had recently discovered the Voyant Stone in Avishae and Rebekah insisted that if they were to use it on Sybilla, she must accompany them. Zohar and Illiam joined her.

Voirrey handed Sybilla over to the Intercessors, holding baby Davina for the duration of the rite. Sybilla did not know if she would survive the ordeal, or whether she deserved to, but she trusted Voirrey with her child's life. Those gathered joined hands and, with the power of the stone, forced Sybilla to a point of crisis, a spiritual precipice that nearly claimed her life. Zohar, who had swallowed Sybilla's blood-tie, felt compassion for her and entered her spirit, drawing her back to life. Waldemar and Amand had not expected Sybilla to survive. Waldemar struggled to master himself, regretting that Sybilla had not died in the Fire of Vaelnyr. If he had killed her then, the Purge would never have taken place. Maeryn sensed Waldemar's intention and Amand's mounting anger. Maeryn used her power to sap her fellow Intercessors of their redness, and in doing so, saved Sybilla's life. Illiam, understanding the grave power of the stone, took his chance and tossed it into the canyon below. Amand responded by trying to strangle him. Rebekah, who had always seen Sybilla as her enemy, was humbled by Zohar's mercy in saving the woman's life. Rebekah could not help seeing Sybilla's spiritual struggle in light of her son's recent death. Privately, the two Skalens formed a Pact, promising to protect the stone from the Intercessors.

Skalens and their Successors, Present Day: The Year 718

Only direct descendants of Skalens may be considered successors. If Velspar does not bless ruling Skalens with children, this is considered a moral judgement on the clan. Lands without Skalens are ruled by Regents named by the Council of Skalens but the laws of hereditary succession do not apply to them.

Nothelm

Skalens: Lenna (65) & Damek Braedal (68)
Successor: Voirrey Braedal (39)
Head Guard: Edric (55)

Vaelnyr

Skalens: Sybilla Ladain (42)
Successor: Davina Ladain (3) fathered by Guardsman Gavril (died age 38 in 714)
Head Guard: Peran (75)

Seltsland

Skalens: Kalet (46) & Magnar Askier (47)
Successor: None
Head Guard: Fenlor (42)

Lindesal

Regents: Haldi Askier (47) & Moriel Braedal (61)
Descendents: None
Head Guard: Grenla (32)

Maglore

Skalens:	Inry (36) & Domhnall Greslet (48)
Successors:	Lilwenn Greslet (10). Second in line Edlin Greslet (8).
Head Guard:	Rayhmer (58)

Brivia

Skalen:	Sidney Karasek (57) is the last living heir of deceased Skalens Emryl (executed age 71 in 700) and Medard Karasek (executed age 73 in 700). Sidney refused his position, instead taking a citizen's oath to demonstrate his obedience to the Council of Skalens.
Successors:	None
Regents:	Olinda (48) and Jemryn Greslet (48) rule in Sidney's stead.
Descendents:	Illiam Greslet (21)
Head Guard:	Kiryn (35)

Avishae

Skalen:	Rebekah (39) & Ulric Elshender (40)
Successors:	Zohar Elshender (21). Second in line Ambrose Elshender (died age 15 in 714).
Head Guard:	John (47)

Before Velspar entered them, they were animals.
There were no spirits then. No 'Velspar.' No realm of
    dreams.
There was no rebirth. No living awareness to feel its
    separateness, and long for union.

This is what they said, those who followed the First
    Diviner. Those who knew a man who was fully
    awake. But surely this is a simplification. What
    were our ancestors one generation before? They
    were not animals, this much I know. I hear them
    whispering from the bowels of the earth. I hear
    their agonies and their joyous cries. As human as
    we are.
I touch my palms to the earth and they sing through
    me like flute song.

The Visions of Intercessor Janek of Avishae, 517.

PART I

THE UNDERTIDE

1

AVISHAE

Intercessor Maeryn advanced upon the Temple stair, the ache in her knees frustrating her ascent. She touched her swollen hands to the cool marble wall, stained these last eighteen years to the colour of rotten teeth. A place misused, but not destroyed. At least not here in Avishae.

At the fourth floor, Maeryn paused, her breath growing short. Through small apertures in the stone, air whisked through and light poured in. She took her time, tracing these perforations; as she continued upward, passing the fifth floor and the sixth, her pulse sounding in her ears.

These sites of ritual and song once shivered with energies. Now, they were as quiet as the bones of the siatka that washed listlessly ashore, and the abandoned nests of the kshidol. The Skalens of Avishae wanted to bring them back, but still they faltered when speaking the holy names. *Siatka of sea, Kshidol of sky. Life bringers. Gatherers. At last breath, guide me to Velspar. Return me to the Stream...*

For good or ill, Skalens Rebekah and Ulric Elshender had participated in the Purge. High Intercessor Camis had instructed them to because he believed in the promise of the Eighth Gate. Those wise thousands who called themselves Intercessors had walked like sheep to the slaughter, doing nothing to fight the madness of Skalen Sybilla's decree. They had welcomed death and abandoned the living souls who needed them.

Maeryn felt sadness about the Purge, and deep regret for not doing more to heal Sybilla of her fears when she was young. But there was no point at which Maeryn regretted her decision to live. She, Maeryn Rosemond of Vaelnyr, Waldemar Rasmus of Brivia, and Amand Angenet of Seltsland were the last of their order. Those Intercessors who accepted execution no longer participated in the flow of the Great Stream, they were no longer a part of Velspar. Like all adepts before her, Maeryn had passed through the Seven Gates of Wisdom and knew there was no Eighth. If the High Intercessors had spent more time practicing Intercession and less seeking visions then they would know this. Life was here. Velspar was here. And now it fell to Maeryn to guide the souls of these lands.

At the seventh floor, she found the small desk and chair where she was to sit each day. They had laid paper out for her. The Visions of Intercessors long dead lined the shelves, salvaged by Rebekah's father, and the Elshenders' allies in Brivia and Lindesal. She was to absorb their wisdom so she could speak on behalf of the Intercessors of this place, whom she had never known in life. And in doing so, the Elshenders imagined she could build a new community of initiates. Did they truly believe that these children of the Meridian Age could pass the Seven Gates? The blinding stone they wore made it so none could hear Velspar's voice. It was unnatural. Still, she must help them.

She smoothed her silver hair, wiped the sweat from her upper lip. The breeze at the window was fresh and bright, pine-scented from the forest below. Maeryn tried to settle herself at the desk. The chair was too small, and it creaked when she moved.

She must fill this page with the truth of Velspar. The new and living truth. If she did not, then it would fall to Waldemar, or Amand. Though she loved them dearly, neither could be trusted with the task. She had seen it in Jokvour. The stone had roused their passions and brought both men close to murder. If she had not been there to hold them back, Waldemar would have slit Sybilla's throat in revenge for the Purge and Amand would have thrown young Illiam into the chasm. All the lad had done was deprive Amand of the stone. No, they could not be trusted in Avishae. But neither would they exile themselves indefinitely. Waldemar had spent almost two years with Sidney Karasek in the Brivian wilds and Voirrey had taken Amand north to a quiet village in the mountains. They would not keep away forever.

Maeryn picked up the quill, running her fingers along its smooth fronds. Her words were a mess inside her. How was she to begin?

The Visions of Intercessor Maeryn Rosemond of Vaelnyr, she wrote.

No other words came.

She rubbed her hand over her heart as if comforting a child.

Above, the domed ceiling formed a lucent halo at the edges of her vision. She tried to calm her mind, to become cerebral, to see all from above. Her gaze drifted to the bookshelves. The volumes there were thick, the leather worn soft from consultation.

She should leaf their pages, fill herself with their understanding, but she could only think: *You were wrong. The Eighth Gate was a false star that burned you blind. You died for nothing and left me here to do this alone.*

She did not write these words. No book of Visions started thus. And yet, this was her truth.

Maeryn wiped her palms, closed her twitching eyelids. There was no way in. She could not face them. Truly, they had abandoned her and she felt righteous in her dismissal of their insights.

This place is no longer holy, she thought. And more than that, Intercession could not be put into words. It lived in the heat of her hands, in her guts, in the aching tensions of the body. Such wisdom could only be passed among the living, mind to mind, palm to palm.

She set the paper aside. Skalen Rebekah had asked her to come here, to cleanse the Temple and begin the rites anew. Though this blessing did not make any of it possible. If she could hold Rebekah's hands and look into her eyes, she would understand. This was a task better suited to one who yearned for hidden knowledge. Her father Landyn, perhaps.

The Temple was not her place any longer. She felt sure of that now. And where holiness had fled, she must follow.

2

SELTSLAND

Skalen Kalet Askier wondered how much farther she would have to go. Flies buzzed about her husband's sweat-damp tunic, both of them knee-deep in boggy mud.

"Really, Magnar, what is the point of all this?" She was growing impatient with him.

He turned to her and grinned, squelching onward. "It seems our friends in Lindesal have caught themselves a magic fish."

"Our friends in Lindesal? You know I don't have any," she said.

"Well, you may feel differently about them when you see the gift they have for you."

Kalet wiped sweat from her brow and grumbled noncommittally.

Back in his trader days, before he had worked his charms on her, Magnar virtually lived in this swamp. Few chose to work in the marshy divide between Seltsland and Lindesal. There was nothing pleasing about the mud. Those who traversed the marshland were perpetually dirty, itching with insect bites, prone to fungal complaints–between their toes, the backs of their knees, and those places where it mattered most.

How had he won her all those years ago? He was just as grubby then as now, stinking of sweat and damp. He galled her daily with his puffed-up schemes. It had to be that smile of his that made him

6

look twenty years younger, reminding her of when they had first met.

She recalled it well enough, that time he'd come to the Skalens' House, reciting the trader's Tally to her late parents. *Aye Skalen*, he'd began, then carried on with the numbers, *two hundred and forty bags of grain, six hundred and twenty sheaves of corn, eighty-seven vials of Alma oil, fifty barrels of wine, eleven boxes of sun-ripened renfruit*, or something along those lines. Her father set his gaze to the parchment and began to write, and, with a jolt to her belly, the brute looked at her. He was hairy like a bear with his thick black beard; the look he gave her like a predator raising his bloody maw mid-feast. She remembered his conspiratorial smile, days later, almost against her will.

It would take many more such meetings, where she would sit alone upon the Skalens' throne, for her to admit–with her smile–that she liked his rough way of talking, his forwardness. After a good long bath, she'd get the stink of the swamp off him. And with her parents plaguerid and almost dead, the only one to stand against the match was Haldi. Kalet sat through her younger sister's talk with more than one roll of her eyes. Power, responsibility, wisdom–who was she to lecture her on such things? Well, Kalet was the eldest, and she had chosen Magnar. Haldi, after many years, had found a match as dull and simpering as she was. Old Moriel Braedal, a man who knew exactly what it was like to lose in the game of hereditary power. They were the two who missed out, who could have brought Nothelm and Seltsland together if it were not for their elder siblings. But they were not the kind to scheme and bring daggers to bear in the night. Instead, they lived a quiet life in the mountains, as if they bore no claim at all, and with great modesty and reluctance they accepted the Regency of Lindesal: defeated lands stewarded by soft-hearted fools. She and Magnar had set them there, just as the Greslets of Maglore had set Olinda and Jemryn up as Regents of Brivia. Placeholders, proxies. Younger siblings. Family members close enough to control, and to deserve a special kind of cruelty.

She followed her husband, through frogspawn and reeds, watching the great orange sun fill the sky. By now, there was no doubt that they had passed into Lindesal. It gave her a weird little thrill, like poking her sister with a stick. She thought that by middling age she would have outgrown this pleasure, but she doubted now whether she ever would. In the distant future, she imagined them, reunited at some feast or another, silver haired and twig-boned, Kalet still poking her with that stick, laughter in her eyes.

Against the sunset's glare she caught sight of a shallow boat, a lone oarsman, his arm resting on his wading pole. Magnar's acquaintance, she presumed.

Magnar waved his arms emphatically.

The hooded figure raised his face but did not speak.

Waist-deep in the water, Kalet struggled to keep pace with her husband, but she was curious now to see what the old man had in there.

The boat sat at waist-height, the man looming silently above them.

Gripping the side of the small boat, Magnar pulled Kalet in beside him and they both peered in. Magnar sucked his teeth. "Well, well. What do we have here?"

The old man grimaced, his mouth puckering beneath the rim of his hood. She heard a butting sound, a muffled grunt. A writhing body half-covered in sackcloth. From under a mop of hay-coloured hair, the young man stared, his bright blue eyes wide with terror. He made a moaning sound, his cries stoppered by the gag. She guessed his age to be sixteen or so.

"This is your magic fish?" She assessed Magnar with raised eyebrows. "An interesting gift, I must say."

"This is no ordinary boy, my love. Calls himself an 'Intercessor.' Too young to be one of the true generation, though. Thought you'd like to take a look at him." He stood back, inviting her to judge the value of the gift.

Kalet looked down at the boy, the Meridian tight about his skull, his hands secured behind his back. "He's a Lindesali by birth?" she asked, still staring down.

"He is, and I'd wager there are more of them festering under your sister's Regency."

Kalet smirked. "Worth questioning, I agree. But we are a fair way from the dungeons. Are you going to carry him?"

"Our friend here will ferry him to the mud flats, and from there I have a few helpers to get him down to the dungeons. If anyone asks, we were out on a lover's walk and found him singing to Siatka in the middle of the swamp."

Kalet scoffed. "If anyone asks? Who is going to ask, oh great and noble Skalen? I swear you concoct these scenarios for sport. Absolute power getting a little dry? Should I introduce a little duplicity and tie you up in the dungeons?"

Magnar winked.

She lowered her voice. "And what of this fellow?" She looked at the fisherman's dour face, his averted eyes.

"An old acquaintance. Used to trade in reed bulbs. Can't hear us. Stone deaf," he said, then turned, gesturing with his hand. "Come on then, friend. Away-o to Seltsland."

Kalet smirked at him, the orange light making him glow all over. His thick hair and beard were iridescent at the edges. She waded over, putting her arms around his neck as he hoisted her onto his back.

"You sure you can carry me all the way home, old man?"

His dark hair was turning grey at the temples, but he was still barrel-chested and hale. He reached back to squeeze her dripping thigh, making her cling tighter, her laughter in his ear.

She rested her head, turning her face to the flaming peaks of the mountain range that would soon dissolve into grey with the coming of twilight. Magnar sloshed onward, his thighs working to a rhythm now, his breath beginning to labour with the task. She turned behind to check the oarsman was still there. It was an eerie sight, the robed silhouette and the dragging motion of his pole; the Lindesali lad hidden there in the boat's cradle. He could not be what Magnar said he was. Only if she entertained the Intercessors' nonsense about the Eighth Gate: the great prophecy spoken with their dying breath. A way of infecting the minds of generations to follow. According to the Intercessors, the Skalens were mistaken in thinking themselves victorious. The Skalens were not executing them; no, they asked for the blade so that they might stage their spiritual revolution. They died so they might *flood the many wombs*, making every child born in the aftermath of the Purge, one gifted with the sight.

Kalet treated that generation with due suspicion but she had long ago dismissed the prophecy. She had scrutinised the newly born, had watched them in their toddling years. When they went about their errands all blundering and shy, she kept them under observance, their stolen kisses and ill begotten pranks. They displayed no special clairvoyance, no propensity for vision or for healing with the hands, for dream-taking or mesmerism. The Lindesali boy would be of similar stuff, she was sure. Still, she would get what she could from him before his sentence was carried out.

Tap tap. The sound of the wading pole. Magnar turned to the oarsman and Kalet slid off her husband's back. With a few careful steps, Kalet tip-toed to a solid patch of mud and waited as Magnar slung the boy over his shoulder.

The oarsman looked on expressionlessly, steadying the boat, and once Magnar had lightened the load, he bowed and turned his craft back toward Lindesal.

In the dimming light, Kalet saw the silhouetted forms of five or six guardsmen up ahead. Magnar waved and two of them came forward, the others ambling over to where horses waited with a litter.

As the two figures neared, Kalet recognised Head Guardsman Fenlor.

"Evening Skalens. This the prisoner?" he said inclining his head.

"Aye, Fenlor. A slimy one. Take him to the Temple dungeons while we get cleaned up. Throw a few buckets over him if you like."

"Very good, Skalen," he said, a little tight-lipped, taking the shivering boy onto his shoulder. As usual, Fenlor addressed Magnar, as if Kalet did not equally command him.

Kalet kissed her husband and slapped him on the back.

He raised his eyebrows, his beard parting in a prideful smile.

One good turn deserves another, was what he was thinking. She could read it on his face. One for you, one for me.

She peered over at him. "Depending on what the prisoner can tell me, there may be cause to send a more significant force into the marshlands to root the traitors out."

He fought a near irrepressible urge to bow his head in gratitude. "My thoughts exactly," he said.

Always a matter of trade between them. The marking of the Tally. One for you, one for me.

3

___

SELTSLAND

KALET ENTERED THE TEMPLE at dawn, the cool of the dungeon below stirring gooseflesh on her skin. It was only her there, and the boy, but he hadn't seen her yet. The other prisoners had been taken up to work the fields. It was not common practice to make them work. The other Skalens generally held to the Intercessors' customs whilst claiming to reject their ways. An Intercessor's first priority was to ensure a prisoner's psychic containment, to prevent red thoughts from spreading among the populace. The risk of that was minuscule, however. In their paranoia, and their obsession with purity, they had lost themselves a workforce. She'd thought Magnar quite resourceful when he floated the idea. In Seltsland, stockpiles rose with no note of it in the Tally. Seeing the prisoners labour in the fields also served as a warning. There would be no quick or noble death for heretics.

She held the key tight in her hand, walking with silent tread.

When she had nearly reached his cell, she stopped outside, pressed her back against the marble, and listened. Though barely perceptible, in time she discerned his breathing. A soft, slow rhythm, as if he were sleeping.

Kalet moved her eye to the opening, looked in. The boy was there, cross-legged on the floor, his eyes closed in meditation, a wall of metal bars between them. She stood before him, perhaps two strides distant. If he was an Intercessor, he was ignoring her. If he wasn't, she need only make a sound to rouse him.

With sudden violence she struck the key against the bars. The sharp chinking sound resounding as the boy's startled eyes locked onto her.

They stared at one another until his lip began to quaver and he took to staring blankly at the floor.

"Give me your name," she said flatly.

A rasping breath preceded his response, as if she had her hands about his throat. "Damyen."

"Well, Damyen, you know who I am, I presume?"

"Skalen Kalet Askier."

"Yes. And you know what you have been accused of?"

Damyen averted his eyes.

"Intercession, Damyen. What do you think of that?"

He did not speak.

"Let us assume that you are what they say you are..." She paused, examined her hands. "The punishment is death, this you already know."

The boy looked blankly ahead in an obvious attempt to master his emotions.

"Now, it seems to me that you are either a liar, or a magical prophet sent to destroy me." Kalet watched him carefully: the tightness of his breathing; the sweat he would not lift his hand to wipe; the feeble attempt he made to regain his composure.

"There may be a third option if you are willing to share what you know... In particular, I am curious to know whether you initiated yourself or if someone took this role upon themselves." Kalet let him think it over.

After a pause, she sharpened her tone: "Did someone initiate you? If you give me their name, I have means to make you more comfortable here. Think about it. If they initiated you, they must have initiated others, and the risk is spread. It need not have been you who spoke, it could have been any of them. And what a cruel fate they have gifted you. First, you are initiated, and now you find your-self in the Temple itself, the place where all the others died. Where they passed through the Eighth Gate! Can you feel them, Intercessor?" She gestured about the dank chamber. "I cannot. I come here often, and there is not a squeak from them."

Still the boy held himself in silence. They always did that. As if they could ignore her and she would simply go away.

"How about I suggest a few names and see if any of them ring a bell?" Kalet paced up and down, considering. "Guardswoman Grenla? No, she is far too aloof. Regent Moriel? No, he mumbles too much. Regent Haldi?"

The boy cut her off. "No one initiated me."

Hmm, she thought. *Haldi.*

Kalet went on. "No one initiated you. Then how can you rightly call yourself an Intercessor?"

"I didn't. I–" he started.

She came up close to the bars. "You must have done something to gain my husband's attention. He is not in the habit of wasting my time."

The boy pressed his lips together.

"Can you feel my red thoughts, even through my Meridian? You must know what I plan to do to you and your accomplices." Her fingers gripped the bars. "But maybe you can stop me? Even Intercession can be used as a weapon if the will is there."

She saw his mind turning over.

"I am all alone here with you," she said. "The guards will not reach me in time if you act now." A prickle of anticipation started in her feet, moved up her legs.

The boy's face stiffened with concentration and she thought she could see his hands grow dark with the ruddy heat she expected there.

Kalet felt a vague pressure about her head. Did she imagine it?

She let out a little sigh, "I can feel you." She had to press her lips to stop herself from laughing as a vein on his forehead began to throb.

"Agh!" she hissed through her teeth, grasped her head as if in pain.

She paused, waiting, almost hoping to see some grit in the boy.

His hands trembled. The pressure–yes, he was doing something–but it wasn't strong. Like a fish beached in the mud, he flapped and flailed toward her, not so magic after all.

She came closer, leaned against the bars, coming down on her knees. They were level with one another and she slid her hand through. "Come on," she whispered. "Come, show me what you can do. Come on." She ran her finger along his bare calf and he shuddered, grimacing, too terrified to recoil. She stopped. "No?"

The heat receded from him, though he was determined to withstand her, to do what he could to hold her off–and maintain some vestige of his dignity.

Kalet looked at him appraisingly. "Damyen. I will make you a promise. A Skalens' Oath, in fact. I will make you a Skalens' Oath. If you extend your hand through the bars of this cell and do exactly what I say, then I will not come in there. The door will remain locked. You in there, me out here. How does that sound?"

His eyelid flickered and he looked as if he might cry.

She extended her hand inside, palm up.

Slowly, he released the fist that sat clenched in his lap, moving it gingerly toward her grasp. Upon touching her, he seemed taken, momentarily, by a wave of nausea.

Kalet held his hand in hers.

If he was still trying his mind tricks, she could not tell. She had never been sensitive to the art, but she watched where the blood went, and his hands had grown cold. Saw him receding into himself, determined to hide in the upper branches until she was gone.

With her left hand she reached into the pocket of her cloak, exhuming first a copper bowl, which she placed on the floor between them, and then the blade.

Her friendly grip grew firm as she twisted his wrist to expose the vein. Pushing the point flat and hard against his skin, she began to lever the blade so the tip formed a little triangle–*ting, ting, ting*–the blood dripped into the copper bowl–his teeth clenched against the pain.

Kalet watched the blood leaking from his wrist, her hands claw-like and locked in position. His chest heaved as he lost his attempt at repose, his eyes like blue eggs in a nest of grimace lines.

Seeing that the bowl was nearly full, she withdrew the knife, placing it on the stained marble floor, using her other hand to apply firm pressure to the wound. Carefully, she wrapped his wrist in clean bandage, tying it off and letting go of his hand.

The boy clutched it to his breast, crying openly now, tears wet and glistening on his freckled cheeks. Kalet crouched, gaze fixed on the bowl as she negotiated it between the bars of the cell.

Then, she lifted the bowl with her forefingers, balancing it between them. She sat back on her knees, raised it, as though to give offering. She felt powerful in this strange arcing posture, tall and ceremonial, her shins cold against the marble floor. Her gaze was fixed on the copper bowl, lifted just above her eyes as she made her silent incantation. She brought the bowl to her lips, the boy's blurred form disappearing behind a circle all copper and red.

From the cusp of the empty vessel, the boy's face reemerged. Anger, horror, disbelief. The bandaged hand hidden under his arm. Kalet tried to read his expression. Wondered what she had done and what the effect might be. Had she consumed some part of his soul? Could she gain his power this way?

Her mouth puckered involuntarily at the sickly taste of what she had just ingested. She tried to become aware of any other sensations in her body. But no, she didn't feel any different.

"Remove your Meridian," Kalet said, surprised by the thickness of her own voice.

He did so, but now he wore an expression of absolute disgust.

Ignoring that, Kalet closed her eyes and tried to focus on the boy. She should be inside him by now. Should be able to make his arms move. Make him bark like a dog or something like that.

After several minutes Kalet let out a frustrated breath.

"Well, that was a waste of time," she said and stood up, taken by a slight dizzy spell.

Damyen glared up at her, still sitting cross legged on the floor of his cell.

"I will get something out of you before your spirit is released."

Kalet wiped the bloody dagger on her robe, returning it to its holster. "Take my advice. Speak the truth, speak all of it, and you will go swiftly to the Stream."

He remained silent as she moved toward the stair.

Before she went out, she turned. From this vantage she could see only his bare feet. "Just know that your struggle will go unwitnessed and that there is no one to betray. You may be thinking of your spirit now, but consider the many ways that pain can mark the spirit. The scars of redness, if you will. You need not take these torments upon you."

She saw him stiffen and tremble, and knew his constitution was weak. A sensitive one. The kind that Haldi would befriend.

"Till morning, then."

4

SELTSLAND

KALET VISITED DAMYEN many times over the ensuing weeks. She needed to injure him quite badly to get the information she needed. By the time she wrote to Haldi to inform her that she had captured a Lindesali heretic on Seltsland soil, one of the boy's arms had been amputated to the elbow, the other at the wrist. His blood did not appear to have any magical properties that she could discern, though she did not discount the possibility that somewhere, latent in the blood, a much-diluted essence might be found. A coveted secret that he was still hiding from her.

The flaying of his right forearm had released the first piece of noteworthy intelligence. He was indeed seventeen years old, and his partners in heresy were all of an age with him. Books had been stolen from the Temple and hidden in sheds, cellars, haylofts. A nest of heretics had gathered the young ones together, given them the books, instructing them to use the Intercessors' visions to remind them of their true nature. They were chosen for the in-born powers they possessed, though if their exertions brought as little as this one's had, they were no real threat. She could just imagine them, young women and men all set about in some dark clearing calling one another Intercessor and bowing their heads, enjoying the danger of the trea-sonous removal of their Meridians, reading aloud the garbled visions

18

of Intercessors long dead and nodding to one another as if any of it made sense.

Kalet had saved her questions about Haldi and Moriel until the moment of amputation but Damyen would not give them up. Perhaps he did not know how the books had been obtained. She had no proof, but Kalet did not think there were many zealous enough to steal the holy books themselves. The true believers had died in the Purge, and those who did not–the half-mad Sisters of Jagoda, for example–were slaughtered years ago. Those alive today were either pleased at the Intercessor's demise or cowards, all.

Cowards could be duplicitous, but they would only be roused to conspiracy if someone more powerful than them had set this plan in motion. It was just the kind of quiet rebellion that Haldi and Moriel would attempt. They would hold no swords, send no rebels into battle, but they would sow ideas.

Well, dear sister, see what I must do to pluck these seeds that you have planted?

She suspected Damyen was telling the truth when he said he did not know the current location of the books, but she did not doubt their authenticity. The tomes that she had burnt for Magnar's benefit during the cleansing of the Temple were substitutes. The true records–some of them dating back to the days of the First Diviner– were in her own secret vaults in the bowels of the Skalens' House. She kept them for her own interest, for her experiments. Magnar was a simple man and she did not need him wrangling with complex deceits. It was likely that she was not the only Skalen who coveted the secrets of the Intercessors but outwardly none could admit it. They had agreed that it was heresy. A flawless pretence, top to bottom. A net to catch up their rivals so they could be eliminated, and such was the true purpose of the Purge. A revolution sparked by Sybilla's lust for revenge, by Damek's desire for a clear harbour, and Domhnall's need to be accepted by the ancient clans. The Elshenders? She watched them tremble in their boots. Fear drove them. The only clans that truly invested themselves in spiritual affairs had died for their principles, which was all well and good as far as Kalet was concerned.

Between his panting and howls of pain, Damyen had recounted what visions he knew. Kalet scrawled them in ink, finding one or two familiar. Then he would grow tired and vague so she was forced to splash cold water in his face. The words fell from his lips, lifeless and dull, and she strained to interpret them. She transcribed what she could, reading them back, adding those marks of expression that his voice lacked. For days, her mind had been a-swirl with disconnected images, cryptic mutterings, and unnatural turns of phrase. Was this the voice of Velspar? Truly?

"The Holy Ones are hiding," Damyen said.

"Hiding where?"

"I will take you."

Her heart swelled with portent.

"Where are they?"

He remained silent, indrawn and smiling.

"Thank you. Praise holy Jagoda."

So... he was one of them. Raised by one of them, she corrected, remembering his age. His mother must have been one of Skalen Jagoda's worshippers. They worshipped her in life, and in death, but especially after the events of the Purge. The details of Damyen's upbringing grew clear in her mind. He would have grown up hearing stories of Jagoda, lovely Jagoda, who had foreseen the horrible events of the Purge and had died to save the siatka from the guardsmen's spears. He would have heard tales of Sybilla's cruelty as she ordered Skalen Cerek's death, leaving Lindesal leaderless and adrift. And at the age of six, his mother would have gone to worship, dancing on the beach with flowers in her hair. But of course, it was heresy to worship a Skalen in this way. And so, the Maglorean guard made their second brutal mark on the pages of history. There was no doubt in her mind that Damyen's mother died that day.

Kalet knew she could use this later but did not want to lead him away from his current trail of thought.

Doggedly, she continued to question him.

"Damyen. Where are they hiding?" She poked him sharply with her nib.

He looked down at the spot of black ink that dribbled down his calf.

His eyes met hers, and she felt the flare of him. *"I will take you."*

She blinked, waiting for him to continue. *"Yes, take me."*

He cackled, then. An uncanny sound that she could only attribute to his delirium.

From there, it was all talking mountains, rattling bones, and the evil whisperings of the stars.

She tried to follow it but had always found the speech of vision to be irritatingly imprecise.

What, where, when, how? She tried to box him in, to gain her coordinates.

It was a messy session, one where she lost her temper. She had left with confirmation that the Holy Ones were hiding far out at sea. Or had she come up with the idea only to insist he confirm it? She was annoyed with herself over that. She must remain patient: observe and analyse.

Today, the boy was much diminished. The youthful flush of fear, the pulse beneath his freckled skin, the startled eyes refracted with the deliberations of one who wants to live–all that was gone. His flesh sagged, sallow and grey. He had willed silence to swallow him, was trying to make himself disappear before his flesh was truly dead. He breathed, his heart persisted, but it was knocking, knocking at the Eighth Gate. He had set his destination. *Take me to the Stream. To the Stream. Velspar guide me home.*

Or, so she imagined. Though surely, he prayed.

Kalet came near. "Damyen," she whispered. "Damyen."

She removed her Meridian but experienced no change in sensation. She knew the blinding stone was powerful, but only for those whose senses were naturally extended. She would allow the boy's psychic tendrils to explore her–though she felt them not–and she would show him what she wanted. Not his knowledge, but knowledge of the Temple books. What was the power of the blood? Did The Holy Ones, Siatka and Kshidol, truly possess their animal counterparts? Why must they ingest the body, why must they taste the blood in order to ferry a spirit home? *Blood*, she thought, *tell me of the blood.* She imagined it, flowing red from cut palms at Blood Call, mixed with meat paste for the Holy Ones, trickling down the Temple dungeon's drains.

He moaned, sliding sideways, doubling over with some hidden pain.

Or was it the topic of her thinking that unsettled him? Anything was possible. Kalet frowned at her mistake, her thoughts running unrestrained. She must not arouse his fear.

How to comfort an Intercessor? Her mind drew a blank. Then, staring at the white-veined wall, she thought of the higher floors. She remembered her own ascent at Blood Call. The scent of burning Alma, sweet and soft in its way. The half-smiles, the heavy-lidded eyes of her Blood Kin.

Kalet went up and called to the nearest guard.

"I need Alma," she said, noticing the man's stilted look. "I must have it. Now, would be best."

"Now, Skalen?" he asked with uncertainty.

"I will ask no questions as to how it was obtained. Just get it to me," she said.

"Certainly, Skalen." The guard bowed, then broke into a jog, heading to the Guard's quarters that abutted the Temple.

Back inside, Kalet left her prisoner for a time, ascending the Temple stair, thinking to put herself in the right frame of mind as she waited for the guardsman to come with the Alma. Each empty, circular room bore the stains of its furnishings. In the marble, she saw the ghostly marks of dark wooden shelves, of meditation stools, hooks in the ceiling where censers once hung, lacing the air with their smoke. Higher and higher she went until she came to the uppermost floor: the seventh, the holy place where the palm was cut at Blood Call. The place that signified the highest form of enlightenment, the Seventh Gate. She looked up. Wondering.

The Eighth Gate, something beyond. A place out there, perhaps.

She wished that she had paused, all those years ago, to interrogate the Intercessors of Seltsland before she sent them to their deaths. A lost opportunity. It had never sat well with her—the silent lines of them, robed in white, murmuring in common prayer—the way they had consented to their own execution. It seemed a trick, and she did not like to look the fool. She had watched for hours, mesmerised by their ecstatic faces. The guardsman's red hand poised to end their life, the way they cried out: *The Eighth Gate is opened!* The repetition of the phrase amongst the carnage and the gurgling drove her half mad. How could those shuffling forward look upon the bloody, shit-streaked robes of their brethren and claim victory? The corpses had to be dragged out the same door through which they entered. The dead and the living squeezed through a common aperture. How could they wear those idiotic expressions of joy, keeping their faith intact? True, there were chinks in the armour–a quavering voice, a darting eye, a shuddering breath–that told her doubt was still possible.

And yet, this process of bleeding out, of burning the body on the pyre, was designed–by the Intercessors themselves–to *destroy* the spirit, or at the very least, to divide it and confuse its path home. She looked out the window over the quiet ocean, a misshapen daytime moon visible among the clouds. Was the promise of the Eighth Gate realised somewhere beyond Velspar's shore? A new world across the sea? They would *flood the many wombs*. Well, they had not done so here.

It was a possibility she had not entertained until this moment, and testing its likelihood, found it flimsy indeed. No, she was letting her jealousy get the better of her. In Nothelm, Damek Braedal had his fleet at the ready, and each time she had word from him, her mind sparkled at the thought. What might they find out there? When it came down to it, Damek and Lenna had signed Sybilla's wretched decree simply to clear the seas of siatka, to overturn the centuries-long taboo against exploration beyond Velspar's shores. It was single-minded madness, and to be frank, she admired them for it.

Her obsessions, however, were not the kind that could be shared. Not yet, at least. She needed more. Needed something certain, something powerful. A knowledge equal in value to the Braedal fleet. Something that could be traded.

5

SELTSLAND

KALET'S FINGERNAILS WERE DIRTY from digging, her nose running from the bitter wind. She sniffed and wiped her face with her sleeve, stalking homeward as quickly as she could manage. Twilight's shawl had lifted, leaving her exposed to others' notice, though she was quite certain no one had seen her bury her treasures, nor had they seen her retrieve them.

With the Skalens' House in sight and time ticking away, she quickened to a jog. The inner pocket of her robe hid the bottled blood, but Damyen's severed hands were more difficult to conceal. The fingers had stiffened and curled so she had to prise them back, binding them with cloth. At present, they were pocketed in the lining of her skirt, giving off an unsavoury odour.

She entered the Skalens' House via the Attendants' passage, taking her relics to the disused cold store behind the kitchens. Her thoughts were divided. Should she dry the Intercessor's hands, salt-curing them as the Attendants did with other creatures? Or was the flesh superfluous? The bone–the enduring core–was that the place where the essence truly resided? If that were the case, she would not want the tacky musculature, the leathery skin. She should set them in a trough of maggots, or a pail of carnivorous fish.

Furtively, she deposited the bandaged parcel, adding the bottle to the shelf among her tinctures and concoctions. Exiting as quickly as she had come, Kalet locked the door and went to the small wash-room. This was her realm, down here. The Attendants she allowed in were the silent type, who knew instinctively that their survival rested on their ability to keep Magnar and Fenlor from discovering her business. Among her loyalists, some were more special than the rest. Her "boys," Magnar called them, for they also attended her in her rooms. Jaret, Colm, and Osmet, her husband hated them all, but he could not lay a hand on them, that she had made clear. She had moulded them to her purposes, had invested in them. And she felt, in all honesty, that after all they willingly endured, she could trust them with her life. In rites of her devising, they had sworn themselves to her.

Kalet above all Skalens. Kalet above the will of the Guard. Kalet alone and to the death.

They kept common quarters down here, away from Magnar's curious eye, sleeping on a roster, so two of them were always ready to assist, no matter the hour.

When a figure emerged in the narrow passage, it took her a moment to register which of them it was. The three could have passed as brothers, like to their mistress in their gaunt features and dark hair. Osmet even shared her cowlick.

Recognising the telltale sweep of his hair, Kalet held up her hand to him. As she approached, she pointed inside the room indicating that she wanted his assistance along with Jaret or Colm, whoever was awake.

With a nod, Osmet disappeared and Kalet entered the tiny lantern-lit space, sitting herself on the stool before the empty wash-basin. Minutes later, Colm came in, recognisable by his burgeoning facial hair and coal-dark eyes. He laid out a large square of black cloth on the floor and proceeded to remove her bloodstained cloak, bodice, and skirts, placing them on the cloth and tying the bundle by its four corners for laundering.

Osmet returned then with a pail of steaming water which he poured into the basin. He exhumed three glass bottles of fragrant oil, unstoppered them and presented each to his mistress in turn.

Lingering on the last, she considered the new and unusual scent. Cool, spicy, and sweet. Kalet raised her eyebrows, impressed. She nodded, confirming her selection and Osmet bowed, barely concealing his smile.

Three drops went into the basin, the rippling water striped with lamp-light. Osmet worked the warm rag over her skin as Colm submerged her hands in the water, gently prising the filth from her nails with a file. Water dripped from her naked body onto the floor, her feet raised on a platform.

With time to think, she went back over her last session with Damyen: the idea that where Intercession lingered, some knowledge of the Holy Ones might still be accessed. Not bookish knowledge, impervious in its poetry, but true instinct such as that of a hunting dog. There had to be a way to transfer and possess that instinct. Though dogs, she knew, could always turn their teeth upon their masters.

Colm patted her dry, paying special attention to her toes. Behind, Osmet laid her clothes and, as she turned, she saw the bronze damask cloak she was to wear to the execution ceremony. Colm gave her a towel to wrap about her, set another down to dry the floor, and went out.

Osmet came in behind her with a comb, and she glanced at him in the mirror. Working the hair free of tangles, he set her cowlick in a decorative loop on her forehead, repeating the shape on both sides. The remaining hair he gathered in a knot at the nape of her neck. Carefully, he set her Meridian in place, inserting obsidian teardrops through her pierced lobes. He stood to the side so she could depart but Kalet gestured to the bottle of perfume once more. He obliged her, daubing it gently behind her ears.

"Thank you, Osmet," Kalet said with a brief smile.

Draping the towel over the back of the chair, she stood in the centre of the room and her boys came to dress her. Practiced in their art, the endless layers of fabric were threaded and tied, tucked and flounced, until she stood perfectly attired. Exiting the dank little room, Colm and Osmet adjusted her skirt, holding it off the ground as she negotiated the narrow stairway.

At the door, they left her, and after ascending the stair, Kalet emerged into the hall near to her official boudoir.

Once inside, Kalet rang the bell. Some minutes later, a flush-faced Attendant appeared at her door.

"Skalen Kalet, how may I assist?" she managed.

Kalet looked the girl up and down. An unmistakable musky scent coming off her confirmed Magnar's activities during her absence. What was this one's name again? Cora? It was difficult to keep the displeasure from her face.

"Please tell my husband that today's executions will commence in two hours. He can travel with me if he is in good order, or he can make his own way, as long as he is not late." Kalet turned from the girl, disturbed by the flush of her cheeks.

"Yes, certainly, Skalen. I will return with his answer." The Attendant went out, closing the door behind her.

Kalet sat impatiently, hearing first the Attendant's hurried footsteps, the closing of her husband's door, a muffled shriek, and then more waiting. She did not have time for this.

Gathering her skirts, she padded quietly down the hall, finding an elderly Attendant at the top of the main stair.

He wrinkled his face in greeting and with reed thin voice gave his *good day*. He resumed his blank posture as if he were a statue animated only for such moments of greeting.

"Good day," she muttered. "Kindly take word to the carriage master below to ready the horses for my immediate departure. Skalen Magnar will follow separately."

"Certainly, Skalen." He bowed as far as his aged neck would allow. "I will make the arrangements."

The Attendant placed his dry palm upon the banister, taking one step at a time.

"I will await him out front," she said, breezing past him.

At the entrance to the Skalens' House, the house retinue kept at a respectable distance, studiously avoiding her attention. She had no wish to engage in pleasantries with them, her gaze darting restlessly between the stable and the distant mountains.

When the horses finally ambled out, Kalet exhaled audibly. She gave the driver a pinched little smile and got in. As they got moving, her thumb moved back and forth over a tender hangnail that Colm had missed. She tried to shake her irritation at Magnar. His exploits distracted her when she most needed to focus. This was her last opportunity to question Damyen before he was put to death. What was the pertinent question she should ask? She must twist him until she felt the thunk of the lock come free.

So diverted was she by these thoughts that she did not even notice when the carriage arrived at its destination.

The driver held open the door and she strode toward the Temple, making directly for the dungeons. Half-way down the stairs, Kalet noticed that Damyen's legs were not visible in the section of floor where he normally sat. She leaned out to the side, looking for him, worried that Haldi had got here early after all. Her heart hammered at the idea of being caught. As she came closer, though, she did see him.

The boy was barely recognisable. He was naked to the waist, wrapped in a meagre loincloth and bloodied bandages. His eyes stared listlessly into the middle distance, his back slumped against the cold marble wall. Was he dead?

She took her key and tapped it on the bars. "Damyen?"

He did not respond.

She slid the key into the lock and opened the door. She paused, holding her skirts high. Blood, piss, and shit, was supposed to run off into the central drain, but the guards had not splashed it out well enough. If there was one thing she could give the Intercessors' credit for it was their ability to keep a clean dungeon. Although, *they* did not have to contend with the challenges of prolonged incarceration or the messy business of torture. When the Intercessors were in charge of executions, the prisoners were kept for no more than a day before they mesmerised them, bled them out in the central trough, and cleaned their bodies for the pyre.

"Guard!" Kalet called.

Heavy footfall echoed closer and when she turned, she was surprised to see Fenlor standing there. "I did not ask for the Head Guard," she smiled. "Where are your underlings?"

"Nothing's below me, Skalen. What need's doing?" Brusquely he made his way down.

She turned to Damyen's cell. "This cell is filthy. I have a few final questions for the prisoner and..." She gestured to the fine fabric she wore, the perfection of her hair.

"You cannot sully your gown," Fenlor said with an unmistakable note of distain. He peered in, wrinkled his nose. "Mmm, not a nice place for a conversation. I don't think the young man will be causing you any more trouble on account of his injuries. How 'bout I take him out, wash him down a bit, and you can have a little talk here on the stairs."

Kalet nodded and stood back as he ventured into the cell. "Hello there young man," he said in a gentle voice as if rousing a drunk from his stupor. "I'll be picking you up now. There, let us put your arms across you like that. There now."

Damyen whimpered.

"There now, boy, I've got you. Up we go." Fenlor grunted as he raised Damyen from the floor.

Fenlor walked out, looked at Kalet, the boy's head on his breast, eyes closed. She knew what the look meant. *You're done with this one. Well, what was it to him?*

Fenlor turned his back on Kalet and set Damyen on the stairs, walking back and forth to cleanse the rag in a bucket of water set beside the blood trough. He was taking his time about it.

"That will do, Fenlor," Kalet snapped.

"Very good Skalen," he said, bowing.

He went to stand on the wall behind her.

"You may go now," she said.

"I hear Regent Haldi is on her way to collect the prisoner," he said innocently.

Kalet whipped around and glared at him. "You did not think to tell me this earlier? Are the pyres ready? The other prisoners?"

"Yep, the bodies are all up, all ready, Skalen. Except this one. Want me to take him? He's almost dead anyway. Don't think you'll get much more out of him now."

"That is for me to decide. Now wait at the top of the stairs and keep a look out. I only need a few minutes, then you can have him."

Fenlor bowed and stepped past her, treading carefully around Damyen, curled there, with his empty eyes.

When Fenlor reached the top of the stairs, Kalet came in close, whispered into his ear.

"Are the Holy Ones near, Damyen? Can you tell me...*where* they are?"

He did not seem to hear her.

Kalet exhaled in frustration.

She peeled away the ragged bandages about his wrist stump. With her finger she touched the bone. She didn't push, couldn't risk the blood staining her dress, but the pain drew him back. He trembled and looked into her eyes.

"You know," he rasped.

Across the sea, she thought, *where Damek is going.*

"Do I?" she asked, needing him to say it. "How do I get there?"

His tongue emerged between dry lips, the words caught in the cave of his mouth. His eyes were still on hers and she knew, now, that there were no lies between them.

He mouthed the word: "Boat."

"Boat," she repeated. A gush of pleasure suffused her.

"Boat," he said once more.

From the corner of her eye, she saw Fenlor's head turn.

"He is ready," she called, a grin pressing at her cheeks as the boy finally broke his gaze.

She stepped away from Damyen who had begun to shake uncontrollably. There was an awkward moment as Fenlor approached and she had to wait for him to scoop the boy up before she could pass by.

Exiting the dungeon she heard Fenlor's cooing *I've got you,* and *this way m'boy,* then finally the garbled moan that signalled his death. What was the point? No one was watching. It was all to show her that he was Magnar's man and that he did not *approve* of her methods. She'd had just about enough of him.

She went out, the wind making rough with Osmet's careful work, and she raised her hand to protect the curls. Quickly, she strode along the ashen path that encircled the burning grounds. The sunken area consisted of seven permanent pyres with a central 'well' in the middle. The well was an invention unique to Seltsland, a way of adhering to the traditional modes of execution whilst accommodating modern practicalities. The proper rite of execution involved bleeding the condemned by slitting the throat.

As in the days of the Intercessors, this sacred substance travelled the length of the blood trough, moving through pipes that led to the sea. The separation of blood from the body signified the first act of disunity, and was designed to confuse the spirit. The body would then be burnt upon the pyre, the shattered spirit unable to discern its way back to Velspar, the communal heart. These spirits, it was said, would be waylaid by the winking light of a thousand burning stars. Spiritual exile destroyed the spirit on its long journey to these false beacons, keeping Velspar's superior light in its rightful state of purity.

In Seltsland, those prisoners who were made to work were brought in chains directly to the burning grounds, their throats set upon the dip in the well's rim so they could bleed out then and there. The well connected below ground with the Temple's existing drainage system.

Kalet approached the Skalens' dais where executions were to be witnessed with due solemnity, seeing that most of the prisoners had already been tied to their respective pyres. Taking up her position, she rested her hands on the wooden railing. Then, noticing the greasy soot that came off on her palms, wiped them on her skirt. From this elevated position, she scanned the road that led to Lindesal.

Fenlor emerged from the Temple with Damyen's corpse. Evidence of his amputations were obvious, even from here. They needed to start the fires now.

A hand on the small of her back made her start. "Magnar!" she squawked.

Magnar leaned in, sniffed her neck, and exhaled in a guttural sigh. "Oh, that is good."

Kalet gave him a sly look. "I knew you would like this one."

"Don't make yourself any more delicious, Kalet, or I will have to eat you up." He gathered the seam of her dress into his fist, squeezing the fabric tight before letting go.

She tried to adopt a more formal posture, clasping her hands and gazing down upon the bodies.

Grudgingly, Magnar righted his own gait, standing tall beside her. "The Guard tell me that Haldi is on her way."

"Yes," Kalet hissed under her breath, "Fenlor needs to get on with it and light the damn pyres."

"He will, he will. Look, he's already got the torch lit."

Magnar whistled sharply and Fenlor looked up. Magnar gestured to Damyen's pyre, indicating that he should light that one first.

Obviously. And thank you for taking care of that, Magnar, Kalet thought, her teeth on edge as her gaze flicked to the road.

Moments later, Fenlor could be seen painting the Lindesali boy with fat, setting the torch to the kindling at his feet. He looked up at the Skalens' dais, watching them for a little too long, Kalet thought, before stepping down to prepare the others.

The air grew thick with smoke, Kalet's shoulders relaxing noticeably as the flames licked higher, hiding the boy's arms, his chest, and sleeping face. She squinted against the stinging air, orange flames roaring bright from the pit. Her cheeks reflected the savage light as she stared at Damyen's pyre. The fat was really taking now. A high flame, especially bright, a leaping shaft of silver at its core. She blinked, determined to see it.

"Did you see that?" She turned to Magnar who stood frowning at a distant patch of sky.

Perhaps he did not hear. He stood, bored and statuesque, thinking of other things.

After a time, the flames receded to their ashen core, revealing blackened bones, roasted skulls, some with stringy hair. Damyen's mangled corpse was just the same as all the others–unidentifiable.

Then, Magnar lifted his voice in prayer. "These spirits, condemned for their red deeds are annihilated here by the will of the Skalens Askier. Velspar bless us in our devotion. Pure is the Stream, clear and bright."

"Pure is the Stream!" the guardsmen returned in monotone.

The Skalens bowed and departed, leaving the men in the pit to clear away the bodies.

Too late, sister, Kalet thought, a spring in her step as she returned to the insight she had extracted. A life for a word, a tantalising word that could lead her anywhere... *Boat.*

6

SELTSLAND

KALET SLUNK DOWN in the copper bathing tub, the water cool enough now that she could submerge her face completely. She tapped her anklet experimentally against the side, listening to the deep clang that it made, the cries of distant cormorants swallowed up in the thickness.

She struggled to identify a persistent high note, raising her head from the water with a great breath of air. She stared at the jangling bell on the wall, moved by a system of levers from the Attendants' quarters on the floor below. Every time she sent them away to see to her own ablutions, she ended up in a situation like this. With quick movements she smoothed the water from her hair, twisting it into a cord to wring it out. She stood, her skin puckering at the chill, dripping water across the floor.

With a violent hand she jangled out her reply–*yes, come up here and irritate me some more*–and set about drying her toes while she waited.

A timid knock sounded at the door.

"Enter!" Kalet called.

A pretty young Attendant appeared. Full lips, honey-coloured hair.

"Skalen, I apologise for disturbing you during your bath but

Regent Haldi Askier has just arrived and is most anxious to meet with you." The girl stopped short, noticing her Skalen's nakedness, and the black look on her face.

"You are new here?" Kalet said, her mouth quirking.

"Ah…yes, Skalen, I started last Avisday."

"You will not be punished this time but do take note. The arrival of a Regent is not sufficient cause to ring the Skalens' chamber bell. An impending attack, the burning of the Skalens' House, the arrival of a *Skalen*, these matters warrant my immediate attention."

"Oh, oh, I am so sorry, Skalen," the girl stammered, her cheeks flushed with mortification.

"Serve refreshments, and I will receive her in the Main Hall when I am ready," Kalet said.

She had almost closed the door when a look of terror took the Attendant's face, "Shall I return to help you dress?" she asked, as if it were a matter of life and death, which it probably was.

"Send Colm," Kalet said, shutting the door firmly in her face.

She would have Colm speak to the girl. A shudder of disgust ran through her. *Shall I return to help you dress?* You shall not.

Roughly, Kalet pulled on her undergarments.

Colm knocked, the sound unique to his hand, like a dropped marble. Silently, he entered, clothing her so expertly with small nudges of his hand that her arms went up, down, this way, that way, without her having to think at all. He drew her corset firm, as she liked it, seating her with a light touch to her shoulder. He collected her thin, quickly-drying hair into a series of ornamental knots before setting her Meridian in place.

She cut a harsh figure and had never been concerned about her beauty or lack thereof. If she had any sentiment about her state of dress it was because it reminded her of her boys and their careful devotion. But on this occasion, she did wish to intimidate her sister, and the sight of fine crows-feet about her eyes, her exposed ears, the fragility of her neck, made her pause.

"Colm? Apply a little more armour, would you?"

She winked at him and the Attendant gave her a faint smile.

Face powder, thick and pale. Rouge. The bitter tang of beetle pigment, to stain her lips. A soft leather necklet hung with a mail of oyster-shell overhung with the heavy chain of her Skalens' medallion. Silver-rimmed earrings of black onyx in the shape of the Skalens' Star.

Better, much better.

"Very good, Colm."

He accompanied her out of the room, slipping down the Attendant's stair to alert the servers that she was coming.

Kalet took her time, smiling at a company of Attendants as they greeted her at the entrance to the Main Hall.

Inside, Haldi sat in a chair by the fire, with only her extended hands visible as she struggled to warm them in the frigid room. Of course, she had heard the squeak of the great doors, the rush of footsteps that heralded Kalet's arrival, but she did not stand. Her hands remained extended, returning to her lap only when Kalet was right beside her.

"Regent sister. What a pleasant surprise." Kalet's adornments tinkled, her heavy skirts whispering across the flags as she came to sit opposite her. The twin chairs were of gold velvet, the tea on the small table lukewarm at best.

"What brings you here? News from Lindesal?" Kalet asked, looking her sister up and down.

Haldi's eyes did not lift from the floor, her mouth pursed in barely repressed anger.

Eventually, she looked up. "A Lindesali citizen was executed here today," she said, and when Kalet only raised her darkly penciled brows, added, "This is not acceptable Kalet."

"Not acceptable?" Kalet mused. She regarded the pathetic figure before her. Her round cheeks and soft-sloping shoulders, her hair barely contained in a lop-sided bun that worked inelegantly around the confines of her Meridian. She had not allowed the Attendants to take her cloak but kept it over her knees as if this was still her home and she could forego formalities.

"I thought you would thank me. Or do you enjoy the business of execution so much? As I remember it, you disliked it most intensely," Kalet said, leaning back in her chair.

"I do what my position demands. But you make things difficult when you threaten the people in my charge," Haldi said.

"The laws are clear. The boy was apprehended in Seltsland and that is where his heresy was committed."

"If anyone can be whisked away in the night and sent to execution, then–"

"Haldi, he has been here for weeks. And this only goes to show that you are not keeping track of the citizens under your Regency."

"Damyen was missing! We were looking for him. This is not a game, Kalet. You should have informed me the moment he was apprehended."

"Well perhaps I do not hold as much faith in you as I once did. How many have you executed this year for the crime of Intercession, for red deeds?" Kalet pressed.

"None. But that is–"

Kalet cut her off. "Exactly. You are not doing your part to defend the Southlands. You want to be the nice sister, offer them leniency and forgiveness all in the hope that they'll love you for it–but they won't. If you want to lead, you must earn their respect through firmness and consistency. If you coddle them, you will see where it gets you. And I'll be the one left to clean up your mess. Even Head Guardsman Rayhmer has noted Lindesal's soft approach, all the way from Maglore! He blames your Head Guardswoman, but it is only a matter of time before he and the other Head Guards learn the truth."

Haldi exhaled in frustration. "Skalen Inry assures me that Rayhmer's reports are prone to exaggeration. It is all in hand. Speak to the Brivian Regents, or the Elshenders, they will tell you what it is like. The threat of rebellion is much overblown."

Kalet squinted at her sister, knowing she was lying. She almost admired the scope of Haldi's deceit.

"Well, whatever the case, Magnar has increased patrols on the Lindesal border."

"That is completely unnecessary!" Haldi cried in exasperation.

"That is for me to decide. And if we continue to stumble across heretics that you have let slip through the net, then that will be the Tally of your failure as Regent."

"Kalet, please. The people of Lindesal are loyal. They all took their oaths. They are sincere. We are a small community there now. Why is it so hard for you to believe that people can be good?" Haldi's hands betrayed the slightest tremble, her palms clammy with the sheen of sweat.

Kalet leaned forward. "Go back and review the grievances brought to you. Bring your Tally into line. You must keep your execution numbers at a healthy rate. Do that, and perhaps I will be able to call Magnar off, give him a new tree to sniff."

Haldi's mouth formed the same pursed line she had worn on her arrival.

"Very well, Skalen," she said, standing wearily.

"Good," Kalet smiled. "I trust you won't be staying?"

"No, thank you. Moriel will be expecting me." She gathered up her cloak.

"Well, pass my regards to Regent Moriel. I hear he has been suffering a stomach complaint."

"He is quite well now, I thank you," Haldi said with a brisk nod, seeing herself out.

As the Attendants fluttered around her sister, their offers of assistance growing faint down the hall, Kalet digested the conversation. She did not need an Intercessor's powers to read the poorly concealed signs of mutiny on her sister's face. The Regents of Lindesal were up to something. She'd let it grow a little larger, just so Haldi thought she might succeed, and then she'd put her in her place.

It was interesting. Not enough, though, to distract her from her greater plans.

7

───────

CIVIT'S RIDGE, NOTHELM

IT WAS A CLEAR DAY in the mountains and the villagers of Civit's Ridge were gathered about a crackling bonfire. Voirrey remained at the back of the group with Sybilla and Amand. Little Davina would not leave the adults, winding herself into the folds of Voirrey's skirt. She was almost four now and should be with the other children but often shyness took her at times like these.

Voirrey looked around. Everyone was here: the town's population amounting to little more than seventy people. They had come with their effigies, following the new tradition that had come to them from the South. Festival was a time for solemn absolution now, and would never again be a time of wild dancing and release. In the days of the Intercessors, Festival had been the one time where redness flowed joyful and free. Excessive emotion was encouraged because the Intercessors were there to guide it. Now, they wound their feelings into the shapes of little dolls, binding them tight so that only the flames could unfurl them, and there in the heart of the fire, those feelings burned in unbroken silence. Voirrey could see that the villagers took the effigies seriously, that the tradition really had taken hold. There was not one among them who had failed to bring one: some stroked their effigies with wrinkled hands, some concealed them as a lumpen shape in a pocket or apron, the children played with theirs, their morbid little forms dangling upside down.

Voirrey did not want to give the address. She wanted them to ask for Amand, the Intercessor she had finally brought them, but they chose Siran Thirwell, a short, jovial man of an age with her and whose sons were always causing mischief. She understood his importance in the community, a man who never forgot a name or a birthday, a man interested in people, but he was no holy man. What good was it to have Siran give a wink and say, *Best to you on your special day*, when Amand was there, ready to perform Blood Call, or the closest they could come to the rite, now that the siatka and kshidol were gone.

She suspected they feared Sybilla, as if Voirrey had come to Civit's Ridge merely to test their allegiances. Yes, Voirrey was the future Skalen of Nothelm, and Sybilla remained Skalen of Vaelnyr, but they were here in spite of all that. They were here as people, to hold this moment of freedom as long as they could. But also to show them how things could be in the North when the torch passed into her hands. All that they had lost in the Purge could be regained. Sybilla, the demon they had feared so long, had been cleansed of her darkness and been forgiven. If Sybilla could be transformed, then any of them could be absolved.

A sharp wind howled through the mountain pass and Davina squealed, burying herself even deeper in Voirrey's skirt, nearly tripping her over.

Voirrey righted herself and crouched down to stroke her hair. "Don't you worry about the wind," she whispered.

"Aunty Voy? Is it finished?"

"They will start soon. You just keep your effigy ready and your Mama will show you what to do." Voirrey smiled at her, glimpsing Sybilla's pinched face, Amand's uncanny stillness, his hands clasped in a formal posture of prayer.

Siran said something that made the sheep farmer laugh. Turning from him with mirthful tears in his eyes, he addressed the crowd. "Aye, now. Here we are, here we are. Let us begin!" Siran loped toward the High Rock, as it was called, though the rock elevated him only a few feet above them.

Weathered faces turned upward to listen, even his boys' pebble-brown eyes ceased their roving and steadied upon their father.

"Our traditions they grow and they change," he said. "Our sacred rites, they change, and sometimes it is not up to us."

Voirrey glanced at Sybilla, trying to assure herself that she was strong enough to hear these words, and that they were spoken without malice.

"We have wise ones here–ones who understand these matters of spirit far better than I. We've had cleansings and burnings and the sweet respite of the Meridian. And now we find an Intercessor sharing the same roof as the Skalen of Vaelnyr, right here in our humble village."

The bonfire fluttered in the expectant silence.

"These are strange times. I know it, and you know it. This is Festival, but it does not feel like Festival. Where is the dancing? Why do we stand here, all grave-faced? Why have we adopted this Southland ritual of throwing effigies into the fire?" He held up the sackcloth figurine in his hand.

Voirrey feared his next words. Where was he going with this?

"I will tell you why. Because Velspar is not something that can be pinned down. We know Velspar in our hearts, whether we perform the rites or not. We listen to the wisdom of our Skalens and Intercessors, oh yes. We respect and honour the ways of old. But in stopping for a time, we learned that Velspar can hear us, the Holy Ones can heed us, wherever we are, if only we bear our naked hearts and reach out. Our Voirrey..." He gestured to her. "She has been our constant, and she will be our Skalen in time. We see the friendship she has formed with Vaelnyr, and we know she is loved in the Southlands. Above all, we know her heart."

Voirrey smiled, her chest tight with gratitude.

"She came all the way from the Skalens' House to this little mountain village because her heart is with us: the people. We thank her, for healing our sick–for bringing us all the Alma we could ask for"–this part he whispered to titters of laughter–"and for showing us that Velspar is always changing. We leave our old rituals behind, because we want to be where Velspar is, now. We follow our future Skalen and listen to her wisdom, even if we do not understand it. We trust in her as our shepherdess."

Voirrey thought this last directive had gone a little too far.

Siran stopped, taking the time to look at each of them.

"Now," he said softly, "come forth with your burden and cast it into the fire. Let go of the past, and all the pain it has brought you. All your mistakes and misgivings, let them be gone and come before your future Skalen to be blessed."

The villagers evened out in a circle around the bonfire, holding their effigies to their lips, whispering to them their confessions, their wishes. Then, all at once, they threw them into the fire. Voirrey watched Sybilla lead her daughter to the edge and help her toss hers in before shying her face from the heat.

Amand and Voirrey came forward together, effigies pressed to their foreheads as they bowed in prayer. She cast hers in, watching Amand's doll of sticks follow after. Small bodies dissolving in the heart of the fire.

"Pure is the Stream, clear and bright," Voirrey murmured, then stood before the High Stone.

Joe Kern came first in line, opening his mouth. Voirrey took the bone-straw, dipped it in Alma oil, and placed her finger over the end to hold the liquid in place. Extending it into his mouth, she released her finger to drip the oil beneath his tongue.

"As one in Velspar," she said.

Joe closed his mouth, swallowed, and bowed. "As one."

Next came his wife Lena, and then the others, shuffling one after another, her refrain and theirs uttered in whisper until only Sybilla remained. Her eyes were red and glossy. Voirrey could sense her fear. She could not bring herself to join the villagers who all sat about the fire. They sat close and leaned into one another, chatting and laughing, their Meridians discarded in a pile.

Voirrey turned the bone straw to her own mouth and received the Alma, leaving a final drop for Davina whose little tongue licked the straw. She drew a dose for Sybilla, the self-same action she had performed when the woman suffered in childbirth to bring Davina into the world. Sybilla uplifted her face and opened her mouth, a tear lodged at the corner of her eye as she swallowed the golden oil.

Voirrey took Sybilla's hand and stroked it with her thumb. "Your red deeds have been released, Sybilla. You must believe that. You must forgive yourself."

Sybilla exhaled long, nodding.

Voirrey led her to the villagers.

"Come on, Vina, who do you want to play with?"

Davina spun around in excitement, losing her balance.

"Siran!" Voirrey called through her laugher. "Davina has started the dance!"

Glancing over, he roared in appreciation and sent the other children to join her.

Holding hands, the children ran in a ring, the taller boys pulling far too hard on the little girl's arms. Still, they squealed happily, apple-cheeked and full of life. Even old Mindy Goodwin joined in for a time.

Voirrey's heart swelled to see Davina among them but behind her she could feel Sybilla, silent as a stone pillar, and wanting desperately to get away.

Meeting Sybilla's eyes, she implored her. "Just come and sit with me on the grass there. We can watch the children awhile and then we can go home."

With head bowed, Sybilla followed, the awakening warmth of the Alma rising like heat from sunbaked stone. The incense of her soul steamed and was buffeted by the winds, and so quietly she kneeled, so still, her expression, that it made Voirrey want to weep. A barb of frustration rose in her throat. She wanted Sybilla to move and laugh and be free, and in looking at her, Voirrey became her mirror: disconnected from the others.

She sat beside Sybilla, the closeness of their bodies forming a grudging solidarity, though Voirrey kept her gaze upon the crowd. She focused on their faces, opened herself to them, tried to feel their proximal feelings. The children, especially. The boys all freckled and reedy, giving their sisters piggy backs. And Davina chasing them and

snatching at their clothes, her fat little face sun-bright and full of
mad glee.

"It's nice to see Davina with them," Sybilla said, her voice seeming
to come from far away. She said it, Voirrey knew, not because she felt
moved by what she saw, but to show Voirrey that she appreciated all
that she had done in bringing them here.

"She is a child, like any other," Voirrey said, wanting it to be true.
Her own childhood had been lonely and cold. And when her father
discovered young Edric in the ranks of the Guard, she had been all
but forgotten.

"I'll get us a drink," Sybilla said, and went off to pour them some
Alma wine.

Voirrey didn't feel like talking anyway. She let her body uncurl,
stretching out on her back, her eyes shaded in the crook of her arm.
The soft beauty of the Alma was about her now, and all her little
worries and irritations seemed inconsequential all of a sudden.

She closed her eyes to the wash of wind, the warm laughter and
crackling fire. Cows lowed in the distance. She could smell meadowsweet and woodsmoke. There were clouds above, voluptuous and
white, performing a pageant for her eyes alone. She watched with
passing delight, her eyes watering, wanting to see what new shapes
the sky would bring.

The children's laughter dissolved about a persistent shrieking.
Davina.

She sat up, blinking the blindness from her vision.

Sybilla abandoned the wooden cups she had been holding
and ran.

Voirrey moved toward them on uncertain feet, assessing the faces,
the tone of Davina's howling. She was hurt, but not badly.

Sybilla gathered her daughter up, and Voirrey examined the girl's
face over her mother's shoulder.

A quivering blood-lip, great sucking breaths, dirt-smeared cheek.
"Hey, Vina," Voirrey cooed, gently touching her hair. "You're okay.
You're okay."

Voirrey noticed Siran watching them.

Sybilla freed her hair, tucking it over her other shoulder. "I think it might be time to go home," she said, rubbing Davina's back.

Voirrey didn't want to go and knew that if given time to dry her tears, Davina would continue to play happily all afternoon. But as the Alma sent her love out from her, it coalesced about Sybilla, about the child. The others did not need her. Not really.

She smiled. "Aunty Voy will take care of you, little one. Don't you cry."

Just as they were leaving, Joe waved. Voirrey worried for a moment that he might come and help them. He was such a kind man, with a soft spot for Davina. He shooed her with his hand. "I'll tell the others. You go."

"Thanks, Joe," she replied, turning away.

And as her little household escaped the festivities, she felt herself relieved.

8

CIVIT'S RIDGE, NOTHELM

THE FIRST WEEKS OF WINTER were always bleak in the mountains. Voirrey had forgotten how cold it could get. She pressed her numbed toes, rocking in her wicker chair to try to bring some feeling into them. Her cheeks were dry from the fire and she had developed a wheezing cough from the constant smoke.

With little else to do, she set about replenishing her medicinal supplies, rolling bandages with agitation. Across the room, Davina rattled the front door. Shoved her back against it, straining her chubby feet. At this point, even Voirrey found herself irritated.

"It's snowing out there, and nighttime. We can't go out." Sybilla tried to take her hand so she'd move away from the draught. "Come on, let's sit by the fire." Davina snatched her hand away and screamed.

Voirrey watched mother and child peripherally as she pinned the latest roll, dropping it into the basket. In the corner, Amand sat, silently, his presence large in the room. Voirrey felt a knot in her stomach, one that she had to focus on to release.

Davina whined, straining harder, staring up at the bolt that she had no hope of reaching. She balled her fists, leaned forward and threw her back into the door–this time hitting her head.

A piercing wail.

"Oh no, what have you done?" Sybilla gathered her daughter up, kissing her and stroking the back of her head.

The little girl looked up, her liquid eyes full of her mother's face, turned soft all of a sudden, and beautiful, Voirrey thought. A smile started at the corner of Voirrey's mouth that retreated when she noticed Amand's eyes on her.

They did not wear their Meridians. Not in this house. Even if the villagers preferred to be cautious.

The people of Civit's Ridge had long been the people of her heart. How many years had she passed through these mountains, taking supplies to the fugitive Intercessor Amand, the old men patting her on the back with tears in their eyes? Civit's Ridge was the safest place she could imagine in this world, and yet, after living here for nigh on two years, she felt more separate from them than ever.

They watched Amand with fear and mistrust and did not want his interference. They seemed not to acknowledge the miracle of Sybilla's transformation. The evidence was before them! If Sybilla–the orchestrator of the Purge–could share a roof with an Intercessor, and trust her only child to his care, then what more proof could there be? The wolf embraced the lamb but still they doubted.

Despite the isolation of this place, and the fact that visitors could be spied at a distance, the villagers wore the Meridian. *But do I not also wear a kind of Meridian when I hide my thoughts within?* Confess it. *Yes, perhaps.*

Voirrey felt a sharp prick as the pin jabbed her finger and pressed it to her lips. *Confess it.* Had that been her thought, or Amand's? She sighed and did not look at him.

They all looked at Davina, the blameless one, who kept peace and goodwill among them. Sybilla looking at the top of her head, occasionally kissing her hair. Amand watching her restless hands. Voirrey observing sidelong, thinking of Sybilla's knees on the cold stone floor.

All grievances were sheathed before the child, but still those dark currents flowed. Could she feel them? An eddy of guilt, a sense of failure and inevitability.

"Give her to me if you like," Voirrey said, holding her arms out.

Davina looked at her shyly, her green eyes round beneath her fringe.

"Come on, your mama is tired."

The little girl trudged forward, her head down on one shoulder, her affected reluctance blossoming into a smile.

Voirrey brought her up on her lap, rocking her as she had done since the day she was born. "Are you a little baby, Vina?"

"No!" she cackled, kicking her legs out.

"Then why are you letting me rock you like a baby?"

Davina grinned and clung to her.

Voirrey shook her head ruefully. "If you turn back into a baby, I'll never be able to take you on a mountain walk."

"You carry me!" Davina commanded, grabbing a lock of Voirrey's blonde hair.

She raised an eyebrow. "Will I? No, I don't think so."

Sybilla still sat by the door, watching them, a gentle smile on her face.

Amand passed between the two women and rustled Davina's hair. "Night, little one."

He clasped his hands behind his back, walking in his slow way down the hall to his room.

"Nigh-night, Ama," Davina called.

When he was gone, Sybilla came and sat in the chair beside Voirrey, keeping to herself as Davina lost interest in play, melting into the soothing warmth of Voirrey's chest.

Before long, Davina took to drooling on Voirrey's smock.

Sybilla returned to braiding her hair. Outside, soft snow fell. Voirrey pulled her wrap about her as the fire bedded down, black coals with hearts of red, tucked among the ashes.

9

CIVIT'S RIDGE, NOTHELM

IT WAS A MILD morning. The mountains shone with runoff, the chill wind betraying the merest scent of blossom. Voirrey went about her errands with brisk step, and felt the whole village astir, eager to meet in this rare moment of sunshine. In the air, she felt the burgeoning energy of spring, an itch of hope and possibility. People who had tightened their cloaks and frowned when last she saw them were full of smiles, all of them asking how little Davina fared.

Presently, she made her way to meet Amand–just the two of them–to perform Blood Call. Not in the old way–the villagers were not ready–but as best they could without Blood Kin or altar, and without the dark-winged kshidol above them.

They prayed to an empty sky, and walked the untrodden path.

It seemed vital to her that they continue the rites. She could not say why, for it was plain that the world of her youth was gone. It was as if she had once sung in harmony with all of Velspar, and for the last nineteen years she had been holding her note in a sea of silence. This is why she treasured Amand. Though, he was only truly at his ease when distant from the town. All winter, he performed his routines with averted eyes. Sybilla had shrunk even further into herself than when they had first met. Each day, the snow drifted down, covering their little home in soft imprisonment. The four of them passed one another, washing and working, moving from bed to bench to chair, and to bed again–but without truly seeing one another. Davina alone seemed bright with life. They doted on her, indulging her every mood so they might avoid meeting each other's eyes and facing the truth.

Voirrey scuffed her feet on the pebbly road, wanting more than anything to perform these rites with Sybilla. To be there when Davina cut her palm for the first time, embracing her heritage and her destiny.

Her eyes traced the roofs of nearby houses, only some running their fires, giving off wafting grey smoke.

Movement caught her eye, and across the way, she saw a dark-haired woman stooping in pain. She started forward. "Mildred!"

Voirrey sped her pace, fearing the woman might collapse.

She reached out with a steadying arm. "Mildred, are you okay?"

Voirrey assessed the woman: she was waxen, sweating, her chest twisting as if the thread of her soul had been pulled tight.

"Ah," the woman managed, leaning herself against the outer wall of the Casterley's barn. "Voirrey, how nice to see you," she said. Her smile belied her pain. "Lovely day for a walk."

Voirrey reached out to touch the woman's face, but Mildred grasped it, as if to say, *do not pity me*. Her grip was firm, her calloused hands work-worn.

Voirrey frowned. "Have you been taking the tonic I gave you?"

Mildred nodded.

"You should be abed. Where is Glenny?" Voirrey looked about for the boy.

"I sent him to the Folshom's." Her breath caught as a new pain started in her breast. "Agh," she cursed, but continued through gritted teeth. "I thought I was having a good day."

Mildred slid to the base of the wall, unable to stand any longer. Anger radiated from her. Anger with herself for being sick, anger with Voirrey for not being able to heal her, anger that she could not even take herself for a walk without help.

Voirrey crouched beside her. "We are all neighbours here. There's no need for you to do this alone."

Mildred's head was in her hands and she glared at the dirt.

"Everything alright, Mildred?" Lena Kern appeared beside Voirrey and set down her basket. "What's happened? Should we get her home?"

Mildred ignored her.

Before Voirrey could explain the situation, Lena was calling for help, and soon they were surrounded by onlookers. The increasing crowd of old women piped in with conflicting suggestions until no one could be heard.

"Oh, you're all hopeless!" Lena cried. "Someone go get Joe and Martin and tell them to come quick."

In the midst of them, Voirrey crouched before the silent woman on the ground. "You're looking a little better." She touched her fingers to Mildred's wrist, sensing the disturbance had passed. "Do you want me to get rid of them?"

Mildred leaned her head back and smiled. "You know, I've been stuck indoors with no one but myself for company. Let them fuss. They won't do me any harm."

Voirrey gave her a conspiratorial nod and pushed herself to stand. "Now, Lena, please be gentle with her and make sure there's someone to sit and talk with her awhile. She can be outside as long as it is warm out, but not on the ground like this. Get the men to take her to the hill and bring her some blankets. I'll be back to check on her in the evening."

The woman bobbed her head as if to thank Voirrey for finally coming to her senses and letting her do what she did best.

"We'll sort you out, Milly."

"Don't call me that, I warn you."

"Oh, you warn me, do you? Feeling feisty, now?"

Voirrey let the voices fade behind her, noticing a chill in the air as she hurried to meet Amand. Sure enough, clouds were darkening at the horizon. For a moment, she thought of going back and telling them to make a fire for the woman, but decided she was worrying unnecessarily.

When she reached the edge of the village, she saw Amand waiting for her like a silhouette in his brown robe. It struck her how wrong it was that he could not wear Intercessor's white. No longer would his raiment remind people of the Temple and its high wisdom. He was a man to hide himself among the crags, to wear his "heresy" like a shadow.

"There you are," he said, his penetrating eyes reminding her that he was beyond such concerns.

Voirrey let out a great sigh. "Here I am." She pointed at the greenish clouds in the distance. "And there are the clouds. Looks ripe to snow again, I'll get grips for our shoes."

He pulled up the rope about his waist to reveal two dangling pairs of metal snow grips.

She laughed. "Very good."

They started out, following the dirt track down for a way, then back up and around until a vast and unpeopled landscape spread out before them. There, the black peaks of Jokvour were dusted white, sloping to silent canyons below.

They walked side-by-side, Voirrey watching the view, Amand slipping easily into his walking trance. To one who did not know him, he walked as any other, but Voirrey knew the rasp of his deeper breath, the stillness of his gaze.

Now and again, she noticed Amand thumbing the scars on his palm.

We will give of our blood, my friend, she thought, *but the kshidol will not come. They will never come again.*

The fact of it left her empty.

She tried to shake the feeling, to let her thoughts and worries drift away.

Amand went before her, his body rocking a little as he walked, humming deep and low. It struck her how alone he seemed. How tragic his pilgrimage. Regret squeezed at her, sickly and persistent. *I should not have made him come here. I should not have torn him from Waldemar and Maeryn.*

Amand turned slowly, his oceanic gaze touching her like an enveloping wave.

She swallowed hard and made herself begin the Hymn. Wanting to be swept up, but not quite managing it:

Swift feather
Traveller,
Blood beaked
Kshidol

Amand's resonant voice joined hers, speaking words of Blood Call—of the gift of life and the passage of the dead. *Holy Kshidol, Father, and bringer of sons.* Amand's seemed to be many voices now. His voice a thread she caught and followed, until they were as birds travelling in formation, to the shape of an ancient song.

In weightless joy, she expanded.

On and on, she held this fragile posture of spirit, heart, and mind. Feeling its perfection, its rightness, the pettiness of thought all sloughed away.

They grew quiet as they reached the crag, where Amand crouched and used his flint to light the Alma. He moved the smoking twigs rhythmically, forming a misty spiral in the sky. He repeated the Hymn until the words were but the shape of his prayers.

Amand laid the smoking thatch between them on the ground. Voirrey breathed its sweetness, her eyes pricking with tears.

They brought their foreheads to touch and her heart bled out all of its poison. Together, their hands reddened with the expansion of their breath.

All is forgiven, and loving, and vast.

She was not Voirrey, a spirit isolated and alone. She was a living embodiment of the Stream. An irruption in flesh of those sacred waters, a vessel and conduit that would flow where all water flows when it is time. Down to the deep. To the larger body. Always there.

In her heat Voirrey shivered, cold sparks falling on her skin as, finally, it began to snow.

"You are crying," he said, his eyes crinkling in a sad smile.

She grasped his hand. "I am."

He looked into her face. "Do you want me to take away your pain?"

Voirrey wiped the tears from her cheeks. "No, I want to feel it."

She realised that she must, or else she would forget the wrong she had done him.

She was not going to speak but then a choked sob escaped her. "I should not have brought you here, Amand, and I am sorry." The meniscus within her broke. "You belong with your own kind."

He grasped her hand where it held his forearm.

"Can you not feel your power, Voirrey?" he asked.

She drew back her hand.

"Intercession flows where Velspar wills," he said, kneeling to extinguish the Alma. "You work with the redness as I do."

Voirrey stood there dumbly, unwilling to think on it. Intercessors were visionaries who could open the lid of the mind and know what lay within. They could read the world around them and see the deeper structures. An Intercessor would know Velspar's will and the right path to take.

He said this to confuse her. She was trying to apologise. If she bore the powers of Intercession, it would be he who cried and opened his heart to her. He exuded holiness, a quietude she could never hope to maintain, but he never spilt his cup.

Voirrey strapped her boots in silence, sifting the resentment within her. This much for herself, this much for the state of the world, this much for Sybilla, this much for Amand. This much for the villagers, her parents, for Meridians, and broken Temples. For uncertainty and loneliness...

But could it be true? She could not think of herself that way. A healer, maybe.

They pulled up their hoods to keep the weather off and Voirrey felt her friend's hand warm on her back. She returned the gesture. Voirrey squinted against the cold, her ears full of the whistling wind.

The dark clouds that brought their flurries were concentrated above them, but as they rounded the bend, Voirrey caught a glimpse of Seltsland, low to the east where the snow never fell. There, slanting golden light split through the clouds. Swampland shone bronze-coloured, like fire oil.

Here they stood a moment to admire the view, taking a few sips of water before continuing on.

Soon the path put Seltsland behind them and they proceeded downhill. The track was narrow here and slippery. Through the whirring snow Voirrey tried to make out the terrain, stepping gingerly over snow-furred rocks and muddy patches that could easily send her over the edge.

Finally, the rooftops of Civit's Ridge came into view. They looked so small, like little bird's nests. She thought of Mildred and the frustration she had nursed over the intervening weeks seemed to evaporate. She still had a role here, one that no other could perform.

She looked fondly upon Amand, his hood flung back in a gust of wind. Despite her misgivings, their time together had refreshed her somehow. He did not need her apologies. He needed her to dip her hands in the Stream and be renewed.

10

CIVIT'S RIDGE, NOTHELM

"MISTRESS! MISTRESS VOIRREY!" The voice was muffled and high, a child, but who? Voirrey pulled the bedsheet clear of her face to listen for the sound, not truly believing in it. A prickle of alarm in the softness of an ill-remembered dream.

But then there was a rapping at the door. Small and insistent.

She sat up in pitch dark, eyes keened as she took her candle to the ghostly hearth.

Outside she heard a sob.

"I am coming!" she rasped, trying not to wake the others as she bent the candle's wick to the slumbering coals.

The little flame stretched and sputtered, hurting her eyes, and she went to open the door.

Mildred's son, Glenny Palmer stood there, tear-streaked, grabbing her arm.

"Come, please, it's Mother. You've got to help."

Fast blood flushed her mind of sleep. "Okay Glenny, let me get my bag."

She went in, stuffed her feet into her boots, drew a cloak about her, and shouldered her medicine bag.

The boy darted in front of her down the street, barefoot and bluish in the dark. She followed with brisk breath, her nightdress swishing as she passed the sleeping houses of their neighbours.

The Palmer's house was up ahead, lamplight ruddy through the open door.

Glenny darted inside and she ran. Bottles clattered at her hip.

Inside, the lamp's flame seemed to writhe, hot and bright, painting the walls a horrifying shade.

Mildred Palmer was doubled over at the table, her face slick and pale. Her son ran past, casting his shadow across her back.

Voirrey approached quickly, with practised calm. Mildred sat with her head askance. The woman's Meridian looked uncomfortably tight about her forehead.

Carefully, Voirrey got the boy to help her lay his mother on the floor and asked him for a pillow. The woman's left side was caught in a rictus that Voirrey was not confident she could undo. It was a miracle that her heart had not given out completely. In her experience, the first spasm would only release in order to prepare for the next squeeze.

Bringing her head low, she turned her face to Mildred's, smiling gently as she began to remove the woman's Meridian. Mildred grit her teeth, her dark eyes rolling in terror.

Voirrey retracted her hands, held them up to show she would not try to remove it by force.

"Mildred, hear me," she whispered. "Do not fear. Do not fear." Compassion flooded from Voirrey's heart. She wanted to take the device from the woman's crown, the barrier that made her feel as though there was nothing on the other side.

Voirrey felt Glenny shuffling beside them, not knowing what to do. She grasped his arm and gestured for him to crouch beside his mother.

"Take off your Meridians; this is your chance to say goodbye," Voirrey whispered gravely.

He looked uncertain, watching his mother, the slight shake of her head. Voirrey felt a surge of pity that verged on anger.

"Mildred, he will not feel your pain. Do not be afraid."

The boy stared, unwilling to disobey his mother.

He turned on Voirrey, his face distorted in fury. "Make her better! Why are you just sitting there?" He balled his fist and punched her arms and chest.

She bore these pangs, trying her hardest not to flinch.

In her mind, the winds of Jokvour called to her with memories of the Stream. Holding that feeling, she spoke to the boy, praying that he, at least, would see.

"There is no remedy for her. I am sorry for this," she said, as gently as she could. "But she is still here, there is still time to help her pass." Glenny did not answer, just stared at his mother, hitching sounds escaping her throat as her body was taken up by a fresh seizure.

Voirrey stood, stepped away. She knew the limits of her gift. "I will send for Intercessor Amand," she said with her head bowed.

Mildred let out a strangled scream, her trembling hands covering her head.

"Mama!" Glenny reached for her shoulder but she did not seem to feel his light touch.

"I will fetch him, stay with her!" Voirrey said and started for the door.

"No!" the boy shouted. "She doesn't want him here." He threw himself over his mother's body, sobbing as she moaned. Long, grief-stricken moans that Voirrey knew well.

In a kind of daze, she went out and closed the door.

She did not know where to go. She could not simply go back to bed and sleep till morning. The woman would die on the floor with her boy crying over her. And when the sun rose, their neighbours would take the body off somewhere.

She could not understand it. There was a holy man in their midst and they would not allow him to do his work. If the dying did not call out to the Holy Ones with their final breath, then how could they be reborn? If the woman's spirit was half-dissolved, she might never find her guide. She thought of going back in, of whispering their names. *Mildred, can you see Mother Siatka and Father Kshidol? Who calls you? Will you return as a girl child or as a boy? Think it now before you are nothing. Intend yourself toward them.*

But she didn't go back. Above her, the scattered stars stared down, watching her as she returned to her own dark cottage and disappeared inside.

Asleep. All asleep. Even Amand.

She glared at his door as if he should know when a spirit was passing. Or did he lay there, eyes on the ceiling, observing Mildred's passage from afar?

Voirrey swallowed dryly and moved through the room.

Picturing him thus, and wanting his company, she opened his door. His eyes were closed, his face grey and serene in the dim. Did he pretend sleep? For a moment longer, she stood, determined to wake him, then turned away, disgusted with herself.

Her stomach clenched in sympathetic paroxysms with the woman whose body must soon find its release.

"Voirrey..." Amand's voice touched her like a hand.

She turned, tears in her eyes, falling to her knees beside him.

"I'm so sorry," she gasped. "Everything is wrong. I don't know how to fix it. I thought I could help them."

Amand sat and touched her shoulders where she kneeled.

The warmth of his broad palms seemed to open her heart, and seeing that his eyes were closed, she let her lids fall. In darkness, hot tears, and love, such love. All her fears and misgivings were as detritus blocking a river–and he removed them. He lifted and freed her, moment by dizzying moment, until she felt the flow of her being restored. It was not him that she felt, it was herself, her best self; purified and reassured.

She opened her eyes, feeling clarified and unmarred.

Amand touched her cheek. "Mildred Palmer," he said.

Voirrey nodded. She went to speak, to tell him of their protests, that he was not wanted but that she, more than anything, wanted him there.

"I will listen from here," he said, moving his eyes to the curtained window. "I can hear her spirit now, and I will not rest until I have delivered her. In the morning, you will prepare the body, and all will be well," Amand said.

"But Amand, they will not let me. I fear that they no longer believe!" Fresh tears sprung from her eyes.

"We do what we can. It is the spirit that travels, as long as you collect a vial of blood we can perform her final Blood Call. Take care that you do not force the people's hearts to close by becoming zealous. These are lessons you taught me, Voirrey. Patience, kindness, imperfection. This is the world we live in now. Above all, we must keep their hearts open," he said.

Several breaths passed and she sat in awe of him.

"Yes, you are right. Thank you, Intercessor."

All will be well, she repeated in her mind.

"Sleep well, my friend," he said, and returned himself to the sheets.

Voirrey bowed and went out.

Sitting in her wicker chair, she chose a vial from her pack, polished it, and stowed it in her pocket, rocking as she waited for the Intercessor's sign.

11

THRALE FOREST, BRIVIA

Waldemar approached the mound. "Ah, dear Illiam has left something for us." He hurried forward, hunger upon him all of a sudden.

This was one of several drop points where the Brivian Regents arranged for supplies to be sent to Sidney. Olinda and Jemryn were Greslets to be sure, but not all Greslets could be counted among their enemies. The Regents' son, Illiam, despite his moment of foolishness on Jokvour, had proved especially loyal to the rebellion. Earlier, the lad had been motivated by a desire to set himself apart and forge his own way–to prove that he inherited nothing from his uncle, the drunken Skalen of Maglore. But this latest act of generosity surely came as penance for depriving the Intercessors of the sacred stone, right when it was needed most.

It was no secret that the young man had captured Zohar Elshender's heart, and the southern alliance was strengthened by such fortuitous interweavings of fate and destiny. The match formed a symbolic link between Brivia, where the boy had lived most of his life, and Avishae. Though it posed a certain threat to his cousin Lilwenn's ascendency in Maglore, the land of his birth. Davina? She still sat in her mother's lap, an ill-begotten child whose very existence brought shame to the Guard. They would use her for their ends, Waldemar knew, or they would kill her before too long. Voirrey's plan to keep the girl hidden in the northern hills was idealistic at best. These young ones would rule, if only they could survive to adulthood. Swords at all of their hearts, that was the truth of it. A sword at Sidney's heart if ever he should stir from his forest hermitage and seek his own inheritance–and his the richest of all.

Waldemar lowered awkwardly to his knees and removed the stones that weighed down the oilskin. Peeling it back he caught a whiff of caraway rolls, a favourite of his from the Skalens' House kitchens in the days when he'd been welcomed there. Illiam had found the recipe somehow, had gone to the trouble of fulfilling an old man's wish. A good lad, he was.

"Sidney, come and look. I can see a jar of honey here at the bottom, and cheese, and even some pork jerky." He rifled through the bundle, his eyebrows dancing at the treasures he had once taken for granted. "Come, Sidney! Let's fatten you up. Got to keep you strong, my Skalen."

The torn roll hung open in his hand. Finally locating the butter, Waldemar unwrapped the waxed paper, his fingers trembling from hunger. Exhuming a knife from his belt, he wiped it on his robe and scraped the heavenly substance thickly onto the roll. He took a great hunk of the buttered bread into his mouth and chewed with his eyes shut tight.

"Mmm, that is good," he mumbled, his beard hopping up and down as he ate.

He could hear Sidney's shambling footsteps as he made his slow approach. Waldemar sat down cross-legged, his knees sticking out from his robe, and grabbed a roll for Sidney.

"With honey, my Skalen?" he asked happily.

Sidney glanced at him with a press of the lips that was almost a smile.

Waldemar spread the butter for Sidney between bites of his own roll, then drizzled the golden honey. As Sidney began to eat, the Intercessor could almost see the sweet flavour as it lit up the man's expression. Simple pleasures, and best they be enjoyed.

Waldemar sucked the stickiness from his fingers with a satisfying pop.

At the bottom of the parcel was a note. The Intercessor held it up to the light and read.

The note was not signed but he knew it came from Illiam's mother, Olinda. The Regents had developed a system of marks to convey information so it could not be decoded by the Maglorean Guard. In the guise of protectors, the Magloreans harried the Brivian population wherever they settled, though they were less inclined these days to pursue them into the thick of the forest. Occasionally, Sidney and Waldemar had been made to hide when they made unexpected patrols, but Thrale was such a vast and untrammelled wilderness that the guardsmen quickly became bored, which made them careless and loud. So, the hermit Skalen (and the Intercessor they didn't know had survived) evaded them easily.

As Waldemar read, he frowned, learning that the Skalen of Maglore, Domhnall Greslet, had been seriously injured in a fall. Olinda did not feel much for Skalen Inry, her sister-by-marriage, yet this latest development put her and the young Greslet heirs in a vulnerable position. Head Guardsman Rayhmer had always been dangerous, taking measures that spat on the sacred tenets of the Guard, but this latest development was dire indeed.

Sidney did not ask what the letter contained, just sat there chewing, enjoying his meal.

Waldemar exhaled a troubled breath. "We need more time. More time," he muttered.

He considered the means by which Rayhmer might be dispatched. Would it be enough? Already Rayhmer's men had that swagger about them. It would be a messy business if the factions of the Guard finally drew swords against one another. Then all pretence of political unity in Velspar would come to an end. The Magloreans would annex this place, removing the rebels and their allies, taking Avishae, birth-place of the stone. He could not lose his chance to unearth what was surely the Intercessors' last inheritance.

He rubbed his temples with forefinger and thumb. "Sidney, what can we do?"

The man did not answer. Whenever Waldemar tried to speak to him of politics, he could not take in the new names–Lilwenn, Edlin, Davina, poor Ambrose and his sister Zohar. Even Illiam, who saw to his survival, was a stranger to him. He lived eternally in that dark moment when his world had ended, when the Fire of Vaelnyr failed to extinguish the Ladain line and Sybilla rose from the ashes to wreak her bloody vengeance.

Following Sidney's parent's execution, his brother, Andrin, ascended as Skalen long enough to decimate the Brivian populace, calling for his people to kill themselves; for faith and for Velspar. Sidney had screamed himself hoarse but Andrin would not stop. He would not listen. The dead lying putrescent in the streets, and finally, Andrin joined them.

It had broken Sidney utterly, and glancing at him, Waldemar was reminded that the wretch was half dead, if not in body, then certainly in mind. By Velspar, he needed Amand. He was the strategist.

Waldemar watched Sidney, who mindlessly stared at the canopy above. If Waldemar had never had that dream of the afterlife, if he did not fear the ashen stains of transgression that it would bring, he could possess the man, make him a Skalen, truly. A Skalen who could put an end to Rayhmer and others like him. Those who sought power over the flesh but who left their souls in disarray.

He swallowed hard, his mouth gone dry. If Maeryn could see his thoughts now... It was a dreadful solution. He wanted to be pure when he stood at the banks of the Great Stream, and such a plan would not only condemn him, but sever his every allegiance.

He clapped his hands, rubbed them together. "We must put this lot away before the ants come! Here Sidney, you carry the blankets, I'll take the food."

The oilskin came together with a rope and Waldemar slung it over his shoulder. He would have to return to the spot to leave his reply but the thoughts swirling through his mind could not be considered wise counsel. He would think on it some more, and by night, he would come. Illiam usually left it a day.

As they returned to their latest campsite, Waldemar composed his coded reply to Olinda.

Caution warranted.
Alert Voirrey.
Lindesali Regents and Elshenders already prepared,
    don't risk contact.
We hide south-east.
Don't bring supplies.
Rouse your brother if you can.

Skalen Domhnall was no friend to their cause but if he was strong, Rayhmer would be held in check for the time being. It was a long shot. The man had been drinking himself into oblivion for nearly two decades now.

As far as Voirrey went, Civit's Ridge was a fair distance, but if they could get word to her, surely she would see that Amand was needed here. He was crucial to the rebel's cause, that was a truth upon which all of them could agree.

But more than that, Waldemar needed another Intercessor, a man of power who could draw close to the stone without losing his mind. In doing this he broke his promise to Maeryn. Like all women of heart, she worried too much. It was her weakness and her strength, and in loving her he must do what his own nature commanded. She would come to see things as he did. She would. And he need not disturb Ambrose's cairn to get at the coveted fragment that the Elshenders guarded, for the black stream ran like a glacier of stone in the earth beneath their feet. Rich with voices, and with promise. The secret to their destiny.

12

THRALE FOREST, BRIVIA

WALDEMAR SAT ON THE BANK of a small creek, one of many that veined the forest, making moss grow thick upon the rocks. The trees here were not so tall as in the heart of Thrale, but familiar species of fungi and flower punctuated the green. Here, at least, he could see the sky.

Waldemar whisked his robe aside as he scrubbed his shins in the water. He placed his old-man feet on a rock and let them drip off, feeling utterly at ease.

"What do you think, Sidney?"

Waldemar knew better than to expect a response, but he liked speaking to him anyway. It was dangerous for an Intercessor to remain too much in the mind. But he also hoped that Sidney gained something from their conversations. To the untrained observer, the last Karasek was a madman, rendered mute by his sufferings. But Waldemar knew the richness of his inner life, the cringing fear of his mother, the guilt that sat upon him in its many layers of sediment, awaiting the movement of speech to unleash the baying storm.

Despite Sidney's dishevelled appearance and rank odour, he had not entirely abandoned the needs of the body. He knew when he was hungry, or when thirst had its claws in him. *Water* was the word he uttered most, and Waldemar made sure to acknowledge him whenever the word passed his lips. No matter the inconvenience, the Intercessor would turn heel in order to find the nearest river, puddle, or pond.

This was how they came to the water's edge and how they had found the profligate mushrooms that now filled Waldemar's pack.

Behind, Sidney sniffed and pocketed something he'd found on the forest floor.

Waldemar smiled and lapsed into silence.

Drawing up water with his hand, he sloughed the remaining grime from his ankles, but did not dare immerse himself fully: he did not like to risk Sidney wandering off.

Waldemar felt the sun emerge from behind a cloud, warm and comforting. It was a beautiful day and for a while he let himself fall into a doze. When he opened his eyes, the brightness was piercing, and he massaged his eyebrows with his fingers to clear his vision.

He glanced about for Sidney, feeling momentarily unsettled, until he caught sight of his scraggy black hair behind a bush. Waldemar had no desire to interrupt a man at his business.

He leaned back, stroking the grey beard that had grown long in the two years that had passed since their party disbanded at Jokvour. Above, golden leaves flitted, the thin bough dipping low at the arrival of an over-large bird. The creature hung upside down, cracking the clustered seeds there. It cawed and several more came, until all he could hear was the crunching and popping of seeds.

Sidney returned from behind the bush and washed his hands in the water, staring up at the birds. Waldemar watched the man's mouth quirk in a rare smile, the pale of his eyes visible as he tilted his face to the light. It was easy to think Sidney's eyes were dark due to his heavy brows, and the shadows cast by his trailing, matted hair. But no, they were a faint blue-grey. It pleased Waldemar to see his Skalen like this.

One of the branches above them snapped and several of the birds took wing, leaving the remnants of their flock to nibble closer to the trunk, their careful movements affording them a greater share of the feast. Standing so near, the stink of Sidney's hair prompted Waldemar to reach for his comb. Powerless to make the man wash,

Waldemar combed his own hair, reassuring himself that he still kept an Intercessor's standards. When he had finished his hair, Waldemar worked the comb from the tail of his beard to the flesh of his cheeks. The sections he had completed took on an airy fullness that made him want for a proper pair of shears.

"We should make camp. I think the weather will hold." Waldemar glanced at the sky. "Over there." He gestured to a nearby clearing.

Sidney was still staring at the birds, but sombrely now, as if he simply did not wish to hear the sound of a human voice.

Waldemar patted Sidney on the back. "Come now, Sidney. Put your pack down and we can gather firewood. Catch a rabbit or two."

Sidney nodded and they walked together, looking for all the world like father and son.

It was a peaceful task, gathering the wood: searching the forest floor for dry kindling in a variety of thicknesses, brushing away leaves and dirt to form a conical cluster that would burn long into the night.

When darkness fell, and the sticks were crackling nicely, Waldemar took up his pipe, pressing dried Alma leaves into its chamber. In the early days of his vagrancy, Waldemar used to toss the leaves onto the fire itself so sweetened smoke filled the air. It was a practice from his Temple days when Alma was held in such abundance that it could be cast freely into the flames without thought of waste. Sometimes if he and Sidney slept in a cave with a narrow opening–in stormy weather, for instance–he returned to this practice, for its gentleness on the dreaming mind. But he and Sidney had taken to the pipe, the hot rush, the flooding of the heart, the effulgent goodness that it brought after two or three breaths.

Waldemar passed the Alma pipe. Sidney's cheeks hollowed as he drew deep, held his breath, and emitted the smoke in twin streams. Waldemar took less, a small sip that he held for effect, then exhaled over his shoulder. Passing it back, Sidney's inhalation seemed to go on and on, the Alma glowing red as the dying sun until he finally let his breath out again. Waldemar saw that there were only ashes left and tapped them out on a rock. As he gathered a fresh pinch of Alma from his pouch, he glanced sidelong. Sidney's eyelids drooped unevenly, his arms draped atop his bent knees. He swayed forward then jolted upright.

Waldemar moved carefully, smoothing the pipe's rim and lighting it with a smouldering twig. He puffed several times to get it going, then presented it to Sidney once more. The man's hand drifted listlessly toward the pipe, one of his eyes completely closed, the other rolling with each slow blink. He sucked, held...held...and breathed ghostly into the dark. His hand had grown slack, and Waldemar extracted the pipe without rousing the other man's notice.

Unwatched as he was, Waldemar extinguished the remains of the Alma.

It seemed that in all that time Sidney had not inhaled, that his previous exhalation imposed a timeless depth upon the surrounding trees.

Waldemar waited. He dusted himself off and reached for one of the nuts they had roasted earlier. Sidney was not asleep. He was frozen, half-poised, half-slumped, as if he had forgotten what he meant to do.

The soft veils of the Alma caressed the waiting Intercessor, making his mind dance joyfully and expand, warming his heart–but all in a way that he could set aside. The wonder of the Alma cleared a central tunnel through which he observed Sidney, the object of his attention. He watched for telltale signs, parchment upon his knee, his quill loaded and ready.

"Mmhh-hh," Sidney groaned, "mmm." He straightened a little, arched his back and slumped forward again.

The fire hissed in the quiet dark and Waldemar began to exert himself over the man, subtly, in the Alma's wake. If his will showed through, if he could be seen by Sidney, then who knew what the man would do? It was not for any lack of affection or caring that Waldemar worked in this way, it was that Sidney was not capable of taking the plan into his mind, of knowing what was best and what was needed. His brokenness left him wide open and that was the way his mother's spirit got in. For all Waldemar's exertions, for all his hours of focusing on her essence–the timbre of her voice, with its cat's rasp–he could not reach her any other way.

"Mmmm," Sidney moaned again, "mmm."

Waldemar felt a tingle of anticipation as Sidney's voice took on a communicative cadence. He paused as if receiving an answer, following with a slow grumbling "mmm" that sounded like a reply.

It often began this way.

Waldemar leaned closer to Sidney's ear, but a little behind him, so if the man opened his eyes the voice would have no owner.

"Skalen Karasek," he said, the safest mode of address, for it could mean Sidney, the rightful Skalen of Brivia and the last of the Karasek line, but it could equally refer to any of the Karasek Skalens who had passed into the Stream, from the First Diviner to his own masters, nineteen years dead. In his mind, Waldemar pictured Emryl, her shrewd eyes and finely wrinkled mouth, her coarse grey hair like a mesh of wire about her face. The way she would purse her lips in such a way that her cheek bones bulged, her jaw delicate and fine.

"Mmm-ah-h-h-h." Sidney's moan brought up strong feelings, a swelling that rose up in him, the breath pouring from his lungs like the final pulse of arterial blood from a slit throat. The air, the sound, and the feeling that came from Sidney's mouth also resembled blood in the way that it pooled about them and did not disperse.

Sidney gasped, his head thrown back, his face possessed by grief, his eyes clenched shut with the force of it. And the gasps from this point on were the gasps of a weeping man. Waldemar watched patiently, as tears ran down his cheeks and into his beard, making it glimmer, leaving tracks of clean skin amid the grime.

"My Skalen," Waldemar gently said. "There are many sorrows, many sorrows, but Velspar is here with us. Can you hear the voices? They are here, they are buried, deep, beneath us. Look beneath you now. Listen beneath. It is as a heartbeat. Strong, steady. You feel it."

Though Waldemar could not feel it himself, except in a very distant sense, he could tell by Sidney's changed expression–the flat calm and piqued attentiveness–that Sidney could. Beneath his lids, Waldemar watched Sidney's eyeballs meandering in their sockets.

"Tell me, which way is north?"

A finger rose on Sidney's left hand, indicating the way. It was miraculous.

"And tell me," the Intercessor said, moistening his lips. "Where can you sense the voices most strongly now?"

For a few moments Sidney remained motionless, save for the fluttering of his lids. And then, with steadiness of hand, he pointed.

Waldemar's pulse ran in satisfied pursuit, a step closer to their prize.

"And in this place, do you feel that they are close to the surface? Do they sing naked to the air, or are they cloaked in blinding stone?" It was always difficult to get Sidney to focus on this aspect of the sensation, but Waldemar lost nothing in trying.

Sidney's hand extended to touch the ghostly substance of his vision. Again, he looked fearful, shaking his head as if he had water in his ear. They spoke to him, Waldemar sensed, they were speaking to him now.

The Intercessor's hand hovered, trembling hot, just behind Sidney's head. His senses keened, and momentarily, he felt it himself. "Ah!" Waldemar cried, losing himself in the moment.

Sidney turned, his eyes sharp on his companion, far too aware.

Waldemar shook his hand and put his finger to his lips as if he had burnt himself.

"Look at me, silly old man," he said and took himself off, the intoxicating sensation of the stone still flowing rich in his memory.

That was enough for one night, he thought. That was enough now.

At least he knew where they must go.

13

THRALE FOREST, BRIVIA

"Get up, Sidney. Come, we must go."

Sidney's eyes opened. He looked at Waldemar, a look of unsettling alacrity, not of accusation exactly, but of awareness. It shamed him, but not for long. Sidney stared dimly into the middle distance, taking up his familiar repose. He did not know. Did he? Sidney did not mind and would understand that sometimes an Intercessor had to override individual needs to access the common wellspring of truth.

Sidney pulled himself up, cupped tepid water from the small pot beside him and spat into the grass. For Sidney, that was the extent of his morning ablutions, but Waldemar had arisen at dawn, as he always did, to strip naked and cleanse the animal musk that accrued otherwise. He moved the dampened rag systematically, starting at the neck and moving down the arms, the torso, buttocks and legs, ending with the feet. The process reoriented the mind, reminding him of the symmetry and structure of his own body. There was an order to things and such order spoke of Velspar's will. The Intercessor's gift also spoke of a deeper order, to the bestowal of insight on Velspar's chosen. Now that his brethren were dead, this holy responsibility sat firmly on his shoulders. He, Amand, and Maeryn, the last remaining links in an ancient chain.

"Come, Sidney, the stone is calling." Waldemar started off.

In the humid air, Waldemar had to focus on the light in Sidney's eyes to bring forth compassion for the man whose hair stank like a clutch of dead ferrets. The Intercessor led on so he would not be downwind but in this section of the forest some pungent flower was in bloom, its orange hollows like orifices, sickening to behold.

In the afternoon, the leaves grew slick with a light rain. The air was still close, but a little fresher now. The two travellers pulled up their hoods and sat beneath the thick foliage of a speckled palm. Sidney's black-rimmed fingers fumbled in his pocket, whole nuts disappearing into his beard. He chewed, surveying their surrounds.

"We are near?" Waldemar asked hopefully.

Sidney gave a single nod and stared at the ground as he finished his mouthful. He looked tense and troubled.

"What do you feel, my Skalen?" Waldemar extended his awareness into the periphery of Sidney's mind. He could feel the war within him, the apprehension and desire.

When Sidney did not answer, Waldemar stood behind him, placing his hands on the man's shoulders. The Intercessor opened the connection and began to draw from him, a hot, prickling sensation moving through his hands and forearms. The feeling was stronger now than it had been on previous occasions. His veins felt thick and distended, the surface of his skin sensitised. Sidney inhaled sharply then exhaled a long breath, the worst of it gone from him now.

His features grew soft and mobile, as if he had just awoken from a particularly restful sleep. He gave Waldemar a flash of a smile. "Thank you, my friend," he whispered.

Waldemar squeezed his arm warmly before going off to relieve himself. For some Intercessors, spiritual waste made their gorge rise, but Waldemar had always suffered the cramps further down in his belly.

After that, they kept a brisk pace, Sidney traipsing determinedly through the undergrowth. Waldemar's old heart pounded as he struggled to keep up, his robe catching on stray branches that barred their way in all directions.

"Sidney! Wait!" he gasped, losing sight of him momentarily.

They were making a steep descent and between the trees, Waldemar caught flashes of the far side of a rocky gorge.

"Slow down! Sidney, it looks like there is a drop ahead."

His movements felt impossibly slow, and like in dreams, the air had a thickness to it, a substance that must be waded through. It was not only he who was affected. Before him, Sidney stumbled in wide circles, clutching at the air.

Waldemar wiped his sweating face with his sleeve and approached the man with caution.

"I feel it, I do. I feel it, Sidney." Waldemar stopped to slow his breath. "It will not evade us. Calm yourself, be calm now."

Sidney released a tearful moan, his grimacing face upturned as his arms grew slack at his sides.

"That's it, shhh, all will be well, my Skalen."

Defensively, Sidney wrapped his arm across his chest. "It is so strong, too strong for me," he wept. "It's too strong," he repeated, shaking his head as he peered over the precipitous drop.

Waldemar caught him, began to draw on him, trying to ease the heat that amassed in him faster than he could relieve it. He could not risk overdoing it, now that they were close, but if he let it build like this, he might lose the man altogether.

Sidney let the Intercessor take his hand and draw him away from the edge. The dense foliage that surrounded them made it difficult to see what lay below. Putting the man behind him, Waldemar craned for a better view through the trees. It appeared to be a barren gorge, a shrunken riverbed reduced to a single stagnant pool. The water was rust-coloured at its edge, darkening sharply at its centre.

"There is a pool there, Sidney. Small, but perhaps very deep."

There did not look to be any safe way down. The rock was mottled with water stains and slick patches of moss. He moved as close to the precipice as he dared and peered round. Soon he spied the grey skeleton of a fallen tree, its roots half clinging to the ridge. Where its tallest branches had fallen, there seemed a distinct channel in the rock. A place where the rain had run the length of the inverted tree, charting its course to the pool.

"We go that way." Waldemar pointed. "And slowly. We must watch our footing."

"Yes, Intercessor," Sidney said, his obedient expression an uncanny reminder of the boy that he had been. And with that shrinking of man into boy, Waldemar felt Emryl's spirit draw close.

The dazed look had re-entered Sidney's eyes and Waldemar had to use all of his will to retain clarity of focus, to remember where they were going and why.

"The tree," the Intercessor mumbled, pointing in the direction they should take. "Go."

Linking arms, they shuffled toward the tree. Clumsily, they made their way over the splintered branches. Part of him knew that the descent could not take long, yet it felt as if the tree went on for an eternity. Waldemar clutched Sidney's bony elbow until it became too much for them to hold one another without falling. From here, he held to the tree instead, Sidney moving quickly ahead of him.

Where the eroded crevice began, his footing slipped. He gasped, clutching his heart and sweating. He must rest here, but Sidney was down on all fours, crawling out of his grasp, sliding head first and grazing his forearms. He followed, skidding, spattering rubble. He fell hard on his hip, but the dull pain was meaningless.

Below, Sidney had reached the bottom. He rushed forward with uncanny speed, then seemingly remembered how to walk. Waldemar hurried down in rushed stride, gaining on him.

"Sidney!" Waldemar called in a warning tone.

The man no longer stumbled. He stalked forward, his spine erect, steps quick and purposeful. Waldemar frowned, realising that Sidney had not even turned to help him when he fell.

Waldemar ran. "Sidney!" he called with growing alarm. He was about to use his power on him, to make him fall, lamb-like, into a doze, but then, at the water's edge, he stopped. Waldemar kept his eyes on Sidney as he closed the distance between them. Sidney stood motionless, his arms hovering slightly at his sides, as if he prepared to fly.

Breathing heavily, Waldemar came up beside him. Sidney stared into the brackish pool, the still water radiant with mosquito song.

The two men stood reflected there in the water, similar in height, dark-robed, and with trailing beards, mouths gaping from their exertions.

Waldemar focused on the hazy pulse of the stone that made his feet tingle, his palms breaking into a sweat.

Sidney raised his left arm and pointed in that same dream-like posture he had adopted that night by the fire. But this time, he seemed to be pointing to his own reflection.

For a moment, Waldemar was crest-fallen. Was it the stone? Something was affecting him, but where was it?

Briskly, Sidney began to disrobe. Waldemar reached for his wrist, fearing what he might do. "Wait! Sidney–"

The man turned and grasped him by the forearms.

"They're here!" Sidney told him. Then suddenly his eyes shot up.

Waldemar looked at the water, the sky. "Who, Sidney? Tell me, who is here?"

Sidney's pupils shrank as he searched the bright expanse above. He shook himself, clutched his head in his hands.

Waldemar stared at him–reading him–sensing the thrum of the stone. He urged him on. Intensified the taste, the urgency of its shimmering call, the touching of two flaming branches–the mind and the idea–becoming one.

With renewed urgency, Sidney stripped off his trousers, his tunic and underthings. The scars on his chest rippled white over his ribs, his lean muscles tense.

After a pause, Waldemar tore off his own clothes and stumbled naked after him into the dark water, hardly feeling the sharp things that pricked his feet. Sidney moved to his thighs and dove in. Waldemar followed, not knowing where to look. He moved blindly, his arms sweeping through the opaque stillness. He emerged, beard and eyelashes dripping.

Again, he dove.

And again.

Each time, waiting for Sidney, watching for the small bubbles of his breath, the wide circlets that sung his passage.

With relief he saw Sidney come up for air, but he did not remain above long enough for Waldemar to speak. He followed, keening his senses.

Sidney moved over places they had already been and Waldemar felt no tangible change in his sensorium. Sidney's movements seemed less certain now, and Waldemar wondered whether the pool was simply too deep. With growing desperation, he scrutinised any nearby rocks for signs of snaking black iridescence.

He could feel the stone, tantalisingly close. The way it whispered as if behind a closed door.

Waldemar dove down, pushing his aged limbs, holding his lungs like a weathered wine skin, taut with air, fierce with promise. But there seemed no forms: no rocks, no weeds, just endless depths. There was no knowing how long it would take to reach the bottom. He turned back, making his body straight as an arrow as he kicked. Moments later his head burst free with a great wheezing gasp. His arms flailed and he could feel a stitch forming in his side. He glared at the desolate shore, the futility of it all.

"Sidney, come back! If it is here, there must be more nearby. Perhaps hidden in the surrounding rocks..." Waldemar said breathlessly.

Sidney looked at him, understanding, and slowly, they both returned to shore.

On the smooth rock at the edge of the pool, Waldemar sat, dripping, hugging his knees, sunlight setting the hair of his legs faintly aglow. A shiver of cold became a sob, his hands gnarled and palm-scarred. Tears fell on the flat of his chest. The wheezy sound of an old man crying.

He looked up and saw Sidney there, not desolate as he was, but with grim repose. His corded hair hung about his thighs. He dressed himself, let his hair soak his tunic black.

Waldemar felt himself reduced in his nakedness and put his underclothes back on. He walked to where Sidney was and sat down.

"You seem calm now," Waldemar observed. "What do you feel?"

Sidney shook his head. "The voices were so strong."

The Intercessor watched him carefully. "And now?"

He pointed in an almost accusatory manner, to the centre of the pool. "It has gone quiet, but it is there."

Waldemar nodded. "If it is there, then it may come closer to the surface in a place nearby." Waldemar said this, but he was not hopeful. If they had the tools to dredge and excavate, if they could command a company of miners to do the work...but it was impossible. There was no man, Meridian or no, who could withstand the power of the stone, or who could be trusted with its safe keeping.

Still, they had found something. A place to be marked out in memory.

Waldemar paused, trying to get his bearings. Fruitless though his efforts were, he tried to align his earlier vision of the dark stream with the geography of Brivia.

"No matter, Sidney. This is a victory for us but let us have a few days to contemplate our plan. Where would you like to go?"

Sidney looked lost and dejected, hanging his head in a way that made Waldemar want to hold his posture a little straighter.

"Let's take a few days in the mountains," Waldemar said. "Give our prayers to Kshidol."

Finally, Sidney looked up and nodded.

"Very good," he said.

They spend some time drying off, eating the oily seeds from a plant that Sidney recognised.

Waldemar made a show of having moved on with his thoughts, of giving Sidney a well-deserved break from the mission, yet just beneath the surface, scenarios and unfeasible plans bubbled and popped.

He needed Olinda's help. It was inevitable. There must be some among the Guard that she could trust, that had training enough to keep their wits. He could shield them. If it was a small number of men, he could do it.

Just as the idea settled, he dismissed it. He risked exposing their greatest weapon to the Guard at a time when they ruled Velspar in all but name. And yet, hadn't the Guard once served the Intercessors? Might not some be capable of it, even now?

There were one or two he had met who might be up to the task. Staunch Brivians who remembered the old ways. Yes, he would have to consider it.

14

ORENHOLM, BRIVIA

WALDEMAR'S LEGS BURNED, the slit on his palm tight after his blood offering to Father Kshidol. As they came back down the mountain, Waldemar squeezed his palm, making it smart, the pain a focal point for his wandering mind. Even during the rite, Waldemar had struggled to focus, going through the motions of chant and prayer with an emptiness of feeling. In his mind, all he could see was the black stream, the question of its source, the extent of its power. He knew that blinding stone was a sure sign that a deeper deposit was hidden beneath. Where one flourished, so did the other: opposed elements caught in some ancient dance. Ever since Sybilla instituted her Meridian Decree, the Seven Lands had mined Blinding Stone, and it was only a matter of time before some unwitting soul tapped that deeper harvest.

Waldemar's stomach clenched with hunger and fear, feeling the urgency of their mission.

Sidney pointed to a bridge below. "We should cross there."

"Yes, good spotting," Waldemar replied.

Coming closer, the Intercessor saw the bridge was not as sturdy as it looked from afar, timber planks hanging off and trailing in the water.

"Wait now, Sidney, this might not be a good idea." Waldemar looked up and down, looking for a narrower place to cross.

Sidney ignored the Intercessor's warnings and started across the bridge.

Waldemar tsk'd under his breath and followed.

Grasping the intact side rope and with cold spray whirring up his robe, the Intercessor made his way, one careful footstep at a time as the fast waters of the Leith tumbled below him. More than once, the ropes gave length and Waldemar braced himself for a fall, but the knots held.

Reaching the other side, Waldemar set his hands on his knees to ground himself. He cast his eye over the tree-mottled landscape, unnerved by the tiled roofs that showed between the branches. Peopled places were places of death for him and had been since the Purge, these nineteen years of vagrancy making his previous life seem unnatural when it should have been the other way around.

According to Illiam's scouts, Orenholm was completely abandoned. In years past, the Maglorean Guard had debauched the place, enjoying dark revelries there at the expense of the Brivian population. The game of cat and mouse ended with a total Brivian retreat into the wilderness. The Magloreans drank up the last of the casks and laid their sweating bodies upon dead men's sheets, growing tired of the place with its haunted streets and emptied larders.

Here, Waldemar saw the place for himself and felt a dread silence in the air. Felt, with his Intercessor's sense, and knew it to be as Illiam had described. A place of memories, swiftly falling into ruin.

Beside him, Sidney paused, casting his eyes across the scene and settling on the stretch of forest beyond, planning his retreat. *No, Sidney,* he thought, *this will be a good place for us to test our strength. Memory peels us as the stone unskins the soul. It will test us, and we must ready ourselves. We must be unflinching and brazen in our fear and our nakedness.*

"Now Sidney," he said, "this time we are going my way. We will go through the great city and see her for what she is. And if there are people there, be assured that my powers are enough to keep them from pursuit."

Waldemar did not wait for Sidney to object but carried on toward the city, scanning the shadows despite himself.

Together they went, he and Sidney, buildings emerging before them, showing their dimensions, their details of mouldering brick and cracked stone, of shadow and window gleam. The path they walked upon, uneven and strange underfoot, a place of life and industry, carved out and silenced. Waldemar's footsteps crunched, signs of the Maglorean presence here evident in piled refuse and rotting bodies, perhaps five years old. Faded curtains hung sadly in windows, broken doors hanging open like the mouths of the dead. A place too far from the whorehouses of the Maglorean foreshore for the guardsmen to remain once the wine barrels had run dry.

Sidney walked on with stumbling gait, passing like a shadow before rotten doorways, his bare feet defiled by the things he trod on. Dank trails of liquid criss-crossed the street, coming from houses they dared not enter. In an alleyway, the half-eaten remains of a dead horse. Waldemar watched, mesmerised by the swinging ropes of Sidney's hair, thinking how much the madman he looked here.

Orenholm was just as broken. No longer a place of food stalls and industry, of gossip and trade. The murmur of life, the sea of voices, the churn of passion and ambition, the sweet smoke of worship–all gone.

The forest had sent its scavengers, its wild grasses and tangling vines. Birds' nests and rat droppings, snake holes and animal tracks. The harder he looked, the more signs he discerned, and in his heart, he ached for the press of bodies, the noise and sweat, the faces like a thousand masks, all unique but composed of a common substrate. In a rare moment of self-reflection, Waldemar wondered whether he quested for the stone because it was this that he longed for. To be an Intercessor once more, immersed in living complexity.

"Oh Sidney," Waldemar sighed, overcome by the sight of this once familiar place. "Do you remember how it used to be?"

Sidney's breath rasped as he walked on, his pace unusually fast, as if he wished to outrun the houses and the shopfronts. It was obvious he wished nothing more than to disappear, back into the hush of leaves and cackling birdsong.

He grunted.

They came around a corner and, there before them, the pearl of Brivia sat like a shocking apparition. Without knowing why, the sudden appearance of the Temple brought to mind Emryl's naked body, grotesque and ageless, a faceless presence ablaze and shining. Its paleness was her shoulder; her cheek shying away. The white robes of his brethren disappearing from sight, as wraiths in a dream.

The smell of the town, already putrid, grew stronger. He found it difficult to take in a full breath.

There was nothing there. Surely, there was nothing there after so many years. And yet the dead horse they had passed could not have been there more than a month.

Her presence was strong here. So strong.

Ahead of him, Sidney tramped on, leaving his heady stink on the wind. As he watched, he saw him as if through his mother's eyes. He could smell the ritual oil she wore, the whiff of cats that always served to dim her glamour and remind him of her advanced age.

The blood, she had whispered, before the Fire of Vaelnyr, *the blood, Waldemar. It runs in my veins. I, and my sons, inherit this. We, the living blood of Skalen Karasek, the First Diviner.* And it was true, none of the other ancient clans could claim this. Their heritage was that of a vassal. The six clans that followed Him.

Waldemar could see Emryl's aged face close to his, her eyes pinning him with preternatural intensity. His heart fluttered at the promise of her untapped power, of revelation so sharp that only the strongest of spirits could withstand it. Sometimes, when they were speaking, the vision came, a deep furrow in her cheek spilling light, that widened painfully until her wrinkled flesh lay like a discarded robe on the Temple floor. A light that receded to the milky disc that shaded her pupil, the coming blindness that had shown her another realm of sight.

She smiled and showed him blue-veined wrists, bid him to touch his fingers to her pulse, to feel it flicker. *Can you feel Him in me, Waldemar? The First Diviner was a man of flesh and blood. Karasek blood. And what do you think became of His scattered spirit?* That was how she had turned him. She had put her hand upon his forehead in an Intercessor's gesture, as if to confirm the source of his holy power. And did it not make sense? There had been but one Diviner, his like never seen again. Skalen had not held himself whole when he entered the Great Stream but had allowed death to scatter his essence among the spirits, his blazing spark reborn in glittering constellation in the form of the Intercessors. It was they who should bear the name Skalen, not the ancient clans. And of course, she counted herself among them.

Even as he sat there with Sidney, Waldemar could feel the throb at Emryl's wrist, how it drew heat to the surface of his skin. His spirit–if she spoke true–a fragment of Him. Her blood, the fleshly counterpart. The possibilities that her initiation promised were dazzling, and he was to be the instrument of her awakening.

In the failed rituals and futile hours of chanting that ensued, Waldemar's hopes fell on rocky ground. But Emryl still held that light within her, the hidden promise that led him back to their bedchamber: the place the other Intercessors could not enter, where Waldemar instructed them. Emryl with her holy inheritances, and Medard, the consort of her womb who had given her two sons in the season of her prime, and who now served her in any way Waldemar designed. He felt a strange sense of pity for the man now, the humiliations he had suffered, the fervour that bid him to cry out for the guardsman's blade simply to follow Emryl into the hollows of death.

Where was he now? Dissolved, like so many spirits, into the common matter of the Stream? Medard did not speak in Sidney's dreams. Occasionally, his body morphed with Emryl's, intermingling and changing sex, but were these simply the echoes of Emryl's visions? It suited Waldemar to think of them this way. Medard had been a dolt, and Waldemar preferred to remember his agonies at the Fifth Gate as the point where his initiation had unequivocally failed. Waldemar merely flattered him to keep in Emryl's good favour.

Waldemar stared at the Temple, seeking Emryl's instruction, the sense of her thick about him, but silent, maddeningly silent. He felt her laughing at him and flexed his fist, the slit in his palm burning.

I am living and you are dead, he thought. *I walk here, among the living. Speak, or do not speak. There are others in the Stream who will teach me all that you came to know and more.*

For a heady moment, he felt victorious. He had let her rule him in death when it was she who had begged him for instruction. He, High Intercessor of Brivia, possessed of a power she could never know.

A sharp pain shot up his leg as he lost his footing, twisting his ankle. He beat his thigh with his fist, trying to master the pain. With head cowed, the Temple flared in his peripheral vision as the sun emerged from the clouds.

Fear stole into him, and he cursed himself.

Before him, Sidney had stopped at the base of the Temple, on his hands and knees. Waldemar watched Sidney's hands, upstretched and trembling. His face was on the cobbles now, and Waldemar limped toward him, unnerved by the sight. Not because he laid his grief at the foot of the Temple, but because Waldemar still could not shake the vision of Emryl's body, could feel her smirking down at them, as if she had brought her son to heel just to show the Intercessor who held the reins.

Waldemar grit his teeth. This was madness. Stupidity and madness.

He came up beside Sidney and offered him his hand. "Come, Sidney, let us leave this place."

Pale eyes looked up at him, helpless and childlike, their whites like fish in the grimy wilderness of his face.

Waldemar continued, "Remember, the grove is this way. Let us go down to the Sea Altar in the morning. We are not far from there now. We will find a place to camp and in the morning, we will go down and give our prayers to Siatka."

Waldemar pulled him up, but Sidney did not let go of his hand. Together they walked, eyes down, Sidney's grip firm and full of need. Waldemar focused all of his attention on Sidney, clearing everything else from his mind. Memories tumbled past, the storm of Sidney's mind charging its course. The Intercessor felt the instinct to run about the town as Sidney had done after his parents' execution. Pleading, grasping strangers by the arm, *No, don't listen to my brother, please, please, you have to live. Don't do this!* The blank faces that would not hear him, the suicidal vortex opening at his feet. Children drowned so their spirits might be saved, the family death pacts, the ones who screamed and were not ready. *Listen to me!*

Waldemar drew the heat from Sidney's spirit, felt the man's anguish flowing through clasped hands.

"That's the way, Sidney," he murmured. "That's the way."

Sidney took a long shuddering breath, his gaze fixed on the distant trees so the town seemed to recede both in his awareness and in Waldemar's. It simply was not real. They passed through a place of dream and could pass out of it at will. There was not a soul here who could tell them otherwise: it was a broken vessel, emptied of spirit, emptied of power.

Waldemar kept hold of Sidney's hand, walking the streets of Orenholm and seeing them not.

"Tomorrow will be a good day, Sidney. When was the last time you looked upon the sea?"

15

____

CIVIT'S RIDGE, NOTHELM

"Good work, Vina," Voirrey said, watching the girl's small hands ineffectually kneading the second batch of dough. "Keep going," she said, as Davina's concentration wavered, drifting to Voirrey's work with the tongs in the heat of the fire.

"Stand back," she warned, depositing the baking tray at the other end of the counter.

Using the tongs, she removed the lid and waved her hands to dispel the steam. Carefully, she carried them to the bench.

She was just tapping the scones out on the counter when she heard crunching footsteps approach the door.

"Hoy!" came a man's voice.

Voirrey looked out, wiped her hands on her apron, and pulled back the bolt.

Siran greeted her with a smile. "Letter, Miss Voirrey. An official one, from your parents."

Voirrey took it. "Well, thank you, Siran," she muttered, perturbed by the unexpected communication. The Skalens of Nothelm would not bother her with anything but bad news.

When Siran remained, she looked at him properly. "Is there something else?"

"No, no, nothing else, Miss. Unless you wish me to pass your reply to the runner?"

Voirrey flipped the envelope over. "There is no mark of urgency. I will send my own runner when I have the time."

"Very well then, Miss. Good day to you," he said, with a bow.

She closed the door and Sybilla entered the room, her head tilted in question.

They exchanged a look.

"Have you seen Amand this morning?" Voirrey asked, noticing his door was open. They should read the letter together.

Sybilla shook her head. He must have gone out.

In the corner of the room, Davina had snuck behind Voirrey's chair, her flour-dusted hands pulling at the wool in her basket, trying her best to wind a ball that she'd accidentally undone. Blankly, she watched the child winding her wool as her mind buzzed with possibilities.

Voirrey flattened the letter on the counter and let out a long breath.

She clicked the wax fastening and opened the paper.

The message was short.

He is gone and if you look for him the charge of heresy will be on your head. Act with wisdom, Voirrey, not childish passion.

Wide-eyed, she flipped the page over. There was no signature, no explanation, though the envelope had borne the Skalens' seal. *Childish passion?* That sounded like her mother. Yet it was decidedly *not* like her mother to send a message such as this out of the blue.

She held it up with trembling hand for Sybilla to see and both women looked to Amand's open door. From the window, cool air seeped into the house, erasing the soft breath of sleep, the homely scents of morning.

Voirrey's arms flushed red and she hit her fist on the bench making Davina start. She tried to think.

Someone had betrayed her, but who? And what did they want? Rageful tears beaded her eyes.

Sybilla whisked Davina to the bedroom where her mumbling voice could be heard: "Do you want to play with Mama's special star?"

Voirrey leant on the bench, accidentally touching the hot pan, the shock of heat speeding her pulse.

Sybilla approached, her close scent like bruised roses. She was placing cool stones upon Voirrey's forehead, crown, and nape, the strap tightening, the storm of sensations quieting, easing, making all things simple and plain.

Voirrey breathed purposefully, putting the letter aside. "Okay," she said. "Okay. This was always a risk."

Her thoughts ran on, weighing the possibilities.

Sybilla's dark eyes searched hers. "Do you want me to go out and see what's happening?"

Voirrey shook her head. Applying logic to the situation she tried to reassure herself that no matter what had happened, Amand was more powerful than a village mob. *Childish passion.* Who would dare patronise her in that way? The expression scattered her thoughts making it impossible to pin the blame on anyone.

She saw Sybilla glance at the metal poker by the hearth.

It would not come to that, Voirrey told herself. Murderers and mobs did not send notes of warning. She was being called to negotiate, that was all.

Hastily, Voirrey went into Amand's room to fetch paper from his writing desk. Amand's simple quarters were as neat as he usually left them, the bed made, his cupboard and stool set straight, but the copper dish where his Alma usually burned was missing. As she scanned the room, she noticed his cloak was gone too. Voirrey went to the window and closed it, pulling the curtains together with tight fists.

In relative privacy now, Voirrey inspected his cupboards and drawers, shuffling through his meagre belongings.

The smell of him wafted up from the bed, the clean scent of lemon balm, the musty man-smell that came upon him when he'd been travelling too long.

Tears arose in a wave of longing, and with difficulty, she willed them away.

"What do you think has happened?" Sybilla stood in the doorway, grave-faced.

"Honestly, I don't know. The note bears my parents' seal, but if the villagers are behind it, they would have to have an accomplice to pull this off. I know they do not want Amand here but this seems a step too far, even for them."

Sybilla nodded. "And if your parents have him?"

"If they have taken him, the only place an Intercessor could be safely contained is the Temple dungeons." Silently, Voirrey continued her thought. The Guard had long been trained to make their minds impervious to the Intercessors' powers. The Guard... would Edric do this, if his mother bid it? It was possible, but again, the note did not make sense. *Childish passion*. Edric was not one to play the emotions.

Voirrey shook her head. "I must make my reply before the runner leaves." Abruptly she turned back to the room to fetch paper and ink as she had originally intended. She rifled through the drawer, finding nothing of use. Sybilla looked at her expectantly as she came back into the room. From under a pile of sewing things, Voirrey exhumed her own store of paper and ink. She shook the bottle in her palms, but when she opened it, the rim was thick with syrupy deposits. She cleaned her tools in silence.

After some deliberation, she wrote her reply.

Send me his mark by sunset this Magsday and name your price.

She and Amand had communicated through a coded system of marks for years. No matter the situation, Amand could tell her much without alerting his captors. If her parents received the message and knew nothing of the plot, then she could claim the missive referred to the exchange of goods. Where supplies travelled long distances, there were always middlemen.

Voirrey waved the paper in the air, blowing to set the ink.

Sybilla watched her intently. "What did you write?"

Voirrey slowed her hand to show her the note.

With an uncertain nod, Sybilla searched her face, needing answers, terrified of what this might mean for the little life they had built in Civit's Ridge.

Voirrey could not think about that now. She had to act. Sun streamed brightly through the window.

"I need to go. I won't be long," she said, and walked past her, out the door.

She looked out, not seeing anything out of the ordinary. The quiet dirt road, a dairy cow led by one of the Forley boys, her bell softly clanging.

The weather was strange. The air unusually still, then the wind would start up, the trees stirred and rushing, the distant valley to the north swirling like a hungry sea. She lifted her senses like a rabbit in tall grass, sifting the wind for the salt-piss scent of the wolf. There was no answer, the Meridian dulling her senses. Who had given Siran the letter? An outsider had been here, and recently. Or was it Siran himself? Could it be?

Rupert Casterley and a few of his farmhands loaded potatoes onto the back of a wagon. Voirrey waved and got the men's nods in return. Did they avoid her eye? Perhaps, perhaps not.

Further down the road she saw Siran chatting with Lena Kern.

"Siran!" Voirrey called, waving.

Lena looked behind, gave Siran a nod and carried on with her errands.

Voirrey approached with note in hand.

Seeing what she held, Siran frowned. "Ah, you missed the runner, he left about ten minutes ago."

She smiled, a little breathless. "Could I trouble you to send someone to catch up with him?"

Siran took the note. "Not a worry, Miss Voirrey." His demeanour was friendly but his eyes lingered on her face. "Is all well?"

She did not feel strong enough to bear his scrutiny at that moment. "Yes, all is well. When your man catches up with the runner, please tell him that I will need a reply by sunset, Magsday."

"Got it," he said, pocketing the letter.

As he left her, Voirrey felt corrupted by the events of the morning, her trust in the people of Civit's Ridge crumbling into dust.

16

CIVIT'S RIDGE, NOTHELM

Listlessly, Voirrey went to the well, and sent the pail down. Her pinched face and fanning blonde hair caught in the water's sheen as she wound it back up. She filled one of the buckets, leaning sidelong as she walked, dark drips falling on the dirt track.

In the distance, she heard horses and turned. She stared wide-eyed in the direction of the sound, but the Casterley's house blocked her view of the road. Her heart thumped, the dreadful sound of their hooves, urgent and out of place. She gripped the bucket, still staring, unwilling to put it down, to alter her movements in any way.

Then, suddenly, they appeared. Four riders. Sleek, black horses clad in the deep green livery of Nothelm. Among them, a face she knew, his short blonde beard framed by a helmet that shined like a beetle's wing. Edric. Her stomach flared.

He spotted her and rode near.

In her rough linen smock and with her hair half-blown from her braid, she stared up at him, feeling unarmored, diminutive. Voirrey's mind spun. Was this the response to her note?

"Voirrey, good day," Edric said brusquely, as if he couldn't stay long.

"Edric. To what do I owe the pleasure?" She smiled as best she could, feeling the slowness of village life upon her despite her fear.

92

He removed his foot from the stirrup and dismounted.

"I've come with a message from your mother," Edric said.

Voirrey's chest grew tight. Could she have been so mistaken in her judgement? But before she could question him, Rupert Casterley approached.

"Welcome, welcome! May I see to your horse, Guardsman? Oh, what a fine creature."

Voirrey used the distraction to catch her breath.

"Yes, thank you kindly," Edric said, with a flash of a smile.

Voirrey nodded in the direction of her cottage so they could speak in private.

She needed to know something of the news he brought before they entered the house and asked in a low voice. "What does my mother want?"

Heeding her discreet tone, he murmured, "The message is for Sybilla."

Voirrey glanced at him sharply, her knuckles white on the bucket handle, her arm stiff from carrying it. "She is in the house."

She walked ahead of him and placed the water bucket by the front door. She knocked twice, which meant, take caution.

A few moments later, Sybilla appeared, fully dressed and wearing her Meridian.

"Guardsman Edric, hello. Do come in," she said.

Edric ducked his head to pass through the doorway, his leathers creaking.

Sybilla straightened one of the chairs and Edric obliged. He looked stiff and uncomfortable, his knees sitting too high.

Voirrey had gone to the bench, quickly arranging the scones on a tray with some butter.

Sybilla started for her bedroom to wait with Davina until he had gone.

"Wait! Sybilla, it is you I have come to speak with," Edric said.

She froze momentarily. "Oh! Very well, I will be with you in a moment," she said disappearing into the little room.

Voirrey put down the tray and sat, buttering her scone without looking at him as Sybilla murmured behind the wall.

Edric leant forward and took Voirrey's proffered knife, buttering his own.

When Sybilla returned, he looked up. "Ah, Sybilla…"

He stroked his beard, a nervous gesture Voirrey recognised, then planted his palm on his knee. The other held the scone, butter dripping onto his fingers.

"Skalen Lenna has sent me here, unofficially, to speak with you." He paused, wiped some of the melting butter on his trousers, then set the uneaten scone back on the tray. "To put it quite plainly, you are wanted in Vaelnyr." His gaze took in the once-fierce Skalen, the scar of melted flesh visible through her thinning hair.

Sybilla's voice was dry. "Has there been word from Peran?"

"Certainly, he is eager for your return." Edric paused for her to reply, and when she remained silent, he went on. "A full report has been prepared for you and I am pleased to act as your escort, but in brief, the difficulty with the Maglorean contingent has worsened and rebel activity is still a threat in the South. Guardsman Peran is concerned that if Vaelnyr remains without its Skalen and heir, that Rayhmer and his men will install themselves there on a more permanent basis."

Sybilla wore a listless expression, as if she could do nothing to resist the tide of fate when it pulled at her. Vaguely, she nodded.

Voirrey chewed her lip. "I suppose my parents are reluctant to commit forces?"

Edric let out a sigh that was almost a laugh. "Well, yes. This is an inconvenient turn of events. If this stands in the way of Nothelm's maiden voyage, your father will have much to say about it."

Meaning, she thought, much to say about her influence over Sybilla and this business in Civit's Ridge.

"My mother?" Voirrey inquired, wiping her hands on her smock.

Edric leaned in. "She takes a graver view and will do whatever it takes to secure the North."

Edric and Voirrey were facing each other now, with Sybilla off to the side, her face dim as she leaned back in her chair. Voirrey sensed a deep trembling in the woman's stillness.

Voirrey smiled officiously. "I understand the situation and I thank you for coming to us but we would like some time to plan our journey."

Edric glanced at the floor. "I'm afraid the situation is of some urgency. If you wish to arrive in secret, you should start packing today," he said. "In the meantime, I will need to arrange lodging for me and my men."

Her eyes narrowed despite her intention to appear non-plussed. "Is this really necessary, Edric?"

He leaned close, his whisper sharp with old resentments. "You can't stay out here forever, Voirrey. And this is not just about Vaelnyr. Your parents are in their twilight years and your father wants to send half my men to sea! Do you care nothing for your homeland?"

No matter how far she fled from her fate, one day, she would be forced to heed his counsel. She, the childless Skalen, and Edric, her Head Guard. No longer rivals for her father's affections, but leaders who must work side by side. For duty. For the people of Nothelm. His sparkling eyes demanded this of her and it was to her shame that she could not answer his call.

Just then, Davina's face appeared in the doorway, the squeaking hinge making all of their heads turn. The girl closed the door again, but not all the way. Her eyes fixed on the stranger.

He took a deep breath, lowered his voice further, speaking to Sybilla now. "These villagers," he waved a finger in the air, "they will be no match for the Magloreans when they come. Take your girl to Vaelnyr and put her in Peran's protection before it is too late."

Sybilla remained motionless. She frowned. "How can you tell me of the Maglorean threat and ask me to ride into their midst? Is Peran still in charge, or not?"

Edric's expression was serious and imploring. "There is no place where your safety can be guaranteed. But I believe we are approaching a tipping point. You have to do what you can to bring stability in Vaelnyr. This cannot wait."

Sybilla gave a barely perceptible nod.

Before she could agree to anything, Voirrey jumped in. "We

appreciate the situation but there is a matter we must see to before we embark on our journey."

He looked at her warily. "How long?"

She thought of Amand, an icy pang in her stomach.

"Two days. Give us two days and we will come."

17

CIVIT'S RIDGE, NOTHELM

ALL DAY, VOIRREY had measured the sun's position as it moved toward her ultimatum. Edric was waiting, but still she had received no reply from Siran.

Sybilla had grown quiet, the space about them shimmering with new fears. Voirrey assessed her unseeing eyes, wondering what she was thinking. She was like a wound that had been bandaged too tight, and Voirrey knew that she would have to work gingerly and with care to keep the way between them open. She could not help her with her damned Meridian in the way.

They had discussed plans well into the night, exploring all the terrible options open to them. Should Voirrey return to Nothelm to try to find out what had become of Amand? Should she go there to reestablish her influence before things moved beyond her control? There were many justifications for her return to Nothelm but in the end Voirrey could not bear the thought.

Life without Davina? The very idea made her chest ache. She could not be separated from them. She could not simply return to Nothelm and resume her old life. It was not enough to heal the sick: she wanted to heal Sybilla. She did not want to bring new children into the world for the sake of it anymore. She loved Davina, and now no other child could rouse her heart. Even the needs of the rebellion, the prospect of Intercession's return, the hallowed rites, the sense of communion, all of that paled in comparison to what she felt for Sybilla and her child.

Voirrey tried to focus, to bring herself back from these thoughts. She unfastened her hair and shook it out, massaging her scalp to ease the headache that had been building all day. Sunset would come before she knew it, and then she and Sybilla would journey into the past–so it seemed–to tread among its consequences like so many shards of broken glass.

She needed to do something.

"Sybilla," Voirrey called to the closed bedroom door. "I'm going to see if I can find Siran."

There was no reply. She waited a moment, sighing, then took herself out.

In the street, she saw one of the Thirwell boys and followed him at a distance. He was heading in the direction of the Casterley's barn.

Sure enough, as she drew closer, she heard Siran's voice within.

She popped her head in, Siran and his sons together with the Casterley boys, rubbing down the guardsmen's horses.

Seeing her, Siran greeted her. "Hello there, Voirrey. These horses, aren't they a handsome lot?"

Entering the stall where he stood, she gazed up at Edric's mount, a glossy black stallion that she had ridden once or twice. Voirrey smiled. "He is a fine one. Moody, though."

"Aye," he said, passing the brush admiringly over sleek muscles. "There he goes! Tossing his mane again. Yes, you are beautiful, I haven't forgotten."

Voirrey did not want to continue this discussion in the stall, fearing her mood might agitate the horses.

"Have you received word from the runner?" she asked.

"No, no. Not yet. But we've hours till sunset." Seeing her expression, he frowned. "Is something wrong? What does it matter if the message is a little late?"

Voirrey let out a tense breath. "I know this might come as a bit of a shock but we are leaving Civit's Ridge in the morning."

"Leaving?" he repeated. "All of you?"

She nodded. "I can't say much more but–"

He held up a hand, ushering her out so they could speak more privately.

Hanging his apron on a hook by the entrance, he called: "Now, boys, be calm in your movements while I'm out front. Don't want any of you catching ugly from a horse's hoof on my watch."

He went outside with her, growing uncharacteristically quiet.

"Now what is this all about?" he said.

Voirrey fingered her braid, eyes on the barn's dim interior. "You know me, Siran. I resent being summoned. But I will return here soon enough."

He scrutinised her. "If there is anything you need, you let me know."

"I will," she said.

When he saw that she would not say more, he gave her arm a squeeze. "I'm going to the Kern's place this afternoon. You should come over."

She nodded, departing before the tears began.

As she made her way back to the cottage, the familiar streets of the town seemed to speed past her, slipping from her grasp. The little thatch houses, the High Rock, places where she had sat with the children and laughed. Her gaze alighted on the Palmer's front step. Haggard yellow flowers still clung to life by the front door, but the curtains remained closed, the whole place suffused with the stillness of death. Was Glenny inside? Or had the Folshom's taken him in? How could she live here and not know?

Despite Siran's apparent warmth, she felt utterly separate from them. Everything her eyes lit upon evidenced her failure. They maintained their quiet ways, refusing to embrace the future she offered them. Perhaps that is what drew her to them in the first place. The way they kept to themselves, disconnected, their settlement dwarfed by ancient mountains.

Now, they hid even deeper in their hollows, pretending to enjoy this latest intrusion, where shining horses brought guards of green leather to sit among them and drink their ale.

She sniffed, wiping her nose.

Soon they would be gone, and maybe that was for the best.

For the remainder of the afternoon, she kept herself busy with preparations for their journey, each hour seeming an age. Sybilla moved about her tasks in silence. Voirrey was in such a state of agitation that she thought it better to leave her alone, taking herself off to the Kern's place despite her misgivings.

She told Joe and Lena the news, who took it in much the same way as Siran had. Immediately, Lena had set about planning their travel provisions, putting together a bundle in the kitchen while Voirrey collected eggs to boil before their departure.

Siran found her in the henhouse.

"Hi there, Voirrey. Lena told me you were out back." He waved the returning message between pinched fingers.

Voirrey's stomach flipped. She took the note from him and tucked it into her pocket. "Thank you. You're a good man." She paused, "Siran, was it the same runner as before? I wonder if you can tell me what they looked like."

Siran went to respond but then a look of vague confusion came over him. "I...Yes, I think it was the same young man. He had brown hair."

She watched him carefully. "Can you tell me anything else about him?"

Siran frowned. "He said he was new, so you wouldn't know him."

"Hmm," Voirrey responded. "That's okay, thank you for the note."

As Siran walked away, Voirrey's apprehension increased. It was quite unlike him to not recall a face. She could not help feeling that he kept something from her.

Not wanting to read the note out here in the garden, she snatched up her half-filled basket and departed, cutting through the back lanes and low fences in a diagonal shortcut to her street. The wind in her ears seemed to erase the world about her, until there was only the note, the numbing rhythm of her foot-fall, and the welcome sight of her own front door.

She went in, bolted the door, then snatched the paper from her pocket. Voirrey stared, her breath fast from walking. *The mark, the mark!* She shook her head, staring, the mark–Amand's mark–a dark sigil that burned its shape into her mind.

Elation and wrongness warred in her so she could not make any sense of it at all.

Distantly she heard Sybilla's voice. "What does it say? Voirrey? Is that his mark?"

Voirrey placed the slip of paper carefully on the bench so she would not smudge it with her tears.

"It says that I should not seek him," her fingers shook. "That this came to him in a vision and that I should not seek him."

Sybilla looked dubiously at the strange markings. "Are you sure it is not a forgery?"

Voirrey shook her head emphatically.

"But what does this mean? What do you think has happened to him?" Sybilla said, wide eyed.

"I don't know, I don't know!" Sobs of anger and frustration shook her body and she leaned her head on Sybilla's shoulder, her limp arms about her waist.

Sybilla embraced her, rubbing her back. She cared, but did she understand? To Sybilla, Amand was always the interloper. Nobody could share this grief. And now the impossible man had done this to her. Stupid, self-sacrificing, proud bloody man. Voirrey sobbed with her eyes closed, lost in a welter of regrets.

There was a tugging at her skirt, and as she looked down, Davina's worried eyes stared up at her.

She managed a tearful chuckle, swiped the tears away. "I'm okay sweetheart, aunty's okay." Voirrey crouched down and cuddled her, the little girl's arms like a vice around her neck.

"That's a little too tight, darling!" Voirrey said weakly and felt her grip release. Voirrey held her in her arms, Davina's head nuzzling into her chest.

"Everything's going to be okay," she whispered, rocking back and forth.

"Where's Ama?"

Voirrey sighed. "Ama has gone somewhere secret. We are going somewhere too." She leant back so she could catch the girl's eye. "We can't talk about Ama in front of people anymore. Do you understand?"

Davina nodded. "But Aunty Voy, he took my acorn."

"Your acorn?" She looked up at Sybilla, who shrugged.

"He gave me an acorn. The top came off and he fixed it. He said it was mine." Davina's frown was deep and serious.

Sybilla nodded. "I remember now," she said to Voirrey. "It was a very special acorn, wasn't it? I think Ama needed it for good luck."

"Okay..." she said slowly.

Voirrey had an idea. "Now, it's your job to find a good luck charm for our journey. We are going to visit Vaelnyr. Remember your mama telling you all about it? The Gulf, the Skalens' House where she grew up?"

Davina nodded enthusiastically and ran to the other room to find something.

Sybilla looked at her. "What do you want to do?"

Voirrey raked her fingers through her hair. "Whatever has happened to Amand, he does not want my help."

Sybilla waited for the rest as Voirrey paced the room.

"I will come with you to Vaelnyr," she said. "We must find our allies there. Only then will I leave for Nothelm."

Sybilla did not argue, quiet in her relief. They could not separate. Not yet, when so much was unknown. Secretly, and despite her fears for Amand, she welcomed Sybilla's silence. They must stand together as long as they could. On that simple truth they could agree.

18

PASSAGE TO VAELNYR

THEY WOULD NOT TAKE a carriage to Vaelnyr, for that would attract too much attention and would not do well on the forest track. Siran, in his seemingly boundless desire to be useful to the Guard, had prepared a wagon. To make it comfortable, the back had been padded with hay mattresses, a canopy erected above them so they might have some chance of disguise. Davina was so excited by her new cubbiehole that she did not appear to comprehend that they would not return. Civit's Ridge, the little house, and Amand, all lay behind them.

Voirrey donned her travelling cloak, her rucksack packed as in the days when she walked the pilgrim's path to Blood Call. In those days, she walked beside the faithful, offering heel balm and cool salves, leaves that, when chewed, would calm the heart and make the walking easier. But the sight of Sybilla, similarly attired, filled her with foreboding. Like a woman brought before the executioner's blade, her face remained a dour mask, her movements heavy and slow.

Edric and his men, smelling of shaving soap and saddle oil, stood off to the side at a respectful distance. The villagers fussed over the visiting guardsmen so they would have nothing to report, but their presence was also a source of genuine excitement. Visitors who left

103

promptly and of their own accord were an interesting diversion in the monotony of village life.

For the first time, she saw herself in their eyes and felt vindicated for leaving.

She held the key to her cottage in one hand and should have passed it on, given the place back to the community, but that would mean this part of her life was over, something she was not quite ready to accept.

Sybilla helped Davina up into the wagon, and moments later, she too disappeared beneath the sackcloth canopy. A swift wind picked up–the winds that were so much a part of this place–drawing her mind to the sheer cliffs and desolate tracks of Jokvour.

Velspar please, deliver Amand from danger, she prayed. *Care for him and keep him safe.*

She could feel Edric's eyes on her, waiting. She kept her back to him, resolute that she would leave in her own time.

She breathed deep of the alpine air, so pure and sweet, she could barely discern the farmyard musk of the town. She wiped her eyes and strode to the cottage as if she had forgotten something. Voirrey put her hand on the front door, feeling the sun-warmed wood. Dry orange flowers rattled in their husks about her feet. They were pretty flowers, almost impossible to kill. Snapping their dry stems she picked a posy for Davina and returned to the wagon.

"Thank you, Guardsman, we are ready now," Voirrey called.

With barely a nod, the guardsmen assembled: Edric upon the driving horse, the others mounted either side.

Voirrey looked behind at the villagers, huddled at interval between the houses. They watched her like a stranger. Siran and Joe raised their hands, Sal and Mindy and a few others waved. She looked at them a moment longer, surprised at her bitterness, at the creeping thought that she would rule over them one day and then they would show her proper respect. They were not worth agonising over. They were weak, that was all.

Voirrey's hair whisked about her head as she solemnly waved her goodbye.

Inside the canopy, the air was warmer and fibrous from the outer layer of sackcloth. Davina sneezed.

The wagon started up, and the two women remained silent for a while.

Time passed and as the light dimmed, Voirrey knew that they had entered the tree-covered pass of the Stetlan Range. She opened the canopy, tying it on either side to let in the breeze. Davina was restless on the bumpy road, leaning close to the edge as she tried to peer out and around. Voirrey had to remind herself that this landscape of boulders and high limbed trees was completely new to the child.

All the while, Sybilla averted her eyes, confining herself to instructions and explanations for Davina's ears. Voirrey piped in here and there, creasing her face in the type of smile people give to children. An expression that promised good intent when the heart had grown too tired for feeling.

Eventually, Davina grew quiet, the Stetlan range behind them now, as they entered the cool and dappled shade of Atilan. Davina clambered over, nuzzled her head into her mother's breast but could not settle there. She fidgeted, crawled about the wagon, and again stuck her head out over the side.

"I want to go home." Davina's bottom lip popped out miserably.

"We are going home." Sybilla drew her near. Kissed her hair.

"I want to go that way." Davina pointed at the track that unfurled behind them. She whimpered and squirmed.

Voirrey spoke to Sybilla, her voice dry from disuse. "She might need to pass water."

Sybilla sighed and stretched. "You're right, we need to take a break."

Voirrey put her head out and whistled.

Eerily, a guard materialised from the scrub. "Yes, Miss Voirrey?"

"We need to stop soon, can you see a clearing nearby?" She tried to look herself, but could not lean out far enough without falling.

He nodded and rode forward to speak to Edric. After some mumbling, the cart took a turn and came to a stop.

Voirrey climbed down first, Sybilla passing the child down.

"I'll take her, it's okay," Voirrey said quickly, leaving Sybilla to herself for a moment.

Knowing Davina would be happier if she went straight away, Voirrey took her behind a tree and helped her move her underclothes clear as she relieved herself.

"Aunty Voy, what's that?" Davina pointed her finger at an inch-worm making its way up a flower stem.

Voirrey crouched beside her, putting out her finger so the little creature could hop on. "Want to say hello?" The inch-worm had its back suckers on her finger, its front ones hovering in the air looking for purchase.

Davina shrank back, shaking her head, but Voirrey knew she wasn't actually scared.

"What about a flower? You can choose one to take with us. Only one though."

The child chose a purple and red flower with diaphanous petals and a trailing beard of sorts.

Voirrey examined it. "Very pretty. And let's get one more for your mother."

Davina had already found something more interesting to do and was picking seed pods from the grass around her. Voirrey stayed behind, looking for colour amongst the brown and green. A sprig of yellow blooms caught her eye, and she leant over a prickly bush to snap the stem, then followed Davina through the bracken.

The wagon was empty. Edric and his guardsmen had gathered with their horses beside a copse of trees, one drinking from his water skin, one taking great crunching bites of apple. They seemed relaxed out here, and she could hear their laughter.

From the edge of her vision, she saw movement and turned to find Sybilla staring up into the leaves. In the dappled light, her dusty travelling cloak blended with the bark of the soaring cypress behind her. Voirrey put a hand on Davina so as not to disturb her mother, whose eyes gleamed with some private sorrow. Voirrey felt she should look away, as if behind her Meridian, Sybilla might be praying.

Remaining quiet, Voirrey took Davina's hand and pointed to a trail of ants whose reddish bodies glowed in the sun. They traced the ants' path in one direction to a broken branch where a wound of dark sap glimmered. Despite some casualties caught in the sticky substance, the colony flowed down the other side of the trunk in a steady line, all the way back to their hole. Voirrey had to remind Davina not to touch them and to stand back, but still her fingers reached.

"Vina, they bite. You mustn't touch. If you put your finger there they will get lost, see how they follow one another? They won't know how to get home if you disturb their path."

Davina wriggled where Voirrey held her between her knees, her long skirt preventing her from escaping backwards through her legs.

Hearing footsteps, she turned. Sybilla approached, and Voirrey saw the tear tracks on her cheeks.

"What have you found?" she asked, her voice thick.

"Ants, Mama!"

"Oh, yes, I can see them. And what is that in your hand?" Sybilla smiled at the bedraggled grass and the half-crushed flower in her daughter's fist. Davina grinned back and opened her palm, the mess of stems scattering on the ground.

Voirrey frowned at Davina with mock offence and shook her head.

"Here," she said, drawing the last remaining flower out of her pocket and handing it to Sybilla.

They heard Edric's voice from the wagon. "We best be off now or we'll lose the light," he said.

Sybilla grasped her daughter's hand and led her back, lifting her into the cart.

Voirrey resumed her position opposite Sybilla and they set off again.

Sybilla leaned back, running her fingers along the blossom tips. Her head rocked with the movement of the wagon, her gaze lost in the verdant passing of the leaves. In the distance, Voirrey could hear a running brook.

The afternoon was warm and with the burlap tied back, the sun poured in syrupy and bright. Davina blinked stubbornly, trying to take in the view, finally losing her battle against sleep. Voirrey smiled to see her cheek squashed against her forearm, the child's open mouth reminding her of a tea-pot spout.

Sybilla held the same distant expression as before and Voirrey wondered with a spark of recognition whether this was the place where Gavril used to take her before Davina was born.

The thought pierced her.

Voirrey had first come to know his name when her rebel allies had sent report that the Skalen of Vaelnyr and her guardsman had been sighted in Brivia. How evil her command seemed in retrospect. *Skalen Sybilla and her guard, yes, kill them if you have the chance, and make it look like an accident.* Because back then she had been foolish enough to believe that Sybilla was the head of the snake and that the Purge could die with her.

Velspar moves in mysterious ways and when Sybilla was rescued by one of Peran's men, she was sent to Nothelm, to Voirrey's very door, for safe haven. Her parents liked to keep their allies in debt, and this favour bound Vaelnyr to the North.

Voirrey avoided the woman at first, knowing that it had come to her to complete the task. Her mind rushed at the terror of it. To imagine herself entering the room, pinning the woman to the bed, smothering her, sticking the knife in to a fatal depth. It made her palms sweat with dread.

At night, Sybilla screamed as if an intruder had come, and Voirrey listened, her heart hammering, and then the sorrowful wail and that name: *Gavril! Gavril, oh.* It was unbearable.

At night, and even during the day, Voirrey plugged her ears with cotton to block out the sound, and when there was silence, she settled on the fact that she could not use her body against the woman. She was a healer. She would give her the medicine she deserved and leave the room. She would go away for awhile. Though every motion of her hands filled her with disgust, the bitter tang of poison unnerving in the air, she prepared a night draught for the heartsick Skalen.

Each day, she stared at the bottle with its dark contents, the oily tincture of Sybilla's demise. If she did not drink it all, it would not work. Voirrey would need to gain her trust.

One day, Voirrey knocked on the door and came in, dressed in her plain woollen smock and apron. Sybilla sighted her with a rolling eye and looked away. *Another Attendant*, she must have thought. Voirrey opened the window a little and came to sit on the end of Sybilla's bed.

"I can help you," Voirrey said softly, looking not at her face but at the unmoving hands that lay upon the sheet.

Sybilla's voice was barely a whisper. "No one can help me."

For the first time, Voirrey looked into the woman's eyes, deep brown, a well of grief so deep it sent a shock through her nerves. She looked away.

A hot rush spread from her ears to her cheeks and the words tumbled out. "Your guardsman–"

Sybilla moaned and turned to the side clutching her belly as if Voirrey had struck her there.

She could see no swelling, but with catastrophic clarity she recognised the sweet scent of early pregnancy that emanated from the woman. *No, no*, she thought, and thanked Velspar through grit teeth that she had not tried the poison on her.

She could not kill a child.

If Velspar had blessed the woman's womb, Voirrey could not be responsible for ending that life. Looking upon her sad form, it was as if sun streamed through storm clouds, the will of Velspar blinding her eyes with some superior wisdom.

She went away to her chamber and disposed of the draught, its scent in her nostrils as evil as the execution pyre. And in the coming weeks she told Sybilla her name, that she was Voirrey Braedal, destined one day to rule over Nothelm, but that here and now she would be a friend to her, that she had delivered many babies and that she would keep the Attendants away if that was what she wished. It was not for Sybilla that she did it, but for the child. The Southland rebels waited eagerly for Voirrey's report, for news of Sybilla's demise, but no word came. The child would be born and then she would decide.

In the garden she walked with Sybilla, in the library she sat with her, and brought to her bed what comforts she required. In time, it seemed she forgot who the woman was, her heart moving automatically to the task, noticing Sybilla's reluctance to accept help, her fear of being touched, feeling such compassion for her–and mercy.

In Voirrey's mind, the thousands of devotees Sybilla had slain equated equally to her own attempt at murder. Never had they spoken of it. Not Sybilla's Purge, nor Voirrey's plot. They did not speak of the reality of things, and this was part of their bond, the river that flowed between them.

In stilted words, Sybilla had told Voirrey of Gavril, of her life in Vaelnyr, but there were so few memories that did not touch upon the Purge. After all that had happened, it was difficult to speak of Sybilla's family at all. Whatever Sybilla was now, she had to be a woman with no past. Velspar had blessed her, first with a child, and then with the miracle of spontaneous Intercession. Her spirit had been flooded and cleansed. In that glorious moment in the mountains of Jokvour, it seemed that Voirrey's shadows were also washed away.

As Voirrey watched Sybilla in the changing light she saw an aspect that made her seem a stranger. The orange of late afternoon knifed her face, bitter shadows falling with the stuttering procession of trees. Her hands–that still held the flower–sat unmoving, as if dead, and Voirrey felt a thrill of fear. By nightfall, Edric would have them in the Skalens' House, the place where Sybilla's family had burned in their beds, the fire of Vaelnyr the event used to justify the Intercessors' annihilation.

Sybilla would be made to take her place at the Skalens' Table, to talk of strategy and bloodshed, to lay traps for Voirrey's allies, to salt the earth where green shoots grew. Voirrey had a part to play in this, and a single misstep would mean their deaths.

Voirrey let her spirit hover above it all, lifting from the telos of her fear into vague rhythms–cartwheels and hoof clop, birdsong, and windsong–that cared nothing for her pain.

19

___

VAELNYR

IT WAS NIGHTTIME and raining when they arrived, the guardsmen's pungent oilskins hastily secured atop the sackcloth to keep them dry. Inside, the air was damp and close. The near-total darkness was stifling and Davina, sensing her mother's agitation, crouched in wide-eyed silence, remaining near to the opening where she could glimpse something of the mysterious world outside. Voirrey moved and sat beside Sybilla.

"Do you know where we are?" Voirrey whispered.

After a slight pause, Sybilla replied, "We are in the back streets behind the old Temple dormitories. When we came down that hill just before, that was when we entered the town. This is where Rayhmer's men were staying. There is a back street behind the main road that connects to the Skalen's House entry. As long as 'Little One' doesn't make any noise, we should be able to pass unnoticed."

The horses' hooves clacked sharply on the wet cobbles. Faraway voices sounded, laughter and yelling–from the tavern perhaps–among the whispering of the waves.

"You there, Guardsman!" The booming voice came like a death knell.

"Evening to you," Edric replied steadily.

"*Head* Guardsman, that is. Thought I recognised you. Well. My eyes are getting sharper by the day." The speaker laughed heartily.

Voirrey put her hand on Davina, willing her to be still. She listened for other voices, guessing from the accent that the speaker was a Maglorean guard on night patrol. Edric's men must have fallen back so as not to attract attention.

Nothing would happen to them, she reminded herself. They'd entered Sybilla's own lands where she was Skalen. They merely came in secret to keep a low profile until their presence could be officially announced. They must be bathed and briefed and dressed in fine regalia. It was a matter of impressions.

The horse snorted rain from his muzzle.

"Right then, Guardsman, must be off: my horse needs a good rub down and a carrot or two," Edric said.

"Wait, wait!" The man called. "What you got in there? If it's weapons, we keep 'em down here now in the new armoury."

"Nothing like that, though a shipment of arms will come from Nothelm within the week," Edric said, and Voirrey made note of this unwelcome detail.

"Good, good. Right then, evening to you, Guardsman," the man said.

The wagon turned about and progressed along a dimly lit street. Edric whistled and to Voirrey's relief she heard the hoofbeat of their entourage rejoining them.

As the path slanted upward, sounds of revelry grew dim. "This is it," Sybilla whispered, her back straight as a rod.

Awkwardly, Voirrey moved back to the other side of the wagon and Sybilla gathered her daughter up in her lap.

Edric whistled twice and with a great clang, the main gate was opened. The crisp sound of wet gravel seemed to go on and on as they were led in a meandering fashion beneath some kind of shelter. Voirrey resisted the urge to peek out.

By the echoing sound and the hiss of lanterns, she guessed that they were positioned at the main entrance.

Footsteps approached and a hand pulled back the coverings. Voirrey sat back as the man glanced at her and then looked upon

Sybilla with familiarity. A look of pained relief overtook his elderly face.

"Sybilla." A smile creased his features and when he tore his eyes away from her, he noticed the child. "Welcome, dear girl," he said warmly.

Holding Davina tight, Sybilla stared dumbly as the man's head disappeared. Moments later, a band of Attendants came to remove the sodden coverings.

Voirrey and Sybilla put up their travelling hoods to hide themselves and Davina clung to her mother's chest, a strange lump beneath the fabric.

The cool air of the Skalens' House seeped over them, the smell of swept tiles and oiled banisters tinged with the unmistakable scent of roses.

The man who had greeted them came to stand before Voirrey. "Welcome, Miss Voirrey," he said. She knew this had to be Head Guardsman Peran, but he seemed so old, so different to Sybilla's descriptions. Was this the man who had carried Sybilla from the fire and set the course of the Purge?

"Greetings to you, Guardsman," she said and returned his small bow.

Edric came to stand beside her and the Head Guards grasped palms. "Edric, you are looking well. It is good to see you."

"And you, Peran," he said. "I'll go with the horses and visit the men in the barracks."

"I'll find you," Peran said, and then turning to the women, he smiled again, as if they were distant relations come home at last. "There is nothing to do tonight. You make yourselves comfortable and we can talk in the morning."

"Thank you, Peran," Sybilla said, her voice almost a croak.

When the Attendants went to escort them up the main stair, Sybilla took an alternate route, leading the way to what must have been her old chambers.

The Attendants followed as quickly as they could, the eldest among them struggling to keep pace.

"Skalen Sybilla, we knew not which rooms you would prefer, so all have been made ready," she said.

Sybilla slowed down a little. Davina was heavy, after all.

"We will all go to my chamber to begin, and then we will inspect the other rooms," she replied curtly.

"Very good," the Attendant replied.

They had entered a long hall dotted with lanterns, each door they passed aglow with a strip of light beneath the door.

When they reached the third one along, Sybilla stopped.

The Attendant curtseyed and stepped forward, pulling a long dark key from her apron. As the door swung open, she held the key out for Sybilla. Grasping it, Sybilla looked about the room, finding the fire low and warm, a canopied bed with a fine crimson coverlet, and a wash basin set on the dresser with towels beside.

The woman made to enter with the younger Attendants behind, but Sybilla stopped her. "Please, leave us."

The Attendant looked mildly affronted, glancing at Voirrey, and then longingly at the child-shaped lump still hiding beneath Sybilla's cloak.

"I've put out some clothes for the child but had to guess at her size, if they are not right, I will send more."

When Sybilla did not oblige the silent request to introduce Davina to the Attendants, the old woman stepped back, adopting a servile rigidity that did not come naturally to her.

Sybilla closed the door with a deep sigh and released her daughter to the floor. As Sybilla turned the key, Voirrey watched Davina's grubby face, her eyes full of wonder. She grasped the bed veils and stared straight up as if into the boughs of a tree, flapping them and watching the soft white fabric ripple.

Sybilla was rigid and did not look like she was about to sit down. Her look was so intense that Voirrey feared to meet her eye. Instead, she focused on the child, holding out her hand.

"Come, darling, let's wash up for bed."

Despite her excitement, Davina went to Voirrey's side and allowed herself to be led to a spot on the velvet rug before the fire. Voirrey lifted the heavy basin of steaming water, the towels slung over her shoulder. She removed and laid out the girl's clothes which all stank of wet sackcloth. With the muslin, she wiped the girl's face, had her lift her arms, wiping and rinsing in the systematic manner of their nightly ritual. When she was clean, the girl sat naked before the fire, rolling on her back and staring upside-down at the vast opulence that surrounded her.

"What about you, Sybilla? Do you want me to leave you to bathe?" Voirrey said, turning.

She was hot in the cheeks and had left her cloak on the chair, but Sybilla sat perched on the edge of the bed, with hers still on, staring at the floor.

Sybilla looked up as if she had not heard what Voirrey had said.

She mumbled absently, "You can go first. I'll go next door and get the water from the other room."

Voirrey waited on the floor as Sybilla went out, returning a few minutes later with an identical basin. She placed it on the floor then went out again, struggling a little with the third basin which must have been taken from the room on the other side. Finally, Sybilla removed her cloak, taking Voirrey's and hanging both on a wall hook.

As the minutes ticked toward Davina's bedtime, Voirrey worried that Sybilla would ask her to choose a place to sleep. It was clear that the refurbished East Wing was where her parents had perished all those years ago, but Lucinda's room had been near to Sybilla's. The last thing she wanted to do was choose the room her sister had died in. Surely, it must be the largest of the three rooms on this side but she could not be sure.

Sybilla misinterpreted the pained expression on her face. "I will bathe on this side of the bed and you can stay where you are." She reached up and let the curtains fall, forming a gauzy shield between them.

Voirrey nodded and could hear Sybilla removing her clothes. Facing the fire, and with her back to the bed, Voirrey took off her clothes, distracted from her discomfort by Davina's kicking legs and bare bum as she inspected the fringe of the rug.

Voirrey smiled and began to wash herself, relishing the comforting warmth of the fire and the heady scent of dried rose petals, piled in bowls on the little table between the sitting chairs. Her lithe figure and small breasts shone in the firelight as she quickly dried herself. She thought she felt Sybilla's gaze on her, but when she found an excuse to turn, she saw nothing but the woman's dark silhouette as she bent to wring out her hair. Voirrey looked away, wrapping herself in a towel, looking at the garments laid out atop a wooden trunk. The underclothes swam on her and she had to pull the ribbon tight just to keep them up. The beige camisole was beautiful against her skin, and even the cotton shift felt soft as down.

Davina resisted the lace smock, but once it was on, she quickly forgot her protest.

Sybilla came and sat beside them in one of the chairs, towelling her hair, and set her Meridian back in place. "I can't believe we are here. None of this seems real."

Voirrey nodded, feeling tired after their long journey and yearning for sleep. "We should get some rest." She paused, waiting for Sybilla to say something, but when she did not, Voirrey asked her outright. "Which room do you think is best for me?"

A flicker of fear passed over Sybilla's face. "Would you be comfortable here?"

"Oh, I don't want to make you leave your own room." She blushed. "This is your room, isn't it?"

"Yes, yes. I just want us to be together tonight, for Davina's sake," she said, looking agitated.

"Okay," Voirrey said, assessing the likely comfort of the cushioned chairs if she arranged them face to face.

"The bed is big enough if we put Davina between us. Do you mind? I don't want–" Sybilla broke off, her eyes growing wet.

Voirrey remembered Sybilla's words, the one and only time that she had recounted her sister's death. *Lucinda was screaming, right there, on the other side of the wall, and I couldn't get to her, I couldn't get her out.*

"Of course," Voirrey said quickly. "Davina needs familiarity right now. We really should go to bed, I am so tired. But we haven't had anything to eat. Can we ask for some milk and bread? Just a light supper will do."

With an air of hesitation, Sybilla rang the bell that hung beside the bed.

Minutes later, the same woman who had greeted them earlier reappeared with lantern in hand. The light illuminated her voluminous grey ringlets and narrow face. The Attendant's curious eyes peeked over Sybilla's shoulder as she received the order for supper.

She went out and when she returned with the tray, the Attendant finally got her wish.

"Well, hello, aren't you a pretty girl?" she said in a singsong voice. "My name is Margret, but you can call me Gretty if you like. What is your name?"

Sybilla stood with her hands on her hips behind the crouched woman, swiftly losing her patience, but Voirrey smiled. They needed as many allies as they could find in this place.

Voirrey rubbed the child's back to say that it was alright, she could speak to the lady.

"Davina," she said shyly, over-annunciating her name.

"Davina," Margaret replied in hushed awe. Her head tilted in adoration and Voirrey smiled again to prompt her departure.

"Pleased to meet you, Davina. We are all so happy you are here." She acknowledged Voirrey and Sybilla with a little nod. "I hope you enjoy your supper, and do let me know if the clothes aren't right."

"I will," Sybilla assured her as she closed the door, turning the key in the lock.

Voirrey sliced some bread and ate it with butter. Davina dipped hers in a cup of creamy milk, doing better these days at not making a mess of her food.

As the fire grew low, the three of them crawled into bed, Sybilla and Voirrey positioned either side of the child. Absently, Sybilla stroked her daughter's hair, and soon Davina fell asleep. When Sybilla's hand came to rest on the pillow beside her face, the women's eyes met.

"I don't know how this is going to go tomorrow," she said gravely.

Voirrey needed to reassure her but felt equally nervous. "Whatever is said, whatever plan is in motion, you just need to draw things out. I will stay with Davina and make sure she is not left with anyone else. Though, we need to make the most of help when it comes. You know I am not going to be able to stay here forever."

"Do you mean 'Gretty'?" she said mockingly. "I don't know where they found her. She's new."

"I'm serious, Sybilla. You will need her. You will need an army of 'Grettys' on your side if Davina is to get along in this world."

Sybilla did not say anything.

Feeling the tragedy of their position and the unfairness of it all, Voirrey went on: "Civit's Ridge was never going to last. I was a fool to believe that we could do what we wanted and forget all of this. I can't help but feel that I have made things worse by taking you away from here."

Sybilla stopped her there. "What you have done for me can never be repaid. I don't say it often enough, Voirrey, but..." She sighed, rolling onto her back. "You saved me. You..."

"It's okay," Voirrey said softly.

"You are a miracle that I did not deserve," Sybilla said, her eyes on the ceiling. "After all the horror, I want to do one good thing. I don't know what that is yet, but I have to be here to find out. I can't hide away anymore."

Voirrey feared her new courage and what it might bring.

Davina's sweet breath bloomed in her face; the child belonged now to all of Vaelnyr. The diaphanous canopy swayed to some tugging draught. So fragile, this moment. So tenuous, the thread of chance they must follow.

Sybilla closed her eyes and Voirrey fought the desire to touch her cheek.

The water of her soul choked with words unsaid.

20

VAELNYR

Voirrey awoke with an air of luxury, stretching her legs like a cat on soft sheets. The dream faded and the details of reality fell heavily into place. She opened her eyes to Sybilla's sleeping form, her face framed by the dark silk of her hair. The veils of the bed moved ghostly as they had done the night before. Voirrey looked down and realised Davina was not there. She sat up and wrenched the veils aside, finding the girl sitting beneath the window, tugging at the drapes. With a sigh of relief, she lay back, her heart skipping like a stone. She turned back to Sybilla who was just waking up. This day was important and they had already slept too long.

Voirrey took herself from the bed, allowing Sybilla her own time to register the facts of morning. It was she, after all, who must face three of the seven Head Guardsmen of Velspar and do her best to conceal her duplicity.

Voirrey rubbed her face. "Vina, what are you doing? You want to look out the window?"

"I can't see," she whined.

"Let's have a look, shall we?"

Voirrey scooped her up and held her on her hip, drawing their faces to the glass. The sky was clear with high streaking clouds. Beneath them were hills of green pasture, the grey buildings of the town forming a crescent about a sapphire bay. Unlike Nothelm with its harbour choked with ships, the Gulf of Vaelnyr sheltered only a smattering of fishing boats. Davina pressed her face to the glass, fogging it up so she could not properly see.

"Beautiful," Voirrey said tonelessly.

"Horsies!" Davina exclaimed, pointing.

"Oh yes, I see. Oh, Vina you are getting heavy, I need to put you down." The girl slid down her leg and went running over to the table where some of last night's supper still sat.

Sybilla came and stood beside Voirrey. "I can have them bring some proper breakfast."

Voirrey waved a hand. "No need to fuss over me, and Vina's already eaten. Can I help you get ready? What are you going to wear?"

Sybilla went to a closet in the corner of the room and flicked through her options. She pulled out a crimson doublet and brought it to her face, sniffing it, her expression souring. "Everything smells like roses. I wonder if it is that 'Gretty' woman's doing."

"You don't like roses?" Voirrey asked, having enjoyed the scent since their arrival.

"My mother used to put roses everywhere. All through the house. Wine red were her favourite. I didn't continue the tradition when I lived here as Skalen. It must be one of the Attendants, trying to bring a woman's touch. This place has been full of guardsmen for four years now." She sighed and placed the doublet on the bed. After some more rifling, she laid out three potential outfits.

"This is for you," Sybilla said passing Voirrey a maroon tunic of silk appliqué Alma flowers. Voirrey eyed it dubiously, but she put it on. Most of the clothing was too big for Voirrey, so Sybilla fitted her with a wrap-around dress secured with a network of interweaving ribbons.

Sybilla glanced at her transformed appearance with approval. "I can braid your hair if you like," she offered.

Voirrey sat obediently in the chair and, despite her reluctance to adorn herself in any way, the feathery touch of Sybilla's fingers was enough to make her relent. Still, looking down at the rich colours of her skirt and sleeves, she felt a bit silly.

When Sybilla was done, Voirrey stood and held out her hands. "How do I look, Vina?"

The girl stared goggle-eyed at her hair as if a bird had taken up residence there.

Voirrey raised her eyebrows comically and reached for a slice of bread.

Sybilla laced herself into leather britches, donning a blouse of heavy black lace beneath the firm velvet doublet. Her own hair, she had swept into an elegant braid that wove itself in and out of her Meridian like a vine, covering her scar completely.

"Will you help me with this?" Sybilla held out the Skalens' Star.

Voirrey undid the fastening and reached around the taller woman's neck, securing it so that it shined from her breast.

Voirrey watched her in the looking glass.

"You look strong," Voirrey said with a laugh. "You look like a Skalen."

Sybilla closed her eyes and took a deep breath, releasing it slowly.

"I need to talk to Peran before I lose my nerve," she said, her cheeks a little flushed.

"I will be here," Voirrey said.

"I think it will be safe for you and Davina to go outside, but don't leave the Skalens' House grounds until we have spoken again."

"Okay," Voirrey said. "Good luck."

Sybilla made for the door.

"Wait! You should eat something." Voirrey ran to the table and cut a slice of bread, buttering it hastily.

Sybilla rolled her eyes and stood there munching until she was finished. "And now, I must go."

Davina's face crumpled as she realised her mother was leaving.

Sybilla crouched before her. "My darling, I will not be gone long. Stay with Aunty Voy." She kissed her swiftly on the brow and went out, making it all seem normal, like it was just another day.

21

SELTSLAND

KALET WAITED in the dark, stretching her legs between the sheets. Her mind ticked. Finally, when she had fallen into a doze, Magnar's great bulk fell into bed beside her, stinking of ale. The hour was late, and she had not seen him since lunchtime. He had come in late several times this week, if he came to her at all. It was foolish of her to treat so carelessly with his allegiance. Like any good Skalen, she assessed risk in the language of the Tally. A dalliance here or there, she was willing to allow, but her husband was gathering a veritable harem about him and it spoke of his neglect.

A neglected husband could be dangerous.

"Spent some time below today, hey? How fare the pups?" he questioned her lazily, as if he did not care, but she caught the hurt tone in his voice. Knew that when he set himself upon Tilly or Naida or whoever it might be, that it was a kind of petty vengeance.

"They do not satisfy me," she said, indulging his suspicions.

"No?" He smiled as she ran her fingers through the dark hair of his chest.

Kalet shook her head.

The smell of him made her stomach coil, a tightness full of jealousy and rage that made her want to hurt him. She scruffed his neck, tightening her fist around a handful of hair. The sting exposed the white of his throat, made his chest rise. His eyes did not wander now. She watched his pulse flicker, waited until she had him entirely in her thrall.

Only me, she thought, *you will only want for me in the end.*

She was a Skalen, of the holy Askier. It was she who made him Skalen. It did not matter how many years had passed since she pulled him out of the swamp. Always, he would bow to her and recognise that he existed at the mercy of her will.

She used her tongue to bring him to this exquisite knowledge and afterward he gazed upon her in a kind of holy terror.

He sighed, still in that thoughtless ecstasy that buzzed in the air about them. He called to her body with his arms and she came into his embrace. A possessive hand cupped her small breast.

Kalet let him recover himself before she spoke, catching the moment before he drifted into sleep. "I met with Haldi the other day," she began.

"Oh, yes?" Magnar replied drowsily.

"I have told her of your increased patrols and that she can do nothing to prevent them," she said.

Magnar chuckled.

"You are focused on the populated areas but we must also move westward," she continued.

He shifted in the bed. "There is nothing but woodland. Or do you mean Jokvour?" He did not sound particularly motivated to pursue her line of thought.

"I mean…" she said, "that we need to forge stronger ties with Maglore so that they leave Lindesal in our care. Once we have allied the Guard of Seltsland and Maglore, the Lindesali rebels will flee south."

He squeezed her against him, kissed her hair. "Got the taste for blood, have you my darling? I thought you might be sending me off for some other reason."

She ran her hand along his thigh. "No other reason than that I know you will hold sway with Rayhmer. I think it's time we invited him to the table. Let him in on a few things. We have played our cards close for long enough."

He scoffed. "Believe me, Guardsman Fenlor has been itching to make sweet with Rayhmer for as long as I can remember." He turned his face to her. "Has he made contact with you?"

Kalet smiled. "No. Nothing from Rayhmer as yet. But if Fenlor brings me more gifts from Lindesal, who knows what wishes I will grant? You can tell him that, word for word."

Magnar baulked. "That was my gift, don't you forget."

He peeled his palm from her breast, traced the line of her hip with his fingers.

"More gifts, more wishes, for you or for Fenlor," she teased.

"Oh, you are a callous woman," he said, retracting his hand and rolling over on his side.

"And your callous woman will be making her own entreaties," she said to the back of his head.

"Oh?"

"I want to talk to Damek. Nothelm have remained aloof of everything since the Purge and I am happy for them to continue in this way, but bound to our cause. The marriage bond between Moriel and my sister will not be any boon to us if those two declare allegiance with the rebels," she said.

Magnar grunted. "I don't envy you that mission."

"Yes, well, we all work to our strengths," she said. "If the weather improves, I might go as early as next week. I'm not sure. I have my 'pups' working on something that might help our case," she said.

A low growl reverberated through his back and she placed her hand there, laughing.

Kalet put her arms around him, wrapping her thigh over his. "You will not harm them, Magnar," she warned. "They're mine."

He held her forearm. "The old rule applies, my darling. If they cross your threshold, they will meet my sword."

"Yes, my love. They know it, and they wouldn't dare."

He made a noncommittal noise and she could tell he was about to fall asleep. "What is this ploy of yours anyway?" he mumbled.

"If I can convince him of the Holy Ones' return, he will do anything to keep the siatka from his waters."

"So, what, you'll have your little laddies dress up in skins and

splash about the bay?" Magnar's wheezing laugh made his ribs tremble. "Ha! That would be a good end for them." He was on his back
now, tears of laughter trailing his cheeks.

"Watch yourself, husband," she chided. "You think you are so
much better than them? How about this: I send my boys to hunt the
siatka and you go with two of your best men to fetch me as many
kshidol as you can shoot down."

Magnar thumped his fist on the mattress. "I accept!"

Ridiculous man.

He rolled over and laid his arm over her chest. "And what will be
my prize?"

"Hmm," she mused. "If you can outstrip my striplings by the next
full moon, I will banish them from the Skalens' House for a week."

"Only a week?"

"Two weeks."

"You drive a hard bargain. Two weeks and I get to slap them
around a little."

"No... Two weeks, and I get to slap you around."

Magnar roared with laughter. "Yes, that will do. A fine wager."

22

SELTSLAND

THE MOON WAXED FAT above the night-black sea. Kalet paced barefoot along the sand, waiting for her boys to bring their quarry. In and around Jokvour, Magnar's search had brought naught but feathers of dubious origin. Although, he had discovered something there more worthy of the hunt. A lone traveller moved in those parts, eluding his pursuers, leaving nothing in his wake but shit and cold campfires.

This was interesting to Kalet, but not enough to lend her mind to it. All she could think of now was that she had a siatka to do with as she pleased.

The previous day, Jaret had come to her, insistent that he'd spotted siatka in the eastern sea. He was confident out there on the water, owing to his early life among the fisherfolk. For over a week, he had taken his little boat, scouting up and down, while Colm and Osmet assisted her with the preparation of the lure. Each day, he returned bitter news.

In the wet room by the kitchens, butcher's waste lay beneath a canvass sheet. The fabric was waxy with fat, the meat stains brown. Beneath the sheet were splintered bones, cartilage sockets with their sinew attached, hooves and other parts unworthy of serving to the Skalens of the House. Kalet had Colm select the scraps most suitable for mincing while she crushed dried Alma leaves into the offering bowl. On a whim, she added a few drops of Damyen's blood. It stank by now, but not much worse than the spoiled meat. As guides for the dead, Mother Siatka and Father Kshidol were drawn to the stench of rot, sending their earthly incarnations to carry what remained of the soul to Velspar's shining furnace.

The meat paste was putrid with death-stench and if this did not bring the water serpents, nothing would.

She sent the three of them out at dawn, watching Jaret curiously as he made a diamond of his hands, and measured the sea. From shore, she watched their little boat, the hook spears glinting in Osmet's hand as Colm began to row.

Kalet watched them until it seemed the black wafer that was their boat became too small to hold in her sight. The rising glare dissolved them, so she had to look away for several seconds to find them anew. Finally, she resolved to leave them to their task and went back to the Skalens' House to prepare the wet room, and her ceremonial space.

By the arc of midday, she had cleansed the wet room of refuse and had prepared her implements. Her stomach gnawed itself with hunger but she could not bear to eat. She went back down to the beach, left her blood-dirty clothes in a pile and cleansed herself in the waves. The water rocked her, like a babe at the ticking of their mother's breast, shushing her impatience, asserting a largeness and strength that dwarfed her. How she hated to wait, to be at the mercy of others. Kalet swam against the waves, reaching the stillness just beyond, and there, she sighted them, the little boat. Relieved, she floated, occasionally lifting her head to check her distance from shore. For a thrilling moment, she imagined the siatka moving beneath her, watching her nakedness like a pale star. It was not beyond the realms of possibility. She twisted upright, watching the water, though even when she opened her eyes beneath the surface, she couldn't see.

Kalet made slow progress as she swam to shore, arriving far from her clothes but near to the path that led to the underside of the Skalen's House. She drew her heavy limbs from the sea and left a trail of dark footprints in her wake. By the time she arrived back at the house, she was dry all over and feeling much revived.

Inside, she dressed herself and, after a light repast, Jaret came barrelling through the door. The boy did not talk much, but the glory of that smile, oh yes, they had done it. Kalet grinned back. "You did it?"

Jaret nodded. "One escaped us, Skalen, but the other we have slain."

"Good, good..." She jumped up.

A frown passed over the boy's features. "To bring the creature without being seen, we will have to take it down to the caves. Bring it up by nightfall."

The temptation was great, so great, but she agreed with his plan.

And now, waiting on the beach, she saw them come, dark figures carrying a shadow on their shoulders, its weight bearing them down. Kalet hurried up the sandy path and stood in the doorway to receive them. Her body fairly thrummed with excitement, breaking into a cold sweat.

She could hear their trudging exertions, the rasp of sand as they finally came within sight.

"Well done," she breathed.

Colm nodded brusquely, the weight of the carcass causing the tendons on his neck to stand stiff at an angle.

"Bring it inside. Don't drag it! Lift the tail," she scolded, seeing the clinging dirt about the underside.

The boys manoeuvred the body carefully. Lowering the great serpent down, they coiled the length of it around the butcher's bench.

Kalet narrowed her eyes, breathing faster than normal, as if she had been the one carrying the siatka.

"The carcass must be washed, and when you are done, I will return with further instruction."

Kalet excused herself then, only noticing once she had left the room how her ears rang with a strange and piercing silence. She focused on the ritual space she had cleared in the adjoining room, lighting the Alma censer that once hung in the Temple's high dome. Behind her, through the door, she heard a sluicing sound, the rush and trickle of a rag being wrung out into water.

Quietly, she opened the door a crack. Kalet stared at the open mouth, at the majesty of the siatka, the milky curve of those teeth, the size of the gleaming black corpse. She watched her boys at work, their hands moving in smooth motions, in caress, almost. Osmet cleaned the head as if he stroked the face of a dead child. His hands moved from the snout to the ridges of the siatka's crown, using the palm of his other hand to deflect the force of the water as he squeezed the rag, working gently around the closed lids.

Jaret, who had been washing the serpent's tail, stood suddenly, noticing Kalet.

"Skalen," he said, bowing.

Kalet pushed the door wide and entered the room as if it had always been her intention to do so at that moment.

With reluctance the last of the three boys put down his rag and stood.

"We will not be able to leave any part of the beast to be found by others, so I ask that you assist me in butchering the carcass."

Osmet looked at the copper bowl she held in her hands, guessing her intention.

Kalet knelt down and took the siatka's head in her lap. Sliding her hand beneath and along the scaled throat, Kalet felt life's fading heat somewhere in the core of that thick and muscular neck. Turning the head to one side, she exposed the throat, and with the bowl positioned beneath, she made the first cut. A gush of thin, brownish fluid splattered into the bowl, slowing to a steady leak.

When the bowl was full, she waved for the boys to use buckets for the rest, and to continue on without her. They were familiar with the methods perfected by Attendants since the days of the Purge. In those days the Holy Ones were first butchered and eaten as a citizen's oath against Intercession. Siatka flakes were rarer now than those made of kshidol flesh and the new generation had, on occasion, taken their oaths using the flesh of sundry birds and common snakes.

Holding the bowl, Kalet walked slowly, the liquid's surface rippling with every footfall. Fearing she would spill the sacred substance, she imagined her hands were made of stone, her breath a gossamer fog, dispersing, and causing no ripple of its own. She knelt and placed the bowl in the centre of the stone floor, arising on trembling legs, shaking the cramp from her fingers as she sealed the chamber door.

The bowl of blood sat upon the floor like a hooded captive, full of presence, awaiting her will. The Alma curled from the ceiling, grey like a network of roots, reaching for the dark surface.

She watched the smoke reflected there, illumined by the light of seven candles. What was it she wanted?

Direction in the dark.

From the shelf she took her sacred object, the gift given her by her father, that came from his mother before him, and so on, in an unbroken line to the very first of the Askier.

Guide my way, she whispered, holding it to her forehead.

She held the diamond-shaped form, smooth and warm in her palm—and bathed it in smoke. Then, by some instinct, she submerged the wooden carving in the siatka's blood. Her hands formed a red-brown halo about the object, and she watched its familiar shape darken. The blood soaked deep, and she had the sick sensation that the substance might destroy its fragile carvings, that all this moisture might warp it and split it in two. Still, she drowned it, watching the Alma dance once more upon the surface.

Blood linked things together; fire tore them apart. These were truths that she had learned. Kalet brought the dripping artefact up from the bowl and licked it clean, placing it damp into the crook of her breast.

Blood of Siatka, reveal to me this secret of the Askier, she prayed, feeling languid and calm in the Alma's haze.

Wet noises from the adjoining room tugged at her attention and she felt that she had done here what she intended to do.

Kalet moved to the doorway, the bloody object still protruding from her bodice.

"The blood is ready for bottling now," she said in a dreamy voice. Osmet was the only one who dared glance at the stains on her breast.

"Extract one of the eye-teeth for me, that one I will take to Damek." Light of step, she wandered to her washroom to change.

23

VAELNYR

Sybilla made directly for the Council Room, her thoughts narrow and clear. There was no hint of Alma in the air, which was to be expected. To share of the Alma showed trust and mutual respect, virtues that found little purchase in new Velspar. Standing before the door, she listened a moment to Peran's muffled voice, then decisively entered the room.

Edric stood leaning against the Skalens' Table, speaking low with Peran, who had seated himself in what was once her father's chair. Behind them, the familiar expanse of grass and sky was bisected by diamond window panes.

Edric straightened. "Sybilla, good morning."

"Guardsman," she said, her inner storm finding him a temporary obstruction, with Peran the full focus of her mind. *Leave us*, she thought.

Peran glanced up at her. "Edric was just leaving." Turning to the man, he smiled with genuine warmth—seeming to give him credit for bringing her back.

A flare of resentment rose in her belly, though Edric did not deserve it. He helped her to safety after Gavril's death, just as he helped her now. It was the associations he brought to mind: journeys of grim obligation, and he the quiet witness.

"Thank you, Edric," she added. "Please send my regards to the Skalens of Nothelm, I owe them much for their hospitality these last years."

Edric acknowledged her words with a bow and departed.

With the click of the door, the room swelled with silence. In her mind, she balanced the stones of her Meridian, safe islands in a treacherous sea.

He just looked at her, taking her in.

"Peran," she said and exhaled long.

"Sybilla," he said, his mouth rising in a half-smile. The expression did not look natural. The left side of his face, the more she looked at it, had a slack quality.

"You have noticed my face," he said, and as he shifted in the chair, she noticed his left hand tremble.

Sybilla frowned.

"I have had a kind of seizure. The healers say that I may return to normal, or I may not." He shrugged. "I am glad you have come home."

Sybilla felt frozen to the spot. He had been the hand at her back, the whisperer insistent on the realisation of her father's mission. The man who saved her from the fire, who saved her from the assassins that killed her lover, who saved her so her child could be born, but who bid her to turn her grief to murder. Peran, steadfast and unrelenting. He had done it all–for her? For love of her dead father? For what?

"Yes," she replied falteringly.

"Sybilla, much has changed." He watched her. "You have changed, I see."

She found herself blushing, looked at her hands.

Peran continued. "There are so many things I want to explain. This silence has gone on too long."

Anger, from nowhere, "In good time, Guardsman," she said, shooting him a fiery glare.

Ashamed, she turned toward the window, stared out as she tried to master herself. The screech of his chair and his shuffling gait disturbed her peripheral vision. What had happened to him? Suddenly, she wanted to cry.

"Sybilla, I am sorry for what happened to Gavril. I never said it at the time and I realise..." He broke off, watching her.

Now the tears were building with a force she could not stifle.

"It is no excuse, but I did not want to put any of it to paper. It was a tense time, politically, and..." He sighed. "The details do not matter, not now. But you must know that I cared for him and that my instruction was to protect you both."

Memories came, of Gavril and Peran, their private chats, the intimation that one day Gavril could sit beside her on the Skalen's throne, the first guardsman to break their vow and pass between these two holy stations. Could the guard who saved her that night have acted of his own free will? Was Gavril's death an accident? She would never know, and it was too late to wonder. Far too late.

She sniffed, wiped her eyes. "I cannot be seen like this Peran," she said.

He nodded solemnly, seeing that he had touched her, her tears alone the admission of the bitterness she had held toward him these past years.

"Then, let us come to more pressing matters. I am not sure how much Edric has told you about the Maglorean contingent, but we have serious concerns about Rayhmer's leadership." Peran's tone had returned to its customary formality.

Sybilla regained herself. "I can see that the Maglorean experiment in Vaelnyr has backfired, but you will need to furnish me with the details."

Peran clasped his trembling hand and straightened his posture. "Rayhmer is a problem. He enlists men who enjoy violence and foregoes their conditioning. There have been concerns about the Maglorean Guard for generations but Rayhmer poses a real threat to the future of the Guard. It is a dangerous business, Sybilla. The cooperation of the Guard has lasted centuries because we are conditioned to the communal need. Our work is without passion or interest."

Sybilla knew that there was some truth to this. She had felt it in the cool reservoir within Gavril's soul. A calm place, sometimes soothing, sometimes so remote it reminded her of blinding stone. The Guard's Way created holy servants, as the Seven Gates of Wisdom shaped the Intercessors. But *without passion or interest*? That, Sybilla would never believe.

Peran went on, tracing the point of the Skalen's Star inlaid in the table's surface. "Rayhmer has overmastered his Skalens and thinks himself accountable to no one. I have tried to rein him in. Edric has helped immeasurably. Guardsman John would never let Avishae fall into Maglorean hands, though there may come a point where he has no choice. I have grave fears for Brivia and Lindesal. Guardsman Kiryn tries to stay out of Rayhmer's way and has abided the 'assistance' of the Maglorean contingent in Brivia for years. Guardswoman Grenla, as you may know, is less obliging."

Sybilla smirked, having met Grenla when she was first appointed Head Guard of Lindesal, though she noticed Peran's omission. "What of Seltsland?"

He sucked in a breath and exhaled, "Guardsman Fenlor is likely to ally with Rayhmer if we do not act. This is why I need you here, Sybilla. If Seltsland joins Maglore it will create a divide between North and South." Peran's cheek twitched, then fell slack as before.

Sybilla paced up and down, the diamond panes flickering with the passing gleam of bevelled glass. She had to protect Voirrey and Davina. This was far worse than she had expected. Seven centuries had passed since the clans had been at war. The coming of the First Diviner brought the Seven together, and as her eyes drifted over the Star that spanned the round table, she felt the weight of what she had done. All of her grief and fear levelled at the Intercessors and now they were gone. She had destroyed the balance and left a crack for Rayhmer's ambitions to thrive. The High Intercessors, if they yet lived, would have pacified him by now. She was such a fool. All she had done, she now realised, was trade the soft tyranny of psychic intrusion for violence. Her Meridian Decree, designed to soothe the passions, to protect the spirit from psychic intermingling, ensured that the only way one could master another was to threaten the animal inside. Violence. Her heart clamoured, fogging her thoughts with swirling terrors. What good was it to protect the spirit if the body could be harmed in innumerable ways? Scenes of barbarity and mutilation flashed through her with startling force.

She looked at Peran, the stoop he had developed, the thinning hair at his temples, the leather of his Meridian dark and stiff, like a brace around something broken.

The door clicked open, drawing Sybilla's blazing eyes.

Peran turned stiffly in his chair.

A guard appeared, one she didn't recognise–tall, thick set, and a little too handsome.

He glanced at her as if she should be impressed. "Guardsman Peran, Rayhmer has sent me. He cannot attend the meeting as arranged and has suggested postponing until tomorrow."

Peran sneered slightly. "Yes, yes. Not to worry. Tomorrow will be fine."

The guard looked furtively at Sybilla once more. "Thank you, Guardsman." He dipped his head and exited.

Sybilla caught Peran's eye with a look of distaste. "Who was that idiot?"

Peran's sudden laugh took him and he clutched his side.

A slow smile appeared on her face.

"Oh, Sybilla." He wiped his eyes. "I have had to suffer so many fools."

Finally, she sat at the table. "I am here, Peran, but I will speak plainly to you now: I do not have a plan." She lowered her voice. "Tell me what to do."

His sigh gave way to silence and it seemed several minutes went by. Was it so complicated he could not formulate his thoughts? Or was it that he could see no way out?

"Just be a figurehead, Sybilla." He caught himself, noticing her frown. "I do not mean to say that your counsel is not of value. What I mean to say is that you must project a strong image. Your presence must be synonymous with Vaelnyr."

Sybilla looked unconvinced.

"You think this is unimportant, but it is the people we must persuade. In the streets they see the Maglorean Guard. We need your presence here. You must use the fact that you have been in Nothelm these past years to our advantage. Show the people that our northern alliance is tighter than ever. We must make Rayhmer focus his aims elsewhere until we can back this image with force." He paused. "And there is one more thing..." Again, he hesitated. "I must name my successor and have them ratified by the Council of Skalens before we lose any more ground. Right now, I think I could obtain their agreement," he said.

Sybilla felt numb.

"You think the Greslet Skalens will sign? I was under the impression that Rayhmer had them in the palm of his hand." Her words proceeded like logic but inside she trembled. For good or ill, Peran was her life's constant. He could not be succeeded. No one would be worthy of that position.

His voice was barely a whisper. "Skalen Inry has not given herself over. She will obtain Skalen Domhnall's mark if it will keep Rayhmer in tow."

Sybilla nodded. "So, who have you chosen?"

"It must be Andrin," he said with a note of apology.

And though she did not like the man, she understood Peran's reasoning–he was utterly committed to the moral code. Whatever social niceties he lacked, he would breed good soldiers, selfless and level-headed.

"You have my support," she said.

His shoulders visibly relaxed.

"When will it be done?" she asked.

"I will send the letters shortly."

She felt relief at his decisiveness and for the first time she paused to recognise him, this man before her who continued to hold her aloft. His sense of duty ran so deep. Not just to Vaelnyr but to her family: to her and her daughter.

"Would you like to meet Davina properly?" Sybilla asked.

He swallowed, and looked at her with tender eyes. "Nothing would bring me more joy."

24

VAELNYR

RAYHMER SENT HIS EXCUSES once more, extending their meeting's delay, but Sybilla could not have been more grateful for the affront. She used that time to take Voirrey and Davina about the places of her childhood. Sad places infused with memory. Curtains she and her sister used to sneak behind, places where her father sat and ate, loosening his collar as if from the Intercessor's yoke. And in those days, the Intercessors did come to the Skalens' House, drifting down the hallway in a cloud of incense.

Sybilla showed her daughter all the secret nooks and hiding places, the places where one could see without being seen, and listen, and learn. Genuinely, she treasured these places, but she realised that as a child of Davina's age, she had mastered silence and had understood the mortal peril of being discovered. In this, she had failed her daughter, who chortled at the acoustics of the great stone buildings and who could be heard pattering along wherever she went.

When Sybilla's shoulders tensed at Davina's sounds, Voirrey seemed to instinctively understand. After all, her own childhood must have been similar, albeit without an older sibling to instruct her. Voirrey trained Davina to walk softly, placing heel and toe, toe and heel, walking blindfolded with arms outstretched to catch her. While Sybilla read her briefing notes, Voirrey taught Davina little sneezes that would not disturb the dust from a moth's wings. She taught her the basic fact–that had somehow alluded her–that hiding meant more than tucking one's head from view.

When it came Sybilla's turn to teach her, the lessons grew less playful, her growing frustration bringing the little girl to whining refusals and tears. Yet Sybilla knew these were the outbursts she had to learn to control. *If you keep very still, you can cry without making a single sound. Just breathe in and out until the feeling passes. Do it with me. In...and out. See? The water leaks silently from our eyes like a trail of ants.* Even Voirrey looked at her disapprovingly after that conversation. So cruel, she felt, and yet these lessons had to outlive her.

Sybilla had lost all expectation of Rayhmer's visit, so felt quite unprepared when Peran confirmed that he had seen the man with his own eyes.

An hour later, they were gathered in the Council Room: Peran and Andrin on the Vaelnyri side, and Rayhmer flanked by guardsmen Sanden and Degore.

At the Skalen's Table, Sybilla listened to Degore, facing him as Rayhmer loomed in her periphery. They had been assembled for ten minutes or so, and had moved from the opening prayer onto the customary discussion of the Skalens' Tally.

Sybilla struggled to master herself after the shock of seeing Rayhmer in the flesh. His height, the intensity of his gaze, the collision of memory and reality as the forty-year-old Rayhmer she had last seen resolved into this man before her. Her sister's words came back to her: *his face would give anyone nightmares.* But no, it was not his face. The moment he entered the Council Room, she felt his presence, the heat of him. He aped the manners of a guardsman when required but as Peran spoke, it was difficult to overlook the disrespect in his meandering gaze. He leaned sidelong in his chair, as if humouring the old man.

Over twenty-five years had passed since Rayhmer had first come to Vaelnyr as Maglore's newly sworn Head Guard. In those days, Peran was a formidable man of strength and intellect whom Rayhmer was forced to abide. Now age was dragging Peran to ground while Rayhmer's strength remained undiminished.

Sybilla thought back to that time, watching Rayhmer from the high window, and then on his last day, when their eyes had met in the hallway. She had seen it clearly, then as now, that whatever he outwardly proposed, he reserved for himself special permission to do otherwise. The Sisters of Jagoda had been the first to discover what Rayhmer's code would allow: against those charged with heresy, anything was permitted. Rayhmer did not participate but he did not discipline his men. According to every law, his men should have been executed for what they had done.

Peran had tried with his retraining camp, to save the Guard from factional warfare. But with little effort, Rayhmer had turned even this to his advantage. Now, it was tradition for Maglorean recruits to spend a summer in Vaelnyr to "realign themselves with the moral code," though Sybilla doubted their Vaelnyri instructors had any power over them at all.

She glanced at Rayhmer, noticing the way his leathery skin still bore the pockmarks of his youth. His calloused hands rested on the table. *He should not be here at all*, she thought. With sickening clarity she realised that she had missed her chance to end him. There was a time when people did what she commanded, and that time had passed. She had turned a blind eye to Rayhmer, as the other Skalens did, leaving it to Peran to fix things. Rayhmer allowed the other Head Guards just enough influence to keep them from acting against him. But the real danger was the rot he had spread amongst his ranks. Immoral men, too many to count, spreading their disease in turn.

As he raked his lank hair back from his face, she shuddered. It was brazen to the point of heresy the way he shirked the Guard's Code. A guardsman must wear his hair short, his face clean shaven until he achieved a high enough rank to grow a beard. It said much of the diminishment of her authority that she would allow Rayhmer to sit before her, beardless with his hair loose.

The men he had brought with him bore a similar air of dishevelment. Degore, a senior Maglorean guard, fidgeted like a dog with fleas, chewing his lip in a grotesque way that made him look like he was blowing kisses. Sanden, that foppish man who had tried to use his charms on her, was there to transcribe the discussion, but the pauses in his scratchings seemed overlong, and she suspected that if she peered over, she would find nothing there but unintelligible cyphers. Their unclean smell was everywhere in the room: the reek of alcohol and unguardsmanly acts. Even the incense could not cover it.

With difficulty she swallowed knowing she could not open the window. Rayhmer's gaze lingered on her, sensing her unease.

Sybilla focused her attention on Degore as he read a seemingly endless list of names from the Maglorean Tally. So many dead. She must take care not to show signs of recognition if Voirrey's friends were among them. She listened impassively and when the list ran to its final line, she allowed herself a moment of relief. The root of the rebellion had not been exposed.

"Thank you, Degore," Rayhmer said, leaning forward. "As you can see, Peran, we are weeding the rebels out, but something is keeping them going. Say what you will of Sidney Karasek, but his disappearance is awfully convenient. We suspect he may have fled to Avishae."

"Avishae?" Peran repeated with incredulity. "Now, this has gone far enough. Our resources are stretched too thin to be chasing phantoms in Avishae. We must hold the centre firm. Do you know how we do that, Rayhmer? We show the people stability. We show them that the time of bloodshed is behind us and that we have created a better society, one worth protecting. These rebels, of which there are precious few, will be viewed as idealists who ask the contented to risk their lives for little reward. Do not go traipsing around, sword drawn–hunting a Skalen, no less–"

Rayhmer cut him off. "With all due respect, the Guard must investigate matters of heresy, no matter who the perpetrator may be. Would you have me simply sit back and wait for disaster? All I suggest is a modest reconnaissance mission to put these rumours to rest."

Peran rolled his eyes, red-faced with frustration. "Then have Edric send some of his men to Avishae–or Kiryn, or Grenla."

Rayhmer smiled at his hands.

Degore appeared to be enjoying the exchange, which meant that Peran's approval was not relevant to their plan. They wanted Avishae, she could see it plainly on the man's unsubtle face. She could not let it happen. Her finger traced the scar on her palm. Rebekah Elshender had asked of her two things: to protect her son's body and to protect knowledge of the stone. Sybilla doubted these men were capable of hearing the stone's call, but to have them in proximity to the cairn was dangerous.

Sybilla intervened. "Guardsman Rayhmer, if it is information you are after, Guardsman Andrin would be a suitable emissary. His recent appointment as Peran's successor creates an ideal opportunity. If there is cause for suspicion in any quarter, he can report back and we can take things from there."

Rayhmer tilted his head back, watching Andrin, who cleared his throat as if on cue. She remembered Andrin's cough, a nervous tic that cropped up whenever he was made to talk to people outside of his moral sphere.

Rayhmer chuckled. "Sybilla, how we have missed having a woman at the table."

It seemed he would not even honour her with a response. Frustration burned beneath her skin.

Degore addressed his superior. "Nothing wrong with a bit of diplomacy, is there?"

The look that passed between them made Sybilla regret her interjection; their hidden plans a twisting snake adapting to new terrain.

"Peran? Andrin? What do you think?" Rayhmer glanced at Sanden. "Of course, you don't get a vote."

Sanden tossed his hair and smirked.

Peran nodded in Andrin's direction so he could answer first.

Andrin glanced at Rayhmer, "Does your intelligence give any detail to Sidney's whereabouts?"

Rayhmer replied, "Baden Forest, most likely. I will brief you on all of that when you pass through Maglore."

Peran clapped his hands on the table. "Well then, it is settled."

When the Council disbanded, Sybilla went out, surprised to see Davina running toward her down the hall with Voirrey in her wake. Voirrey caught her under the arms and to Sybilla's chagrin, Davina squealed, high and piercing so that all the men turned.

Voirrey let her go and Davina ran to Sybilla, coming up short a few steps shy of her mother, finally noticing the people watching her.

Sybilla brought her near.

"Got yourself a wild one, eh?" Rayhmer's said.

Sybilla turned, her palm on Davina's head. Gave a tight smile.

He crouched in front of her, close to her daughter's face. "No need to hide in your mother's skirts, girl. You'll be a big Skalen one day."

Davina pressed herself against Sybilla's legs but by some miracle, she did not hide her face.

Peran interjected. "Good day, Miss Davina. Out for a walk, I see?"

Sybilla took up the thread. "Yes, I did promise to take her to meet the new lambs."

Rayhmer gave Davina a wink that made Sybilla's stomach twist, then stood, belatedly acknowledging Voirrey. "Miss Braedal." His smirking tone was lost on none of them and Sybilla blushed.

Voirrey seemed little concerned with him. "How is it, Guardsman, that so many years have passed without formal introduction?"

Rayhmer inclined his head, a loose section of hair momentarily obscuring his face. He shook it free and smiled. "I hope that such meetings will occur more often. Guardsman Edric is a fine emissary, but you are right, all would benefit from closer relations between North and South."

The conversation dwindled and Sanden produced some matter of urgency that required the attention of his compatriots. Peran and Andrin remained, and all seemed to wait for the other men's footfall to fade.

Andrin looked stiff and uncomfortable and was about to depart when Peran stopped him with a meaningful look. Dutifully, Andrin bowed to the little girl. "Miss Davina," he said, looking as if he had been made to bow to a small dog.

"This is Guardsman Andrin," Peran said, "He is a good man, you remember that."

Andrin took the compliment with a stately grimace and bowed once more.

Sybilla took the opening, "Andrin, this seems a good opportunity to thank you for accepting Peran's bestowal."

"Thank you, Skalen. But it is my hope that I remain in Peran's shadow for many years to come." After a pause, he continued. "My mother suffered a similar ailment and made a full recovery. With Velspar's blessings, he will regain his sword arm before long," he said.

Sybilla felt Davina begin to fidget. "Nonetheless," she said. "We are pleased with Peran's choice." She looked down. "Now, Davina, would you like to go and see the lambs?"

The little girl nodded vigorously, casting Andrin a wary glance.

Taking their leave, Sybilla and Voirrey helped Davina down the stairs, not wanting to draw any further attention if she tripped.

Once outside, Voirrey looked at her and without words Sybilla felt her understanding, her concern, the release of harboured tension, the visceral unease of having Rayhmer approach Davina like that.

They made their way across the field, Davina running on ahead and pouncing on the dandelions in her path.

After Sybilla had told Voirrey the latest from the council room, her friend drew into herself. Voirrey had this way of seeming unassuming and kind, but when faced with matters of politics, her eyes grew sharp with the ticking of inner logics. Whether she accepted her birthright or not, Voirrey had been trained as a Skalen and when such moods took her, Sybilla could almost sense Lenna's shrewdness, Damek's proud isolationism. All Sybilla's lessons came from her sister, redacted and softened for the second born who had seen too far into her father's soul.

Sybilla kept her silence as they rasped through the meadowsweet, not wanting to disturb Voirrey's thoughts.

"Tell me again about Andrin," Voirrey said, her head down.

Sybilla sighed, trying to dissect her dealings with him over the years. He was dismissive. He rarely looked her in the eye. Always, he had had that nervous cough. "He is a man of the Code. That is why Peran chose him, because he is respected by his peers and his compass is set straight. He is not a man that can be swayed by emotional appeals or justifications. I think that is why he does not like conversing with people outside of the Guard. He has never said as much, but I always had the impression that he saw such people as being unclean, or incomprehensible in some way."

Voirrey considered. "All we can do is try to forewarn Maeryn that they are coming."

Sybilla looked at her. "How? I have no contacts here that could be trusted with a coded letter."

Voirrey sucked her teeth in frustration, and Sybilla could tell from her expression that this train of thought had reignited her fears for Amand. Still frowning, she looked at Sybilla. "Do you still sense the connection with Zohar?" she asked.

Sybilla shook her head.

"Don't tell me *no* like that Sybilla; think about it." Voirrey's tone was uncharacteristically sharp. "I'm sorry," Voirrey added, softening. "But I want you to try this before you tell me it is hopeless."

Sybilla's heart was racing, the unnatural sensations of Jokvour returning to her, the slipping of another's spirit beneath her skin. "I will," she said. She could not help but feel that there was more to this. Was it a test of her dedication? A test to prove that Velspar's will still moved in her? Or was it that Voirrey could not face the rebels now her loyalties were divided?

Voirrey snapped off a stalk of grass and twisted it in her fingers. "If Rayhmer brings things to a head in the Southlands, my promises will be put to the test. Being with you, with Davina..." She tossed the mangled grass aside. "How am I to explain it?"

Sybilla remained silent.

"If my allies are to risk their lives, they will expect everything from me. Once I believed it all, Sybilla. I put the fire in their eyes with the strength of my conviction. And now I have nothing to give. I have nothing but fear. Fear that I will lose you–" Voirrey broke off.

In the distance Sybilla could see the ewes all yellowish and grey, flanked by milk-white lambs. Davina called out and pointed but Sybilla's attention remained with Voirrey. Her words struck deeply and Sybilla did not want to do anything to break the spell.

Voirrey went on. "I knew things would be different once we reached Vaelnyr, but all of this is moving so fast and I feel like I am walking blind. Honestly, I don't know what to do."

The thought came over Sybilla like a cold shadow. The only way to arrive at their future was to walk into the stronghold of their enemies and keep their faces straight. It was no gift to share their fears together, Sybilla realised. Only blind fervour could save them now, and where was she to find it? She could not leave Voirrey to do this alone.

Sybilla watched Davina chasing the lambs, the sheep bleating their reproach. She recalled her last visit to Maglore when the Greslet children were young; Skalen Domhnall impersonating animals to make his daughter laugh. The man was a fool and a drunkard but Skalen Inry was a mother, like herself. One who would do anything to protect her children from war. Perhaps Davina could be their point of understanding.

Sybilla proceeded cautiously. "I think we should travel to Maglore. You still have people there, near the border?"

"Yes," Voirrey confirmed.

Sybilla pictured their journey and felt unexpectedly sad to leave Vaelnyr so soon. "We'll go with Andrin, on his tour. He will not allow any harm to come to us."

Voirrey looked at her in guarded assent.

She would do this, she would take all that was precious to her, walk through a sea of knives and come out the other side. It was the only way. Sybilla searched for that old fire that had burned brighter than the pain, that had turned her family's assassination into a holy war. It was long gone, but she remembered how it felt in her chest. Tightness, heat, and rage.

"We must do this, Voirrey. Our hiding places are gone."

25

MAGLORE

Sybilla's eyes were swollen from sleeplessness and still the horses trudged on. Darkness was wet upon the untamed grasses of Marain, the velvet night twinkling on high. Voirrey's head had fallen forward, rocking with the movement of the carriage, her blonde hair covering her face. Davina was tucked in against her.

The hulking shadow of the Maglorean Skalens' House stood against the star speckled sky, an uncertain mystery solidifying as she watched. Inry's lavish gardens appeared as a ragged black crest either side.

She nudged Voirrey awake and the woman blinked blearily, rubbing her face.

"We're here?" she asked.

Sybilla nodded and peered once more from the window. She could see them now, a company of guards milling down from the Main Gate.

Voirrey tilted her head to see Davina's sleeping face, a smile tugging at her lips.

"We should wake her now," Sybilla said, knowing the way her daughter could cry if torn prematurely from sleep.

Gently, she moved her arm out from under her so the girl flopped onto Voirrey's side. Voirrey's fingers moved through Davina's dark hair, and the sleeping eyes opened. A scowl, but no cry. Davina tried to wriggle back into position.

"No darling, we are almost there, it's time to wake up now," Voirrey said.

Sybilla patted Davina's knee. "Skalen Inry has the most beautiful gardens. We will have to go and see them when the sun is up."

Davina crawled onto her lap and looked out the window.

"Where?" Davina said. She rubbed her eyes. "I can't see."

Sybilla pointed. "Over there, but it's too dark now. You'll see in the morning." As she looked, she saw only the grey outline of untidy shrubs, their protrusions unsettling somehow. She could smell the lilies in the wet grass, their sickly scent reawakening her memories of this place.

"Skalen Inry is very kind and has children of her own for you to play with," Sybilla said, feeling a dull pain as she brought Lilwenn and Edlin to mind. Gavril had sat beside her at the table, squeezing her hand, the little girl taunting her younger brother in a game of Guess. They would be older now. The girl had been six, she remembered, so now she must be eleven, and the boy nine. Had that much time passed?

Peering into the dimness, Sybilla saw Andrin up ahead. A contingent of guards came to meet him. The carriage lagged behind and Sybilla could not make out their conversation.

The carriage stopped and Sybilla exchanged a look with Voirrey.

After ten long minutes had passed, a group of guards came down to offer escort.

One popped his head in the window: "Evening, Skalen. Guardsman Andrin has gone up to the barracks. Given the hour, you might like to go straight in and break bread with Skalen Domhnall. He's up and waiting for you in the Main Hall." He waited a moment and when Sybilla did not respond, he gave a quick smile. "Night then."

Sybilla found the guardsman's manner a little familiar but she reminded herself that the Maglorean Guard had suffered a generation of poor leadership and she should expect the bare minimum in this place.

More guards came from the shadows, milling about the dark hillside. With a sharp whistle, the iron gates drew apart, allowing them entry. As the carriage came to a halt, Sybilla waited, she and Voirrey listening intently to the dispersing guards. Were they leaving?

Sybilla opened the curtain and the same guard that had spoken to her earlier flashed an officious smile. "He's inside," he said, as if she were a bit dim, pointed to the open door and went off.

Sybilla and Voirrey stepped out of the carriage, and into the deserted courtyard. "Come on, Davina," Sybilla whispered trying to sound unperturbed.

There were no Attendants in sight. What was happening here?

Eager to find Domhnall, Sybilla led them in, making for the Main Hall.

Reaching the threshold, her heart sank as she entered the dark and seemingly empty room. Two wall lamps guttered in the gloom. She was about to walk out the way they had come. They would simply go to the Guard's Barracks and demand to see Andrin.

At the far end of the room, she heard a sniffle, a wheezing cough. With a jolt she saw him. He must have been there the whole time. Grasping Davina's hand, she approached the Skalen's Chair.

Domhnall's cheeks were sallow above the thick mass of his beard. His hair had grown past his shoulders and she could not discern the boundary between his dark clothes and the shadows of the room. Sybilla caught the gleam of his eyes as he watched her. But did he see? From his left hand dangled a tarnished goblet that pattered liquid on the floor. Beyond the damp scent of stone, she caught the smell of bile-riddled wine.

"Skalen Domhnall?" Sybilla called.

His head jerked a little and to her horror, the man loudly passed wind, grunted and slumped back in his chair.

"It is Skalen Sybilla of Vaelnyr, and Voirrey Braedal of Nothelm. We accompany Guardsman Andrin on his tour of the Seven Lands."

Domhnall made a scoffing sound. "Tour, eh?" he mumbled. "Come to see the Maglorean puppet show? Few more actors for our troupe, eh?" Davina wisely hid herself behind her mother.

Sybilla blinked, still in shock at what Domhnall had become.

"Thank you, Domhnall," Sybilla said, haltingly. "We will take our leave now. Where are Skalen Inry and the children?" Sybilla asked.

He turned his face so she could barely make out his form. A choking sound, a gasp. Sybilla turned to Voirrey, was the man going to vomit?

Voirrey frowned and shook her head slightly.

"Inry..." he croaked, her name barely audible.

He was crying.

Voirrey grasped Sybilla's arm and the three of them padded quietly from the room.

Sybilla considered the men outside, who best to speak to, unable to shake the sense that they had walked into a trap. Peering down the shadowed hallway, Sybilla began to walk.

Voirrey tried to stop her, wanting to talk, but Sybilla was running on instinct now. "I think I remember the way," she whispered, grasping her daughter's hand and leading her onward.

Voirrey tsk'd her frustration but followed.

They padded down the hallway. Sybilla's mind raced, trying to make sense of things. If Rayhmer meant to kill them, he could have done so on the road–blamed it on bandits. Why did he bring them here and expose so much? Something was wrong here. Very wrong.

This was not a Skalens' House any longer.

Sybilla heard a disturbing sound coming from the end of the passage. She froze. Was that Inry's chamber? What was happening here?

She wanted to tell Davina to cover her ears but they were too close. The child's body was already rigid with fright.

Sybilla pointed to indicate that they should pass the room and turn left where the hallway ended. The beastly sounds grew louder as they passed, filling Sybilla with such panic that she wondered if they should try to flee. Where was Andrin?

Sweat ran cold down her neck, her legs tingling as they passed the corner. She had not been in this area of the Skalens' House before. If they were to double back, she should do it now.

Sybilla stared down the passage, and with a shock registered a face...a girl in a white nightdress crouched there in the dark.

Voirrey drew up beside her, also noticing the girl. At first it looked like she would run, but then she saw Davina.

Confusion. Fear.

"Lilwenn?" Sybilla whispered.

The girl clapped her hands over her mouth and motioned toward the doorway.

The three of them followed the girl into a dimly lit chamber, so dishevelled and mouldering that it made Sybilla's skin crawl. The dark-haired waif shoved them toward the back of the room. "Behind the canopy," she said, then hurried to the door, roping the handle to the dresser leg with practiced movements. Sybilla and Voirrey moved quickly with Davina into the cramped space.

With spidery limbs, Lilwenn negotiated the sheets piled on the floor and climbed up on the bed. She drew the door-facing canopy, and opened the other side, where her visitors hid.

She stared, studying them, as if they were a clutch of jewels she had snatched, and in the safety of her hovel, she opened her hands to examine them.

"Mother said you would come," she said in her thin voice. Her expression was destitute and strange.

Voirrey crouched before Lilwenn, who had shuffled forward to the edge of the bed. "Things are bad here, aren't they?"

Lilwenn gave the barest nod.

"Where is your brother?" Voirrey pressed.

The girl's eyes grew unfocused, then with stiffening jaw, she met Voirrey's stare. She pointed to the wall, indicating the adjoining room. "You can't get in. They let mother and I out of our rooms but they are punishing him now."

"What have they done to him?" Voirrey asked.

Lilwenn's face crumpled. "I told him not to, but he tried to attack one of the guards. They just lock him in there and won't let him out. When no one is watching, I slip crusts under his door."

Voirrey took a shuddering breath. "Is that what you were doing just now?"

Lilwenn nodded. "It will not be safe here for long. I don't know what they want with you."

Sybilla itched in the pause that followed. Voirrey's eyes searched the ceiling and Sybilla prayed that she was coming up with a plan.

Eventually, Voirrey broke the silence. "I am a healer, Lilwenn, and I might be able to help you. If you'll let me, that is."

Lilwenn remained wary.

"If we remove our Meridians, I can take some of this pain from you. Just enough so you can think clearly. We need to think clearly so we can make the right choices."

Lilwenn's eyes darted to the door.

Voirrey waited but did not get a reply. "Please, let me help you."

Sybilla scooped Davina up and took her to the other side of the room. Voirrey and Lilwenn spoke in murmurs for a time and then from the corner of her eye Sybilla saw the girl remove her Meridian. Voirrey gently clasped her forearms, keeping her eyes on the floor. Moments later, the girl's head craned, her teeth set in a horrible grimace.

Davina pressed her face into her mother's chest and Sybilla tried not to let the fear take her. The room had no window, but she guessed they had a few hours till dawn broke, then they would not even have the darkness to hide them.

Voirrey released her hands and sat back on her heels.

Lilwenn seemed frozen, her face tilted upward, her eyes shut tight.

Sybilla looked at Voirrey expectantly, but it seemed she was not finished. Leaning forward, she whispered in Lilwenn's ear: "Tell me his name."

Lilwenn's choked whisper brought nausea to her limbs. "Degore," she managed with a gasp as if Voirrey had cleared her throat of a chicken bone.

The girl leaned forward, her face buried in her hands. "He is with mother now," she said without looking up. "He will not come here tonight."

Sybilla was desperate to escape. "Lilwenn, you know this place: how can we evade the Guard? If we can just get out of here, we have forces at our command that can save your family. Help us. Please."

Lilwenn watched Davina with deadly resolve. "You must pretend you never found me. Hide yourselves till morning. At table, suggest going on an outing somewhere in Maglore. They are different during the day, almost normal. In the beginning they let us out of the gates but Mother and I were too scared to run. If we had run, we might have escaped. Every night I think about that, imagining the ways I would do it. Feel myself running and disappearing from sight..."

Sybilla glanced at the low-burning tapers about the room, fearing they were losing precious time. "Where can we hide till morning?"

"Go to the end of the eastern hall and into the orchard. They won't look there because there is no way out," Lilwenn said.

"Will you come with us?" Sybilla asked feeling ashamed at the thought of leaving her.

Voirrey shook her head. "Lilwenn is right, she cannot be seen with us. She will be safe here till morning."

Sybilla knew that Voirrey spoke reassuringly so they would not lose themselves to fear. No one was safe here and they were abandoning this girl in the slim hope of saving their own lives.

Lilwenn came forward and unwound the rope from the door, seeming far older now than she first appeared.

Voirrey whispered something in Lilwenn's ear then urged Sybilla on, her hand pushing the small of her back. With the drums of terror filling her mind, she did not even turn to look at Lilwenn as they left. Silence burned in her ears as they passed Edlin's door. Sybilla felt a wave of unaccountable sorrow and almost turned back, feeling a presence like a familiar hand, but Voirrey urged her on.

The lead window was ajar as Lilwenn had said it would be.

"Go through darling. We are coming, too." Sybilla guided Davina through.

Voirrey's lithe form went after and Sybilla unhooked her cloak where it had snagged on the hinge. Crouching down on the stone floor, Sybilla fed her arms and head through, trying to keep herself calm as her larger hips pressed tight through the space. Voirrey came and supported her forearms on the other side. Voirrey had to pull her so she could get past her knees and Sybilla fell heavily on her, then scrambled to one side, breathless and faint with stress.

Voirrey stood and pulled Sybilla to her feet. "We must get among the trees."

Before them extended an overgrown orchard, the central garden of the Skalens' House that had once been Inry's pride and glory. Holding Davina's hand, Voirrey and Sybilla darted into the trees.

Rotten mandarins squelched black under her feet, the low branches forcing her into a crouch. There were peach trees too, and plums. When they had gone deep enough to feel themselves hidden, Sybilla swept a clear patch of ground and the three of them sat. Davina hid herself in Sybilla's lap, anxiously twisting her mother's hair around her fingers, and it was a miracle that she could keep herself quiet so long in a situation she could not possibly understand.

The two women sat opposite each other, eyes locked. *What will we do? How can we protect Davina? Is Andrin already dead?*

The sharing of these questions required no words. Voirrey tapped her Meridian and glanced at Davina, whose stones remained safely in place. The two women removed their Meridians and brought their foreheads to touch. Rarely did they commune in this way, but within seconds, the horrors of Lilwenn's youth were inside Sybilla's mind. She tried to breathe steadily, to bear the experiences that seared her nerves.

Sybilla thought absurdly of burying Davina in the orchard to protect her from a similar fate, a thought that she shook off, finding it made of Lilwenn's memories, of hiding here before the fruit had fallen, back when Edlin ran at her heels and they stowed their treasures for safe keeping. Later, when the warmth had gone, they hid other things. A hole for her father's wine bottle, the dark liquid sloshing as they ran. A hole for her mother's comb that she dug so fiercely into her scalp that her hair matted with blood. A hole for Davina, ran Lilwenn's wish. *Beautiful girl, hide her among the trees where he'll never find her.* Death is better than this.

Sybilla's will railed against the flooding memories, poisonous and sick, thoughts that once inside her mind would never leave her. Disgusted by her own skin, by the bruises and the scent of him that would not wash off with the meagre water they provided.

"Sybilla…" Voirrey whispered sharply, squeezing her hands. "Hold yourself to the side, let it pass."

Sybilla made a noise but could not find Voirrey in the tumult.

Sharp nails dug into the flesh of her arm and Sybilla opened her eyes. Voirrey. She tried to hold her image, the branches above her like guardsmen's shadows.

Voirrey's lips moved, and slowly the words resolved themselves "…we need to know this. Ignorance is dangerous now. Observe, but do not feel. These are but incidents. See them listed in the Tally. See the occurrences, the inferences, the risks, but this is not for you to feel. To feel is more dangerous than ignorance. Do you understand me?"

Sybilla blinked, heard the wind rustling softly among the leaves. "Yes."

Her hand shook as she reappointed her Meridian.

Sybilla began to think out loud. "If we flee, they know we will go to our allies and the moment we accuse Maglore, Rayhmer will have reason to act. They are tempting us to this outcome by flaunting their crimes. They might let us go, as a matter of strategy."

Sybilla felt suspended above a precipice. The moment went on and no answer came.

Finally, Voirrey spoke: "They might, but there is no way of knowing their strategy… All I know is that they have enslaved the Greslets by ransoming them to one another. Any one of them might escape if they tried, but they know it will mean the others' death." She gave Sybilla a pointed look. "We need to make a decision, here and now, if they try the same with us."

Sybilla stared at her, unable to answer.

Davina seemed to have fallen asleep on her chest, though her left eye remained partially open. Sybilla's throat surged with tears and she shook her head. *Not Davina.* Sybilla kept shaking her head, tears falling on the child's supine form.

Voirrey reached out and touched her arm. "Davina's life over ours. I understand."

The words came like a slap but Sybilla could not deny them. She stilled, mesmerised by Voirrey's apparent calm. Within, her spirit warred between a desire to grow utterly numb, and a burning rage that demanded she expose the evils here. But neither of these options were open to her.

If she lifted the mask, she would confront Rayhmer and Degore in their animal form, faces flayed and reeking, the self-same demons she had run from all of her life.

For Davina, she would face them, fully conscious, alert to the arousal of their redness, quenching it in the Intercessor's way: with coolness and deflection.

26

MAGLORE

SYBILLA AWOKE with Davina in her arms, her clothes damp with dew. She had fallen asleep against the slim trunk of a peach tree, its gnarled bark pricking her back, though they had not slept for long. She leaned forward a little and tried to release the tension in her neck. Voirrey's hair spilled pale next to her, the woman so small when curled on her side.

The orchard had kept them safe for the night, but what now? Her stomach roiled. The appalling facts of the evening seemed far worse now. She felt her daughter's skin, all clammy with dew, the leaves above her speckled with black mould. Beside her, Voirrey lay, sinking into the wet earth, like a peach fallen from the bough.

What was the time? Early morning, a little after dawn. She tried to remember the orchard when she had come here with Gavril. The waxen green leaves, the purplish tips of the lemon buds, the bees all dancing. That was Inry. That was what she had brought to Maglore with her youth and her ridiculous oiled curls. Something vivacious and alive. The place felt cursed now.

Rayhmer's face loomed in Sybilla's mind, making her legs weak. She breathed the cool air that rustled the leaves, testing it, trying to separate her fears from what was real. A bird started up its call, brash and chortling.

Sybilla reached for Voirrey. Mauve half-moons circled her eyes, but she sat up promptly, shaking out her hair.

"We should not have slept," Sybilla said.

Voirrey stared in the direction they had come the previous night, mind ticking.

"What are we going to do?" Sybilla prompted.

Voirrey turned to her. "As mad as it seems, I think that we should follow Lilwenn's advice…"

Sybilla waited for her to go on.

Voirrey rubbed her face trying to wake herself up. "When I entered Lilwenn's spirit, I understood the pattern here. There might be a time to run, but the path out of here will be a dance of instinct. We cannot confront Rayhmer, no matter what he or his men have done."

Sybilla understood what she was saying, having felt the truth of it the previous night. "Edlin suffered the worst because he showed them a mirror…"

Voirrey continued the thought: "…and Domhnall is the freest of all because he offers no resistance."

Though Sybilla could follow the logic, there remained no means of escape, no way of protecting themselves from the horrors that Inry and Lilwenn suffered.

"We buy ourselves time," Voirrey muttered, almost to herself.

Sybilla thought of Peran, elderly and frail. Of Guardsman Edric in far distant Nothelm, and of their allies in the South. Rayhmer could send letters in her hand, could have her agree to anything with Davina in his grasp.

Sybilla shook her head. "No one will come for us."

The women shared a look of despair.

Voirrey's mouth formed a grim line. "We convince them to let us outside the gates and when the moment comes, we run."

"Convince them, how?" Sybilla countered.

Voirrey chewed her thumbnail. "We appear weak, and the Guard believe they have the run of Maglore. This is how the people of Maglore survive the day. They suffer in silence and the Guard believe that they have the population under their thumb. We must do the same."

While they talked the sun grew brighter, the moment for action drawing near.

Sybilla shook her head, thinking the plan dangerously absurd. "So we just turn up at breakfast, and say...what?"

Voirrey stretched her legs. "We say that we met with Domhnall and then Davina ran off. We could hear her in the garden and came out to fetch her."

At this, Davina finally admitted that she was awake by stretching out her arm, though Sybilla had felt her wakefulness for some time. The child listening to the booming of her mother's heart.

Sybilla kissed her daughter's hair. "Morning, my darling," she said gently as fear sparked cold in her stomach. She checked with Voirrey once more: *we are doing this, then?*

Voirrey nodded.

Turning her daughter to face her, Sybilla went on: "We are going to go inside in a minute."

Davina reached into Sybilla's cloak to find the Skalen's Star that hung about her neck, fiddling with it and twisting the chain.

Voirrey came closer and rubbed the girl's back reassuringly. As she did so, Sybilla noticed the ruddiness of her hand. She was leeching away her daughter's fears. A lump rose in her throat, of gratitude and longing. If only Voirrey could do the same for her, but she could not ask it. Sybilla did not believe it possible that Intercession could leave the healer untouched by the poison they removed.

Gently, Sybilla nudged her daughter from her lap and stood. Voirrey came and brushed her down and the two women fixed each other's hair.

There was no point discussing things any further. They must face their fate with dignity and pray that Peran would send forces to save them before it was too late.

"I remember a door, over there." Sybilla pointed through the dappled shade, the light having shifted from grey to pale gold.

Voirrey looked dubious.

Sybilla walked a few paces in that direction.

Taking Davina's hand, Voirrey followed Sybilla, crouching to pass beneath low branches. Sure enough, the door appeared where Sybilla expected, gleaming in the sun. They might already be at table.

Feeling herself observed, Sybilla knocked loudly on the door, the lie ready on her lips.

First silence, then footsteps started from the far end of the hallway. Closer they came like a battle drum.

"Hello again, Davina." Rayhmer smiled, his dead eyes fixed upon the girl. He tore off a hunk of bread and chewed, staring at the women that surrounded him with their small defiant chins, their averted eyes. Inry hid the marks on her skin in her high-necked blouse. Lilwenn, her hair a little greasy for his taste, looked skittish as usual. He observed Sybilla, back from her convalescence. And the keen one, Voirrey. The two of them bound at the hip like a mated pair. Then, there was the girl... Davina. Such danger in that small face. Such quiet danger.

Her round eyes returned his stare.

"You caused us a lot of worry last night, but no matter. I can see you have an adventurous spirit. Not to be put to bed like other little girls," Rayhmer said.

Inry, who sat beside him, coughed, a short and ragged sound that she sought to contain in her mouse-like fist. Her dark ringlets jangled in his periphery.

Voirrey piped in, "Rayhmer, tell us, when will Andrin be presented to the Skalens?"

Rayhmer slowed his chewing, tapped his butter knife on the table. "Skalen Domhnall is feeling poorly and has asked not to be disturbed. It may be a couple of days."

Voirrey sipped her tea, glanced at the Attendant entering the room and the guardsman by the door. "In that case, it might be a nice opportunity for our party to complete a tour of Maglore. I am sure Davina would like the chance to see the countryside and to spend a little time with the Greslet children."

Rayhmer chewed his bread, considering which of the planned scenarios he would put into play. All had beneficial outcomes for Maglore.

He decided to begin with a light touch, to test their mettle. "Sadly, young Edlin has the same complaint as his father," he said. "We fear it may be contagious. Best he rest up for now."

Sybilla shifted in her chair, reached for the honey. "Inry," she said, her gaze trained upon the drizzling golden stream. "It would be a treat for Davina to see the swans on the lake. She has never seen a swan in real life."

Inry's face cracked into a smile, her voice thin and breathless. "Oh, that would be so nice. Like your last visit." Her face collapsed momentarily as if she had been struck, then recovered just as quickly.

Rayhmer leaned back in his chair, his arms hanging wide as he regarded them. "A nice day for it," he said, turning to Inry. "Lilwenn might bring Edlin a swan feather, for his collection?"

Sybilla felt the heat in Rayhmer's tone, the threat against the boy's life. Again, she felt the pull of the boy's absence, as if he prayed to her from the confines of his room. *Make them forget me, make Mother and Lilwenn go.*

Inry smiled, her watery eyes betraying her sleeplessness and fear. "Yes, he would love that."

She fell quiet and concentrated on her food. She held the tepid porridge in her mouth and it was only with difficulty that she swallowed it down. The longer Sybilla focused on the woman, the more she felt the dreadful clang that resounded in her—shock waves from events she could not see.

Rayhmer stood and patted himself down. "It has been a pleasure to take breakfast with you, but now I must see to my duties. You enjoy a day in the countryside. I'll prepare an escort out front."

Sybilla fought the urge to ask after Andrin a second time, but could not afford the risk.

"Thank you, Rayhmer," came Voirrey's reply, which began the muttered chorus.

Rayhmer went out the door and the guard left with him. Two

Attendants remained, and with bowed heads they collected Rayhmer's plate, reaching furtive hands to tuck away other bits and pieces.

At their exit, Lilwenn kicked her mother's leg under the table. Startled, she looked up.

"Yes, I am finished. Let's go," Inry said automatically. "Sybilla, Voirrey, are you ready?"

Voirrey reached for some more bread, two slices disappearing into the pocket of her skirt along with the knife. "Yes, let us go."

Inry, startled at her action, scanned the table and began stuffing dried fruit into her own pockets. Sybilla, too, took a knife.

The two women started for the door, Lilwenn, Sybilla and Davina following their lead.

Sybilla ruffled her daughter's hair in feigned lightheartedness, leaned down and whispered. "Not long, darling, and we will be out in the open air."

27

MAGLORE

THE LAKE was empty. On the far side, trees leaned in with shadows of deep blue, the scum-coloured water rippling sky-white.

"Do the swans still come?" Sybilla asked Inry, her hair blown back by the wind. If they could not find the swans, this would be a short trip indeed.

The carriage they arrived in disappeared down the road, but Rayhmer had left a healthy entourage behind. The guards fanned out, forming a perimeter, while the women did their best to ignore them. The plan was not going well.

Lilwenn was down in the reeds with Davina while Voirrey looked for hatchlings.

Inry's eyes, greener than Sybilla remembered, surveyed the water. "I don't know, Sybilla."

Inry strolled–aimlessly, it seemed–and Sybilla followed.

They were moving out of earshot now, but Sybilla noted the closest guard, his arms folded across his belly, sword at his hip. Inry fixed her eyes on the picturesque landscape, as if committing it to memory. "I look around me–at this place, my home–and I feel I am a stranger here." A note of hysteria entered her voice. "I look at the trees, Sybilla, and it is as if they are not really there. It is like I am still inside. My garden–" A stifled sob escaped the woman's throat, her expression transforming into a grimace that might distantly pass for a smile. She shielded her eyes from the sun as the tears ran, leaving dark spots on her blouse.

Sybilla felt it, a dread so consuming it blackened the windows of the soul, so that nothing felt real. "Inry, you can't worry about that right now. This could be our last chance to escape."

She shook her head. "You ask me to sacrifice my son. Do you know that? They will murder him if I leave."

Sybilla sensed the guards' positions, their relaxed postures. Heard the swallows singing in the trees.

"And what if you stay? No one will come to save you."

Inry's eyes grew dark with memory, recognising Sybilla as she had been the day they first met, burnt and bleeding and full of rage. She had survived and had exacted brutal vengeance against her enemies. All of them, now dead.

Sybilla could see the spark of courage in her slowly come to life.

"We need you, Inry. We need each other."

Over in the rushes, Voirrey rose to her feet. Inry watched Lilwenn grasp Voirrey's arm, her face suddenly slack with horror.

The words leaked from the edges of her Meridian like fire's heat, *no, no, no.*

Inry whispered, "It's too late." Her eyes were set on her daughter. "Lilwenn's been drugged. She cannot run. They do this, they always do this."

The look that Inry gave, flat and knowing, chilled her to the marrow.

"I will not leave her."

28

MAGLORE

DAVINA'S DUSTY travelling dress caught on a submerged branch at the lake's edge. She turned, but Lilwenn had already come to unhook her. The older girl smiled warmly. "Can you hear that?"

Davina listened past the crickets' accordion song to hear their high keening. She looked up for confirmation.

"Watch your step, Vina, they are small and you don't want to tread on the nest," Voirrey said absently, watching Sybilla and Inry move up along the bank.

Their situation was hopeless, utterly hopeless. They waited for their moment, like a shard of sunlight from a cloud-banked sky: to run, and run, and have blood spill hot from their throats. Death hovered about them in the balmy air, the sweet spring breeze so gentle as to be cruel.

"Lilwenn, don't get your shoes too deep in the mud. We must be ready," Voirrey said, turning to check Sybilla's expression.

The plan was to buy as much time as possible while Sybilla and Inry plotted their escape. Inry alone knew the lay of the land, the places where they might find shelter. Lilwenn had seemed strong in her survival instincts the night before, but now... her hands flopped heavy as she walked and Voirrey was finding it impossible to gain her attention. All of them knew that this little escapade was permitted only because Rayhmer was certain of his power. He already had the Greslets on a chain and he seemed quite confident that Sybilla would take the yoke through fear alone.

They must show their fear through perfect obedience and not give his men any reason to use force. That is, until the decisive moment.

Voirrey thought once more of the direction she should run. That way.

She turned with irritation to Lilwenn who did not seem alert to the task.

Lilwenn clasped her hands to her cheeks. "Davina! I can hear the baby birds. Listen–"

"Lilwenn!" Voirrey hissed. The young woman made a vague swatting gesture. She expanded her arms and swayed, the sun on her drowsing lids. "Lilwenn, if we are separated, find your way to the river. If we hide inland, they will run us down. Lilwenn?"

Slowly, the young woman opened her eyes, one rising slower than the other. "I dreamed I carved a tunnel with mother's comb all the way to the water, to a great river," Lilwenn murmured, staring now into the mud at her feet. "This water is stuck."

Davina's dark head popped up a few paces away. "Aunty Voy, I see something, come and look!"

Voirrey noticed Lilwenn begin to waver and reached for her arm, her healers' instinct taking charge. With cool fingers, she felt at the girl's wrist, counted, noticed the clamminess of her skin and thick, slow breaths. Something was wrong. Poison?

"I want to see them, the little birds," Lilwenn said.

Danger swarmed Voirrey's senses. "Okay, Lilwenn, I will take you there, hold my arm." Voirrey's assessment ran from poison to sleeping draught, observing the telltale bloodshot eyes, the thick breath and rapid pulse, the dreamy movements that gave way to smiles. An Alma concoction laced with lincado root powder. Voirrey judged that she would feel the effects by now if it had been mixed into her own breakfast. Sybilla and Inry still walked upon the bank, with only Sybilla's face visible to her. They showed no signs of faintness that she could detect, but Davina?

"Vina?" she called.

The head popped up again. "Here." Davina looked tired but not at all drowsy.

Carefully, she guided Lilwenn forward. *Sweet Velspar, what are we going to do?* she thought. Everything was falling apart. The girl was like an anchor, dragging them to the deep.

Davina pulled the reeds to one side, showing the nest where two chicks screeched their soft song, all beak and fluffy grey down.

Lilwenn hugged herself. "So small," she whispered.

Davina laughed with delight, but when she caught Voirrey's expression, she looked unsure.

Voirrey pulled Lilwenn down among the reeds, loosened the girl's Meridian, unclasped her own, and pressed their foreheads close. Lilwenn jerked back but soon relented. Through the aperture of her mind, Voirrey impressed her message. *We run. We run, or we die. Run any way that you can and do not stop no matter who falls. Run and get to the river.*

Voirrey set the girl's Meridian back in place with trembling hands. Doused in the muzzy glow of Lilwenn's otherworldly euphoria, she too felt the temptation of oblivion.

When she looked up, Lilwenn's expression blazed, sharp and bitter. Her eyes roved about her, checking their surroundings, looking for guards. The motion unsteadied her, and she fell to one knee.

"Bastards," she spat, eyes locked with Voirrey's. "Bastards, bastards."

"Shh, Lilwenn," Voirrey soothed.

All three of them jumped at a loud cracking sound in the reeds. Crunch, crunch, crunch, and the swan emerged, great black wings arched in a territorial display.

"Okay, move back from the nest."

Voirrey saw Sybilla and Inry watching them, their expressions too distant to read. The road behind them let up a cloud of dust and Voirrey squinted to see what was happening.

Voirrey gestured with her hand for the women to come down to the lake and after some hesitation, they came.

Sybilla made her way down with Inry behind. For the Guard's benefit, Inry called to Lilwenn, "What have you found?"

Lilwenn met her mother's eyes as if it would be the last time they'd ever find themselves here. With a tremble in her voice, she replied: "The swans are still here. Four chicks and a mother."

Inry's eyes twinkled, a sorrowing gift in her smile. "I'm so glad."

Voirrey could see the pattern enacting itself once more. Despite Lilwenn's earlier outburst and Inry's apparent agreement with their plan, the Greslets could not make themselves take the final step. *Run, we have to run!*

The crunch of the carriage wheel could be heard now with the beating of hooves, the whole scene about to be stripped away like the painted backdrop that it was. Voirrey's palms had begun to sweat though she would not loosen her grip on Davina's hand.

Sybilla now stood beside them, her breath tight in her chest. The slightest shake of her head told Voirrey that Inry and Lilwenn would not join them, though this came as no surprise. Voirrey returned the signal and they prepared themselves.

The perimeter guard loaded into one of the arriving carriages, their replacements coming down to wrap things up. Four men, this time. The women pretended not to see them coming. Continuing the pantomime.

Sybilla's blood sharpened in her thighs as the guardsmen formed a line, giving their gesture for the women's return.

She read them from left to right like a sentence in a book: stranger, the guard who drew the gate, Degore–then her gaze snagged–Andrin. The words were out of her mouth before she could think. "Andrin! You must come and see this."

The entourage with their folded arms smirked at him. Andrin did not register humour, here or at any time Sybilla had known him. He started off toward them, clearing his throat, and for the first time, Sybilla found the tic endearing, his presence a gush of feeling bound up with Peran's recent kindness and the promise of his protection.

She came up on the bank, actually grasped his hand to lead him to the nest. In none of his manner did he betray that this was not her usual way with him. He followed, his distracted expression appearing strained. Their backs to the guards, she spoke quickly and low. "We are prisoners here?"

"Yes," he confirmed.

"You must kill Degore," she said, and at that moment the mother swan came clacking toward them. The father followed, returned from his foraging, and they found themselves surrounded.

Andrin ducked to avoid the darting beak of the first swan, a spectacle that the guards on the bank found endlessly amusing.

He brandished a stick, putting Davina behind him, adopting a defensive posture that exceeded the requirements of the situation. Voirrey pulled Lilwenn close and led her as Andrin's long arms swept Sybilla and Inry out of harm's way. Inry teetered, her shoes mudstuck. Sybilla helped her, and it seemed that time skipped forward, the way to the carriage, that last taste of freedom. Over, before it could be savoured.

Inside the carriage, Voirrey sat between Davina and Lilwenn, with Sybilla and Inry opposite.

To Sybilla's horror, Degore squeezed in next to Inry, and through the window, the two remaining Maglorean guards shouldered Andrin along. As he climbed up with them to the driver's bench, he caught her eye, the gateman smacking Andrin's behind.

The horses started up, rising to a steady clip. Sybilla struggled to keep the wild look from her eye as she waited for something to happen. Moments dripped lazily into the pond of time and despite Andrin's presence above her, Sybilla sensed something foetid awaited them. She could almost taste it—dank and bloody.

"Nice day, ladies?" Degore said to no one in particular.

Sybilla noticed his chubby hand resting on Inry's thigh. Lilwenn glared at him, her eyes fierce though her arms drooped at her sides. Voirrey held one of Lilwenn's hands and was doing what she could to calm her but it would not last long.

"Got to be careful of those swans. Got a nasty bite."

Inry stared straight ahead, her glassy eyes wide and unblinking. Even Voirrey ignored him. Sybilla's mouth was so dry she did not trust herself to speak.

Degore whistled a tune, looking dull-witted and smug. Eventually he stopped, chewing his lip in that same grotesque way he had in the Council Room in Vaelnyr.

Feeling as if she might vomit from the tension in the air, Sybilla focused on the trees, the long sweeping movements of the high wind, the sky beyond, cloudless and blank as if it refused to bear witness. They were half way to the Skalens' House now. How was that possible?

Suddenly, the carriage lurched and Sybilla gripped her seat. There were shouts, scuffling. The horses went faster.

"Hey!" Degore cried, attempting to stand but the carriage swerved and everyone went sliding. Degore's shoulder thunked into the side door as the horses raced on, and the women scrambled away from him. Voirrey threw her body over Davina and Lilwenn, bracing them as she gripped the handrail.

Sybilla was pinned behind Inry, and Degore had just made it to his feet when a swordblade punctured the roof above their heads. Everyone screamed as it jabbed down.

"Fucking maggot!" Degore, bug-eyed and sun-blind, tried to locate his attacker. The blade came down fast, halving his ear, biting into the bone of his skull, once, twice, then the man tumbled, gouts of blood drenching his neck. He roared, sucking ragged breaths.

Inry's feet shot up to get away from him and then she started kicking. She got him in the face several times but could not put him down. He just kept coming, moving like a drunkard, his hair matted with blood. Sybilla squeezed from behind Inry and as Degore attempted to gain his balance she drove her boot down on his hand. Inry reached over him and yanked at the hilt of his sword but could not get it free.

Above, Andrin was fighting both of the remaining guards.

She could hear them cursing. "He's cut the bloody reins!" and seconds later a sword came arcing down through the torn roof. It clattered on the seat and as Sybilla looked up she saw the guardsman snap Andrin's neck. He fell, tumbling from the carriage, back there in the grass.

Inry snatched up the sword and thrust it into Degore's back. It did not go in all the way but his body quaked in agony and Sybilla reached forward to add her weight. Both women rammed the sword down until something cracked, and as the resistance went out of him, so spread a terrible stench.

The fierce expression on Inry's face wavered and her mouth fell open in a silent scream. Both of them let go of the sword as if it were on fire.

"We have to get out of here," Sybilla said and turned to Voirrey who prayed forcefully into Davina's hair.

Inry wiped her shaking hands on her dress. "Give me Lilwenn," she barked, and Voirrey released her.

The girl stared at the corpse as if in a dream. Her mother grabbed her hand and yanked the door free. "We're going to do it. Just like we always planned. We go together. Now!"

A moment later, they were gone.

Outside, the grasslands rushed by, but not so fast as before. Once the two remaining guards got control of the horses they would be done for.

"Quick!" Sybilla called, clambering over Degore's body.

Voirrey followed with Davina whose eyes were wide with terror. Sybilla grasped her daughter's hand. "We are going to jump now." She had a good grip on her and could not wait for her to respond. Voirrey had her other hand. "One, two, three, jump!" They were airborne but a second before falling hard in the grass. From atop the carriage one of the guards saw them. "Hey!" he called, and his torso disappeared from view.

"Run!"

They went blindly toward the trees.

"Get on my back!" Voirrey crouched and Davina got on, arms and legs wrapped tight around her.

Farther down the field, Sybilla's heart lurched to see Inry had done the same, Lilwenn's body flopped over her, the woman struggling desperately to gain speed in the long grass.

They laboured on, staggering and panting, and Sybilla knew that somewhere up ahead they would find Andrin's body.

Sybilla darted her head around. The carriage was still moving away from them.

She ran harder. "Get in the trees," she gasped. Voirrey ran, moving faster as the grass grew thin at the wood's edge.

Realising she could no longer hear the rattle of the carriage, Sybilla turned again. Two little specs in the distance, two men, trudged toward them. They did not move quickly, owing to their injuries, but that did not mean they could not catch them.

She pushed her muscles to move, amazed to find Voirrey gaining ground even with Davina's weight on her back. Inry had almost reached the trees.

A high whistle sounded and Sybilla turned again. A third man was coming from a barn house in the other direction and with him dark shapes. She heard them now. Dogs.

The sound of the dogs was far too close, the savage barking, their quick sound behind her, and then she was down. Burning teeth sank deep into her calf, the snarling head worrying at her flesh. She screamed as, far ahead of her, Voirrey pushed Davina up into the branches, her skirt whisking into the leaves. She balled herself, hiding her face but could not free her leg that sang with a lacerating agony worse than anything she had experienced in her life.

The high peel of the whistle and the dog raised his bloody maw. A rhythm, two whistles, pause, then one more.

The dog fled back down the field and now there was nothing she could feel but pain. Dragging herself on her elbows, she tried to stand on the other leg but it had turned to jelly. She willed herself to look down, saw the blood, everywhere, blood. A note sounded but she could no longer tell if it was the whistle or the herald of unconsciousness. Whiteness, and a buzzing in her ears; the high note rang on.

THE LONG SHADOW

29

———

AVISHAE

EDITH LIT THE Alma with her back to them, the pine-scented air giving way to her smoky caress. She began her signal, her left hand drawing the Alma thatch left and right in a sweeping rhythm–down and down and down, and then the upsweep. The smoke arose from her body in a column, slowly rising, climbing the breeze. Seven cycles, and her heart was pattering. She watched the blue patch of sky, the white clouds like friendly spirits peering down and passing on.

With her right hand, she took up the drum, flicked it back and forth to the thump of strung stones. The call began somewhere deep in her belly, rising to a wailing cry. All was His name. *Kshidol, the Father, come to me. I call thee down. Holy Father, Kshidol.*

On high, a dark shadow sliced the daylight, his wings broad upon the air. Dark, they flickered–his brethren. The meat-paste lay prepared in a wide copper dish upon the stone and as they flocked, she breathed the musk of their bodies–their strange purplish scent– and stood back from them. She could feel the heat of them, their power and their majesty. An eye fixed on her, the beak tilted sideways so she could see the grey tongue working at the meat paste. His shining black feathers gleamed oily along the length of his neck.

She looked away.

The meat paste contained the blood offerings of her people, the inhabitants of the Raeburn camp, and others who had come back to the old ways. Three drops for each man, woman, and child, in case the enemy came before the next anniversary of their birth. In case these holy beings were shot from the sky like the rest of their kind. In case this was the last time she would ever call them down.

The meat itself was a mixture of lamb and pheasant, kneaded with Alma and spices.

Her attention drifted back, the one who had watched her now showed her his back, his neck deep in the bowl. She longed to stroke him, his glorious wings, and as he twitched, feeling the encroaching presence of his neighbour, the wind raised his feathers, revealing his tender skin. He shuddered, one of his feathers stuck up at an odd angle.

Then with a shock of movement, the first of them took flight.

Not yet, she thought, *stay with me.*

Others began to flap their great wings, raising dust, so that she had to shield her eyes.

Behind her, Edith heard Maeryn's warbling voice, calling the prayer of thanks and it was only then that she remembered the others. Reluctantly she joined Maeryn in the prayer, in the signal of farewell that sent the glorious kshidol upward and away. She squinted, tears coming easily to her eyes as the last of them departed. The air shivered, but all too soon, it grew still. Why could she not hold his gaze? She should have touched him this time. Why could she not fly with them and see with the eyes of the Father?

A kind of melancholy descended on her and she harkened to the comfort of the Alma.

Maeryn's voice neared, and then she felt the old woman's hand on her shoulder. The heat of her touch made Edith's emotions swell, reaching a cascade that swiftly petered out. The Intercessor was drawing her back.

No, don't take me back, I want to be with them, she wheedled in her mind.

Maeryn came before her, took Edith's face in her hands. "Bless you, dear girl," she whispered.

Edith refused to open her eyes.

"Bless you," the Intercessor continued, urging her to let go of the connection to the winged ones.

Edith nodded. She could not hide her face, as it flexed in paroxysms of grief.

"Bless you," she whispered once more, her words the vessel of some deeper message that spoke to the fundament of her being.

For a moment, she felt that she was falling and her eyes burst open.

Maeryn's eyes were there, the dark centre refocusing, the blue starburst a web of interminable depth.

Edith gasped, swiftly regaining herself, finding reality in the hammering of her heart. She felt the clothing of her spirit reassembling–her reservedness, her sceptical nature, finding themselves intact once more.

Edith lowered her eyes and Maeryn released her.

The old woman waddled a few paces and plonked herself on a fallen log. "Praise Kshidol, Holy Father," she breathed, closing her eyes.

Edith glanced at the patch of sky above. Six adults, she had called this time, and two juveniles. Pride rose in her chest.

All these years, she had been the only one brave enough to call them. She had brought Ma Bet with her, and Landyn Raeburn, and Rowan. She had brought Zohar here once before. All must keep this secret close when, for all the Elshenders could determine, the kshidol were completely extinct on the mainland.

Only then, as she thought of Zohar, did she remember her cousin's quiet presence. Edith turned to her and smiled. As the smoke cleared, she saw that Illiam had moved right up next to Zohar. They stood so close the back of their hands were touching, their heads tilted at an identical angle.

The sight broke Edith from her thoughts with a snort of laughter, and like magic, their hands retracted. Why did they try to hide it when everybody knew? Illiam stepped forward, his short curls damp from the climb, his cheeks red for no other reason than that she had embarrassed him in front of the great Intercessor Maeryn.

He came and inspected the bowl. "They ate it all?" he asked.

"Seems so," she said, stating the obvious.

He thrust his hands into his pockets. "There were more this time?"

She nodded, and from the corner of her eye she saw Zohar sit down beside Maeryn to share some food from her pack.

Illiam expended his awkwardness in a litany of mundane questions and observations, before resigning his gaze to the view. The high clearing overlooked the lands of Avishae, and out there the afternoon sun painted the pasture gold. Haydentown lay to the east, by the river, with its tiny windows gleaming.

She liked Illiam, but not here, in this sacred place. She knew that he was peering down the mountain, calculating the value of this position should hostile guardsmen arrive from the mainland. Every time Zohar brought him to the camp, he got like this. He stiffened up, acted like an emissary abroad–like Zohar's personal bodyguard. Wasn't he needed back in Brivia? Surely he could not remain in Avishae indefinitely.

Ultimately, Edith knew that Illiam was afraid of the kshidol. Not in the way that she was, not because they were supernatural beings, but because they might attract the wrong kind of attention. Standing before them, feeling the kshidol as she did, she could not trade that for fear of the Guard. They were mere mortals. And if they came here?…Well, she just couldn't imagine it. Mainlanders went to the Skalens' House and departed the way they had come. That was how it had always been. Even Sybilla, with all the horror that she had wrought in the Seven Lands. Even she had not set foot in Baden forest. This was Raeburn land. Her forest. And the kshidol would always be welcome here.

Edith chewed her lip, began to pack away her things. She scrubbed the Alma on a rough patch of stone to remove the ash, then wrapped it in cloth. The hand drum and flint, she placed carefully in her satchel.

She glanced at Maeryn, her dewy face upturned to the sky where the kshidol had departed. Her eyes sparkled and for a sour moment, Edith yearned to have been a part of her generation. To see the arcing wings of the Father in their multitudes, free about the skies, descending in worship, day after day at the sky temples of Velspar. The siatka, too, they had known in their multitudes...not these barren oceans. Now, there were only fish with their dead eyes, flailing in the fishermen's nets.

She retrieved the bowl from the stone and crouched, wiping out the remains with a handful of leaves. Zohar approached with delicate footsteps and Edith smirked at the sight of her skirt, the ridiculous outfits she wore for Illiam. Edith stood, wiped her hands on her britches.

Zohar smiled, shading her eyes. "You are amazing, Edith."

Edith's gaze went anywhere but her cousin's face as she waited for the compliment to end.

Still Zohar stood there, her red-blonde hair glowing in the sunlight. "Maeryn says it, too."

Edith swallowed awkwardly and searched about for more dry leaves.

"You have a gift," Zohar went on. "You must choose some of the young ones to teach."

Edith nodded impatiently. "I will. I will. I said it last time."

"I know you did, but who?"

"Rowan," she countered. "I brought him up here twice last week. And, he helped me mix the paste earlier this morning."

Zohar was unimpressed. "Rowan? We both know he does not connect with them as you do. You need to find people like you who can draw them close. And if need be, will them away. You do more than wave incense around. They come to your spirit's call."

Edith's stomach fluttered. These must have been Maeryn's words. Was it true?

Catching Zohar's gaze, she relented. "Okay, Zohar. I'll do it. I will. I'll find someone."

Zohar raised her eyebrows. "You might actually have to talk to people to do it."

Edith rolled her eyes.

"Seriously, Edith, things are getting really bad on the mainland.

We have to be ready. Illiam's scared, I'm scared, and even Guardsman John says we have to prepare."

Edith returned her look.

Zohar went on. "The Raeburn camp is protected by a wooden fence. If the Maglorean Guard make war in Avishae, you will not be safe here. I need you to understand how serious this is and to keep our family safe."

A shiver ran down her spine. "Yes, cousin."

Her words seemed to hang in the air as the four of them collected their packs and started back down the mountain. These words of foreboding clung to her like spiderwebs, leeching the joy from an otherwise perfect day. The distant sun passed its pale light through the pines as the dampness of late afternoon gathered about them. She frowned at the figures in front of her. Zohar and Illiam walking side-by-side, Maeryn behind them, bracing her weight on a branch.

What would she do if the mainlanders came for the kshidol? Rage sparked inside her.

They would not touch them. Not while she lived.

Zohar was right, she could not do it alone.

30

———

AVISHAE

REBEKAH GLANCED at her husband who sat hunched over the table preparing the Alma. The wind was high, screaming up the Tower's facade, making it seem colder than it was. Her gaze moved about the wall-hangings of cornfields and farmland, as the thrumming breeze set the strings of the lute buzzing in the corner. These were improvements that lifted the space somewhat, but the past remained like a faint smell, a bitter grime that marked the walls with the sense of anguish and tears.

She sipped her lavender tea and paced, feeling that despite his invitation, the room did not have the space for her.

"Won't you sit down, love?" he bid her, shielding the Alma bowl as the breeze picked up. "And close the window if you could."

She nodded, placed her cup down.

Reaching out the window to the extended pane, she was met by a blast of salty air that sent her hair arcing. Below, waves crashed upon the high black cliffs of the Skalen's House. She sealed the window, and in the close quiet, the room felt even smaller.

She sat down as he sparked the flint stone, staring listlessly into her cup. The surface quivered, fingers of flame appearing at strange angles as Ulric lit the tapers. Placing one of the candles below the copper mesh, he waved his hand to get it going and soon the Alma began to crackle and smoke.

Finished with the task, Ulric's warm hands enveloped hers with a reassuring squeeze. Rebekah looked into his eyes, those familiar eyes that were a mirror for her sorrow. Right there was everything she had been avoiding. His love.

Her throat tightened and she gave his hand a pat, then set her palms about her teacup.

The smoke curled upward, meandering about them, then streaking outward toward the window seam. "It's going to storm today," he said and the goodwill in his voice made her feel ashamed.

He was alone in his grief, just as she was. Why did she hold herself back like this?

A cascade of feeling flowed from her and she set the cup aside to grasp her husband's hands. Meeting her eyes, he accepted her silent apology. She nodded, and finally the tears came.

She feared to connect with him, to see in his eyes their son's death. And now that the Alma had given her the courage to really look, she saw him there–her Ulric–how lonely he was and how she had abandoned him.

"There are some storms that I welcome and some that I do not know if I can withstand," she said, releasing her hand to wipe her face.

Gravely, he nodded, massaging his bearded chin between finger and thumb. "I once thought it wise to give myself to the people of Avishae, that anything I could do for them was worth the price. But now, I think of all the time I wasted, while he was growing up. His life was unfolding without me–" He stopped.

"Not wasted, my love, never wasted," Rebekah countered, hating to see him like this.

"You can't know that, Rebekah. No. I have to speak the truth to you now. There were days when I prayed so hard to remove the redness from them that it made me physically sick. But there were other days when my thoughts were wisps on the wind and I knew that it was not helping them. Still, I stayed up here because I couldn't bear to face the world we had created. If I had spent more time with him, if…"

Ulric's shoulders shook, and Rebekah went to him. He came into her arms and they swayed together in a desperate embrace. "And now, I am doing the same with Zohar," he said over her shoulder. "She lives! She survived an ordeal I cannot even begin to understand and yet I can hardly speak to her."

Rebekah stroked his back.

"She knows, Ulric. She knows you love her." Rebekah felt a fresh wave of sobbing in his chest.

He stood back, swiped at the tears on his cheeks, blew his nose on a pocket linen.

Rebekah wiped her palms on her skirt, her heart throbbing like a drum.

"Zohar will be alright. She is old enough to share this burden with us." She paused, finding her thoughts well-formed on this point after long discussions with Maeryn. "We are getting older, and if anyone is to survive this mess, it must be Zohar. Do not forget that she will have Illiam at her side. He is a fine young man, and one day, he will make a good Skalen."

She went on. "Maglore seems to be an insurmountable threat and I do not know how we will reach the other side of things with the Greslets, but as a Greslet, Illiam holds the keys to peace in the South."

He seemed calmed by this.

"You are right," he said, finally.

Rebekah felt the way was open between them now as it had not been in months.

"We will do this together," she said, the Alma warming her to the topic. "Guardsman John is preparing the townsfolk. There will be death but it will not be a slaughter. He believes that Maeryn can help. He has explained it to me, but I have not yet discussed it with her."

Ulric looked up. "What do you mean, 'help'?"

"Ulric…" she said, placing her hand on his arm, "we can teach the people to fight but, in the end, Maglore has the numbers to destroy us." She stopped him before he could argue. "Even with Brivia's help."

"Go on…" he said, guardedly.

"It is a tactic that Intercessor Camis shared with John before he died," she said.

Ulric pulled away from her. "Camis!" he hissed.

She knew what he felt, that Camis' warnings had doomed them all. High Intercessor Camis, who had assured them of the unavoidable nature of Sybilla's purge and the promise of the Eighth Gate. That the promise remained unfulfilled was the greatest tragedy in recorded history. The willing deaths of thousands–for nothing.

"Think what you will of Camis, but he was a powerful Intercessor, and one who thought strategically. He entrusted this knowledge to John so that it could be used in dire need," she implored, unwanted images streaming through her mind of what would happen if the Magloreans came for Zohar. Rough hands and blood. The screaming of her last living child.

He nodded and gazed out the window. A bright shaft of sun came upon his face that made him squint. The air in the room was soft and milky with smoke.

She watched him, the golden light that tinted his eyes.

"Tell me, then," he said, the fight having gone out of him.

Rebekah took a breath and exhaled slowly, noticing the wash of fatigue that had come over her.

"John believes that if Maeryn were to harm the invading army–in their minds–before they come ashore, that a full-scale battle will not be necessary."

Ulric had turned toward her and now his face was entirely in shadow, the window's light blazing about his head. Her heart leapt to an unexpected canter, feeling his judgement.

Rebekah chewed at her lip, repeating the words as John had spoken them. "The Guard are trained from childhood to attain an equanimity of mind to protect them from the corrupting influence of red thoughts, and Intercessors are their mirror, in a way. Their mastery of red thoughts allows them to ease people's suffering, and… to increase their suffering, should they wish it." Rebekah paused.

Ulric's voice was tight. "Can she do that? A whole army? Doesn't she need to focus on one person at a time? I thought she needed to touch the person.”

Rebekah blinked, tried to focus on his face. “If we use the stone–”

“The stone?” He was standing up now, unbounded anger rippling off him in waves.

“Please, love. Please. Sit down. We would mine it, it wouldn’t be from Ambrose. Never that. Please, just listen.” Rebekah knew he was seconds from charging down to the Guards’ quarters and laying fists on John.

“If we let Maeryn use the stone, her powers will be amplified. He says that an Intercessor can direct their will in this way. The Guard can withstand it. And we can protect the people with Meridians.” Rebekah felt the room was too hot, hated that they were fighting again. But it was too important. This could be the difference between life and death for all of them. “I trust her, Ulric. She would not bring harm to us. I saw her in Jokvour...how she controlled two other Intercessors and kept all of our passions in check. She has the strength to do this.”

Suddenly, his arm shot out and he punched the wall with the side of his fist. An anguished sound tore from his throat, and it was not from any physical pain.

“What else can we do, Ulric? You tell me a better plan!” she cried.

“There isn’t one. There is nothing we can do but die fighting. But that thing is not holy! It brings nothing but death. On that count, John could not be closer to the truth.”

Rebekah took a gentler tone, knowing that all he had seen of the stone was what it had done to their son. He had not been there in the mountains to witness Sybilla’s transformation. “Any weapon can be righteous in the hands of the good.”

Ulric scoffed and Rebekah shrivelled a little inside, recognising the facetiousness of her own assertion.

“I have not even asked Maeryn,” she said. “She might refuse.”

“If she is all that you say she is, she will refuse,” Ulric returned, acidly.

She picked up her teacup and tossed the water on the candle, the

Alma swirling in a mess of tea and ash. "Maybe," she said, and left by the stairs.

31

AVISHAE

ZOHAR AND ILLIAM walked through the forest, hand in hand. Everything was possessed of the dewy warmth of late spring and, through the trees, she could see a clearing. Dappled light shone warm upon the emerald grass, scattering like fish in a pool.

The day was perfect. When she glanced at Illiam, he too seemed to shine. A wave of unease passed over her as if she might find her brother's body again, rotting at the foot of the oak, a plait of hair between his fingers.

Illiam smiled and picked up a stick to run along the passing branches. In the flickering shade, she remembered Ambrose–so young–whacking leaves with a stick as he ran. She felt it coming, a lightness in her legs as if she were disappearing. An intangible sense of wrongness threatened to swallow her. Her feet moved–she saw her feet proceeding–but all seemed pale and distant. Something shifted in her mind, distorting the birdsong and for a moment, she could not sense Illiam at all. She gazed up at the glassiness of the trees, their branches snatching at the light and blurring it in diluted streaks.

A rush of blood came and she grit her nails into her palms.

Help me, Velspar, she prayed. Fearfully, she looked for Illiam, finding his figure but paces away. *Bless us, oh Velspar, keep us in your holy light.*

Illiam came near and squeezed her shoulder, his touch both safe and familiar. He wore a half-smile, one meant to cheer her, but she sensed a deeper comfort from him. She smiled back, the weightless feeling commencing its retreat.

"Come on," he said and ran on ahead.

She did not run, but felt the pull of his anchor and followed. *We are safe here*, she told herself and did her best to believe it. Ahead, he stopped and found a place to rest.

He was lying on his back, a stem of grass seeds in his hand, and he patted his chest for her to lie with him.

Zohar knelt and curled in beside him, hearing the vibrant patter of his heart.

"Such a beautiful day," she said.

An intake of breath from him that drew into a lingering pause.

His heart was slowing and she watched his hands as he stroked and plucked the grass seeds, flicking them one at a time.

"It is a beautiful day, but...?" he prompted.

The warmth of his chest was comforting, and as her body opened itself to the sense of him, she felt the strange interflowing that they shared. It had been that way ever since the night when they encountered the stone that had killed her brother: where horror set them flooding into one another, their edges dissolved in a maelstrom of tenderness and confusion. Before that night, they had barely known one another and might have taken a lifetime to grow their love, but now, nothing would separate them.

The stone and its like lay shrouded now, their power dulled by blinding stone. Zohar knew where she ended and where he began. But always, they inclined toward one another, watching and sensing, seeking to close the distance. And what had seemed unnatural–even scary–in the beginning, now urged them, by some strange alchemy, to become a single being who walked in two forms.

They resisted this and made a habit of reinforcing the line that distinguished them, and yet, she had to remind herself that he did not always know what she was thinking.

"I think I have been too much in my own head lately," she murmured, speaking her thoughts aloud, but not necessarily addressing him. She frowned, feeling that her sense of alienation required some confession. "Sometimes, I am afraid to look into your eyes. I don't know why. There is a goodness in you…" She trailed off, losing her courage.

He stroked her back. "There is nothing in you that can hurt me," he said. He did not go so far as to say he had seen it all, but she knew this was what he meant.

Perhaps it wasn't a confession he needed, she thought. At least not in words.

She stared at her own pale hand lying on his chest, feeling his gaze there too. It was as if she could see herself through his eyes, that when her attention mirrored his, her own senses dimmed. She focused on her fingers, on the texture of his tunic and the pulse beneath. As her hand moved, she felt the tension in his flesh. His palm still stroked her back but in a way that urged her to lift her head, and once she did, his kiss drew every part of her to worship.

She ran her fingers through his short-cropped curls and closed her eyes. Moving her face against his, she drank the scent of him, reading him with her hands until all was blindness and heat.

There they lost themselves–his breath was her breath, her heartbeat his–until they were nothing: nothing but shivering flesh and darkness.

Nothing. Nothing. Nothing.

She panted into his hair.

And as her pulse slowed, she seemed to remember herself like a distant dream.

The dirt grazed her bare knees, her feet were tangled in her clothes. They were outside, and the breeze brushed over her skin, soft and warm.

Twice, she kissed his cheek, and he smiled, eyes closed in a kind of stupor. Zohar sat up, covering her breasts and refastening the hooks of her bodice. Her body felt heavy, as if she had just walked out of the sea. This body, her own, was heavy and real and alive.

She wandered the glade, feeling that all things between them had been restored. How simple and how perfect things could be when she trusted him. She plucked flowers as she walked, and returned to find him unmoved, the smile still lingering on his lips. If only she had her paints with her, she thought, admiring the planes of his chest, the light and shadow, the crest of hair beneath his upstretched arms.

Crouching beside him, she laid a clutch of snowdrops on his chest, making him flinch at their unexpected coolness. Illiam roused with a grin and dressed himself. Then, hand in hand, they meandered back to the village.

When they drew close to the paddock, Illiam spoke, "I haven't received word from my parents in Brivia for a while now."

Zohar looked at him and waited for more. She did not want him to go back there though she knew how he worried about his parents, and Sidney, and their allies who would feel the brunt of whatever was coming their way.

Illiam went on, "I'm worried that this means it is not safe to send messengers, which means that the Brivian coast is not safe, and the Brivian coast–if I stand on that mountain there–is but a stone's throw away."

She sighed, not wanting to let go of the good feelings of the afternoon.

"We're running blind, Zohar. We–"

"Please Illiam, you can't be thinking of going to the mainland. Not now. Your mother is smart, she will know what to do."

He did not immediately respond.

"I know she will do what is necessary, and that our people know how to hide. But war? Generations have passed without knowing what war looks like. The clans are divided and without a decisive tip of the scale, the threat of invasion might never end. Do you understand that?"

His words sat uneasily with her. A *tip of the scale* meant so many dead that one side could no longer hold its claim. The cold feeling crept once more into her limbs, needing her to take notice.

"I understand, but I can't think beyond Avishae right now. I have no power over what happens on the mainland."

He went silent for a time and she knew her answer had not pleased him.

"Whether we like it or not, we have to think of the mainland.

Every night I am kept awake wondering what has become of those who are in this pact with us. Not just the Southlanders, but those we stood with at Jokvour. I believe Waldemar will keep Sidney safe but what of the party that went north? We have heard nothing reliable about Sybilla, Voirrey, and Amand."

Illiam watched her expectantly.

"What? Do you think I know something? I don't. They went to some town in Nothelm to live a simple life, just as we are trying to do here."

His eyes implored her.

She knew that he could not put the break with Amand to rest in his mind. Surely the Intercessor's anger had cooled by now but it left the space for doubt in him.

"Do you think Amand plans to move against our cause?" she asked.

Illiam shook his head. "It's not that. I just…"

Zohar was not enjoying this conversation and wished he would get to the point.

Illiam walked beside her, watching his feet as he spoke. "I don't want you to take this the wrong way, but sometimes when we are close, I feel her in you. I fear things are not well with Sybilla and if this is true, we have cause to worry about the North."

Zohar felt a shadow cross her heart.

Quickly, he went on, "I can feel you pulling away from me, right now, I can feel it. You don't need to do that Zohar. It is not a bad thing. I just, I feel something that is not you. It passes by and then goes away, but it feels like her. It reminds me of her. You must feel it too."

She did. Whenever the feeling came, she pushed it aside, distracted herself, did anything she could to keep it from her heart, but still it lingered. She let out a frustrated breath. She had swallowed the blood-tie and she guessed that the stone had played a part in galvanising its power. She had bonded herself to Sybilla and now she could not undo it.

"I don't know why I did it, Illiam. It was a stupid mistake and I regret it, but it doesn't change anything. Honestly, Mother and Maeryn make out as if it was an honourable thing. Like I did it on purpose. I didn't know what I was doing! I just saw it there, and I knew I needed to keep it from Grandfather. I swallowed the thing and now I'll never be free of her." Zohar realised she was talking too loudly and that the Kinnon's cowshed was within earshot.

She rubbed her face.

Illiam spoke quietly. "I didn't mean to upset you. I just have a bad feeling and now is not the time to ignore our instincts."

He reached out to squeeze her arm, his voice softening. "I don't want you to think that Sybilla is anywhere in my mind when I am with you. It is just–I look at you, and know that there is danger coming and I have to keep you safe. Nothing can happen to you, do you understand?"

"Sorry, Illiam," she said, feeling awful, "I just...it's hard to accept that my spirit is bonded to hers for life. I want my will to be my own and if I lose focus on that it feels like everything will fall apart. When we were there, on Jokvour, I felt for her. Somehow, I went all the way into the heart of her suffering and would have done anything to spare her, but now, she lingers at a distance and my old feelings come rushing back in and I hate her. She ruined everything and if I let myself too close to her, even in my mind, I fear I might forgive her again."

Illiam reached for her hand to help her over the fence. "Would it be so bad, to forgive her?"

Zohar balanced her weight on him and put her legs over, one at a time. When he released her, she glared at him.

"Zohar I am serious. You can't hate something that lives inside of you. She is a part of you now. Like old age. No one wants to grow old and rot away but that's what happens. She is there and I think that you need to make peace with that," he said.

Tears burned hot in her eyes. It was Sybilla's fault that Ambrose was dead. She couldn't even say it out loud because she knew it sounded mad. Ambrose had killed himself, the stone had killed him. But somehow, Sybilla had blackened his heart. She had created a world that was hostile to him. A place of death and isolation where he could never thrive.

"Just think about it," he said. "I won't mention it again because I can see that it hurts you. But please, promise me you'll think about it."

She strode through the high grass, crushing it beneath her feet as she went. "Fine," she said, struck by an incredible sense of deja vu.

Just then, Zohar noticed Tom, the Kinnon's boy, running toward them. His expression was frantic but he did not yell out.

Zohar spun around, looking behind her, and at the barn, as Illiam ran forward to meet him.

The boy's freckled face was bright red from running, his breath heaving in his throat.

"Put on your Meridians!" he gasped.

Zohar did not immediately move and in impatient terror he repeated his plea. "Miss Zohar, they are here!" More gasping. "The Magloreans."

Her flesh went cold and she went fumbling in the pockets of her skirt for her Meridian. Illiam did the same.

"Slow down, boy. Slow down. You saw Guardsmen from Maglore?"

Tom nodded, taking a great shaking breath.

"Okay," Illiam said. "Okay. How many did you see?"

"Three," Tom said.

"Only three?"

"There could be more, I don't know." The panic was creeping back into his voice.

"But you saw three," Illiam went on. "Do you know where they went?"

The boy pointed toward the Skalens' House.

Zohar piped in now, feeling her wits returning to her, the Meridian collecting her thoughts into some kind of order.

"Tom, what did they do here?" she asked, looking for signs of their passage.

"They came asking for water," Tom said and cleared his throat.

Zohar and Illiam shared a look.

"They didn't harm anyone or threaten you?" she asked, her heart skipping.

He looked down at his half-laced boots, shook his head.

"It's going to be okay, Tom. We knew this might happen and that's why we've been doing drills. Do you remember what to do?"

His wide blue eyes came up to meet hers. "I ring the Meridian Bell."

"That's right, Tom. If you ring the bell, then everyone will know to wear their Meridians, and everything will be fine. If they came asking for water, then they are not an army. Illiam and I will go now and warn Guardsman John," she said.

The boy's shoulders relaxed a little. "Thank you, Miss Zohar. Sorry to have bothered you. I will go now and ring the bell."

"Good, Tom," she said.

The boy whistled for his horse and had one leg in the stirrup when Zohar realised they would need the horse themselves.

"Have you another horse we can ride?"

"Round back in the stables," he said, making to alight from the saddle, but Illiam stopped him.

"Don't get off, go ring the bell. We'll get ourselves a horse."

The boy clicked his tongue and set off, his mare striding fast through the yellow grass.

Zohar ran after Illiam and it was well that he could calm his voice around the animals. The ageing mare bowed her head and nuzzled his hand, and he let her out of her stall. He saddled her faster than Zohar imagined he was capable and soon they were on their way, she clinging to his waist as they advanced up the hill.

"When we go in," he said, "I'll take the horse through the training yard and find John. You go up and see what is happening. Once John knows, I'll join you."

Zohar didn't say anything.

"It's probably nothing," he said. "Sometimes small wandering parties are sent scouting through Brivia. They don't find much now that the locals are hidden in the deeper parts of the forest. It can be a tiresome job. Maybe they got bored and wanted to see Avishae."

The horse was moving at a steady trot, so as not to arouse suspicion.

"Even that worries me," Zohar said.

"It is worrying, but you've got to realise that most mainlanders have never set foot in Avishae. Could be curiosity that brought them here, and if we give them nothing to see, then they'll go home and tell that story. It might be good for us, in that way." Illiam's voice was over-bright and Zohar had not shaken her nervousness.

The gate was before them, open as they had left it, the Avishaen Guard milling about as they usually did.

Illiam brought the mare to a stop by the stone entryway and helped Zohar down.

"See you inside," he said, and led the horse away with his head down.

Zohar hitched her skirts and crossed the courtyard. Once inside, her eyes faltered in the sudden dimness, a figure moving toward her from the hall. Seeing it was Elspeth, she relaxed a little. Her Attendant came close and made to brush dust from Zohar's skirt, whispering. "Three guardsman from Maglore upstairs with your parents." She drew back and smiled, speaking then in a louder voice. "Welcome back, Miss Zohar, I trust you enjoyed your walk?"

"Yes, thank you. Illiam will be up shortly and we will take tea upstairs." Zohar said.

She took the stairs quietly, a little slower than her normal pace, listening intently for any noise in the rooms above.

Mumbling tones, male–not hostile–her father, formal-sounding, the clinking of tableware.

The doors to the Main Hall stood open, breeze from a seldom-opened window sloughing dust down the hallway. She smelled honey, waxed timber, and the faint tang of sour sweat.

They saw her. Three bearded men sat across the table from her parents, their eyes lingering long enough to break the conversation.

Her father turned.

"Zohar, please come and join us," he said, and held out the chair to his left.

As she sat down, she heard the distant ringing of the town bell. One-two-three, pause, one-two-three. A longer pause, and then the alarm repeated.

"Our guests visit from Maglore," her mother said. "They have been telling us of their travels."

Zohar smiled noncommittally.

"Yes, Miss Zohar, the wilds of Brivia are a sight to behold," the middle one remarked, his pouchy eyes glimmering with some secret amusement.

"Brivia is most beautiful," she said. "In what region are you stationed?"

"Oh, you know, all parts. We move about," the first one said, taking a rather dainty bite of honeyed bread.

Illiam entered then, striding quickly to the table.

Her mother gave him a nod of greeting. "Please, join us, Illiam."

He sat next to Zohar, glancing at the three men. "Hello guardsmen. I don't believe we have met. What brings you to Avishae?" He helped himself to the food laid out on the table, and poured a round of wine.

"No, I don't think we've met. Redmund and Dojo here are from up near the north border, and my name's Tirus. I grew up in the port town. I must say, it's mighty nice to meet a Greslet so far from home. Though I wonder if you remember it, having left so young?"

"Dojo, that's an unusual name. Is it short for something?" Illiam asked, focusing on the thin man.

"Oh, that's just a play name," Tirus said, taking charge of the conversation once more.

Glances were exchanged in taut silence.

"Please, Tirus, tell me something of my homeland. As you say, I have not seen it for many years. How fares my uncle?"

"Oh, we are not so high ranking to have met your uncle!" Tirus replied.

Zohar saw her father frown, and from what little she knew of the guardsman's code, this was indeed unusual.

"What of my young cousins then? Surely Skalen Inry still parades them in the finest silks?" Illiam's smile receded, finding that even this well-worn jibe did not arouse a knowing smile.

Somewhat belatedly, Redmund piped in: "Yes, the young ones are hale and strong, I hear."

Zohar stomach would not unclench and she dearly wished that these leering dimwits would speak their purpose and be done with it.

Zohar's mother spoke. "I thank you for taking tea with us, guardsmen, and you are welcome to remain in the guards' quarters until you are rested for your journey home."

Her father stood, signalling a premature end to the meal. "Well met, Tirus, Redmund, Dojo," he said in turn.

Zohar and Illiam stood and the guardsmen followed suit. Dojo licked the honey from his grubby fingers then wiped them on his britches.

"Shall I walk you down, guardsmen?" Illiam offered, and it was only by the unusual forwardness of his manner that Zohar could tell how terrified he really was.

"Certainly, Master Illiam, that would be a rare privilege," Tirus replied, taking one last sip of wine.

As they went out, Zohar listened to their chatter, walking a little way behind.

"Have you had a chance to see Haydentown?" Illiam asked.

"Oh, no, we came by the mountain track, always nice to get out for a bit of a hike. You like the outdoors, Master Greslet?" Tirus said.

At that, Redmund winked at Dojo, giving Zohar a brief leering glance that made her ears burn. With a wash of fear, she wondered: *Could they have seen?* She kept her posture very straight, walked a little slower to widen the distance. She felt very keenly that she and Illiam had survived this day by a blade's breadth. Illiam was right and she'd been foolish to ignore the fact for so long.

Nowhere was safe. Despite the town meetings and the drills, Avishae was not prepared.

32

AVISHAE

THERE WERE GUARDSMEN everywhere, wandering about and trying to look as though they were usually allowed here. Even though Edith knew the Avishaens were there to protect the camp, their presence put her on edge. Above, by the Raeburn gate she could see Rowan hiding in his bird's nest, his darting eyes visible even from below.

She hoisted herself up the ladder and shoved her way in beside him.

"Why are they here?" Edith whispered, scowling, and of course she meant the three foreigners who were the cause of all this fuss.

Rowan shifted awkwardly with both hands raised, trying to move clear of her body. He seemed equally disturbed by her invading his watchpost as he was about the arrival of the mainlanders.

She moved her face close to his ear, "You think they are here for Maeryn?"

Rowan glared at her. "How am I supposed to know?" He elbowed her in the ribs, making her sit back.

"Ow!" she yelped. "What's wrong with you?"

Rowan stared at the guards from beneath dark brows. "I want them gone Edith and you are going to make them suspicious."

Edith gave him one of her deadpan looks. "I'm only doing what you do every day of your life–sit up here and spy on people. Besides, it's normal for thick-headed villagers to stare at strangers from the mainland." She pulled a face, half-crossing her eyes.

Rowan ignored her, but she did not feel like leaving. She leaned back on the timber frame, her hair flickering from the entrance-facing viewport.

Noticing how filthy her nails were, she went about cleaning them with her small knife.

Rowan was hunched forward, watching with the intensity of a cat.

Eventually, he gestured her to come forward. She slipped the knife back into her belt case and crawled in beside him.

His tone was careful. "They are searching for something," he said. "Watch. One goes into a hut, another goes behind, and the third stands watch in the centre."

She looked sceptically at the dark-haired man standing below. He did not look like he was capable of doing anything so systematic. Then, she saw the stocky one emerge from behind Ma Bet's hut. Moments later, the tall one came out. They switched. Black hair went in, stocky stood vigil, tall one went out back.

A gnawing unease took hold in her stomach. *Maeryn.* Or did they know about the Temple books? They could not know about the stone. The people of Avishae barely understood what it was. And if the mainlanders had heard anything, they would know where it was hidden, in her cousin's belly. Poor Ambrose, up there on the hill beneath a cairn of blinding stone.

Edith watched, wide-eyed as the stocky one went into Maeryn's hut. Seconds stretched.

Come out, come out, she thought, *come on.*

The guard emerged, tripped on the step, said something to the tall one who seemed the brains of their operation. They moved on.

Edith let out a long breath but continued to watch Maeryn's hut. Nothing stirred. Perhaps it was that she was not accustomed to wearing the Meridian at camp but she felt a certain numbness had come over her. She could not protect her kin if she could not feel them. The thought brought a chill, though it was clear they were not to fight these men today. She felt, with her spirit, for Maeryn, but could not feel the Intercessor's presence at all. She wanted to take off her Meridian just to see but would not risk it.

She tried to stretch out her legs. "I don't know how you stand it up here, it's so cramped."

Edith rolled her shoulders and stretched her neck from side to side.

"No one asked you up here," he said grumpily.

Truth was, she didn't trust her temper if she went down. Didn't trust herself to act normal when what she really wanted to do was hold something sharp to their throats and tell them to get out of her camp.

Rowan was her safety net, endlessly worrying and warning her of dangers she would not have heeded otherwise. The other Raeburns abided her moods, her special status with the kshidol up in the mountains, but they didn't dare tell her what to do. Rowan could not help himself, just like she couldn't help feeling sour most of the time.

Working against her instincts, Edith stayed put until the guardsmen left. Landyn remained a long time watching from the open gate. She stared down at his bald head wondering what he was thinking.

"Rowan," he called without looking up. "Help me with the gate."

Edith trailed Rowan down the ladder and together they pulled the gate closed.

Villagers emerged cautiously from their huts, a quiet tension in the air.

Landyn turned his piercing grey eyes on Edith. "Build a fire. This place must be cleansed. But don't light it till they've gone a good hour on the road."

She nodded and set off, giving instruction to the younger Raeburns as she went to the Alma storehouse to gather fronds.

Passing the farthest hut, she glanced in through the open doorway. Paused.

Quietly, she entered, tapping on the door with a gentle sound.

"I am here, Edith. Do not fret." Maeryn's voice emerged from the dim room, weary-sounding.

Edith's heart warmed with relief.

"Come in for a moment, dear."

Edith went inside, finding the old woman tucked up in bed, the light from the doorway illuminating her face.

Maeryn patted the corner of the bed and Edith sat down.

"They do not know who I am. I tested the guardsman's mind. They do not know of the stone or of anything that has been happening here. They were searching for fugitives." Maeryn gave her a dark look that made Edith deeply uneasy.

"Who?" Edith whispered, having no idea what the woman would say.

"Take that thing off and I will show you their faces as the guardsman pictures them," Maeryn said.

Edith slipped off her Meridian, and the Intercessor reached for her hands.

"Touch your forehead to mine," Maeryn said, closing her eyes.

Edith swallowed, not having done this before, and came closer. The Intercessor leaned gently forward and guided Edith's head.

A disorienting swirl of blackness, a hallway draught, the sweet scent of hair oil, lilies... a woman was there–beautiful–in a layered silk dress. A Meridian hung with pearls that shook among shining dark ringlets. Her pinched and tired face, so pale. Another was near her, like a ghost, a girl who disappeared, running in her nightdress, a sick feeling like she was falling down a hole.

Edith gasped, pulling back. Maeryn's soft face rose before her, her pupils dark–too deep–like the place the girl had fallen.

The scent of woollen blankets, the first smoke of the fire–these things brought her back. She looked away, heart still racing.

"Who are they?" Edith asked. She did not recognise them, but for some reason she feared to know their names.

Maeryn's eyes seemed more normal now, and she moved her legs out from under the blanket, rising to join Edith. "Skalen Inry Greslet and her daughter Lilwenn. I am sure of it."

Edith helped her to the doorway, knowing the old woman's knees hurt.

The Intercessor's thoughts moved far above her, but all Edith

could think of was her kshidol. *They can't come here, they can't,* she
thought.

Maeryn's look was stern with judgement.

The woman and the girl, Edith felt them once more, suffusing her
like a scent on the wind. *You will protect them,* Maeryn's eyes seemed
to say. *You must.*

33

SELTSLAND

THE RUNNER BURST into the dining hall where Kalet sat eating her breakfast, his face scratched and bleeding.

This was it.

She stood, eyes wide with impatience as she waited for his message.

"The mountains," he gasped. "By the..." He struggled again for breath. "...river–"

"Oh for goodness sakes, stop talking, you fool, and take me there!" Kalet roared, and the two of them went sprinting for the stables.

Kalet rode as fast as her horse would go, right on the heels of the runner's brown bay. Her charge slavered, almost bucked as she dug the spurs again. *Intercessor*, the lad had gasped, his eyes round with terror. *Intercessor*, somewhere in the mountains. It was the fugitive Magnar had been hunting for uncounted cycles of the moon and whom Kalet had agreed warranted her personal attention.

Almost there, she could see them, a great pack of guardsmen straining on ropes, at least twenty dead on the ground.

She pulled on the reins, slowing the beast, though he stamped and circled, snorting from his exertions. Kalet pulled more softly, trying to soothe him with her voice though her own eyes were black and wild. She searched the sea of helms, finally stilling her mount enough to disembark.

Where was he?

Then, through the press of bodies, she spotted him.

There. Oh yes, the lad was not wrong.

She could feel his power. Her legs trembled, and not simply from the ride. She felt a profound strength-sapping nausea the closer she came.

His clear eyes blazed, the rope tight in his teeth, the swooning guardsmen pulling him in one direction then another. One had managed to tie the Intercessor's leg to a tree before expiring on the ground.

Dizzy, she looked down at the nearest corpse, face all scratched with blood-dirty fingernails. She kicked the man in the stomach to make sure.

Dead. *Amazing*, she thought.

She wore her Meridian but maybe it would not be strong enough. She dislodged the helm from the dead guardsman and wore it as a second line of defence. All helms were lined with blinding stone these days.

"Skalen!" a guardsman cried, the rope he held wrapped tight about his own waist.

Kalet's breath caught, the Intercessor finally making note of her.

"I know you..." she croaked, feeling her throat contract.

He was an old one. An original. She had seen his face at Blood Call, she was sure of it.

His cheeks were grazed and there were rasping red marks all over his skin. The guardsman behind him, poised to wrap a rope about his neck, grew vacant, the coiling length pooling at his feet. The guardsman vomited on the ground and lay moaning in foetal position.

"Intercessor," she managed through gritted teeth. "You were born of these lands, which makes me your Skalen. By your oath you will serve the Askier. By your oath!"

Kalet fell to her knees, her heart seemingly too big for her chest, thumping so hard her vision could not retain him. He was fading before her in a white nimbus, he was fading. *Intercessor!*

34

SELTSLAND

THE INTERCESSOR hung upside down, his face swollen both from the last beating and from the blood pooling there. She stood outside the bars of his cell nervously tapping her foot. This interrogation technique had seemed like a good idea the previous evening, but now she worried that it might have unintended consequences. Might swell his brain to the point of death. And all before she had got what she needed out of him.

Both Kalet and her prisoner wore Meridians and she could tell that, this time, she had a powerful specimen in her midst. Even with his eyes closed and seemingly unconscious, he could make her stomach turn, and almost make her faint. Her assistants in torture had been replaced several times. Most of them now convalesced in the guard's barracks. One or two of them were dead.

Somehow, Kalet had been able to withstand his presence, though she was frequently ill and kept a bucket nearby for such moments when the bile came creeping up her throat.

She pursed her lips.

"Guardsman!" she called.

A moment later, Burnley appeared, a stocky guardsman of advanced years. "Yes, Skalen?"

She looked at him dubiously thinking he would be the third casualty by afternoon.

"I'd like you to take the prisoner down, clean him up, and give him something to eat. I'll be back a little later."

~

When Kalet returned, the Intercessor was sitting upright, one leg up, one down as he leaned back in the cot the guardsman had set up for him. *Was this the Intercessor's powers of persuasion at work? Or some sneakiness in the guard's ranks?* she wondered.

He was chewing on a chicken bone.

At her arrival, he smiled.

She matched his cocky expression with a squint of the eyes. *Got yourself a chicken bone and think things are going pretty well. You won't be smiling when I'm done with you*, she mused.

They studied each other.

He looked so familiar. Every now and then, his pale eyes would move to the left, and the feeling would catch her. The expression transcended the bruising, calling forth a memory too deep or insignificant to clarify. She was certain that he was a Seltslander.

"You smile, Intercessor, and I think I know you," she said, in one of her friendly moods. "Will you not give me your name?"

He paused his eating. "We are the same age, you and I."

She believed it, but his skin bore its sun stains. He had lived a life beyond the white robe of his station. He had survived where all others had perished. Or were there more of his ilk out there in the mountains of Jokvour?

"I will remember you, I am sure," Kalet said, taking it as a challenge.

The Intercessor went back to his eating, working his teeth about the fine bones so as to leave nothing behind. His wrists, scorched red by his restraints, gave way to sinewy forearms. He was lean, but not entirely malnourished, which either meant that he knew how to survive in the elements or he had help.

He placed the bone neatly at the foot of his cot and wiped his hands, folding them in his lap. The hands, like half-moons, cupped one another. With a strange nostalgia, she recognised the meditative posture, saw the training and purpose in his every movement. The calm rhythm of his breath.

"Will you work with me, Intercessor?" she asked. "Will you tell me what I need to know? I recognise your rank and know that you will not be broken in the usual way. I am willing to do things a little differently, if you are agreeable?" She found herself leaning forward, appealing to him.

His eyes did not leave her as a little smile quirked at the corner of his mouth. "I am agreeable."

She nodded.

"I will send blankets and a wash basin," she said, and went out.

All the way up the stairs, she felt light, full of comfort and tender joy. The gentling breeze was delicious on her face as sunset broke red over the marshlands.

35

───────

SELTSLAND

KALET ARRIVED at the Temple at dawn. The distant sun peeked like an eye above the rim of the ocean, casting the pinkish glow of its sight. *The dawn sees me*, she thought, but no other would dare come near. Kalet looked up, knowing the Intercessor was there in the upper window, but could not see him for the shadows. The faintest scent of Alma incense blew on the breeze.

In her dark cloak, she hurried to the barred door and fumbled with cold fingers for the key. A nervous sweat chilled her as the heavy iron gate opened: today was the day she tested him. She locked it behind her and went up the dewy marble stairs. By the time she reached the seventh floor, her heart was pattering and she had to take a moment to catch her breath.

In the dim, circular room, she stared into the shadowed furs that warmed his bed, and as her eyes adjusted, saw his eyes gleaming there. On the floor beside him, glowed the incense embers, tiny points of light like a hovering constellation.

She took a tight-throated breath and exhaled. "Ready, Intercessor?"

His eyes held hers a moment longer, then he arose, coming to his full height, at least a head taller than her.

They sat on prayer cushions in the centre of the room as pale light filtered in through the teardrop apertures that surrounded them.

He took the ceremonial dagger in his hand and made a series of intentional incisions about his wrist and forearm, avoiding a litany of unhealed cuts until blood dripped steadily from his upraised elbow. She caught it in the copper bowl, counting the drips until a reasonable half-cup had accrued there. Gently, he scraped the surface of his skin with the flat of the blade, sending a final dribble into the bowl.

He cleaned his wounds with a wet cloth, binding the weeping sores until they calmed.

Meanwhile, Kalet added Alma wine to the bowl, stirred it with the tip of the blade and began to drink.

Nursing his arm, the Intercessor went to the window facing the sea, the sun golden in his face, making his eyes seem as jewels in a bright river.

Kalet drank slowly, knowing this gift was hers and flowed freely. She felt it in her mouth as a kind of alchemy, rich and sweet, charged with an otherness that her spirit recognised.

As the blood came into her, she felt compelled to calmness, to a peace beyond understanding. And in this peace, such puzzles as she had worried over for years became simple and orderly before her mind. She felt that her most daring expeditions into the unknown were as fumbling and stupid as a child building castles out of mud. Castles that melted away in the superior order of falling rain. Essence returning to essence. The Intercessor's blood, his presence, cleansed her somehow, stirred little used instincts to waking.

She set out the food she had brought, and they ate the dense bread and seedfruit in silence.

Seven shafts of light illuminated the space, strong shafts from the east and pale from the west, gleaming in an airy circlet in the centre of the room where the high altar once stood.

She cleaned her hands in a basin of salt water that the Intercessor kept in the corner and wiped them on her skirt.

Over the months of their arrangement, a certain trust had been built, and Kalet felt a sense of fellow feeling with the man that was entirely new to her, though not entirely unpleasant.

By now, she had guessed his name but had not spoken it. If, by some chance, she was wrong, she felt that to speak it might break the spell of her dominion.

"Come, Intercessor," she said. "I have something to show you."

This would be the test of his power, his usefulness to her. The artefact she was about to show him was the very seed that had sparked the heretical obsessions of her girlhood and had made her the Skalen she was.

She placed the wrapped object in the convergence of light and stood back.

With her permission, the Intercessor came forward, unfolding it until the flat wooden diamond sat glowing in the palm of his hand. It was strange to see its familiar form, its carved design in another's hand. She watched him inspect it, the crudely carved sun at its centre, the bisecting line joining point to diamond point, the pattern of dots, mirrored above and below, darker now for the kiss of the siatka's blood. He turned it over and read aloud the single word written there. A name, a prayer in some lost language of the ancient clans, a curse–she did not know.

"Solska."

A droplet of blood rose from his wrist wound and he placed the object down to press the cloth to it.

She did not feel she could say the word aloud, though it seemed his voice still held its holy resonances in the Temple's inner dome.

She felt the thrill of his blood in her, the rush of mingling that brought his soul flooding in. "It reminds you of something, does it not?"

He reached for it again, tipped the diamond this way and that. "It is like the Eye of Velspar, though here, the eye is made of flame, and there is no separation between the twin mouths of the Holy Ones. Though the diamond is bisected. It might yet be..." He trailed off.

She waited for more, his gaze betraying the value of the thing that he held.

His fingers traced the pattern of dots.

"Above and below," she interjected. "As a mirror." She came forward on her knees, unable to hold herself back as she intended to.

She pointed at the pattern of dots. "Above, below. These are stars, Intercessor. In the sky and reflected in water."

He looked at her, his eyes gently parting the reeds of her mind to reveal the root of her knowledge. She felt it and did not try to stop him.

"It is old, isn't it? Older than the First?"

She smiled faintly, the scum of heresy rising in her throat. "Older than the Battle of Jokvour," she murmured. How delicious to say it out loud, to an Intercessor who could not accuse her or take a knife to her throat, who was forbidden to move against her.

In her mind, she pictured the scene of the original clans at war. The Intercessor before her loomed in her periphery, seeming divine beyond his station, as if she sat before Skalen Karasek himself. And whispering from her, victorious and devastating, the knowledge of something that came before.

The Intercessor's pupils widened, and she realised how close his face was to hers. Too close.

Abruptly, she looked away.

She felt nauseous, almost drunk, and made a quick assessment of her surroundings. The knife still lay on the floor.

"I have never understood the heresy against the stars," Kalet said, her heart stuttering.

The Intercessor replied with the oft-repeated refrain: "The stars lure us away from Velspar."

"Away from Velspar and towards what?" The excitement of her blood showed in her cheeks.

He looked at her with his wide, seashell eyes. "What I have learned of the stars I learned in the silence that followed the deaths of my brethren." A mist of thoughts seemed to steal him from her. "There is no secret knowledge that the Intercessors have held back. I learned by looking into the darkness with my own two eyes."

A flare of anger writhed within and yet she felt fixed to his will, his message, that was deceptive in its simplicity. She could feel the waves of his power like silently expanding wings. If she turned her eyes askance, she would finally see herself bound in his clutches, cocooned in the fine web of his spirit.

Again, the Intercessor's pupils seemed to grow, like abyssal pools. "There is another who looks into the dark," he said, his voice large, his breath herbal on her cheek.

She intended to leave but remained unmoving. She swallowed, tasting in the air the boy Damyen that she had killed, remembering the word he'd gifted her.

"Damek," she whispered. She pictured the man's face with his blue-grey eyes and wolfish beard, and then, in some dark doorway, a flash of blonde hair, a bird with flapping wings, pale and frantic, searching for the glass-bright sky.

Rapidly, a sense of normalcy established itself about her, and when she turned, the Intercessor sat several feet from her, the object secure in its wrappings.

She stood, stumbling slightly. "Thank you, Intercessor. I shall return tomorrow."

Time skipped in disorienting rhythms as she exited. The winding stair circled, descended, and seemed never-ending. An anxious feeling came upon her and she realised she had left her Meridian up there with him.

Madness.

She continued on, not trusting herself to go back in. It was madness to sit so close with him. To let him wield a knife. To be with him without protection of any kind. Her desperation for insight made her take risks she would never have contemplated in the past. She felt an exhilaration of shame to know that he had laid eyes on the deepest secret of the Askier, a clan secret that she had not even shared with her husband.

Locking the gate behind her, she resolved to leave him a few days. Let him get hungry and remember his place.

She would go north, to Damek. She had been planning to see him regardless. She would take the device to him, let him sketch its shape, and see what he might give her in return.

Kalet went the long way to the Skalens' House, wetting her feet in the shallows as she trod the sandy shore. She thought of blonde hair, of the terror that accompanied the vision. It was a vision, of that she felt sure. She had experienced something like this with others of his ilk. When the pain made their blood race and their eyes grew wide, the momentary thrall they held her in was not without its gifts. Like a wolf taking the rabbit's head gently in its jaws, once inside this place of ultimate danger, she could catch a glimpse of *their* hidden place. And in the Intercessor's she had seen this woman, this bright-haired runaway of whom she had heard tantalisingly little over the past few years. Voirrey Braedal.

36

MAGLORE

SYBILLA MUMBLED through the pain. Her mouth did not want to move and when she tried again, all she could manage was an inarticulate cry. When her eyelids would not obey her command, she raised her eyebrows as high as they would go, considered using her hands to open them manually. Hands, hands. She could not detect the existence of such things.

There was pain, but where? The static hiss of numbness prickled, hid the location from her. Deep and ragged and very bad. *Open!* She raised her eyebrows again, this time, the lids separated. Dark stone walls, blurring lashes, a figure by the window. Her eyes closed again and like a drop of ink in water, her mind swirled, lost time. She tried once more to open her eyes, one of them rose full wide this time. He stared at her–the man–with his full black beard. He stared as though this was all a dream. He would give way to another form, turn into a blackbird and fly away, turn into a black dog and eat her alive.

Her heart began to race.

The eye that worked tilted down, registering a bedpost, a twisted sheet, a blood-mottled bandage she could not distinguish from the sheet. She could not make sense of her body's shape. What was that part that stuck out to the side? The eyelid closed once more, and inside her mind, she looked down at the parts of her that lay sleeping. She was wrapped like the Intercessors used to wrap the dead. But, no, she was not dead. She had not been cleaved into seven pieces. The pain flowed through many channels–so deep its cry. Somewhere in the lower realms, it came for her, skittering up through the bones of her face.

I live. That is all I can know... But where is Voirrey? Davina? These thoughts were located in place and time, in the living waters of reality but she was not ready to drop that anchor. She let her mind dissemble and drift. She seemed to travel, to speed forward, until all was caught up in the blur. Until the blur lost colour–grew dark, sunk low–and in that inner pool, silence held her. Suspended and weightless, she was. An awareness unbounded and without edge.

Sybilla writhed, surfaced with a gasp, and sank back down into the pool. Sometimes it was the pain that roused her, the knowledge that hands touched her body. She would stare at the blurred face before her–Domhnall again–with his puffy eyes and grave expression. He was unwrapping her, the sting of blood-stuck bandage, the trickle of water in the basin dripping from a squeezed rag.

She was gone again–floating in a liquid realm alive with dark vitality, but her own light was dimmed. Her soul so quiet, so still, that the darkness did not converse with her. It went about its connections, its expressions, permutations and unfoldings. It rippled through her translucence and she felt it possible to dissemble further. She could cease to hold her centre, and simply let go.

"Agh!" Breath sucked sharply through her teeth. Her lungs, like dusty old sacks, nudged at her heart.

The curtain danced, a long and drifting extension, then fell flat.

She could not see anyone in the room, though behind her there was a disorienting hollow sound: stumbling footsteps, a clatter, a deep wheezing cough.

Sybilla blinked to wake herself, chasing the sound for its origin. Her body struggled to regain its autonomy, to integrate its pieces, like a puppet on twisted strings. Her elbows shifted back and she pushed, trying to lift her head. The movement seemed to peel her from the bedsheet like a scab. Her nerves sang with over-wakefulness, the emergency of life a frantically clanging bell. Sybilla's eyes were open now, fully open, and though her head swam with sluggishness, waves of cold revelation assailed her. She tried to move her feet, but there was only one shape down there, only one peak ridged with flexing toes.

She pulled back the sheet, saw the bandage, the stump, the weeping stains all over the mattress, and now she feared infection but did not dare to look at the wound. I have no foot. My foot is gone. The dogs...

Her mind bore into the memory, tried to fill in the gaps, but there was nothing there. The farmer striding toward her, the teeth ripping at her flesh, the stink of the dog's damp fur. She remembered Domhnall shifting her to her side and cleansing her skin... Where was the rest? What had happened to her?

Then, her mind tilted, expanded. Voirrey and Davina clambering up into a tree. She wanted to die. There was no way they could have escaped. Were they here? Surely she was a prisoner of Maglore. She cried out to the person coughing in the other room.

"Help me, help me!" she panted. "Help me!" The veins in her neck clutched at the words.

Someone shuffled through the echoing hall. Grunted. His footsteps were close all of a sudden. He turned to her–it was Domhnall alright–and he was stone drunk. He looked at her. Sniffed, and wiped his nose on the back of his sleeve.

He plonked himself on the side of the bed and held out the bottle of wine he was drinking. A flicker of wisdom swam in the dirge of his drunkenness.

She reached for the bottle, but her hand was so weak she could not grasp it. He lifted it gently to her lips and the sour dark flowed into her mouth. She swallowed, the taste ringing on her tongue.

They shared the bottle this way, silently and all the way to the bottom, until Sybilla felt herself glued to the headboard, and Domhnall slumped forward on his knees.

"Lie down," Sybilla said, numbly, and he curled himself into a ball beside her.

She stared into the middle distance, unable to close her eyes. "Are they dead?" she whispered.

Domhnall breathed a heaving sigh. "I don't know," he said, his back beginning to shake with tears. His wet sounds continued and her mind drifted away from him.

Slowly, she tried to gather the pieces. *If he does not know, he has not seen them.* Degore was dead. Surely, he was dead. And then, with regret, she felt sure of Andrin's fate. Rayhmer lived, yet he had not come to torment her. Why? And why would he put her into Domhnall's care? She had not seen an Attendant, nor any sign that they tended to this room. Edlin? Did he yet live? The thought pierced her with horror, knowing that there had been no one to pass scraps to him for days, if not weeks.

Right now, Rayhmer could be moving on Vaelnyr, could have declared against Peran's Guardsmanship. Now that the hidden conflict between Maglore and the old guard of Velspar had found its flash point, anything could be in motion. She wheeled back the circumstances, this way and that, trying to determine ways that she could have averted this. A strategy to distract herself from the hollow in her arms, the forehead she longed to kiss, the hands she longed to hold. *Gavril, if they are dead, care for them. You must.*

She thought of the Holy Ones then, of Siatka and Kshidol, and for the first time in her life, she did not fear them. Their primal song was a part of the dark reverberation that had moved through her, that had recognised her–that drew like among like. The flesh budded, bloomed, and fell, but in the deep, she saw the order of constellations, the eternal spinning of fragments into points of brightness. She was a point of brightness, a gathering of fallen threads.

Where, now, was Gavril? Her parents? Her sister and grandfather?

In her stupor, she drew them close in her mind, calling to them, through flesh and aether.

Always, we will draw near to each other; always we will flock to the gate of life to renew our love. We cannot be separated. She told herself. *There is nothing they can do to separate us, not ever again.*

37

MAGLORE

SYBILLA HEARD the bolt clunk in the Main Hall behind her. Domhnall shuffled back with their breakfast. The faint scent of baked rolls roused her senses, made her wonder at the fickleness of her own body, how it could hunger and feel the satisfaction of a meal at a time like this.

Sybilla used her arms and good leg to push herself to the edge of the bed. They would not give her a walking stick, of course, but she used the bedpost to stand, leaned there until Domhnall appeared in the doorway.

The room they lived in was never intended to be a bedchamber. It was the Guard's anteroom, a place where armoured men would wait during the Skalens' audiences, eyes upon the silent lever on the wall that, when pressed in the arm of the Skalens' throne, would alert them by flipping a wooden circle from its black face to red. They did not have such a thing in Vaelnyr and Domhnall had shown her the mechanics of it for a brief moment of distraction.

Every waking moment was harsh with the reality of their situation. Ideas of escape floundered against the bolted door, and the row of men that remained below, ready with their arrows. For their passivity, they received their rations and survived another day.

When Domhnall took to the bottle, Sybilla sank into her inner pool, that dark place where she extended the confines of her prison. The peace she experienced there was so profound, so simple, that it reminded her of those days in her youth when her grandfather trained her in the rudiments of Hiatus–the Guards' Way. He had tried to show her but she had been too young to understand. With her imperfect understanding, she had equated his teaching with the Meridian, though they were not the same. The darkness was not a place of confinement and hiding. It was not a place of deadened emotion.

All the people of Velspar became a myriad of temporary forms, and she, herself, an alloy of those who had lived before. She felt the alchemical strangeness of her own flesh and blood. Of Davina, who had been born of her and yet was a complete mystery.

There was the surface–all urgency and feeling–that the Meridian could mask. There was a layer where the red roots of passion reached into the soul. And there was her deep place. Constant and eternal. Part of her was there, and through that quiet substrate, she felt Voirrey and Davina remained beside her, in a place beyond words.

Sometimes, she reached that place, and sometimes she didn't.

For much of the time, she lived in Domhnall's shadow where it was impossible not to despair. He lived each day on the precipice, not knowing what had happened to his wife and children. One day, the Guard would ascend and there would be no more Skalens. They would never leave this room. Never. Sybilla shuddered, felt the fear like a strong wind lifting at her sleeves, the breathless desire to run, to wrench one of the Attendants through the door and strangle them until they were dead. Then, to run. *Escape! Escape!* But she would never run again.

Domhnall set down the tray. Bread and butter, water in a jar. He came near to give her his shoulder as a crutch, helping her to hobble to her seat.

"Thank you," she said, with more sincerity than she dreamed she could bestow upon this man.

They ate silently for a time. The window made its displays of freedom, showing the world that existed out there: a grey glaring sky, wind in the distant trees, Guardsmen like figurines dotting the hill.

"Domhnall, I want you to try again with me today," Sybilla said, firm this time.

His eyes moved evasively. "It is pointless."

"Our lives are pointless," she countered. "We exist merely so Rayhmer can wheel us out and prove that we are not dead."

"Can you at least let me finish eating?" he asked, chewing at a dry crust.

Sybilla didn't say anything. She waited, feeling the tide of that other realm, needing to take him there. As she prepared herself, she could almost feel her grandfather in the room, as if she could borrow his essence from the hillside of her mind.

Eventually, Domhnall finished eating, gulped from the shared water jar, and brushed the crumbs from his beard.

"Close your eyes," she said.

The man's left-cheek trembled, a tic that Sybilla had come to know. She persisted. "Inry and Lilwenn may yet live, but they could be far from us. I feel Edlin here, still. You must reach out to him with your spirit."

He glared at her, but followed her lead in removing his Meridian.

"Grow quiet and still," she murmured. "And do not think of him until you are there."

She left off with words, allowed the sensations of her body to quieten, the interactions and desires of the day to settle like dust in a windless room. Her leg throbbed and she focused on the sensation, its strange pulse, its urgent message. *Yes*, she said to the throbbing, *I can hear the urgent message. I hear you.* The pain of it listed away.

Birdsong.

Domhnall's breath.

The action of blood in her stomach, taking mouthfuls of bread down to its lair.

Birdsong again.

Dimming.

The prickling of sound–bright, dull, bright–a long note of silence.

Dimming.

A thought trickling in, *I must help him, I must find Edlin, Edlin might be able to save us, Eldin might...*

Dimming.

Birdsong, close and distant.

Fall away, deep.

She could sense it nearing, the flowing dark, and turned her inner eye to Domhnall. His skin was tender as if wiped with alcohol, his expression cowering. His guilt was a shroud of shadows. She looked into those shadows and knew them. Watched them grow gauzy, giving way to her probing.

Her spirit led him the way she and Voirrey had gone with Davina that first night: the hallway that led to a juncture. She sped past the entombing silence of Inry's chamber, turned left. Past the low-angled windows that opened onto the night orchard, for though it was daytime, her memories painted that place, provided a map for her to follow. Imprints of Voirrey and Davina ran with her, stared at the sliver of light beneath Lilwenn's door. Behind her, Domhnall almost vanished away. She turned fiery eyes on him and he shrank before her, receding and growing young until he was that man again. Ruddy and cocksure, intoxicated by Inry's perfumed curls, in the days before his children, in the days before...

His face grew dusty and vague. There was a fire between them, a campfire in a cave. She looked around her–moonlight, firelight–in the mountains of Jokvour. Domhnall's face came and went, a flickering apparition in his dark travelling cloak. There was her father talking to him, a cupped hand whispering into an absence where Domhnall's face should be...

Domhnall had flooded her mind with shared memories from before the Purge, anything to keep from having to open Edlin's door. She did not fight him, knowing she could not press him too hard.

In Jokvour, the young Domhnall stared, his face squirming between its aspects, settling in a horrifying countenance, deathlike and pale. An old man, luridly aged, a distortion of Domhnall's features–not him at all. His dying father, this must be.

Domhnall's hands clawed at this face, crumbled it into dust that left wafting clouds in the night air. Sybilla's father watched her, with flames in his eyes. Her lost foot kindled, her leather boot sucking tight to her flesh. Flames shivered through her, bright and evil, transforming her body into a promontory fire, a torch on high among the ruins of Velspar.

Between the leaping flames she caught him, the young Domhnall. He turned, dropped his cloak, and then it was a boy who was running. A boy stumbling down the jagged rocks, running from his father's wrath, from fate and burdens too heavy to bear, from all the things he thought he wanted. Running for his life.

Sybilla clutched her leg, grit her teeth in pain. The room smelt of damp stone and breadcrumbs, of that sad bearded man. She rubbed her eyes, trying to regain her bearings. Domhnall's head was in his hands.

Shame hung about them, in what he had failed to do, and in the secret parts of him that she had seen.

"I need a drink," he said abruptly and stood.

Sybilla listened to his footsteps, the pop of the cork, a swigging sound.

She smashed the table with her fist. "Dammit!"

Every time they tried this, it was the same result. They made it to the hall, past Inry's bedroom and then... timelines fell apart. Though she had to admit that they had made it a little further this time. They had turned. They had seen Lilwenn's door.

Sybilla craned her neck around the frame, tried to see where Domhnall had gone. He sat in his throne, no doubt, and wouldn't see her until he was good and drunk. He would sit there marinating, slurring at shadows, until the need to piss brought him stumbling to the chamber pot.

Sybilla hopped to the window and sat at the small table, determined now to focus her mind elsewhere. She watched the clouds, thin and rippled on high, and stormy out at sea. She could see the guardsmen out on patrol but kept herself aloof of them. She watched the grass, like velvet, with its short and silken fibres. The window's edge gifted her vague scents, distant cook fires and sweet flowers. In the end she could not tell if she smelled the lilies of the hill with her senses or her memory.

Thoughts of Inry took her back to the task at hand and in her mind, she said to Domhnall what she did not dare to say aloud. *Your son is dying and he is right there down the hall. He is there, within your reach. You must find him before it is too late.*

She heard him groan. A horrible sound, a wound she had opened in him.

She left off, shifted her thoughts so she would not have to bear his tears. She knew, more than anyone, what it was to be powerless to protect the ones she loved. It was cruel the way she prodded him, taking the art of healing that Voirrey had taught her and fashioning it into a key. She did feel for him, but what of her own grief? It hovered above her like a layer of smoke, numbing and insidious. It had forced her into the deepest extremities of her being, had cracked her shell. But still, she could not face it. In her mind–in reality as she lived it– Voirrey and Davina were neither living nor dead. They were within her, presences that guided her, because she must arrive at her destination. The mission was everything. The end point that required everything of her if she was to escape.

38

MAGLORE

Voirrey scrambled up the branches, Davina climbing close to the trunk.

The dogs, she could hear the dogs, and Sybilla screaming. Awareness of her hands and feet paled at that sound. *Hold on, hold on.* She gave herself the order, forced her heart to retreat from the sound. It came back. A swarm about her. *Sybilla!*

Davina's startled face came into view, the whites of her eyes showing all around, her dark hair disappearing into the leaves. Voirrey came to her senses and eased herself closer to the girl. She touched her back briefly, tried to smile, but tears choked her. That scream. *Sybilla–please you must live. How will we get out of this?*

Voirrey looked past her feet to the ground. The guards had not followed them and as she focused, she could hear hoarse voices at the other end of the field. "Inry!" one called, then the other. "Inry! Don't do anything silly now." The difference in tone was like the swinging of a pendulum. They followed, and there was menace in their tone, but little sense of urgency. This told her that they must be confident their escaped charges would be picked up further on. How thickly did their patrols run?

A whistle peeped from the other direction, sounding several

times, and Sybilla's voice grew quiet. Voirrey knew she should flee but could not leave. She listened, set her listening to the burning silence that was wind and leaves, that was grass and insects calling–the textures of life that got in the way of what she needed to hear.

Softly, a voice. "Back now. Sit, boy. We're taking this one."

The sound of torn fabric, then quiet. Eventually she heard him grunt with effort, and guessed he was lifting her, would carry her back. Take her to Rayhmer.

Voirrey remained frozen in the branches. She listened, heard the guardsman's voices moving farther away, the horses set loose, the dogs barking in wild circles, faster than her feet could run.

Beside her, a trickling sound caught her and she turned to see Davina had wet herself.

She closed her eyes a moment, remembering the child.

There was no way she could leave her here alone. "Vina, we're going to move through the branches and go that way." She pointed north-east, moving away from Inry and Lilwenn.

The trees were old and high, and they made good progress before the branches lay beyond their grasp. Distance was the only protection she could offer the child even if their progress felt like betrayal. She had left Sybilla, had left her with their enemies, injured and without ally. It was almost too much to bear.

Davina's arms and legs were scratched and she had pushed her little muscles to their limit. The past two tree crossings had almost seen her fall.

"Okay, stop. We will come down very quietly and see if we can walk from here. But if you see anyone, you just climb as high as you can."

Davina nodded.

As Voirrey's foot touched the earth the expression of nerves seemed to make the woodland sing her presence aloud. She froze, looked about slowly in all directions. The Guard had not found them and could not see them here. Voirrey took off her Meridian, bound it around her arm. Davina slid down, her crumpled face full of shame. She held her damp, dirt-smudged hands either side, and could not wipe them clean on her wet dress.

Voirrey crouched in front of her, whispered, "You cannot worry about this, Vina. Wipe your hands on my skirt, it's okay."

Davina shook her head violently, the coming tears making her shoulders seize up about her neck. The chicken soup smell of piss had taken on an unpleasant metallic tang from sitting on the skin too long, but Voirrey had ceased to experience disgust at malfunctions of the human body. They were signs she could read, a language clearer than speaking.

Voirrey hugged her close and soon her squirming gave way to squeaking sobs. So much grief in her tiny body, her mother...

Voirrey had to think of her that way, had to force herself to think of her, not by name, but as the child's mother. If she thought of Sybilla in all that she was, she would drag the girl back with her to Maglore and to the vilest of deaths.

She considered their trajectory, knowing that if she could make it to Brivia, or even Lindesal, that they might yet rescue Sybilla. Her parents in Nothelm would not stand for this, and even if Peran was weak, he still commanded loyalty enough for his men to fight. Maglore could be brought low at her hand.

Clear of her Meridian, Voirrey turned her senses to their surroundings so she would be forewarned of attack. She held Davina's sticky hand, walking purposefully, knowing by the prevalence of ferns that there must be a water source nearby. Davina stopped sniffing after a while and there were no human sounds that Voirrey could detect beyond that of their own footfall.

They must have walked for close to an hour before Davina tripped and grazed her knee. Voirrey put her on her back and continued on but every time the child started to fall asleep, her arms would relax, so that Voirrey had to lean forward to keep her in place. After another hour of walking like that, Voirrey knew she could not go on. She went to her knees, whispered to Davina as she slid her off into the leaf litter. She led the child to a nook among the tree roots where they both lay down. Voirrey scattered leaves over their bodies, though such camouflage would only fool someone at a distance.

Sleep snatched her up with its weightless buzzing and its thickening silence. And in the warm dark, Sybilla was there. A presence. She was whole–Voirrey felt it. Or did she wish it?

She lives, Voirrey told herself. *She lives and I will save her.*

39

MAGLORE

CRUNCHING footsteps. Voirrey blinked the haze from her vision, heart pattering, pin-pointing their location. Davina was still fast asleep and Voirrey crouched in front of her, listening. There. Two figures in dark clothing. They did not look like guards.

The taller one had a stoop and had the slow movements of the aged. The shorter one, definitely young, occasionally took the elder's arm. They were not guards but they still had eyes to see and Voirrey did not doubt that they could get a message where it needed to go.

Remaining stock still, she resolved to conceal herself behind the trunk of the tree, with Davina somewhat hidden among the roots. Voirrey shifted her weight, moved agonisingly slow as she inched herself behind the trunk. It was no longer safe for her to peer around to map their location. Her heart thudded into the smooth bark at her back, listening to their meandering tread. They came ever closer, the rasping voice of the old man now audible and the piping reply of the youth. She could not make out the words but she soon realised that their call and response had shifted from its earlier pattern of conversation into a kind of chanting.

A bird cawed loudly above her, and she cursed, listening keenly in the silence that followed. The old man: "A child is welcome at my hearth."

The youth, "A child and a friend."

A brief pause, their slow steps crushing the leaves.

Again, the old man, "A child is welcome at my hearth."

The youth, "Aye, a child and a friend."

Could her Brivian allies have heard of her flight? It was possible if they had sent scouts to follow the Vaelnyri entourage.

"...a child and a friend." Came the youth's voice and Voirrey slid her head sideways, looking out from behind the tree. They were a small distance off. Davina's face was framed by dark hair, all too visible among the leaves.

The old man repeated his refrain and Voirrey's voice, choked with fear, came calling. "A child and a friend."

Their footsteps stopped abruptly.

"A friend is welcome at my hearth," the old man replied.

Voirrey came out from behind the tree, locking eyes with the man as she crouched beside Davina. "Whose friend?" she questioned with threat in her tone.

He closed his eyes, his gnarled hands clasped at his chest. "A friend and a child," he whispered.

40

MAGLORE

THEY SAT AT THE fireside in the old man's home. His name was Teppin. His grandson, Sam. They were friends of Inry. Teppin had been telling a story about his younger days when he worked for Inry's father. He had not been a kind man and had died years ago, but the old merchant had loved his Inry, had paraded her around the docks since she was Davina's age. And Inry had made many friends that way, friends who had not forgotten her, her beauty and her spark, in these long dark years.

Inry and Lilwenn were safe, he told her. Some small injuries, but their pursuers had not fared so well. Teppin's considerate descriptions "in front of the child" meant she could not determine the mechanics of their rescue. From what she could gather, Teppin's friends had killed the two already injured guards and their bodies had "vanished." Inry and Lilwenn were being looked after but they would need to leave that place soon. Voirrey and Davina needed to leave, that much was certain.

Teppin–whose shelter she very much appreciated–was a kind man, yet one prone to spontaneous outbursts that would leave him crying tears of joy. On this count, she feared his judgement was not sound, despite his good intention. But upon seeing Davina's bewildered, dirt-smeared face light up when he told his stories, she resolved to let her recover here a little longer. Sam, the grandson, was keen and industrious, preparing meals and tidying them away, helping the old man to his bed of an evening.

Davina, now bathed and clothed in a brown peasant's smock with cream embroidery about the collar, looked as a little girl should. She lay restful in Voirrey's arms, her combed hair petal-sweet from the bathing water Sam had prepared. She should live like this always, like Voirrey had wanted for her in Civit's Ridge. Not running from violent men, not propped upon a Skalens' throne, witness to death–endless death–in her name.

Voirrey watched Teppin, restless in his cot on the other side of the room. The low fire set his wrinkled face in relief, accentuating the obscure tilt of his ill-fitting Meridian. A deep frown burrowed shadows into his skin, and he rolled to one side, grimacing through whatever plagued him. Suddenly, his face changed, and Voirrey glanced away, thinking he had woken. Watching him once more, she saw that he was definitely asleep. His brows rose slowly in surprise, his mouth fell open, then pressed together in a gentle smile.

The sleeping man's smile remained as shining tears tracked his temples. She reminded herself not to drift too close. She could not take any more of other people's tragedy. It was there in the house, though she tried not to see. It was there in the carved toys–wooden piglets and frogs–that he gave Davina to play with. In the way he huddled on the side of the mattress, never crossing to the empty side, pulling the embroidered quilt up to his chin.

People were missing. People who should have lived.

Voirrey reached beneath the top layer of her skirt, feeling her pockets for the last of her supplies. She still had several vials and resolved to keep the rest for the times to come. But right now, she needed to rest in Velspar's embrace.

Gently, she pulled the stopper with her thumbnail, measured three drops beneath her tongue, and sealed it once more. Settling herself on the bedroll, Voirrey continued to watch the man, his face growing distant as the room took on a comforting softness. She felt herself let go, her body at peace here. This was a safe place after all.

And as her thoughts wandered, she felt as if some old woman

rocked her, stroked her hair, a woman whose dry hands smelt of violets, the creases of her fingers stained green. Teppin whistled a merry tune, and she could hear the cowbells softly ringing. While the old woman was here, there was no need for worry. No need for upset. There were strawberries in her apron, and a summer breeze blew through the doorway.

41

MAGLORE

Davina hugged Teppin's knee, nearly toppling him. He chuckled, patted her hair.

"You'll see old Teppin again. Don't you fear."

Davina stared up at him, eyes choked with tears. She held the carved piglet in her fist, the one with a little heart carved into its belly, her arms stiff by her sides.

The wet fields were quiet, dawn's chill enfolding them in mauve unreality.

"I don't want to go away," she wailed. "I want to stay here." She tugged Voirrey's hand trying to pull her back inside the cottage. The world around them remained still, even the birds had not woken with their morning cries.

Teppin bowed his head, Sam mirroring the old man's gesture as he looked regretfully at the ground.

"No, lass. I promised Skalen Inry, you see. A promise is a promise," he said.

Davina's grip loosened, and her head drooped in weary resignation. She let the piglet drop to the ground.

"No, oh no, child." Teppin said and tried to get himself down on one knee. Sam held him back and reached for the carving, holding it out to Davina.

Sam did not say much, but he spoke now, "Grampy Teppin carved three piglets, only three. They are very special, not something to throw away. You've got to keep this with you always, to remember us."

Davina looked up, nodded, and held out her hand.

"One is for little Asher," he went on, "one is for me, and one is for you. You've got to keep this little piglet so you'll never forget."

Voirrey sucked in a sharp breath and exhaled. They had to get moving. "Come on, Vina, we have to go now."

With relief she watched Davina take the carving from the boy's hand and put it in her pocket.

Teppin smiled. "I will stay here and keep the cows company. Sam will take you where you need to go." He waved and shuffled back into the cottage.

"Back soon, Grampy," Sam called. The young man smiled. "This way."

Voirrey and Davina followed him through the wet grass, moving back into the forest. The blue dress Voirrey now wore was beautifully embroidered, like Davina's, but in a simple style commonly worn by the farming women of Southern Velspar. She still wore her leather boots and had traded her old clothes for a travelling satchel. Teppin's garden had a good selection of herbs, and she now had the beginnings of a medicine kit. She had an ointment for infection and had been gifted a small measure of fever tincture, a valuable medicine that she would not have been able to distil without proper equipment.

Voirrey pulled Davina nearer, ensuring that they followed Sam's steps exactly. Glancing behind, she could see the cleft their footfall had left in the grass. When the dew lifted with the warmth of the sun, the grass would spring up and cover their tracks, but that would not be for another hour or so. They hurried on, Voirrey's toes cold in damp leather, her skirt dragging heavily.

They entered the thickest part of the forest as the sun came up, the previous night's rain still pattering from the canopy. Sam moved them tirelessly on, Voirrey's feet growing blistered and numb. He had offered to carry Davina and had done so for some time, but now it was her turn again.

"Nearly there," he puffed. Then, in a quieter tone to Voirrey, "She okay with dark places?"

Voirrey shrugged. She would have to be. There was only one way out.

They stopped to relieve themselves in the bushes, sat for a moment to eat some food from their pack, and followed Sam into a sort of clearing overrun with blackberry.

Sam reached into his pack and pulled out two leather cloaks. "Do you want me to take her through?" he asked Voirrey.

"Davina, can Sam carry you again? We have to cover ourselves so we don't get scratched by thorns." The precaution was not only to preserve their skin, but to ensure the thorns did not collect fragments of their clothing.

The little girl nodded and climbed up on his back.

Voirrey helped drape the cloak and tied it loosely at the front.

"Might be a bit sweaty in there but we've got to keep the hood over you. Sorry." Sam used his walking stick to part the brambles.

Putting on her own cloak, Voirrey mirrored Sam step-for-step, moving close so the parted canes would allow her through. Still, she felt the thorns scrape the leather, scoring this false skin, and inevitably reaching her own in biting pricks and minor scratches. By the time they made it through the worst of it, her hands were covered in tiny lines that stung with purple juice.

Removing the cloaks, the three of them stood among overgrown scrub with barely a place to set their feet, but as Voirrey looked around, she saw the shadow beyond: the tunnel that was to take them to safety.

Thirsty, and well aware that the water skin Voirrey carried would not take them far, she fed Davina as many blackberries as she could manage, stuffing dark clusters into her own mouth, trying not to bite down on the seeds. Her stomach was a twisted knot and she could hardly distinguish the sweet from the tart–all was bitter fuel for their journey.

Sam came close to Voirrey, spoke low. "If the tunnel has collapsed, you will have to come back, and if that happens, you should move north-east through the forest to join the river north of the town. If you do get through, there will be a boat waiting for you on the other side."

Voirrey searched his face. How could he be sure? A tunnel such as this could not remain secret for long, though it was well concealed.

"And if we must go further up river?" she asked.

"It will be more difficult for us to leave a boat where you are sure to find it. The less time you spend wandering the riverbank the better," he said.

Sam looked at Davina and pressed his lips into a smile. "Safe travels."

The sounds of his departure were careful and sparing, a boy who had been raised hunting game.

Voirrey checked her pocket for the tapers Sam had given her and drew out her flint stone.

Davina's eyes were ringed with fear and she had taken herself as far from the tunnel's opening as was possible without moving into the blackberry vines.

Voirrey bent down and removed both of their Meridians, held the girl's hand. Davina had become used to this by now and knew what to do. Their foreheads touched and Voirrey began to draw the heat from her, the vibration of her terror like a mouse shivering in her hand.

When Voirrey opened her eyes, Davina was okay again. The redness Voirrey had taken remained beneath her skin, a toxin that made her feel sick and irritable and if they had not been on the run, she would have screamed just to feel some kind of release. As it was, they had to keep going, so Voirrey lit the taper and took her hand.

Inside, the air rushed cool on her cheeks, giving her hope that the tunnel remained clear. Davina walked beside her like a sleepwalker, the taper illuminating as much as it blinded, leaving its hot wax in searing drips on her fingers.

Voirrey, with all the pain that lurked beneath the surface of her mind, decided that it was too late for fear, too late to wonder what was on the other side. They had entered. Their fate already given to Velspar's mercy, and the river's tide.

42

PASSAGE TO BRIVIA

Voirrey ran, swift and quiet, with Davina's small arms almost choking her. Ankle deep in freezing water, her numb fingers untied the rope. Plonking Davina into the boat, she levered herself in, the craft tipping precariously.

She set the paddles and began to row in awkward shaking movements, cowering in the accusatory light of day. The rope trailed stripes in the water. No arrow came whistling toward them, no guardsmen flocked to the shore. They were alone–as far as she could see with the peasant's hood about her head.

The current ran weakly this part of the River Nanthe. She rowed and rowed, grew tired, and began to sweat in her cloak. The whole time, Davina's face was blank, like one of Teppin's carvings, a face frozen and numb. Voirrey tried not to notice the girl's hands fiddling with the piglet figurine. She was taking her away again. To what safety? She commanded nothing here. No armies, no allies.

When the riverbank showed only lush grass and thickening trees, she took off her cloak, passing her hand over her sweat-covered brow. Crickets creaked the song of high noon, and light gleamed off the water.

Already, she was sunburnt, and Davina's cheeks were rough.

"Are you thirsty, Vina?" she asked.

The girl nodded.

At the end of the boat was a piece of sackcloth with something under it. She rifled through the disordered objects: a fisherman's hook, a net, and with relief she spied a set of wooden cups. Her throat ached for water, but she knew Davina could not swim so did not want to risk upending the boat by leaning too far over the side.

With an irritable urgency in her veins, Voirrey tied the cup handle to a length of twine, tested the knot, and lowered it down into the river. With a quick tug, she drew up the half-filled cup and swallowed its contents with an involuntary gasp. She filled it again and passed it to Davina. Her poor chapped lips curved about the cup and she swallowed with that same gasping reaction. How could she let the child grow so thirsty? Voirrey felt a pang of conscience.

She refilled the cup and both of them drank again.

Davina had never been this quiet. In Civit's Ridge she cried and screamed, laughed, and threw tantrums. She was curious and stubborn–sneaky at times. Now it was as if the child's soul was a kite hovering a small distance from her body, the blank expression on her face the only sign that she still held tight to the string.

It was a matter of survival. Voirrey knew this.

"Vina, put this over you to keep the sun off," she said and shaded her with the hood of her cloak.

Voirrey took up the oars and continued to row, watching with eerie fascination as the Brivian forest turned golden in the afternoon light.

She rowed like this, on and on, until the rhythm stole her bearings.

At some point, between the movement of the oars, and her weary moments of rest, Voirrey felt the current take hold. The Brivian wilderness loomed about her on either side, the orange blaze of sunset dissolving into black.

Voirrey could not row anymore. She simply could not go on. Her head hung in desolation, her hands limp at her sides.

They had fled into an abyss.

Davina, who had sat balled up in Voirrey's discarded cloak, stirred and crawled over to hug her aunty's belly. Voirrey's tears came in deep shuddering breaths. Davina held tight to her, patting her hip with her tiny hand.

How will we survive this? Voirrey thought. *We are lost! Lost! Sybilla... how could I leave you behind? And Amand, where did you go?* She called to him in the old way, called his name, and waited.

A light breeze stirred the water. Crickets in the leafy dark. She sniffed, sighed, tried to calm her tears. Tried to listen.

Amand, she called, urgent and strong.

Nothing.

Sybilla, please, Sybilla hear me...

For the barest moment she felt her presence, as if she'd passed her in the street. Fleeting and gone.

For the first time in her life, Voirrey felt that she had been given more than she could take. She held Davina's warm body close. If Voirrey did not keep her from harm she would die like this, a flower bud, secret and unknowable. To die out here, in this nothingness, seemed the worst fate of all.

Voirrey cursed herself for letting an addled old man give her advice. Still, they had made it this far. He had told her that Inry and Lilwenn had escaped. That they would be waiting at the shore for them when morning came.

She was tired, so very tired.

"Vina," she croaked. "Have you ever seen stars like this before?"

They shuffled down, deep in the boat.

Davina nestled close. "The moon is glowing," she said with her dry voice. "It has a rainbow."

"Sleep now, darling," Voirrey said, unable to keep her eyes open any longer.

There was nothing she could do. A prayer began in her mind, *Davina, please, Davina...* but sleep was already closing in.

43

BRIVIA

THE SUN RAGED, bonfire bright and all-seeing. There was no shelter, no reprieve, no end to this burning; this flame would not tire, this relentless light. The great unblinking eye of the sun continued to watch her, its vigil unbroken since the beginning of time.

End it, she prayed. *Hide me.*

In darkness, silence. In silence, rest. Davina was in her arms, and forever would remain there, the crescent moon and her tiny star.

Awaken! the light commanded. *Awaken!*

Her lids stirred. A squirm of colour.

The voice deepened. *Awaken*, it said, sounding familiar. *Awaken.*

The voice nudged at her memories, raised her face up.

"Voirrey, you must wake up. The child is here. Davina needs you. Come now." A man's voice, aged and strong.

With dawning realisation, she recognised the voice. Waldemar. Another voice, murmuring. Amand. *Oh*, her stomach tipped, her vision exploded into spots, and through the blinding chaos she sensed shadows, tall trees and damp earth, the weight of Davina's head still pillowed on her breast.

"Vina…" she tried to say, but her mouth was too dry.

"Wet that cloth and put it to her lips, Sidney. Yes, that's it, damp the lips."

A sensation like melting ice, a droplet coursing her cheek.

"Vina," she said again, husky like an old woman.

"Aunty," came the small voice quite close to her ear.

"My eyes," she said and tried to move her leaden hand.

"Take off the bandages Sidney, she is with us," Waldemar said.

Gentle hands fumbled about her face with a stench that made her gorge rise, and then in a flood there was colour, and there was light.

Her eyelids stung but she could see Davina's foggy outline–and Sidney, and Waldemar. It seemed her whole face was wet, and when she touched it, her fingers came away with traces of greenish gel.

Burned, she must have been burned very badly by the sun.

"Amand," she said, and moved to sit up.

She couldn't see him. He had been here.

Voirrey looked at Waldemar, disorientated by his changed appearance, the length of his wisping hair and beard. "Amand!" she cried, watching Waldemar's face. Sombre, unmoving, not jumping to explain.

"He was here," she whispered under her breath.

Waldemar's face twisted in real pain, and she felt it, his hand spread upon his heart. "We do not know where he is," he said.

"How can that be?" Voirrey's throat constricted. "He was here just a moment ago."

The Intercessor was crying, though he breathed evenly. "Part of him was here and has been with us for some time, but he will not tell me of his location. He has built a heavy ward around this and I must trust his judgement."

He wiped his eyes, and grew still, apparently collecting himself.

Like a change in the wind, Voirrey felt her emotions soften and grow distant, recognising at once the Intercessor's technique.

Take it away then, she thought. *I will find him on my own.*

Waldemar reached a hand to help her up. "What matters is that you are here, Voirrey. Thank Velspar for your return." He smiled.

Sitting upright, but too dizzy to stand, she moved her head to the side, noticing the wildman beside her. Sidney. Sidney Karasek.

Her mind was reeling.

Davina sat cross-legged beside her, in the same dress as before but wearing a crown of vine leaves. Her lips were scabbed, and there was a sore on her cheek daubed with the same gel that covered her own face.

"How did you find us?" she asked, that haze of unreality clinging to her so that she could not be sure that this was not a dream. She could be dying right now, out there in the boat, her mind dancing absurd pirouettes, snatching up people and places, trying to hold onto something.

Waldemar looked down, tapped his hand to his heart. "If you felt him here, then perhaps you will believe my story after all." He crouched down before her and eased his old bones to the ground. "Voirrey, it was Amand who led us here, to you."

Her heart started up again, bubbling in her chest. "What else do you know? You must know something of him."

Waldemar raised his hand. "He wants only for your safety and for that of the girl. He does not want me to pass into his suffering."

Her breath caught. "Suffering?"

Waldemar smiled ruefully. "An Intercessor can bear more suffering than you can know. And when I have delivered you to safety, I will go to him, wherever he hides. I swear this to you."

This was Amand's way and knowing the truth of it, she felt strangely comforted. Waldemar was probably the only person who could find Amand. Now that her emotions had eased a little, she saw the value of this moment. Waldemar was a powerful Intercessor whose help could be crucial to her in the times to come. She must show him her good intentions and bind him to her plans.

Waldemar drew some cured fish from his pack, folding it in a thick orange strip of fruit or vegetable–she could not tell. He passed a portion to her and Davina, then held out a handful of seeds drawn from his pocket. Her body screamed for nourishment and she had to fight the urge to shove the whole lot into her mouth. Pouring the seeds into the pool of her skirt, she started on the fish, tasting little but salt.

"Are there others here?" Voirrey asked, wondering if Inry and Lilwenn had arrived as Teppin promised.

"Allies?" Waldemar asked. "Oh yes. We will be able to find safe shelter for you."

Voirrey looked around, seeing nothing but forest in all directions.

Waldemar went on, "We keep to ourselves. They do not know we are here, but there are settlements south of Lake Nanthe where the guardsmen seldom visit."

Settlements. Not an army, not anything that could be brought to bear against Rayhmer's forces. Just people, hiding among the trees, hoping to evade capture.

He focused on her. "Where is it that you want to go?"

She could feel the pressure of his attention all about her head but was too tired to erect her inner wards. Now that her senses were returning to her, she knew that he had taken her Meridian to keep the channel between them clear.

There was no point in concealment, not now, when she needed his help and trust.

She shifted position, the seeds almost tipping into the dirt. "Come, Davina, eat these with me."

She scooped them up and let half trickle down into Davina's hands.

Voirrey ate the seeds, collecting her thoughts.

"We were in Civit's Ridge, as you know. Amand went missing and not long after that Edric came from Nothelm, calling Sybilla to Vaelnyr to deal with the Maglorean presence there."

Waldemar nodded and Voirrey went on with her story, telling him of Peran's ailment, of Andrin's death, and the horrors of Maglore. After her first stumble, she referred to Sybilla not by name but as the 'Skalen of Vaelnyr'–knowing how he hated her–and relayed Teppin's fragmentary account of Inry and Lilwenn's escape.

Once he and Sidney had eaten their meagre rations, Waldemar sat back and packed his pipe. Voirrey shivered, finding the slightest breeze feverish to her skin despite the warmth of the day. Sidney exhumed a coal wrapped in grass and broad leaves, using it to start up a small fire. Distracted, Voirrey felt Davina leave her side.

She turned, hearing the child urinating behind a tree.

Voirrey could not help but notice the change in her. She had learned to see to her own needs without the help of adults, and the brutal necessity of silence. Davina did not return to her lap but wandered about nearby, inspecting a patch of spotted fungi with a stick. Voirrey watched the girl's face, a version of her future self residing there–so precious, so perilous–and then, just as quickly, the moment faded.

"She'll not wander far," Waldemar said, as if he were expert in Davina's ways.

Voirrey watched him as he started up the pipe, his bushy eyebrows high as he puffed at the smoke.

"Have some," he said, holding his breath.

She nodded and took the pipe, smoke roiling from his nostrils in wide plumes.

Voirrey took a scorching draw, and with another breath, a feeling arose in her–of homeliness and comfort, of rightness and peace. She smiled at Sidney, noticing his eyes for the first time as she handed him the pipe.

Waldemar spoke. "If Inry and Lilwenn are here in Brivia, I will find them. But the question remains: where are you all to go now that things have taken a turn in Maglore?"

Voirrey went to scratch her face and realised the gel was still there, and began wiping it instead with the hem of her skirt.

"I had not thought that far ahead. For now, I just need Davina to be safe," she said.

Waldemar collected the pipe from Sidney's outstretched hand and sucked on it once more.

"You could remain hidden in the Brivian wilderness for the rest of your lives. That is the truth. They will never civilise this place. Even Orenholm has given itself up to the vines."

He offered the pipe to her but she refused, feeling dizzy and a little nauseous from the fish she'd eaten.

The Intercessor continued. "You could remain in Brivia, but I think you have a greater plan here, Voirrey."

A sharp pain lanced her stomach and she doubled over.

He reached his hand to steady her and she waved him away. "I'm okay. It is passing. Just feel a little sick."

He blew smoke into the filtered light above, the shaft interrupted by a pair of darting parrots.

"Maeryn is in Avishae. She will help you," he said, a vague bitterness in his voice.

Voirrey looked at Davina, wondering how she would fare in Brivia if taken in by one of the forest families. It did not seem right. This place, so wild, and yet far too close to Maglore. Waldemar was right, now that she was here, Avishae did seem the safer haven.

"Could you get us there? To Avishae?"

He closed his eyes and smiled.

44

BRIVIA

Voirrey and Davina followed the boy through the trees, amazed at his blackened feet, and how he moved from rock to branch to earth. Davina took to the task with relative ease, and Voirrey wondered if, in time, she could learn the forest as the Brivians did.

Ahead, Voirrey made out a smattering of huts, though she still found it strange that nothing in this place could be seen from a distance. All was hidden and woven in, pocketed among the trees.

The boy peeled back a branch to let her pass. "There she is, Miss."

A short distance away, Voirrey saw a thin woman sitting on a log with her back turned. She wore peasant's clothing, her hair shrouded in a brown wrap.

Voirrey grasped Davina's hand, not trusting to leave her with anybody, even Waldemar. She felt nervous, as if when the woman turned, she would not have the right face.

"Hello?" Voirrey called.

Warily, the woman turned.

Inry, oh Inry, it is you, she thought, and rushed forward.

It was a moment before she looked up.

Her breath caught at the sight of Davina, a look of shock passing over her as if the girl were a phantom. Then Lilwenn was there, wrapping the child in her arms, laughing and squeezing her like a lost puppy returned home.

"This is unbelievable," Inry breathed, finding Voirrey and glancing behind her where the boy had disappeared.

They waited until Lilwenn and Davina moved out of hearing.

"Sybilla?" she whispered.

Voirrey shook her head. "The dogs–" she began, swallowing hard.

Inry held her gaze, careful not to rouse Davina's attention away from Lilwenn who was showing her how to extract seeds from large, fleshy pods.

Recognising Voirrey's difficulty, Inry looked down at her hands. "If she survived, they will have her in the Skalen's House by now."

An inner numbness kept Voirrey from shuddering. If she allowed herself to think of Sybilla at all, she would not be able to go through with the plan.

Inry sniffed, scratching her thumbnail. "Degore is dead. I would not worry about her in that way. Rayhmer will keep her alive as long as she holds value, and he has not played his cards yet."

Inry knew Rayhmer better than anyone and though the thought of Sybilla twisted her gut, these words secured her resolve, helped her to feel that hope was warranted.

Voirrey took in the dark rings under Inry's eyes, the frail elegance of her dirt-stained fingers.

"Let us walk," Voirrey suggested. Then, understanding Inry's worried glance, she assured her that they would not allow the children out of their sight.

The two women strolled together, circling their charges at a distance.

"You must wonder how I found you," Voirrey started.

Inry shook her head. "I wonder at nothing anymore. We just keep running and no one has stopped us. All I can think is that I have one more day with my daughter."

Voirrey stepped lightly through the ferns, not ready to speak.

Inry went on. "It is a terrifying feeling. I keep running, but it feels like I have leapt from a cliff, and I'm waiting to hit the bottom. They find us, or they don't, my son lives, or he doesn't. All I can do now is keep Lilwenn near and try not to lose my nerve." Inry's eyes were fearful, and her fingers gnawed at a stray thread at her wrist.

"You are right, Inry. Nothing is certain," Voirrey said. She sifted her thoughts: she felt bonded with the Greslets now, even if she could not share all that she felt. She could not speak about Sybilla.

She took a deep breath. "Nothing is certain, but I do have a plan. I want you and Lilwenn to come to Avishae with Davina and me. I think you will be safer there."

Inry's eyes seemed to say, *Brivia, Avishae, what is the difference?*

"And what is the rest of the plan?" Inry asked.

"I know my parents have spared little thought for the Southlands in recent years, but once they understand the extent of Rayhmer's corruption, they will act. I have just come from Vaelnyr and the Guard there are eager to throw off the Maglorean yoke. And it is not just that. I have allies here, as you do." Voirrey tried to read Inry's expression. "Not just friends who would keep me hidden, but friends who in recent years have kept their own counsel and who might easily be judged as heretics."

Inry glanced at Lilwenn and Davina as she spoke. "I have had my suspicions about my Brivian hosts, but now you confirm it for me. I think in the past I would have quailed at the thought, but here I am, and here they are, giving me shelter."

"I am glad you see it that way," Voirrey said. "The Elshenders in Avishae, your sister-in-law and her husband in Brivia, even Haldi and Moriel in Lindesal–they all want an end to the ways of the Purge. No more heresy, no more Meridians. They await their moment and when the Braedal and Vaelnyri forces come from above, the Southlands will squeeze Rayhmer out."

Inry tilted her face upward, searching the dark lacework of the canopy. "And the Askier?" she asked.

"They will fall where circumstances lean, just as they have always done. If I can just make it home, I can bring forces and put things right."

Inry's tone grew cold. "You speak of war, of the Maglorean yoke... What of my people? What of Teppin–and Sybilla–and my son?"

Voirrey flushed. "If we succeed, it will be the Maglorean Guard who are put to the sword. The Guard must cleanse their ranks. I will do everything I can to keep your people safe but there are no guarantees. In truth, I do not know what the Counsel of Skalens will do in a case like this, but believe me, I will do anything to get Sybilla and Edlin out." She pointed a reddening hand at Davina. "That child will not be made an orphan because of me."

Inry was silent and they continued walking, their dizzying track reminding Voirrey of the bandages she once rolled, one after another, by the fire in Civit's Ridge.

"I know you mean well," Inry said in a faraway voice. "And maybe it will work. I have no ready alternative."

"It has to work," Voirrey said with conviction.

"I'm tired of walking in circles, aren't you?" Inry said with the barest hint of a smile.

She looked over to where Lilwenn sat, carefully balancing a leaf on Davina's head. "Yes. It is ridiculous, I know. I just love to see them together. Like sisters."

The women stopped to watch the game. The leaf had fallen onto the ground and now it was Davina's turn. She collected a handful of leaves and placed one on Lilwenn's head. Immediately, it slipped from the young woman's ebony hair. Davina hastily added more, cackling as they fell. She threw handfuls and Lilwenn followed suit.

Inry sighed. "How long until we leave this place? Have you people to take us to Avishae? I am working with borrowed allegiances here and do not have anyone but you as a friend."

Despite the many things she had told Inry, she realised that the woman perhaps did not know the rebels harboured Intercessors. Ones from before the Purge.

"Inry... there is something I have not told you. This may be difficult for you but we travel with an Intercessor. A true Intercessor."

As expected, the Skalen's face paled.

"And that is not all," Voirrey went on. "There is another, in Avishae. It is their protection that shields us. They are the reason I can have faith in my plan. They are powerful allies, Inry."

The woman's lips parted but no words came. It seemed a torrent of memories flooded her, dulling her vision of the here and now.

She swallowed dryly. "How can you trust them?"

Voirrey gave her a look of understanding. It must be terrifying for her, to face one such as Waldemar or Maeryn after needlessly slaughtering thousands of their brethren. After trying to wipe them from the earth.

"I trust them because they work for the good of those I love," Voirrey said. This was not quite true, but it was what she needed Inry to hear. "Of all those who draw breath in Velspar, who should they hate more than Sybilla?"

Inry shook her head, having no answer.

"When Davina was a babe, the Intercessors stood with Sybilla in the mountains of Jokvour and proved to me that they walked the path of forgiveness and peace. Even Sybilla, they forgave. Even Sybilla." Uttering these words, Voirrey shivered. Tears streamed from Inry's eyes, these words accessing the deep water of her soul, a guilt so well hidden that even she did not realise its ongoing power.

Lilwenn turned at the sound of her mother's crying but the woman could not stop.

"Oh, Voirrey..." she whispered. "I'm cursed. All of my family are cursed. For what we did to them!"

Voirrey stepped forward, dared to place a comforting hand on her arm. "There is no curse, Inry, not anymore. You'll see."

Inry's sucked in a breath, wiping her eyes. "When must we leave?"

Voirrey looked about them, through the weave of the trees. "As soon as we can."

It was dark and Voirrey waited in the abandoned fort, dew dripping on the timbers in a slow staccato rhythm. Davina was asleep on the boards and Sidney was out communing with the horses. Waldemar sat opposite her, sunk deep in trance, his shadowed posture reminding her achingly of Amand.

She stood and looked over the railing, staring in the direction of the settlement. Dully, she listened to the forest's symphony. The crickets and frogs, the whirring of unseen wings. The plash of leaves as shadowed creatures leapt from branch to branch.

Who knew what was out there? She felt blind. All that spacious detail hidden within the silhouettes of ancient trees. Occasionally, she saw movement and looked in that direction, but her sight was too weak. And whenever she heard the mumbling of Sidney's voice or the huff of the horses, her attention receded, drawing her back from the forests' depths.

This fort, this little structure, gave her the sense that she was set apart from the wilderness out there. That she was safe. Still, the water dripped and mosses grew, and soon these timbers would be soft enough to crumble. The fort would thunk in pieces to the wet earth and in a season or two, new shoots would grow, until there was nothing left at all. Brivia was a strange place, wild and green, where people were made small in the scheme of things.

Small, she felt, in comparison to the task before her. So very small.

Voirrey watched the dark glint of water on wood, the grey ferns beneath her. Was it that her eyes had adjusted, or was the darkness fading?

Something caught her eye down on the forest floor, and lazily, she turned her face. This time, she saw what she had been waiting for.

They emerged from the trees. Two cloaked figures, slender as wraiths, a wrapped bundle carried between them by lengths of rope.

Voirrey whistled. Soft, like birdsong.

Pale faces upturned in her direction.

A shiver passed through her as Inry whistled back.

45

BRIVIA

SIDNEY MUMBLED something to Waldemar, pointing the way they should go. The horses were barely making any progress, turned around by swathes of low vines and patches of marshy ground. Voirrey shared a glance with Inry, wondering if they would ever make the coast. Lilwenn, for her part, did not look at anyone, save Davina. Having seen into the girl's soul, Voirrey knew the fortifications she was building inside. Against the Intercessor and his wildman, against the men in the Brivian settlements.

On horseback, Lilwenn rode at the front of the double-saddle, wearing her mother like a protective cloak.

Sidney's horse shied and Voirrey instinctively crouched, expecting guardsmen.

"Snake," Waldemar assured them, sounding little concerned. "A big one, but he's moving off. Pull up and wait a moment."

Sidney shushed his mount, the horse moving awkwardly back.

Waldemar sighed. "I think this is a good place to leave the horses anyway. They do not do well without a wide track."

Voirrey tried to rouse her body from numbness, the seemingly endless ride having rocked her into a stupor. She nudged Davina. "We need to hop off now, darling."

Once they dismounted, Sidney walked the horses off into the

trees. She prayed that he knew where he was going. There were no landmarks here that she could see, no rock in the shape of such-and-such, no wide-branched tree on a hill. The vines and ferns seemed to grow by the day, transforming and uncurling, great trees of the past collapsing on their neighbours, leaving wounds for wet rot. The forest seemed to digest itself, and as they passed through it, they were at the mercy of its hungers.

"Waldemar," she called. "The day is growing dim, do you think it safe to sleep here?"

Voirrey glanced at Inry and Lilwenn who leaned wearily against a tree, their clothes filthy and damp.

The Intercessor sighed, packing his pipe. "I too am weary and must consider our direction from here. I sense people nearby but I do not know if they are the friends we are searching for."

Voirrey nodded and turned to Inry. "If you can find a dry spot to sit, we will rest here until Sidney returns. Waldemar is deciding our direction."

Inry nodded, holding up the fabric of her skirt as she touched the damp roots of a large tree. She urged Lilwenn to sit down.

As Voirrey took Davina to relieve herself, she sipped her water skin and thought of Lilwenn: how grey her face, how dead her eyes when Davina was away from her. Her tormentor was dead, Andrin having given his life for this, but Voirrey wondered if there had been others. She wondered if, without Intercession, Lilwenn could be free at all. She would not ask Waldemar to do it, though it was in his power. Maeryn would be better suited to the task.

Waldemar struggled to light his pipe, finding the coal he carried had almost died of humidity. After a few false starts, he roused the spark and puffed at his pipe staring fixedly through the trees. She watched his face, waiting for the moment of decision but his frown only deepened.

Hearing shuffling, she turned, stiffening, marking Davina's distance from her and places to take cover.

She recognised Sidney's smell before she saw his dark figure, and overcome with relief, commenced to shake her body of the relentless tension that plagued her of late. Her neck was so stiff from the ride that she quickly regretted moving so freely, feeling her shoulder pang.

Sidney approached Waldemar and the two of them mumbled under their breath.

The Intercessor tapped out his pipe and pointed it through the trees.

"That is the way we want to go," he said, tugging on his beard. "We should go as far as we can before dark. That way, we will be able to make the straight tomorrow." He looked behind him. "Okay, let us go."

Voirrey took Davina on her back and the group fell in behind the Intercessor.

They stopped to drink and chew their meagre travel rations over the intervening hours, moving to the forest's strange choreography of angled steps, twists, and curtseys, the little ups and downs and skirting circles that the animals here knew by instinct.

Still, Waldemar did not stop, and Voirrey fixed her sight on the dull shape of his silver hair knowing that he would only take them this far by dusk if there was good reason for it.

Then, without warning, he stopped.

Voirrey glanced about to check that Inry and Lilwenn were close. She could sense little with her Meridian on, and with Davina on her back she could not very well remove it. In the drip and rustle of the forest, she strained to listen, and then she smelt it–woodsmoke. After a moment, she heard a man's voice and distant laughter.

Waldemar's hand, barely visible, pointed and held up four fingers. Then, when she thought he would urge them back, he spun his finger to indicate their surrounds and held up three fingers. Travelling guardsmen, then.

Could he stave off the attention of seven men? And how would they find their way to safety once they lost the light? He turned to them and made a down motion with his hand. Voirrey let Davina slide off her back and ushered her near, lowering onto her belly. Inry and Lilwenn were right beside them and lay within arm's reach.

Waldemar and Sidney moved off, their quiet noises now indistinguishable from those of the forest. Voirrey felt the wet earth imparting its cool touch from breasts to thighs, and she dreaded a night spent here if the Intercessor did not return. Voirrey reached out her arm to hold Inry's hand, slipping her Meridian. She could sense Waldemar, but only indistinctly. The guardsmen–when they grew quiet around their fire–she could not sense at all.

Inry pressed her hand in return, and was holding herself still, but Voirrey found herself increasingly distracted by Lilwenn's breathing. She sensed the tightness of the girls' throat, the pace of her heart, and Voirrey's own breath began to move in sympathy. She reappointed her Meridian, resting her head on her forearm. She had to trust Waldemar, she had to wait.

Time dragged by and with it went the light. Voirrey blinked and could barely discern the difference between open and closed, such was the pervading darkness. She chanced to raise her head above the fern cover and could see the faint glow of the guardsmen's fire in the distance.

There was a cry, coming from the opposite direction, and in yet another direction, the sound of scuffling. Shouts arose from the main group and there was a great commotion in the trees. Even if they brought torches, they would be fire-blind, she told herself.

A gurgling scream. Too close. And off in the distance, the clash of steel. Death screams.

Voirrey grit her teeth. *Be silent, be still, we are nothing, do not find us.*

She smelt Sidney, knew that he could not sense them as Waldemar did. She could hear him grappling from tree to tree with heavy breath.

She licked her lips, tried to remember the exact sound of the night bird's whistle. The sound from her lips made her cringe in fear.

Sidney returned the whistle, and soon enough she felt his patting hands feeling the earth beside her.

"He is hurt," Sidney whispered in his deep, rasping voice.

"Are they dead?" she returned.

"All dead. More than we thought," he said.

"We do not need to whisper then?" she asked.

She suspected from the pause that Sidney was shaking his head, but finally he confirmed this with words. "There is no one to hear us. Leave the child and come." He tugged on her arm.

"Wait," she said. "How far?"

"Not far," Sidney said.

Whatever that could mean. She sat up, taking Davina's hand and placing it in Inry's. "I will return. Stay here."

"Please Voirrey, don't go!" Inry whispered.

Voirrey knew her fear but could not give herself a moment to doubt. Without Waldemar, they would never make it to Avishae.

"Davina, you will be safe here with Inry and Lilwenn. The worst is passed," she said with all the assurance she could muster.

The girl started to cry, and Voirrey did not stop to shush her. She must be allowed to cry sometimes.

Sidney had already started to move off, impatient to get to Waldemar.

Voirrey followed, seeing that he moved in the general direction of the fire.

She did not know what she trod on but felt living things scatter from her path, and as her hands grappled the tree trunks, she touched upon cool scales that she hoped were beetles. Her arms mapped the way before her, though still she bumped into branches, passing through sticky spiderwebs that made her whisk her hands through her hair.

She followed the sound of Sidney's footsteps and wheezing breaths. He tapped the tree trunks with a stick as he passed. She returned the sound with the side of her fist until she could snap off a tree branch of her own.

All the way, it seemed, she trudged through deepening space, surprised by the level of the ground, and the absence of things she expected to touch.

Eventually, the fire's glow brought form to her surrounds and she moved more quickly, the scent of blood making her skin prickle. Several bodies lay sprawled, their expressions frozen in agony where they fell. One guard still held the sword that he had plunged into his comrade's belly and Voirrey knew this to be the Intercessor's work.

The vibrant hiss of the fire carried on, the damp timbers boiling off thick smoke.

Sidney moved before her, stepping over the bodies, leading her around to the other side. There, Waldemar lay, breathing the shallow breaths of a body in great pain. Voirrey knelt beside him.

"Waldemar," she said gently.

His eyes snapped open and he seized her arm.

"I had them, I don't know what happened. I had them," he said, eyes wide.

She ignored the pressure of his fingers, scanning his body for injuries. The worst she could see was a deep wound in his upper arm that had bled profusely into the dirt.

From her pocket she drew out her cleansing tonic, poured it directly over the wound so that his fingers dug into her flesh.

There was little in the way of clean cloth anywhere in this place but she had to keep pressure on the wound. She considered burning it shut. Hesitatingly, she drew out the butter knife she had taken from the breakfast table in Maglore. She held it to the flame. With the other hand, she pinched the wound tightly and though blood still flowed from it, the pressure she exerted had some effect.

Voirrey pressed the scalding metal hard against his skin as the old man shook with agony showing all of his teeth. Sidney paced nearby, his underlit face looking young and fearful.

He looked at her, wanting to help.

"Only with clean hands, Sidney. Best I keep the pressure." Her hands were fully occupied with the task.

"If you can reach into this pocket here..." She gestured with her eyes, "I have Alma oil that you can give him."

Sidney came by and pulled out one of Voirrey's last remaining vials. He sat above the Intercessor and took Waldemar's head in his lap. The old man held out his tongue, sweating and straining, but conscious enough to know that Sidney was about to give him relief.

After a little while the oil took effect and Waldemar's face turned to the dwindling fire.

"We are not safe here," he mumbled. "We are not safe, Sidney."

A filthy black hand touched his hair.

Voirrey watched the tender gesture and knew Sidney would look after him better than she could from here.

She stared back into the black expanse from whence she had come, wondering if she could find her way back to them from memory. Now that there was no need for silence, she made the bird call several times, hoping that Inry would know what that meant.

Waldemar murmured in Sidney's ear, loud enough for Voirrey to hear though he seemed unaware of her listening: "The Magloreans are on their way, Sidney. The full contingent. We are on the wrong side of the forest. We must hide in the east and wait for your mother's instruction."

Voirrey frowned at this last part, attributing the mistake to his delirium. *The full contingent.* He must have read this in the guardsmen's minds. By Velspar, she prayed for the sun's light so they could leave this cursed place.

Such faith she had placed in the ageing Intercessor, but as he lay upon the ground, she realised his frailty. They had to make it to Avishae. There they would be able to hide behind great walls and gates. They had guardsmen and horses and weapons of every kind. There, they would stand a chance.

46

NOTHELM

"SKALEN KALET," Damek began, his arms outstretched.

Kalet gave him a tempered smirk.

"Magnar did not join you on this visit?" He peered past her into the dark carriage.

"Skalen Magnar is busy taunting our siblings in Lindesal," she said.

Damek let out a bark of laughter that filled the night air with the cloud of his breath.

"Well, a little taunting will do them good. But you will not bring harm to my blood." He pointed a finger of warning at her.

She came to stand beside him, ever surprised by the cold that lingered in Nothelm, despite the warm day that she'd passed travelling. She put on her cloak, eager to change the subject. Kalet knew that Damek's concern for the Southlands had no weight to it. Moriel was off limits, even Magnar knew that.

She threaded her arm through his. "I want to know about your boats, Damek."

He gave her a curious look.

"I am not teasing," she said. "Perhaps in the past I said some things that may lead you to suspect my interest, but I assure you that I have well and truly changed my tune."

The night's sky glittered above, a chill breeze playing about Kalet's exposed ankles.

"Well, Kalet, you have just risen in my esteem." He pulled on her arm, leading her away from the Skalen's House. "Tell me, have you designs to build a fleet of your own?"

"Damek, I am not here to steal your secrets."

"Hmm..." he replied, not believing her.

"Really, Damek, I do not wish to compete with you. Though I am curious to know what is out there, beyond Velspar's shores. I would like to see for myself."

Damek's eyebrows shot up, surprised she would venture so deep, so early. "You wish to sail?"

Kalet hid her smile in her hood.

"Like you, I have a passion for discovery," she replied.

Damek's breathing was a little laboured, she noticed, and as he inhaled, his throat caught on the cold wind. He coughed, releasing her arm and slowed their pace.

"That I understand," he said. "Yet, if we were to discover new and peopled lands, there may be significant danger in such a mission. Is your curiosity as strong as that?"

She cackled at this.

Damek looked at her curiously.

They continued walking down the poorly lit street, the milky stars dominating her vision. Damek bypassed the main road with its echoing voices and took Kalet down a narrow stair that led directly to the foreshore.

Even before they turned onto the boulevard, Kalet could hear the ruffling of the sails.

Kalet slipped on the wet stone and caught herself.

Damek kept going, moving habitually, like a sleepwalker, and Kalet hurried to follow him.

At the end of the wall, the docks opened up before her. Moonlight shone upon the sea among the great hulking ships. She had not expected them to be so tall. Fat-bellied and creaking at their ropes, darkly bound wings a-flutter. Damek stopped to behold them and turned to her with a wide smile.

Kalet shook her head from side to side, speechless.

His smile grew, then after a pensive moment, his gaze fell to his feet.

"Kalet, this is my life's work. It is all I think about. I visit my ships every day. I dream of them. And when I am needed at the Skalens' Table, I find myself lingering by the window, watching that fair horizon," he said.

Kalet's eyes shone with understanding. "Lenna does not share your interest."

Damek sighed. "She does not. And this damnable business in the South threatens everything that I have built."

She felt the need in him, the weakness, and positioned herself to make use of it.

"Seltsland is here to bar the Southland rebels from your lands. They trickle in from Lindesal but none passes our net. Eastward of Jokvour at least."

Damek smoothed his beard to a point. "You wonder at our relations with Maglore. It is natural that you should, but that is Lenna's arena."

Kalet changed her tack. "There is another force gathering in the South," she said toyingly. "One you cannot afford to be ignorant of."

Damek's arms were folded against the rising wind.

"The siatka return," she said.

Damek's breath caught and he began to cough again. When his eyes reached hers they were streaming. "You are not serious," he managed, a scowl on his face.

Kalet ran her eyes up the length of the mast as the tied sails fluttered with greater ferocity. "I have the carcasses," she said. "And if you don't believe me..." She trailed off, drawing the siatka tooth from her pocket and watching his eyes widen in horror.

Kalet levelled him with her gaze. "For every prisoner who claims the powers of Intercession, we find an equal number of siatka." This was of course an exaggeration, but she was pleased by the effect this had on him. "Seltsland is at the fore in this fight, and only because the other lands grow lax in their patrols."

"You think they are calling them somehow? We've had no sightings in Nothelm and we are already venturing farther from shore than ever," he said, beginning to entertain the consequences this would have for his fleet.

"I think," Kalet said carefully, "that your daughter has much to do with it."

In the moonlight, Damek's features appeared even more pale. "What in Velspar's name are you saying, woman?" He panted slightly, his chest heaving up as his throat grew tighter.

Panic, she thought, and like a spear thrown blindly into the waves, her intimation had struck truth. Always, Voirrey flitted at the edge of her prisoner's mind. Why? What connection could there possibly be between this Intercessor and the heir of Nothelm? It wasn't love. Not that. No...it was some other kind of fateful alliance. That is what it felt like. He watched over her, protected her somehow, which meant she was important to him.

At first, Kalet had been unsure, but then she had dreamed Voirrey's face, tear-stained and pleading. *Amand!* she cried, the forest in her hair. Such a dream. Like a glass shattered upon the surface of her mind that left nothing but dazzling clarity. *Amand!* Voirrey had cried, with such strange familiarity. The remainder of his name emerged like a figure from the dark: Angenet. That was it.

"What are you saying?" Damek repeated, a bark of anger in his voice.

Kalet resolved her features, made herself cold. "I have an Intercessor in my dungeons–a real one from before the Purge–and he knows your daughter."

"Who?" he shot back.

"He is a Seltslander. Intercessor Amand Angenet," she said.

"And what has he to do with Voirrey?" he asked, though his voice did not contain the outrage of one confirmed of their daughter's innocence. And yet, if he were to admit suspicion of her heresy before another Skalen, his daughter's execution would be assured.

Kalet saw two figures by the docks looking at them, scenting the danger in their conversation.

"Answer me, Kalet. I'll not broach slander against my blood," he said, rounding on her.

She extended her arm. "Come, Damek, we are all family here. We can discuss this with Lenna over a hot meal."

He shrugged her off. "Tell me now. Tell me what you know."

"Or what? You will deny me the hospitality of your House?" She was playing with him now but knew she shouldn't push him too far. "Okay Damek, okay. I do not have any great case against Voirrey, nor would I wish to mount one. One day she will inherit Nothelm and I want to be in her good graces as much as I do yours. We have never been close, but the bond shared between the Braedals and the Askier is the last thing I would undermine. I want to protect her from whatever foolishness she might have got herself into. It is difficult to be born to power, to be of an age to wield it, and be hamstrung by circumstance. The woman has not had the opportunity to prove herself. She has not had a cause to fight for."

"She is a healer," Damek said weakly.

"Yes...and a sympathiser."

Damek glared at her, his mouth a thin line.

"Do you even know where she is? The few leads I have followed have grown cold."

His eyes glazed over in thought. "Vaelnyr. Edric escorted her there with Sybilla and the child."

"How long ago?" she pressed.

"Three months?" he said, frowning. "I will admit, she has not been replying to Lenna's letters. But we have had more pressing matters to contend with." The look of concern shifted. "You know, she has always done this. Voirrey grows restless and argumentative and then she just goes off for a while. I'll send Edric to Vaelnyr to check on things and then you'll see that all of this is ridiculous."

She let him hang onto that thought and without further conversation, they started making their way back to the Skalen's House. The night was quiet, too quiet for such delicate conversation.

Kalet spoke in a low whisper. "You may be right about Voirrey, but it does not explain the Intercessor's interest in her."

Damek gave her a warning glance. "Do not speak to my wife of this. Not yet."

Kalet nodded without conviction.

He chewed his lip, a plan taking shape in his mind. "Will you delay your prisoner's execution? I would like to question this man."

"The Intercessor is yours to do with as you wish," Kalet smiled. "Seltsland grants you the right of execution according to the laws of Velspar," she recited in accord with the custom.

"Thank you, Skalen," he paused. "Is there something you seek from me in return?"

This was the moment she had envisaged, and now it had come.

"I want to go past the horizon, Damek. Whatever is out there, I want a share in it. Promise me this and Voirrey's indiscretions will disappear."

Damek nodded, sighing heavily.

"Okay, Kalet, you have my word."

47

NOTHELM

KALET AWOKE in a strange bed, the window opposite her not to the west as in her own House.

She drew the bedsheet around her and looked out upon the harbour.

In the dark, the ships had seemed apparitions, but they were real enough. With a tug of longing, she watched one of the boats go out, their wide green sails like the vast copper skirts she wore on her wedding day. New and glorious. The promise that all that would come was yet to be.

The boat would not go far. These were practice runs, careful loops stitched to shore.

Kalet performed her ablutions automatically, barely conscious of her movements. Not knowing what the day would bring, she dressed in formal britches, and a golden tunic overlaid with a lace of Skalens' Stars.

Before breakfast, she wandered the halls, drawing suspicious glances and deep bows from the Attendants. She peered down at the inner courtyard with its topiary sculptures, cool in morning's shadows.

Eventually, she found the library. A handsome room with a roaring fire and a patterned tile floor. Kalet investigated the spines, discovering the categories that subdivided the shelves. Agriculture, botany, mathematics, moral treatises authored by Skalens of old, the obligatory Visions of Skalen Karasek, and a small selection of lesser visionary texts. Kalet made note of this these minor 'hereticals' and moved on. There were commentaries on the Skalens' Tallies, organised by year, a full shelf of 'dramaticals' with more than a few 'lover's fancies' dropped in among them. Kalet smirked trying to imagine Lenna, with her stiff posture and her pointed chin, answering to some of the lines hidden between those covers.

The shelf at Damek's eye-height contained the most extensive collection of maps that she had ever seen. She drew out a few volumes and flicked through the pages which featured endless diagrams of Velspar's topographies and rivers, of mountain ranges and the composition of rock and loam. Kalet looked carefully at the spines, noting a thin volume with extensive wear. She slid it free, examining its unmarked cover. Inside, to her surprise, Kalet discovered a set of poems, accompanied by illustrations. There was one page where a thumb had rested, so often and so long that the page bore a yellow mark.

If all the seas were gone, I would walk unhindered.

Down the mountain to the valley, from the valley to the mountains new.

Kalet paused, picturing this seeming law of nature. For both sides of a valley do rise. Did Damek imagine–in this very room–that he could walk to the bottom of the sea, and from there, ascend? His first intimation that beyond Velspar there must be more.

Her fingers began to sweat with the overbearing warmth of the fireplace. Kalet looked out the open door and saw no one near. She placed the book back in the shelf, drawing out volume after volume, looking for images that resembled the diamond of Solska. She didn't find anything, and soon became discouraged, exhaling sharply with frustration and rolling her eyes at the uselessness of the words, the waste of time and ink. After flicking through a particularly pompous account of Braedal history, she gave up all together.

She shook her head, stalking toward the dining hall. If Damek had anything of remote interest, he would not keep it in the main library.

"Skalen Kalet," Lenna called. "I am just finishing up my breakfast but there is plenty here for you. Please help yourself."

Lenna had more wrinkles than last Kalet saw her, though her greying ginger hair looked just as severe. The older woman's pin-prick eyes regarded her as she stood, gathering a stack of papers in her arms.

"Good morning, Skalen Lenna. Do not let me keep you, I can see you are busy," Kalet said, seating herself and perusing the delicacies on offer.

"Quite busy," Lenna said cattishly. "Each day that we stave off war with the rebels is a quiet victory. Damek doesn't appreciate this, but I'm sure you do. After all, you are much closer to their strongholds."

Kalet appraised the woman. Her manner was sharper than necessary. She was suspicious of Kalet's interest in her husband. Worried, perhaps, about losing another piece on the board to this shipbuilding nonsense.

Kalet picked up cold meats with her fingers and a piece of dark bread. "We have a firm grip on Lindesal, I assure you. No rebels will make it north of the Askier." She took a mouthful of the delicately sliced meat. "Or are you inferring something about Vaelnyr?"

Lenna pursed her lips. "There is rot all the way down the west coast. Vaelnyr is neither here nor there. But Maglore..." She sucked air through her teeth.

Kalet narrowed her eyes. "You think that they have plans beyond quashing the rebellion?"

"Of that I have little doubt. The rebels have not staged any great attack. Maglore pursues them as a part of its expansionist regime." Lenna leaned one hand on the table, balancing the papers on her hip. "And this has me wondering about Seltsland's position."

Kalet bit her bread with a little more tooth than was necessary, making the woman wait until she had completely finished chewing. Kalet took a sip of watered wine.

"It is wise that you wonder at my motives, Lenna. People are too trusting these days. But let me put it plainly. Rayhmer is a good dog.

He sniffs out heretics and lays them at our feet. He hopes one day that he will stand on two legs and wear this fine medallion." She tugged on the Skalen's Star about her neck. "If there is one thing you can rely upon it is that I will never relinquish my power to a dog."

Lenna scoffed and let out an amused sigh.

"Yes, that is a fair assessment of things..." She was still smiling. "We do not correspond nearly enough, Kalet. Let us change that. There are many small threads in the weave of things that have grown loose these past years. I need people about me of sharp wit and steady resolve."

Kalet did not feel affection for the woman but recognised a useful alliance when it was offered. Kalet pointed a greasy finger at her. "You and I, Lenna, we will get things in order."

The older woman nodded and went out.

As Kalet finished her meal, she considered the ways she might play her hand. She would not cede power to a dog but her unfruiting womb and her age dictated that she must cede power to someone. Withered sacks, salted beds, was that all that remained of the holy Askier? Somehow, Kalet could not truly believe in the reality of her own demise. It was not the end. She would not be the last.

This knowledge burned in her blood and would not be silenced. Oh Haldi, so accepting of Velspar's curse, so willing to bow her head in shame and prostrate herself. She truly was a dead fruit, ever sacrificing, ever giving in to her sister, the reddest apple on the tree.

She thought of Voirrey, still of child-bearing age, a threat to Kalet's plans. She turned the possibilities this way and that. By the ancient laws, only direct descendants could be named Skalens. But with two of the Seven Lands already under Regency, the Council of Skalens might reconsider the laws of succession. At some point, they would have to.

There were a few Askier stamens left in the garden that could shake their seeds upon Braedal soil. A childbearing alliance between Seltsland and Nothelm would galvanise what Haldi and Moriel could not. Cousin Lamrach, perhaps? Uncle Samat?

A child, Kalet could mould. And then, sweet Voirrey could meet her natural end.

She was not committed to the plan, exactly. The variables made her dizzy.

Kalet came back to herself, her hand hovering claw-like by her cheek, her unblinking eyes full of fervour. She felt it rise, this insufferable intensity that had no outlet. One day, she would slip into the lock and know her moment, but that day had not come. She forced herself into retreat, the roots of her teeth throbbing.

Closing her eyes, her thoughts continued to scramble in all directions.

Voirrey.

She tried to focus on her, to hear her desperate voice, but there was this damn buzzing in her ears. Kalet pushed her thoughts doggedly to the point of childbirth, imagined herself taking the child, slitting Voirrey's throat.

Again, her thoughts recoiled like an overwound scroll.

She took a deep breath and exhaled.

My child. My heir.

She pictured him, knowing that he would have to be a boy, and that his hair must be dark. Her heart sunk. Lamrach and Samat were not dark. No. Voirrey was all wrong. All wrong. That the child might be born blonde filled her with sudden and unaccountable disgust.

She discarded the thought, feeling this was the last thing she should do. Sometimes her ideas went too far. She knew this, but the realisation left her heart thudding in the afterglow. More than ever, she must keep her wits. She breathed.

Something else. There would be another way.

48

SELTSLAND

Kalet returned home to Seltsland by riverboat, feeling restless and pacing the deck. She liked the sting of the wind against her cheek. Staring at the shining water she tried to imagine that this was it, that she was out there on Damek's great ship, first to see, first to touch, first to know.

The trip to Nothelm had refreshed her, had given her the perspective she needed.

Now that she had traded the Intercessor as a part of her bargain, she was determined to squeeze all she could from him before payment was due. Sunlight gleamed like silver scales across the surface of the water. She squinted, considering her options.

Her tongue worked at a piece of meat stuck in her teeth and as it came free, an idea struck her. The problem of the Askier line had been lingering in her thoughts, but suddenly she saw a new path, a lightning bolt that shivered with certainty. Reflecting on the dark realisations of her early marriage, Kalet had first blamed Magnar and had taken things into her own hands. Many had tried her womb and failed. But was this because they were unworthy? Was it that her womb awaited the Intercessor? Velspar had brought him to her very late–she had just turned 47–but her bloods still came like clockwork and the Tally proved there were women older than she who had received Velspar's blessing.

As the idea expanded in her mind, she relegated her plans for Voirrey, considering instead how she might use Amand's loyalties for her own ends. Her heart bounced, saying, *yes, yes, this is it.* She knew this feeling. Often it evaded her, but she was persistent. There was no filth she would not wade through to chase the snake of wisdom and now she had hold of its tail.

The riverboat came around a bend, and as the Skalens' House appeared in the distance, she fell to wondering how Magnar had spent his time while she was away. She would have to see to him too. No use upsetting the man by making him suspect her adultery.

She imagined his ruddy face, his chest swollen with pride. A babe in one arm and she in the other. A half-smile formed on her face.

"Skalen, we are soon to dock," the boat's captain told her.

Kalet nodded and remained where she was. Now that she looked for it, she could pick out the wooden platform that zig-zagged the marshland, ending in a small port a little way down river. Figures stood waiting for her, ready with her palanquin. As the boat drew up to port, she recognised the four guardsmen and accepted their salutes.

She did not like to ride by palanquin but the marsh was no place for horses. Accepting the indignity of being carried thus, she perched herself upon the little shaded seat and let herself be hoisted in the air. There was a backward tilt to the palanquin owing to differences in height among the men, and all the way she could not get her thoughts straight for the labour of their breath about her feet.

When they had made it most of the way out of the marshes, Kalet decided she'd had enough and asked that they let her down. She left her baggage with them and strode on at a pace, enjoying the balm of afternoon. Passing over mangroves and still water, the mud crab stink of Seltsland greeted her, familiar as the scent of her own body. She walked for an hour or more, her ankles throbbing with insect bites as she reached higher ground. Sprawling figs ran their roots across her path, and long after she had passed them, she could still smell their musky fruit on the soles of her shoes.

There upon the hillock, she stopped and regarded the Temple. In the end, it did resemble a giant phallus. A laugh escaped her and she shook her head at the absurdity of her task. He was not an unattractive man, but sexually, he was cold as a dead fish. Once they passed their initiations all of them were like that. She began to have her doubts. Were Intercessors even capable of performing the act?

It was an experiment worthy of her effort, one capable of yielding the highest reward.

She tried to think of everything she knew about Intercessors, and planning her seduction, she made herself laugh out loud.

"Oh," she sighed, wiping her eyes.

Deciding she was not in the right frame of mind to make her attempt, she turned back toward the Skalens' House. With slow meandering steps, she eventually fell into more serious contemplation.

A high dose of Alma. Bloodletting in his tender areas. And then? Surely, he was a man like any other. She would make herself clean and adorn herself with siatka extract, pop a kshidol feather in her hair. And if that didn't work, there was always Voirrey's life to dangle before him.

Could it be so easy?

She sensed that this new plan might put her too close to the source of his power. Dangerously close. He might even kill her.

This did make her frown.

It would be like walking into the jaws of the siatka. Like stepping off a cliff and expecting to fly. And that was why she alone could succeed in this. Only she would attempt such a thing.

It was her last chance. She was owed this chance. In her mind, she could see the child, a boy, small and serious, like Osmet. The Askier, an arrow loosed before her birth that would keep flying through the generations, unstoppable. The idea gripped her, though when she thought of the task she must perform, when she thought of the Intercessor, her thoughts clouded and swarmed.

He would not be like the others, she thought, with uncharacteristic foreboding. Nothing like the others. The time of laughing was over.

Kalet sat at the breakfast table, pondering. This plan of hers must be put into motion as her final act before sending the Intercessor to Nothelm. That gave her precious little time to fill her stores before his heart stopped altogether. Her thoughts nattered on with such practical business yet each time she contemplated her plan, doubt struck her. Would she really climb the Temple stair and do what she intended?

He will not get the better of me, she thought. *I have him.*

She grit her teeth, angry at her recent indecisiveness. Magnar had just returned from his latest trip to the mountains and she knew that she would have to work her will by nightfall, or never. It was an opportune day in her cycle, which she could naught but take for a sign. She would have him, and that was that.

A flush of heat suffused her neck and she felt a strange constriction that scattered her thoughts. The feeling confused her momentarily but immediately afterward she felt angry. She was not fool enough to miss the changes the blood had wrought in her. Vivid dreams, sudden startling impressions, sounds, scents, all full of import and foreboding. It was as if she had previously seen the world only in blues and reds and now the full spectrum revealed itself. Her moods were hot and savage one moment, and maudlin the next. Some of the Attendants whispered that she was undergoing the change of life, but that was not it. It was a metamorphosis with no precedent, and the fact of it thrilled her.

Or at least, it had up until now.

Shut up. Stop it.

A rush of apprehension snaked the core of her bones.

She was her own master and would not be cowed. She made her thoughts run louder, pushing those other currents down.

Yes, she was changing–she was drinking of his power and now it was hers.

Intellectually, she wondered how it worked. According to the Intercessors, blood magic was heretical because it pierced the wholeness of the self and was therefore an act against Velspar's divine will.

Velspar wove the threads of personhood, loosening only those strands that were divinely loosened, unweaving all in death. And yet, she thought, life was a series of perforations and interminglings. The more Kalet took of him, the wider her personhood stretched. She did not lose anything of herself in this one-sided exchange, but gained and gained, taking on new dimensions. The others she had drank from may have tossed a jewel or two into her pot but this one was the wellspring.

Even Magnar noticed the change, and looked at her with renewed curiosity.

Come back from his latest mission, her husband gave her a wink as he joined her at the breakfast table, pulling her onto his lap.

"Oh, my taloned wench…" He squeezed her, sniffed her neck.

She dug her fingernails into the flesh of his forearms and smiled, happy for the distraction.

The Attendants in the room fled, cheeks ablaze.

"You smell," he sniffed again, burying his face in her meagre breasts. "…interesting. I can't place it."

He frowned at her but did not expect a serious answer.

She watched his pupils intently, noting that they wavered a little, just as his nostrils did. She had bid Osmet to incorporate higher doses of the holy extracts in her perfume. Distillations of siatka were drawn from all body parts, bone marrow and glands, scale and rendered fat, but thus far, they had only desiccated remnants of the kshidol, and a dwindling supply of feathers.

"I can't be giving away my secrets now, can I?" she teased and got to her feet.

He leaned back, smiling broadly. "I will quite happily lavish you with secrets, my love. Which would you like first?"

Kalet sat on the table and took up a small knife, using it to slice a warty looking renfruit. The flesh inside was a rich orange and beautifully firm.

"The biggest and the deadliest, please," she said and ate a slice of the fruit.

"Well now, I have met with Rayhmer in the Maglorean foothills and I believe we are close to forming an alliance. He has not said as much, but I would wager that his price will be a happy accident that sees Grenla removed as Head Guard of Lindesal so he can establish someone more amenable to his methods."

Kalet held out a piece of fruit to him and he leaned forward to eat it from her hand.

"And do you know who that might be?"

Magnar finished chewing. "Fenlor has a few in mind."

Kalet was genuinely surprised. "Fenlor agreed to this?"

Her husband frowned at what he deemed to be an absurd question, assuming it impossible for his Head Guard to have a will of his own.

"As long as you are also happy with the plan, this is what we will offer Rayhmer when the time comes."

Kalet turned and poured herself some spiced tea. "I'm happy," she said absently. "But don't let him get out of hand. I don't want any of his damn men in Seltsland. That is where I draw the line."

Magnar held up his hands. "Understood."

Kalet warmed her fingers about the cup. "And what of these other secrets of yours?"

Magnar folded his hands in his lap. "Got a few more for your dungeon...if you've got the room?" The note of jealousy in his voice was unmistakable.

Kalet's expression grew cold. She did not want him near the Temple, not now. Her possessive instinct was so strong she could almost see herself, a wildcat with a great dead beast in her lair, hissing, where her husband stood, peering in. She tried to hold onto her rationality, to behave as was reasonable in this situation.

"I will make room on Lindesday." She smiled, secretly unmoored by these words of commitment. Two nights, that gave her. One for her Intercessor, and one for her Skalen.

"Thank you, my love," she said with a lingering kiss. "I'm glad you're back. I have a truly excellent bottle of Alma wine to share with you. If you aren't too tired from your journey, that is?"

His hungry eyes drank her in. "No, not too tired."

49

BRIVIA

WALDEMAR WINCED at another shooting pain in his arm but held to the lip of the boat, wading into the current up to his knees. Sidney passed the rope to Voirrey and stood back. The current tugged on them and then the Intercessor was forced to let go, the tiny craft wobbling free of his grasp.

He held his hands in prayer, bowed to them.

Voirrey returned his gesture, the Greslet women silent at her side.

They floated like a dead leaf upon the waters.

My gift to you, Maeryn, he thought.

He stood where he was, the tide tugging at his shins, not ready to turn his back. *If I crossed into Avishae, might she accept me after all?* The possibility made his heart ache. Despite his feeling, Amand needed him. That was the truth of it.

Amand's visitations came to Waldemar jagged and anguished, red as fire's haze. He was in dire need and mortal danger. And yet Amand did not cry out to be saved. He spent himself for the greater good. A little on Voirrey, the rest on this directive that Waldemar must come. *Follow the blazing of my star.*

Sidney had gone foraging and Waldemar took this time to consider his journey. Sidney would survive without him. He knew how to hunt and how to hide.

But, no. He could not leave him. He could not be parted from his Skalen. A hapless friend with the frightened eyes of a child, and the vessel containing all the Karaseks that had been or would be.

He would have to take him. He might have to insist on cutting his hair. If not for the distinctive look it gave him, then for the rousing smell. They would have to get word to Olinda and arrange passage through Brivia and Lindesal into Seltsland.

Seltsland, where the light of Amand's shattered spirit shone its desperate beacon.

I am coming, Amand. Waldemar thought, wiping selfish tears from his cheeks.

50

PASSAGE TO SELTSLAND

WEEKS BEHIND them, weeks playing dead in farmer's carts, donning disguises, meeting eyes with new acquaintances and testing their commitment to the cause. Waldemar an unnamed Intercessor, Sidney, his mute companion. They moved from Olinda's inner circle to an extended network of 'friends.'

They had made their way past the largest danger, the Brivian contingent of the Maglorean Guard stationed along the Brivian Road. Yet, when they reached Lindesal and met with the Regents there, Haldi and Moriel helped Waldemar to appreciate the expansionist threat posed by Seltsland.

Surely this is what had prompted Amand to desert Voirrey? Some vision. Some terrible insight had driven him back to the land of his birth. Whatever it was, it had got the better of him. But all that was about to come to an end.

Waldemar and Sidney floated a little way out from shore, eyeing the secluded inlet.

"As good a place as any, Sidney," Waldemar said, glancing at his companion.

A warm smile spread across his clean-shaven face. Sidney's eyes crinkled, the feeling strangely infectious. Sidney, how well he looked! His hair cropped short, his face so clean Waldemar could see the constellation of moles on his skin. His hands! With their pink finger-nails and tiny black hairs. He was a new man. He seemed less mad every day.

Sidney's smile widened so his rotten teeth showed and Waldemar laughed.

"Whatever happens, Sidney, let us take the time to appreciate this place. Behold, Seltsland!"

In the distance, the city of Seltsland emerged from the dusk with the gleam of first torchlight.

Waldemar turned them toward shore and that night, they roasted shellfish in their fire and gathered their strength.

51

SELTSLAND

W ALDEMAR BALANCED in the branches of a tall tree, Sidney down below, looking conspicuously human since his haircut.

Through the shifting leaves, he stared at the Temple. *My friend, I am here*, he whispered across the intervening air.

For several days Waldemar had watched from this vantage. The area about the Temple saw a steady trail of guardsman, milling about like so many ants. But none entered the Temple. Waldemar felt certain, from his visions, that Amand was in there. He was imprisoned there but Waldemar felt a certain retraction of his powers. Had they weakened him? Tortured him? Why had he not been able to use his wiles to escape?

He watched and waited, considering his plan. If he hid Sidney somewhere safe, he could pass by night among the Guard and learn who held the key. It was not difficult to make a guardsman's mind wander in this day and age. When they served the Intercessors, they had taken the art of Hiatus seriously: the still centre that held them aloft from the Intercessor's realm of influence–of redness in the blood. These days, he doubted whether guards were taught anything but how to wield a sword.

Decided in this, Waldemar came down from the tree and sat with

Sidney awhile. They ate some mushrooms and Waldemar told Sidney his plan. They rested on the hillock in the sun, unnoticed by the villagers below.

At sunset, Waldemar went back up the tree to review the track he intended to take. The Temple shone blazing, the sun painting its colours on the distant sea. And then, as if a spider had crawled upon his arm, Waldemar saw a figure moving past the Guard's posts, saw them parting, and finally the cloaked figure stood before the Temple gate, opened it, and went inside.

Only a Skalen could enter thus. And only a woman could be so slight. So, Kalet visited him then. She had taken a personal interest. A fact that would complicate their escape.

Waldemar moved his hands over the stubble of his chin, staring and seeing nothing, focusing on Amand with his inner sense. He was there, pulsing strong, and then that strange sense of dilution. Waldemar re-doubled his focus, but Amand would not let him into his bodily experience. His skin-sense. Instead, his friend showed him visions of Voirrey. *Danger. Voirrey.* Amand insisted.

My friend, I have seen her safe to Avishae! The child is safe. Voirrey is under Maeryn's protection. Rest your worries. I am here to save you! I will come this night, when the Skalen is gone.

Waldemar reached yet further toward Amand, seeking intimacy with his spirit, which had gone silent. He felt the roughness of the bark, the looming distance below, his arm wrapping about the branch just in time to prevent his fall. He needed to set himself upon the earth and stop this foolishness of staring with his eyes. The black shadow of the Jokvour range had plunged the lower half of the Temple into shadow so only its bright tip showed. With trembling arms, the Intercessor descended the tree, meeting Sidney's eyes when he reached the ground.

He sees my fear, Waldemar thought, *and he, too, cares for Amand.*

"Sidney, please, keep a lookout. I must immerse myself in meditation and listen keenly for our friend's voice."

Faithful Sidney nodded and stood watch.

Waldemar let go of his body, seeking that voice of reason, his sensible friend, this man of strategy, kindness and daring. Amand. He was paying a price of the spirit, a deep price. Waldemar could feel it, and could not intervene. Amand consented to this bargain, whatever it was, and raised his hand to his friend, barring his entry.

Witness this, dear friend, and do not rush to your outrage. Do not come to my rescue.

With difficulty, Waldemar relented, and was let in.

Amand was there, glowing before him in twin posture. The light from him escaping.

Fear clawed at Waldemar and yet he let it flow from him.

Watch where I go, Amand said, his golden face smiling.

Waldemar did not want to look away from him, fearing that if he did, Amand would disappear completely. It was as watching the death vapours at execution, the air of the spirit let free to mingle and disperse. Freedom. Annihilation. And the prayer to Velspar.

Watch, my friend, the shining eyes half-lidded, the gold of him leaking like light beneath a closed door.

Waldemar widened his vision, watching the diffusion of his spirit like pollen on the wind. Then he saw it, an unnatural backward trickling, a siphoning off of living spirit into a new vessel. The realisation came upon him, dark and evil. Amand murdered himself! Steadily, deliberately, with such sacrilegious magics as to make Waldemar shudder in the depths of his soul.

Do not abandon Velspar, Amand! Waldemar begged him. *Please, I am here.*

Amand's spirit was thin but unwavering.

Trust in me, Amand said. *Follow me where I go. I am not alone.*

His voice was fading, though only because he wished it to fade. Waldemar felt himself returned to his body, to wet tears on his cheeks, and to Sidney's concerned face.

After a long silence, Waldemar hung his head. "He does not want saving. He has bid us gone."

Sidney looked to him in confusion but Waldemar could not answer his questions. He took himself back up the tree, unable to leave his vigil.

Below it was full night, the town a-glitter in low torch-light, the

Temple, to all eyes, a place abandoned to the turning faces of the moon.

The spider emerged in the dark hours of morning. As Waldemar watched, he saw her glow, the wine of Amand's spirit poured between two goblets. Bitter tears filled his eyes.

Follow me where I go.

52

AVISHAE

Edith submerged her feet in the waters of the straight. There were smooth pebbles on the shore, blue-brown in the sun, and the occasional rust red. Then under the gleaming sheath of water, their colours ran deep and lustrous.

Rowan sat farther back on the grass, scowling into the sunlight. He thought their mission ridiculous. The Intercessor had told of fugitives from the mainland that would arrive any day now. Edith had explained this to him but his world had always ended at the boundary of the Raeburn camp. She was at pains to convince him that it was all of Avishae that they must defend. It was a truth that she had recently come to herself.

On previous visits he had sketched a few rough maps, agreeing that it was necessary to know these borders and places of natural ingress. As she demonstrated, it was only when you stood on the shore that you could see the invitation that a tree's shadow offered to the weary traveller. Only when you walked the riverbank, up and down, could you see the natural coves, the undulations that welcomed the eye, the places that promised shelter.

She plunged her swollen hands into the cool water, slipped reeds through her fingers–listening, always listening, to the chirruping of crickets and birdsong. People thought of the straight as a border, a watery road to travel down. It brought supplies in crates and canvas sacks, but with her hands immersed in these waters, she felt its layers–warm and wide, a cool wisp, and pale fish darting. The great forest of Brivia bowing her branches, reaching for the Avishaen canopy, though their distance was insurmountable. She recognised the history of this place, of seeds cast by breeze and by bird to the other side. Gifts and connections that the water helped sprout, despite the lingering taste of ocean salt.

"Edith! Come on. I want to go back now." Rowan's voice was sharp and irritable.

She turned around, ruddy cheeked and smiling.

"I'm sick of this," he said, dusting his pants. "You can find your own way home."

"Hey!" she called, shaking droplets from her hands, her feet finding careful purchase as she traversed the pebbled shore. "I'm coming, okay? I'll have you back in your pen by sunset, don't you worry."

Rowan rolled his eyes.

She scanned the Brivian coastline, finding it distant and blurred. Strange that she could see so much more with her eyes closed, with the deeper senses of her soul. All Rowan saw here was the threat of exposure, the anticipation of enemy boats and a distance too far to run.

Why this spot? Why did she return here, particularly?

Guardsman John's patrols also trod the Avishaen periphery, and maybe they would be the ones to discover Inry and her girl. But Edith thought not. In Maeryn's uncanny gaze, in her penetrating voice, Edith felt this to be a fated thing. There was some presence with her that made the skin around her eyes relax, the scent of lemon balm in the air. It washed her senses clean and focused her eye like an arrow tip upon her prey.

There, and...loose. It was that kind of feeling. The knowledge that the arrow had struck, the certainty, the weight in her step as she went to collect the body.

Perhaps tomorrow.

"Have some of this before we head back?" Edith suggested, extracting a small packet from her belt-pouch.

His mouth quirked in a reluctant half-smile. It was renna gum. You could chew it for hours and after a little while you started to feel happy and light. Tasted good too, spicy and sweet.

"You made it?" he asked, taking a piece from her outstretched hand.

She nodded, knowing that he appreciated the extra spice she added that left the mouth tingling.

They popped the gum into their mouths and started chewing, Edith wrapping the remaining pieces and tucking them away.

Moments later they grinned their pink teeth at one another and Edith growled.

She broke into a run, reaching the cove seconds before him. Beneath leafy shadows they darted and raced, sweating and panting, breathing out the stitches in their sides and heading on again.

We'll need to be fast to survive, Edith thought. A thought like a spear, and she pursued him, feeling her legs burn, her throat rasping, her heart a desperate drum.

53

AVISHAE

REBEKAH PULLED her cloak around her, more against the darkness than the cold. They had built a bonfire a little way outside of the Raeburn camp–a halfway point between the place where she had grown up, and the Skalens' House where she now ruled.

Even after all these years, she sought to avoid incensing her father by making him attend the Council Room. Always, she came to him, and on neutral ground. That was, until that dark night when Velspar had stolen her son. Her last trespass into the Raeburn camp had almost severed her relationship with her father. She remembered it as a dream: Ambrose dead, the moon in the sky, the wafting resonance of the stone–*the stone, the stone*–and her father gone. The surge of rage, of injustice, the mark of the thief on him as she pictured him in her mind. She pursued him with her guards, with Zohar and Illiam staggering beside her like an unholy apparition.

She had taken the axe and broken his door. To this day, it did not seem real. As a child, that door had seemed impenetrable. He closed her in, he shut her out; that door was her father's will. And how easily the axe reduced it to splinters. She passed through it without mercy, without needing to bother with the latch. What was it in her racing heart that kept her standing as the stone drove him to agonies there on the floor? What was it that made Zohar open his secret box and swallow the blood-tie hidden there? They had all played their parts in this surreal play. The impossible spark of Sybilla's blood, enemy of her heart, now flowing within her daughter's veins.

Vividly, she recalled the figure of Sybilla, there in Jokvour, bidding Rebekah into the cave as if calling her to her death. They were enemies, and yet they both were Skalens and together they had sworn a Skalen's pact: to hide the stone in Avishae until none remembered its awful power. And now, here they were, she and Ulric, her father and Maeryn, gathering to discuss what should never be spoken, to do what should never be done.

She glanced over to where her father sat, Landyn Raeburn, with his bald head and grey stubbled chin, the orange of the flames eclipsing his storm-grey eyes. She read the tension in the sinew of his forearms, the flexing of his fingers.

A wave of nausea took her and she began to sweat, removing her cloak.

Ulric put his hand over hers, spoke low. "Come and sit the other side of me, you are getting all the heat there."

She nodded, and moved to sit beside Maeryn, whisking her thick hair off her neck and gathering it over one shoulder.

"Landyn, sprinkle the Alma, would you please?" Maeryn smiled. Rebekah found the Intercessor's appearance strange now that she had taken to braiding her silver hair. She wore a colourful woven blanket about her shoulders and Rebekah wondered what life the woman might have lived if she had never been called to her role when she was but a girl, in Vaelnyr.

Her father actually smiled as he regarded Maeryn and Rebekah felt wounded by this new camaraderie between them. By logic it was a good outcome, but she did not like the idea that her father might influence Maeryn in some way when she was not there.

Sweet Alma smoke hovered in the air and Rebekah took a deep involuntary breath that sent her blood flowing to a softer rhythm.

"Thank you, Landyn," Maeryn said, as he sat back down on the log. Her eyes twinkled in a smile.

"We have come together here to speak plainly of the dangers we face. Let us not mince our words here tonight. Let the Alma clear away the desire to hide our true intentions, let us be of one mind together at this fire. Let us speak our fears and listen as to the sound of a child's first words, with the will to understand." She paused, and Rebekah felt the swelling of her heart, the need to speak. "Are we together now?" the Intercessor asked.

Rebekah held her hands in prayer at her naked forehead.

"We are," came Ulric's voice on her left, and she looked up to find tears shining on his cheek.

"We are," came her father's voice.

Rebekah felt the words emerge from her. "We are," she said, feeling the Alma more powerfully than normal.

Maeryn whispered, "We are," her voice like an echo in the trees.

Silence descended with its nocturnal noises, the breeze at her back suffused with nightness, the star-stained air, a sort of etheric perfume, all black and cool. Why did this feel like danger?

Rebekah's eyes shot open. "You have brought it here!" She struggled to focus her gaze on her father, on Maeryn. Her fear darted between them, rebounding and rebounding.

"Peace," Maeryn said, and a golden sensation spread through Rebekah's heart.

From the folds of her heavy shawl, Maeryn drew a pendant. The wet-looking stone flickered with inner fire—with hidden song—seed shaped in the Intercessor's hand. Maeryn's eyes danced with that same fire, with that same song, and then, with a movement of her thumb, she slipped the stone into its casing. A sudden absence followed as if all the world had grown dim. Rebekah felt her wits return, her thoughts setting themselves straight.

Maeryn's look was gentle now, and utterly composed. All that wildness gone. "Rebekah, I know of your Skalens' Pact and I apologise for going ahead with my experiments without consulting you. There are things that one must discover firsthand."

Rebekah could not hold back the words. "My father knew?"

Maeryn nodded. "He has been helping me." She turned to Landyn. "Your father is better than I with the written word and he has been studying the Temple tracts. I know you set this task to me, but I find I can make connections more easily when he reads the visions aloud."

Rebekah felt a lump rise in her throat. She had wanted to tell Maeryn of Guardsman John's plan in private. Was it too late? She felt the pressing of secrets, of old jealousies. The primordial fear her father inspired in her.

"If you were not afraid right now Rebekah, I would fear for Avishae. And you too, Ulric. You are wise to fear. Your son died for this knowledge. He did. He died for this knowledge, and he holds it before you. I know now, that we must not look away."

Rebekah shivered, awe and terror warring in her opened mind.

"Tell me," Rebekah said breathlessly.

Maeryn looked to Ulric and Rebekah saw her husband nod.

"Firstly, I must assure you that Ambrose's stone will never be disturbed. Your father, too, has sworn this. The fragment that you keep, Rebekah, remains where you have hidden it and will not be taken from you. The sliver in my possession was taken from a sea cave on the west coast of Avishae. I believe it is the same place where your son discovered it," Maeryn said.

"It is accessible?" Rebekah said, her lips growing numb.

"The young can access it. Not an old woman like me. Rest assured, the boy who helped me has no memory of the experience. I had to stabilise his mind as he went in, to bolster his defences. He was able to hold the stone in his hands without losing control, but only with my full concentration," Maeryn explained.

Rebekah pictured the scene uneasily, feeling Maeryn's power not as a protective force but as a dangerous entity that she had invited in. *What boy?* she thought. *All here are my people. What if the plan had not worked?*

"Death surrounds us, Rebekah, make no mistake," Maeryn's voice sounded uncharacteristically harsh.

Rebekah cowed, unprepared for the sting. These past years Maeryn had been as a mother to her, who had forgiven the monstrous thing she had done. The Intercessor had forgiven her. Hadn't she?

"It comes down to this, my Skalens. I can wield a stone of this size.

When it is encased in blinding stone, its power is silenced. When it is exposed, it reaches for consciousness like a flower does the sun. This intermingling...I can only find its like in the Intercessor's initiatory trance. It is a profound mixing of spiritual substances where the will is easily overcome. As a trained Intercessor, I can maintain my will with a stone of this size," Maeryn said, pinching the pendant between finger and thumb.

"You have tried a larger stone?" Ulric asked.

"Slightly larger. It has been cast back into the sea," she said, not elaborating further.

Rebekah thought of the Skalen's Pact, the sense of Sybilla's presence arising unbidden like mushrooms from damp wood.

"*Protect the stone, keep it safe. Keep it hidden. In memory of your son and his sacrifice.*"

"*In memory of my son and his sacrifice, I swear.*

Blood of my palm, I swear."

"Read the passage, Landyn," Maeryn said.

Her father extracted a leather volume from his coat, his fingers alighting on a slender leaf that he had stuck between the pages. He looked at her hesitatingly, a wounded look about him that squeezed at her heart.

"I never told you this, Rebekah, but he came to me before it happened. Ambrose came to me. He was not acting like himself. He had a gash on his forehead." He gestured to his own. "Just hidden by his hair." Her father's lip trembled. "He asked about the Eye of Velspar, an eye hidden in the earth. His words reminded me of a passage I had read in the books left to me by Intercessor Camis. This book, in particular. *The Visions of Intercessor Janek*, written some two hundred years ago."

He tapped the open page.

"I read these words to him:

Veiled Eye, Eye of Stone,

Living Stone, of Velspar.

Voices Buried in the Earth

Waking, Voyant, Heralding."

"Then he looked at me. Looked *into* me," her father shook his head. "So much power, Rebekah, you do not understand. Then, he seemed to grow fearful and almost ran from the camp. He did not return to my confidence in his final days. He went out on his own, after that. He gave himself to the power of the stone."

Ulric leaned forward, his face drawn by grief. "Show me that book."

Landyn passed the open book, hesitating for fear that it might be tossed into the fire. "You are right, Ulric, there is more. Like any visionary text it meanders through realms that we cannot hope to map to our own."

Ulric frowned, tipping the page to the fire's light, reading carefully. Rebekah squinted to catch the words over his shoulder.

Suddenly she saw it. "There!" she cried and pointed to the words.

Rebekah looked up at her father. "He speaks of the Eighth Gate." She turned to Maeryn. "Is this the only book where it is mentioned?"

Maeryn nodded. "The only one where it is named as such. There are many references to gates in the visionary texts but it is more likely that they refer to the Seven Gates of Wisdom. I believe that Intercessor Janek encountered the stone as your son did. It is possible that other Avishaen initiates knew of the stone, or that Janek passed his visions to his brethren by psychic bond."

Rebekah held up her hand, feeling overwhelmed. "But what does this mean? Does Janek explain the meaning of the Eighth Gate? Is the prophecy true?"

Her heart was beating so fast she thought she might faint.

Ulric looked at Landyn. "This section is bound with a different thread." His tone was accusatory.

Maeryn cut in, "Yes, the original volume in Landyn's possession did not contain the section about the Eighth Gate, but the text and paper match. Look at that stain there, it matches perfectly. Which means that Camis entrusted the most valuable piece to his *Skalens* when he made you stewards of the Temple library."

Rebekah watched Ulric, his thoughts plain on his face. *Why did we not read the holy tractates? Why did we not seek an answer? At the crucial hour, we gave up our faith.*

Ulric looked up at Maeryn. "I don't understand these words. I feel dizzy just reading them. What does it mean?"

The Intercessor took a deep breath. "Janek conceives of the stone as a petrified river. You will see half way through the inserted section, he says, over and over, *the Great Stream does not flow*."

Ulric flicked through the pages, finding the passage, and he read aloud.

"Blood flows, for life is movement,
Death, without time, is still,
The Great Stream takes what life releases,
Makes it unmoving and infinitely dense.
The Great Stream it does not flow..."

Ulric trailed off and Rebekah shivered, imagining Ambrose, his youthful face, his eyes peering into the sickening depths of the stone, beholding his own death.

Rebekah scratched nervously at her thumbnail. "Is that what it does? It brings death?"

The Intercessor exhumed the pendant once more from her shawl, handling it with care as if it were a creature that she did not wish to startle. Rebekah found herself cringing, anticipating the stone's thick waves of magnetism and having no way to protect herself.

Maeryn turned the pendant in her hand, leaving it safe within its shell of blinding stone. "There is a woman, Catla, that the Intercessor Janek loved. She was a weaver. When the pox came, she grew ill, like so many others, and was taken by a terrible, maddening thirst. She ran through the forest and threw herself from the cliff, falling to her death. Grief-stricken, Janek, went down to the water to search for her body so she might receive holy burial. He did not find her but he said that he heard her, *inside the womb of the earth*."

Ulric stopped her there. "You believe this refers to the cave where Ambrose discovered the stone?"

Maeryn and Landyn both nodded.

The Intercessor went on. "He believed that he had discovered the physical location of the Great Stream."

"This is ridiculous," Ulric broke in. "The Great Stream is a state of... *non*-embodiment." He struggled to find the right words. "It is not a place or a thing. It cannot *be* anywhere."

Maeryn held up a finger. "And yet... the spiritual bodies of Siatka and Kshidol exist in physical form. They possess the physical but are not one with these forms. In a very real sense, *we* are Velspar. We, as Velspar, possess our bodies, and then, when these bodies perish, where do we go? Where do we linger before the moment of rebirth? We are told, again and again, not to look to the stars, not to go out there into the vastness beyond. We must remain here, in this place, where spirit resides."

They lapsed into silence, listening to the fire's crackling flame.

Rebekah found her thoughts returning to the story of Catla, of her voice emanating from the stone.

"Maeryn, is it really possible that the stone absorbs the spirits of the dead?" Rebekah said, trying not to look at the pendant glowing dully on the Intercessor's breast.

Maeryn remained silent, extending her fingers toward the fire's warmth, seemingly in deep thought.

The Intercessor's voice was soft. "I cannot say. Janek believed so, and I suspect that Intercessor Camis and other Intercessors in Avishae came to this view." She shook her head. "But there is a piece missing here. The prophecy of the Eighth Gate foretold that all the Intercessors that died in the Purge would be reborn. They would 'flood the many wombs' as it was said. It would be a spiritual revolution... Janek's writings do not speak of return."

Ulric was still reading. "You are right, Maeryn. From what I can see, at least. But what is this about the Eye of Velspar? I understand the symbolism from the Skalens' Star, the mouths of Siatka and Kshidol that together form the eye of Intercession. Does this mean that the stone can see us? Does it have a will of its own?"

Her father had remained silent this whole time, but with a gesture of Maeryn's hand, he cleared his throat. "Janek speaks of the stone as something that can trespass into our spirit, as an Intercessor might. He refers to it as a mixture of voices. A river of spirits–of people who have passed into death. This seems to include spirits who did not receive holy burial, as in the case of Catla."

Rebekah knew that he was thinking of Ambrose, was trying to save his grandson's spirit from dissolution, even now. Still, she blamed him. She looked in her father's direction but did not quite meet his eyes. "All of us here have felt the power of the stone. We have felt its will, and to me, it is a will like wind or lightning. Without being bound to a body, it cannot share our hopes and fears or have any kinship with us."

Rebekah felt Maeryn's attention lingering about her head. *She knows, she knows of Guardsman John's plan*, she thought, now fearful.

Ulric closed the book, rubbed his face. "Maeryn, you know our grief. Do not give us hope if there is none."

Rebekah knew that he spoke not of the Eighth Gate and their absolution as Skalens, but of the possibility of contacting their son.

Maeryn tossed a handful of Alma on the fire, renewing the sweetness of the flame.

"The Great Stream was only meant to flow in one direction. Death cannot be undone. You cannot afford to believe otherwise. We must–all of us–take care to focus on the living." She paused, sat forward. "If we survive this time. *If.* Then we will speak long into the night of prophecies and deeper meanings. Rightly or wrongly, I rejected the promise of the Eighth Gate. This stone, I take as a gift from the holy Intercessors of this place in order to defend the people of Avishae. I will harness the power that they give me and take no more than I can wield. I will protect your daughter and all who live here." Maeryn's hand drew about the stone, clasping it in her fist.

Rebekah shivered, a powerful effervescence washing over her, prickling the hairs on her arms.

"What will you do?" Rebekah asked, feeling both terrified and strangely elated.

Maeryn met her eyes. "I am an Intercessor and my job is to heal. I draw the redness out. In another time, I would have reached into Rayhmer's spirit to leech all that was rotten there. My brethren would have cleansed his ranks and those men would have lived. That is impossible now. I see it."

Ulric's voice was tight. "You will kill them, then?"

Her father's gaze flicked nervously between them.

She smiled bitterly. "Together, Skalen. You with your sword, and I with mine."

54

AVISHAE

Maeryn wiped her clammy palms on her kirtle. Her heart fluttered, the pain in her knees was unusually strong as she wove her way along the coastal track. The stone rested malignantly above her heart, silent in its shell.

She needed time alone. Away from Landyn and his hunger. Away from the freckled children with their hard, dark eyes–looking to her as their protector. Away from the Skalens and their guilt.

"Nearly there," she muttered, breathing heavily. "We've walked greater mountains than this."

Each step sent a wincing pain, making her waddle even more than usual, but now there was no one to make fun of her. No one to smile knowingly and laugh with her about the indignities of age. No Waldemar.

Inside, she kept her heart closed to him, just as she kept herself closed to the Eighth Gate. Too much pain. Too much mystery.

Her stringy grey hair danced as she approached the cliff edge. No matter what she told Ulric and Rebekah, some part of their boy was still here. Not a spirit, fully formed and conscious. No. She just felt him here, as if she had seen his figure walking, dark curls shrouding his eyes. There were others too. So many.

Echoes. That is all that they were. And yet...

Maeryn sat on the cliff edge in meditative posture, breathed in deeply and exhaled. With eyes closed, her heartbeat seemed impossibly loud, the sun illumining the dark with its red coronas. The wind hissed in her ears, and then the hissing softened. She followed the eddying sound, her heartbeat slowing, her limbs growing lighter. Her edges expanded, until she knew herself to be something more.

With this same crystalline sense, she had once felt the presence of the Holy Ones. Of Kshidol on high and Siatka below. They were still there, but it was as if the world had grown larger, and they had shifted back to make way. They were small, now. Deflated of worship. Melancholy spectres fading with the birth of new generations who did not know their song.

She slipped the stone from its casing–just a crescent–and felt it burn like a knife against her palm. Immediately, she felt a dark weight about her, a spark in her belly that thrummed with a feverish pulse. A denseness, an overcomplex pattern presented itself to her mind. A dizzying succession of likenesses, all unique, all named, all desperate and entreating.

Maeryn waited, unmoving, allowing the swarm to immerse her.

They were all about her, fragments, the glinting wings of a thousand bees, and she the old oak, the steady surface they crawled upon.

They would not harm her, she told herself: she must let them in.

She exposed the stone fully to her palm and darkness raged, deafeningly fast. Rasping screams scorched the fibre of her being. Sighs. Voices drawn thin. A deep and hollow sound, or was that the wind? The wind was so loud–the salt wind, and the other wind, that loosened the senses.

She let it take her. Faster, faster, until all that remained was the circle of her palm, the spinning voices, the circling song. They penetrated her, thousands upon thousands, found a deeper layer. She knew this place, the point of crisis that she strove to release in others. The place that made them cry out and go limp, and then the redness came flowing out, leaving them empty.

It was the gush of blood when the spear was pulled out. Childbirth and death. The eclipse of the self.

The voices tugged at that part of her, pulled it almost clear. In a glorious rush she expanded, flowing outward in endless waves.

Part of her did not want to return. And yet, she was strong, far stronger than the stone. She drew upon the tide, gathering herself up in the undertow.

Her sweating fist still held the stone, her body resolving. She felt the pang in her knees, familiar pains, the scents of her body.

She held her fist firm, her grasp on the present, her anchor to life. *Life*. This. Now.

The voices stilled and gathered about her, watching, recognising that she was not like them.

She, alone, was whole.

Slowly, and with unyielding will, she gathered them, held infinite eyes transfixed to her bright burning centre.

Bid them to follow her.

Later, in her hut, Maeryn watched the candle flame gutter and flash. Watched the ruddy light dance its last and perish. Smoke was sharp in her nostrils. The glowing ember faded into pure dark.

It brought to mind the winking stars, phosphorescing in their own dark river. She wondered...thinking of Ambrose and the way he had died. Of the woman Catla in Janek's fevered visions. And of the Holy Ones, how they had seemed so distant.

It was likely that High Intercessor Camis had not simply read about the stone in Janek's tractate but had communed with it as she had. Did he believe the stone to be the embodiment of the Great Stream? What, then, was the purpose of the Holy Ones? Why worship Mother Siatka and Father Kshidol if one could travel to the Stream directly?

Maeryn found her thoughts unravelling and running on in a way that was not usual to her mind. With a thrill she wondered if she was finally experiencing the elusive sensation her brethren spoke of when Velspar illumined the intellect.

The thrill was immediately followed by a vertiginous sense of horror: the sickening magnitude of the High Intercessors' decision to pursue the Eighth Gate, to believe they could master the stone, and therefore master death.

She saw it so clearly, the fading ember lingering ghostly in her mind. According to the rites of holy burial, the body must be divided into seven parts. Not simply to make it easier for the Holy Ones to consume the flesh, but because none in death remain whole. To divide into seven pieces, gave order to the rite. To divide further was to destroy the spirit by making it unrecognisable to itself, whereby it would forget its destination. All in the Stream was chaos and mixture, but the Holy Ones persisted as great images of intent.

Her brethren had abandoned those images and had chosen a new orientation. They had died–wilfully abandoning the Holy Ones–for the promise of the stone. Whatever they had expected, Maeryn knew that they had not remained whole in death. She felt them all. Voices, fragments, a cacophony of disembodied consciousness that yearned for what it had lost. To be born unto this world, and to live, for a time, undivided.

She concentrated her recollections, tried to isolate the fragments, to recognise them as Intercessors she had known in Vaelnyr. It was impossible to be sure. Either the stone had the unique power to absorb fragments of spirit loosed by death, or it truly was the Great Stream arrested in motion, a Stream indifferent to the ways in which time unfurls a body, carrying spirit from birth to death like a great wave.

Wave after wave, returning.

If that was true, what did it mean for her to use the stone in the way that she intended? The vertiginous feeling returned, reminding her of that moment in Jokvour when Illiam had tossed another stone into the chasm. Was that what she should do now, before it was too late? She had already exposed Edith to its power...

Guide me, Velspar. Help me to know what is right and what I must do.

Maeryn reached for her flint stone, struck up a new flame to write by. She drew out the volume that would be her own–for it was true, she could not know the course of her life and how close she might be to the end.

With a curious feeling of nervous anticipation, she wrote: *The Visions of Intercessor Maeryn of Vaelnyr, the year 719.*

Hereupon this day, she continued, *I hear the spirits of the Stream calling for rebirth. The Holy Intercessors spilt their blood into the Temple troughs, and that redness spread about the sea. Their bodies were burned, all in hatred by those who had slain them. Into Velspar's heart they flooded, bright and strong, no longer recognisable. And here they cry out, they lift the earth with their song, they burst out and bleed from the caves in crystalline streams. In a Great Stream that shakes this land with its birth pangs. I await their coming with reverence and trembling, seeing in their sacrifice, that same excess of death that gave rise to the First Diviner's holy visions.*

I await the word and will of Velspar, for I am, and I remain, holy in my servitude.

55

AVISHAE

Edith sat on the banks of the straight, a little further north this time. She skimmed the unreal horizon, the forest out there that harboured so many savage men. They would come here to kill, to enslave, to uncover all that was hidden here and destroy it. She put her mind through scenarios, fighting techniques that Guardsman John had taught them these past weeks, tactics of subterfuge and evasion.

Right now, Rowan was helping the Sherburns with the Skalens' House defences. Blinding Stone—as much of it as could be mined—was to be brought to the Skalens' House to line the lower floors. Rowan could not swim, so he could not help them chip it from the jutting rocks that littered the Bay of Knives. Instead, he worked at the Skalen's House, laying the tiles, fixing them like interlocking scales all up and down the walls. Edith had never seen him this scared. She could hardly imagine what Landyn had said to make him journey so far from the camp to work with guardsmen and men from the town.

Edith tugged at the pendant Maeryn had given her, afraid to open its shell. Each night, Edith visited Maeryn, to hear her wisdom and discover what more there might be to her vision. In the Intercessor's smoky cabin, Edith heard stories of Maeryn's youth and the Temple of Vaelnyr. To Edith, the Intercessors had always seemed clean-handed, doing their holy work with their minds. But Maeryn's stories helped her to understand the nature of redness, and the way it was married to the flesh. Maeryn taught her sacred chants with tears in her eyes. Edith listened, confused, striving to remember these things. Did the old woman think that she was soon to die? The thought harmed her in a deep place she thought forgotten, reawakening feelings about her own mother's death all those years ago.

Maeryn had given Edith a pendant similar to her own. Its blinding stone shell contained the barest sliver of the stone. She was to keep it hidden. From Landyn especially.

Redness, Maeryn explained, *is the fire of life. It is not evil but can be tipped out of balance. Intercessors maintain the sacred balance, and few can be trusted to interact with such forces. You, I trust, Edith. Even the kshidol bestow their trust. You will not master this in the time we have left, but you must do what you can to balance the redness when the Magloreans come. Fight in the ways that you know but if the time comes, the stone will help you. Remember what I taught you. Never act out of fear. They are enflamed with redness, and all you need do is focus on its diminishment.*

Pass that dish, she said. *Now hold it over the flame. As you move closer with your will, you starve the flame and ease it out of existence. See how the flame perishes?*

Maeryn had explained to her such things that she had never had cause to consider. That without redness, without inner heat, a body could not exist at all. The spirit in contact with flesh creates this burning, this holy fusion, a tension of substances that accounts for all of human life. And its increase, at times, is necessary. It must flare to bring about new life and without it, no child of Velspar would be born. It flares in passion and in inspiration, just as it does in acts of courage and depraved violence. It is for the Intercessor to know when the inner fire takes on an unhealthy cast. This is why only the initiated can manipulate its heat, for it is essential in so many ways.

Edith heard a noise behind her and turned. She studied the leaves, the bouncing branch and bird wing. Water sounds and breeze and the rushing of leaves.

It will not be today, she thought, and turned her mind back to

Maeryn, to the cascade of sacred knowledge she had poured upon her, trying to catch it all.

The stone would amplify her qualities, her aptitudes, as it would amplify her weakness and her fear. She knew the state of mind that brought the kshidol. It was a familiar posture that she could slip into at will. That was why Maeryn had chosen her.

She held the pendant in her palms, tapping her foot, daring herself to unsheathe it.

Chewing on her lip, she released the shell-seal, feeling the stone's energy through that fine aperture as she traced it with her fingers. Hunger and heat tingled through her. Closing her eyes, she focused on the posture of Blood Call, of the sacred chants and the sounding drum. *Higher, I am. Singular and with a directness of will. I command you and will not be dissolved.*

Her inner words grew silent as she discerned a change in the stone. A compression of movement, and a corresponding clarity in her awareness. She smiled, pleased with herself. *Do not push it, Edith,* she told herself, sealing the shell with a click.

Tucking the pendant beneath her tunic, she stood, stretched, and crunched her way along the riverbank, taking a slightly different path than the one she had come.

She had just entered the trees when she felt something beside her. She turned, not seeing anything unusual. Remaining still for several moments, she considered it wise to make her way directly home, remaining hidden from sight.

She deviated from the natural gaps in the trees, bending and crouching to negotiate the low and tangled branches. Soon she was covered in scratches, hair awry, and had walked herself into a patch of forest so overgrown she could not progress in any direction. Frustrated, she snapped a branch that barred her way and threw it to the side.

Suddenly she stopped, unsure of what she had just seen. A low ridge of rock with a long shadow beneath: had she seen movement there?

Quietly now, she stalked forward, easing her bow from its case.

A yelp sounded, and deep in grey shadows she saw the shuffle of feet.

Their hearts pulsed like beacons, and she could sense them there.

"Inry?" she called in a loud whisper.

She drew closer, her eyes adjusting to the contrast, a crouching figure resolving from the shadows. Too young to be Inry, but not a child.

"What do you want?" came a woman's voice, resonating from deeper beneath the overhang.

Edith understood their fear and did not hesitate. "I am Edith Raeburn, sent by one who wishes your protection."

She waited as the dark haired woman from her vision emerged, touching the silent girl's shoulder as she passed. It was her.

Moments later, a blonde woman strode from the cave, her features obscured in a shaft of light that shone through the trees. A small figure followed her, a child that clutched her skirt.

"Please," Edith said, addressing Inry with a breathless laugh. "Who are these others? And tell me you have no more hidden in there."

56

MAGLORE

Sybilla heard voices but could not determine their location. She lay in bed, her arms like feathers, and it seemed as if her body levitated in the air. Shockingly, a man's face appeared, looming close. She tried to move away but knew now that something was wrong. She'd been drugged. And over there, three men stood, chuckling.

She tried to see them, to hear them. What were they doing here?

Beside her, she felt the cool stones of her Meridian and as her fingers rested there; a slight clarity came.

The men laughed again. Rayhmer, and two others: one who wore the uniform of a foreign Guard. How hard it was to think! She stared, slumped sideways on the bed, drooling.

The strip of bronze upon his surcoat. A guard of Seltsland, here?

The other man, who had come forward to inspect her, now glanced once more in her direction. He was more richly dressed but his grizzled hair made him look rough. She knew this man, she knew... and in a timeless moment she felt herself back there, on that fateful day when she had called the Skalens of the Seven Lands to avenge her parents' deaths. The screams of those who would not join her resounded in her ears, and that man's face leered down at her. "You have our oath," he had said, with that same look of amusement that he wore now. Skalen Magnar Askier of Seltsland.

She let her eyes glaze over, listing as if she had lost consciousness. Her fingers anchored to the disc of blinding stone. *Protect me, keep me*, she prayed.

She scanned her body for injury or violation, finding nothing suspect. But where was Domhnall? He was not in the bed. She searched for the scent of wine, perhaps vomit, that might suggest he had simply passed out somewhere on the floor.

The room smelt strange, all sour sweat and grass. She could not remember anyone coming in before them, Attendants or otherwise. A chill of fear came over her at this dark place in her memory, a missed beat, a rift in the progression of things.

The voices continued their garbled murmuring.

They moved across the room from the bright window to the door beside the bed. Rayhmer's pocked face appeared at the corner of her vision.

She heard a crunching sound, a plaintive moan from beside the bed. Domhnall.

"Well, Rayhmer, looks like you have everything in hand here," Magnar said, a smile splitting his beard.

Her eyelids seemed frozen in their half-closed position.

"Just a bit of insurance, should we need it. There are a few pieces missing from the board, but they'll show up soon enough," Rayhmer assured him. "Let me take you down to the docks, find something more to your tastes." He gestured at Sybilla who tried for her life not to move.

They went out. She heard the bolt of the Hall door and then the spreading stillness of their solitude. She pressed her numb lips together, wondered if she had strength enough to speak.

"Domhnall," she murmured.

A noise, of crying, ragged breath and desolation. He was not grievously injured. He would live.

She closed her eyes, clutched her Meridian in a burst of heedless joy. Rayhmer had not found them. Voirrey and Davina were safe.

Though Domhnall lay weeping on the floor and her lips could not move to smile, her heart swelled with relief.

57

———

MAGLORE

SYBILLA AWOKE feeling as if she had been asleep for days. Her mouth was unbearably dry and it hurt to swallow. She touched her neck feeling lumps on either side. She was sick, which explained the headache, the tenderness of her skin.

Beside her, Domhnall lay as he often did, on his back like a fresh corpse. He looked waxen and she wondered with a start if he truly was dead. She watched his chest but it did not seem to move at all. Eventually she saw a stray nose hair flutter and calmed herself.

As unlikely as it seemed, his presence did bring her comfort. He suffered with her, which meant she could not leave him to suffer alone.

She sat, reaching for the snapped-off chair leg that served as her walking stick and limped to the window. The hillside was empty, with not a single guardsman in sight. She glanced into the dim Hall, listening. Her thoughts ran on and finally she heard the clunk of the heavy bolt, the scrape of the food tray. The Attendant's footsteps receded.

Sybilla sat a moment longer, trying to process what Magnar's presence meant. An alliance with Seltsland was unprecedented. Seltsland had never bothered itself with the Southlands. Even Vaelnyr, its direct neighbour, was met with disinterest. Her entire life she had thought of Seltsland as an extension of Nothelm; the Askier a clan that kept to themselves. For a moment, she wondered if Magnar had disposed of Kalet, if the world had gone that mad.

These thoughts circled in her mind as she hobbled past Domhnall's sleeping figure and into the Hall. When she reached the food tray, she did not bother to take it back with her to the table but sat there on the floor, chewing distractedly. The tasteless gruel was warm at least. She kept the stale bread and an apple for him.

Sybilla pocketed these items and shuffled back to the window, leaving the tray behind. For hours she sat, occasionally sniffing the apple, savouring its scent. And the entire time, not a single guardsman passed. A few peasants, a horse and cart–and nothing more.

Domhnall made a gasping noise and she looked up. He often awoke like that, bolt upright, wild-haired and sweating, his mouth a great O. His palms gripped his knees as he tried to steady himself. He coughed. Paused. Then a protracted coughing fit ensued that made his body curl in on itself.

She brought him water which he gratefully received between wheezing breaths. He did not look well at all.

Watery eyed, he stared at the table, eventually noticing the apple.

"I saved it for you," she said, and tossed it to him.

He caught it, held it to his heart like a beggar.

She smiled. "Enjoy it, Domhnall. It is a good one for a change."

She turned her face from him, observing the scene outside. She knew it so well she could picture it with her eyes closed: the hill in the foreground, the edge of the Skalens' House to the left and, in the far distance, the sea. To the right, at the bottom of the hill, ran the road, the fringing wood. The sky draped coloured veils over the scene in accord with time's passing: from grey dawn to bright day, the brief exuberance of sunset settling into pitch.

Small figures entered and left. Horses, guardsmen, the occasional donkey. Sometimes there were flowers on the hill, tiny flowers of white and yellow that danced when the wind blew.

"Something is happening," she said. "The Guard are all gone from the hill."

Domhnall munched the apple with great relish, the juice of it wetting his beard.

"Could be something," he said between mouthfuls. "Could be nothing."

Despite his good temper, despite the apple, despite what passed for a good day here in their prison, she could not help but fear. *They'll show up soon enough*, Rayhmer had said.

Soon enough for him to destroy all that she cared for in this life.

"And if it *is* something?" she searched his face.

He swallowed, let the apple core hang limply between finger and thumb. His eyes grew hazy with old pain.

With a rare pang of anger towards him, she let out a hissing sigh. "We must try–something. There are ways out of here but you need to try."

With agonising slowness, he gathered himself up out of bed, placed the juicy core in front of her, and wandered from the room. *Back to the cask*, she thought. *The second I say anything, the second he feels anything real, he goes back to the cask.*

She tapped irritatedly on the table, tried to think. Scenarios presented themselves, each ending in her own violent death. And yet, her mind kept returning to that dark hallway where Edlin was. In her meditations she passed him, small and impassive. So alone! If it were Davina in that room, she would have braved anything. She would find the strength. Why couldn't he?

58

MAGLORE

THE BED WAS EMPTY beside her. No doubt Domhnall had fallen asleep in the Skalens' throne. She took her time combing out her greasy hair with her fingers, braiding it and setting her Meridian. She relieved herself in the chamber pot and removed her threadbare sleeping gown. Bathing water from several days past sat in the corner of the room all filmed with dust. She stirred it up so she could imagine it fresh. Sybilla washed, the cold water drawing gooseflesh, and proceeded to eat the remains of yesterday's meal: a few oat biscuits with butter.

She saved one for Domhnall, spreading the butter thickly as he liked it, then hobbled with her stick into the Hall.

"Your meal, Skalen," she called with good-natured sarcasm.

He was slumped in his old throne, where she expected him to be.

The reek on him was especially bad this morning and she screwed up her face as she nudged at his shoulder. She thought his chest covered in blood until she realised that it was simply a spectacular wine stain.

"Domhnall?" she said, placing the biscuit on the arm of the chair so she could give his shoulder a shake. The moment she touched him, she knew something was wrong. His skin was cold, his wine-

311

stained lips cracked and pouting from his beard, and yet he did not drool. He did not blink. As she reached to touch the pulse at his neck, she felt the absence of him.

"No," she whispered. *No, no, no.* This could not be real. She stared at the cask. He drank like no man she had met before, but he drank, he slurred and he slept and that was it. She went over to the cask, crouched down so she could weigh it in her arms, knowing the Attendants had only brought it yesterday. It did not seem like much, not enough to kill a man. With creeping dread the suspicion landed in her mind. Poison. Saliva pooled in her mouth, wondering whether her food had been tainted also.

She pressed her eyes, tried to think, feeling Domhnall's body as a diseased thing that might infect her. He was corrupted; he was flesh commenced to rot. She was trapped in here with this horror.

Sybilla moved away from him, from the wretched stink of wine.

Soon, an Attendant would come for the tray.

Often, she had imagined smashing past the Attendant as they opened the door, strangling them with her bare hands. Nervously, she tapped her stick, realising as she did that it was probably the best weapon she would find.

But would they come? If it was poison, what would be the point? At this stage it did not matter. If there was any chance the Attendant would come, then she must take it. If by night they did not come, she would know, and she would try the window. She might make it, even with her leg as it was. If there were no guardsmen below to watch her scramble the tiles.

She sucked in a panicked breath. Her time in Jokvour had left her with a fear of heights, a bloodless trembling that she feared would seize her the moment she passed the sill. The fall would be fatal, unless she could find her way to the raised courtyard where Inry's fruit trees grew. Even that way, she would have to fight her way in.

Sybilla moved across the Hall and stood beside the door. Her heart hammered in her throat. Each minute seemed an unbearable eternity as she waited for the sound of footsteps.

More than once, she imagined them, anticipated them into existence, straining to hear above the laboured sound of her breath. Then finally, she was sure. The footsteps came, were coming toward her, unhurried, something tinkling on the tray. She heard them stop, the closeness of this person on the other side of the door, setting the tray down with a grunt. *An old woman then*, she thought.

The keys jangled tortuously and she heard the lock release. From the corner of her eye, she saw the dark line of the bolt move clear.

The door squealed open and Sybilla pushed it hard, opening it to its full width before descending upon the crouched woman with her little white cap, smashing the stick down on her head. Hitting her again and again. Aged shaking hands crossed to protect her face.

Sybilla could not hear anything but the burning in her ears, the fallen woman slumped forward with blood matting the grey curls at the nape of her neck. Red on her apron, on the stone floor, in a mess all on the food tray.

With blazing eyes, Sybilla dropped the stick, crouched down and reached her hand into the mess she had created, searching for the key. She would not look at the woman. Quickly she extracted the cold iron ring and its promise of freedom.

The stick was in her hand again and she laboured on in jerky movements, half running, half limping, unable to stop the shuddering in her chest.

No one had stopped her, no one pursued, and even if they did, she would have kept going.

Down the hallway, past Inry's chambers, past Lilwenn's room, and suddenly Edlin's door was before her, just as it had been in vision.

She pulled out a key, tried it, and dropped them on the floor with a crash. *Damn shaking hands*, she cursed herself, *dammit*. She tried the next one, focusing intently on her movements until the click came. Sybilla exhaled deeply, pocketed the keys, and pushed the door open.

"Edlin?" she whispered. "You are free!" She called into the dark: "You have to run."

The room was cold and smelt of damp linen and mice. She wondered if somehow he had been moved.

Eerily, the boy's wan face came into view, squinting into the light.

The floor was covered in sheets, bundled in odd formations as if he had built himself a nest.

"You have come," he rasped.

Sybilla blinked, her eyes watering. "Yes," she said, unable to focus on him, extending her hand. "Come, this is your only chance. Come!"

Sybilla leaned on the doorway, feeling faint.

Edlin nodded with that same vague expression his father often wore, making tears rise in her throat. "Come!" she repeated. "Tell me the way out."

"Over there," he said, looking over her shoulder, wide-eyed.

She turned, screamed at the sight of the grimacing Attendant. An old man, tears of rage running the channels of his face, teeth bared. "You killed her!" He seethed and before she could raise her hands to stop him, something heavy collided with her head in an explosion of pain.

Sybilla rushed backward in limitless dark.

Fear.

Fear bright and blazing when all else was swirling pain.

Something in her turned, an impression of the doorway, the boy standing there. Edlin's tender smile. A familiar smile. How much he reminded her of her grandfather. He moved closer, held what must be her hand and spoke in a voice that was everywhere.

Hover, as smoke before the wind comes and know that I am with you.

Yes, she thought, *it is you. Galen, my grandfather.*

She drew herself close to his presence, afraid to allow herself to know anything more. She could hear the slithering of dark scales, a whisper somewhere down the hall. *Siatka,* she thought, and tried to hide herself.

The boy's childlike eyes spoke to her in silent communion. *Mother Siatka will come if you want her to, or we can go together.*

The memory of her grandfather's death resounded in her then, with the Intercessor's refrain: *he has gone to Siatka to be reborn a girl child.* Thus the holy woman had said, but her grandfather had moved his spirit otherwise and had chosen to be born a boy. He willed it because he would not abide their counsel.

The fact of it shocked her. His spirit walked outside of ritual and was not destroyed. His presence bid her to take this leap, to walk as he had walked.

Still, the teachings of her youth tolled about her, doom-laden as war drums.

Do you know the way?

What will become of me?

Do not look at the stars!

They moved upward, outward, spreading to encompass so many things that her fears seemed abstract and strange. Fragments of her soul darted like birds in the panic of what was happening to her.

One flying fast to the south. *Davina!*

Another for Voirrey.

Another–

The boy drew her back to him. *Not yet*, he said, and she obeyed. *Remember*, he instructed. It seemed that her eyes were full of tears, for he blurred and shifted. She felt her grandfather's smile, a wisp of him, a stray thread woven through the boy's fingers.

She trusted him. Trusted him more than any other, living or dead.

Where are we going?

He bid her to look down, and beneath her rushed rooftops, forests, and fields.

She saw the people as living flames–surging, dimming–reaching out to one another to become something larger and more bright.

The boy urged her deeper. The dark river flashed in her awareness.

Do not be frightened, Sybilla, the boy said. *In many lives we have travelled near to one another. Each death fractures us, but stay close and we will not be lost.*

She saw the truth of it, that he was Edlin and yet part of him she had known by another name. Only part of him. Just as she was Sybilla who had lived as man and woman and had been known by many names before.

They were descending, passing through the stuff of matter as if it were little but shadow and light.

We separate so we may yearn for unity. We see ourselves in others... Her grandfather's voice now, growing distant on the wind, the wind itself growing louder, a thousand voices burning bright. They streamed through her like water, parts of her coming away, pieces she once thought essential that she now knew were not. She held her centre, an orb that would not be divided.

Sybilla. Pure, and warm, and bright.

PART III

———

THE GATHERING

59

AVISHAE

DAVINA WAS CURLED in Voirrey's lap like a bird in her nest. This was the part where she must say goodbye. She must tell the girl that she would be safe here in Avishae without her, and that she would be back as soon as she could. The warmth of Davina's body melted into her, softened her heart, and she couldn't move. They had been taken to the Raeburn camp, and she had heard that Maeryn lived there now, though when they arrived Maeryn had been up at the Skalens' House.

The shock of recognition still unnerved her. Maeryn and Rebekah, Zohar and Illiam. Their fates so strangely tied. She met Skalen Ulric, Guardsman John, and Rebekah's father Landyn, of whom she had heard much, both good and ill.

There were too many people in the Skalens' House, stonemason's tools incessantly tapping downstairs. No one slept, or if they did, they awoke at so many intervals that it seemed an age had passed in just one night. They had slept there two nights so far. This morning, Davina's nightmares had set Voirrey's heart racing and now neither of them would sleep. It was dawn and she remembered as a child how much she had loved to watch the sunrise over the ocean. She was about to tell Davina this, but thought it trivial, considering the circumstances.

The morning was chill with dew and a restless wind whistled along the cliff. The pink glow of morning was faint, already fading into the blue of day. Down on the sand, the sea burst in tumbling waves that loosed a veil of rising mist. Voirrey rested her cheek on Davina's head. Soon she must go. She would never be able to save Sybilla and Amand with a child to worry about. It was a miracle she had taken her this far.

Voirrey's face tensed as she mulled the words over in her mind. *Davina, I love you more than anything but I have to leave you here...*

Davina, your mother is in great danger...

Davina, Amand is still missing and we need his help...

Vina, my love, my dear...

The tender warmth of the child's body did not want these words. Must she break this embrace, fill her eyes with tears? Must she wound this child? Already Davina knew the necessity of silence, the need to disappear from sight. She knew danger and the hollows she must hide in. Voirrey provided some small shelter where her heart could rest. Who else could do this?

I will return to you, Voirrey said in her mind, though her conviction could not erase the doubts that plagued her. Her mission was impossible. To traverse the length of Velspar alone and in a time of war. If she did not leave before the Maglorean invasion, she might lose her chance. Only she could mobilise reinforcements from the North to crush their enemies into dust.

Voirrey kissed her hair. Wrapped the cloak around her against the wind.

Not today. She would not leave today.

60

AVISHAE

Voirrey carried Davina back to the Skalens' House where Guardsman John and Illiam were talking at the gate.

"We need to move them now," Illiam was saying.

Guardsman John shook his head. "Soon, Illiam. But the simple fact is that only a fraction of our people will fit in the fortified rooms. You put people down there too early and the whole place will fester. Either that, or you'll find the fighting men wandering up the hill to visit their children. When the time is right, you and Zohar will lead the evacuation."

Voirrey walked inside without their notice and took Davina up to bed.

Leaving Davina in the room, she turned the key hoping the child would not wake wondering where she was. She needed some peace, some time to think. A sense of unreality had suffused her spirit since their last night in Brivia, her determination scattered like sand.

As she pocketed the key, Inry appeared from the room beside her.

"Is Davina in there?" the woman asked, resembling her former self now that she'd been given some fresh clothes and jewellery.

Voirrey nodded.

"Don't do that," she said, shaking her head at the locked door. "Please."

Not wanting to upset her, Voirrey reversed the motion of the key and left it open a crack.

Inry fiddled with the necklace about her throat, a thin silver chain that Rebekah had gifted her.

"It's not that we are not grateful for the Elshenders' hospitality, but Lilwenn and I agree that we would prefer humbler accommodations," Inry said, her freshly washed curls now showing their streaks of grey.

Voirrey considered the common architecture of the Skalens' Houses, how this place must seem like a reconfigured version of their home in Maglore. Their prison. She knew that there was no way Inry and Lilwenn would allow themselves to be locked in the safe rooms that the men were building downstairs. So, what was the alternative? Haydentown sat on the banks of the river and was by far the easiest place for the Magloreans to disembark. If they sent men through the mountain range at dawn, they would smother the Raeburn camp by nightfall. The farmland that flanked the valley might be safe for a time but it was no place to make a stand. She wondered about Landyn's idea to row people off shore but all agreed that the common folk of Avishae were not known for their sea craft. The Sherburn brothers, whom she had briefly met, said that they and a group of fishing families familiar with the treacherous Bay of Knives could take people off shore if it came to the worst, but that Avishae was better served if they stayed to fight. In short, no place was safe.

Lilwenn appeared next to her mother, her dark wavy hair hanging lightly on pale shoulders. Now that she was clean, a collection of scars could be seen about her throat and collarbone. Voirrey looked away.

"No one is going to stop us if we try to leave. Would you feel better in the camp where Edith first took us?" Voirrey asked. The truth of it was that she had been waiting for an opportunity to take them to Maeryn. At least this way, they came of their own accord.

Inry looked at her daughter, who nodded her assent.

"I will take you now while Davina is sleeping," Voirrey said, peering in the door. "But let me first tell the Elshenders that she is here on her own."

"Thank you, Voirrey, we will ready our things," Inry said, and the Greslet women returned to their room.

The previous day, Davina had really taken to Zohar, laughing and cuddling her, playing with her hair. Voirrey had expected this, on account of the blood tie, but was perhaps making more of it than she should. Voirrey found herself watching Zohar, looking for signs, for Sybilla's telltale mannerisms, but there was no way of knowing for sure. Her affection for Davina was indisputable but when Voirrey caught her eye, there was no connection. They were strangers. She tried not to be hurt by this, or to let herself doubt that Zohar was the one. She had to care for the child.

Even if there was no blood imperative at work, Voirrey knew Zohar had a kind heart and the capacity for great courage. She had met Zohar's personal Attendant Elspeth who seemed a capable young woman, and most of the Attendants here seemed trustworthy. In her mind, she tested all who might cross Davina's path, determining the community of Avishae to be better than most.

Voirrey peered down the hall wondering where the Attendant's bell was. She went downstairs and eventually found an old woman in the kitchen who called Elspeth from there. Elspeth told Voirrey that Zohar was speaking with her father, and said she would bring Zohar back to Voirrey's room.

Voirrey agreed and made her way back.

A short while later, Zohar appeared, her face weathered by long and sleepless nights. Everyone had that look about them lately.

"Hello Voirrey, are you well?" Zohar said and made the effort to smile.

"Zohar, it is good of you to come. I have Davina asleep in the bed and must go to the Raeburn camp for the afternoon. Could I entrust her care to your Attendant?" Voirrey asked.

Zohar peered into the room, her hand moving to her heart as she watched Davina. A smile tugged at her lips. "Let me do it, Elspeth," she said and turned to Voirrey. "I would be happy to mind her. There are so many people about and everyone is at their wit's end with preparations. You have given me a good excuse to sit and collect my thoughts."

Voirrey felt awash with relief. "That is so kind of you," she said, watching Zohar as she reclined on the settee. "I will return before sundown."

Voirrey closed the door behind her and then rapped gently on Inry and Lilwenn's. The Greslet women were dressed in riding britches and long tunics, their hair veiled. Without a word, they made their way downstairs and to the stables where people moved about with great purpose. Voirrey saw Illiam hauling sacks of grain and called out to him.

"Voirrey!" he panted. Then, recognising his somewhat estranged kin, he bowed. "Aunt Inry, Lilwenn, are you pleased with your quarters?"

"Hello, Illiam. Yes, the Elshenders are looking after us very well." Inry broke into an overripe smile, her tone nattering. "Oh, it is so good to see you here. What a stroke of fate! We are off to the camp now with Voirrey, but I do hope there will be many opportunities for us to talk when time allows. I feel it was only yesterday you were a boy playing hide-and-seek in the orchards in Maglore."

Illiam laughed softly at the memory. "Yes, Aunty, it has been a long time." He turned to Lilwenn. "And you, cousin, are you well? It must have been an arduous journey."

Lilwenn nodded but kept her eyes down.

Voirrey felt the awkwardness of this reunion, the years changing each of them beyond recognition.

"Illiam, could you help us find a couple of horses?" Voirrey broke in. "Just to go to the camp and back again."

He wiped his face of sweat and hesitated. "It is not a good time to be venturing anywhere. You know they are almost upon us. There have been sightings along the Brivian coast."

"We will not be long," she assured him.

After a breath he relented. "Okay, okay. You can take my horse, the chestnut mare in the last stall, and Zohar's horse Silvey is already strapped with a double saddle."

Voirrey bowed her head. "Thank you, Illiam."

Inry and Lilwenn bowed appreciatively, then hastened to the horses.

Voirrey gave him a sympathetic smile. These bonds would take time to re-tie.

The three women rode at a steady pace, following the way they had come two days prior. Inry's veil flew free and her hair bounced in the sun. Though the sight should have cheered her, after all that had happened, Voirrey felt the encroaching shadow of Maglore.

They were coming, Illiam had said. It could happen any time.

Inry and her daughter rode before her. They were like cracked vessels all stuck together with honey; the cursed flies would find them no matter where they fled. Voirrey tried not to think of things that way, her fear numbing her senses to the sweetness of the meadow and the shushing pines.

Maeryn would fix them, she thought. She could heal them of this curse.

Voirrey rode her horse harder, as she could not have done with Davina in tow. The fair wind cooled her face and she actually laughed. It was a mad laugh, and Inry, a short way off, turned and smiled. Lilwenn kept her head down and sped forward.

"That way," Voirrey called, pointing where a track opened up between the trees.

They slowed a little, the horses negotiating the low branches. Grey-brown rabbits scattered in her periphery, hiding among patches of wild Alma and bellflower. Soon enough, they came upon a copse of oak trees and the perimeter fence of the Raeburn Camp beyond that.

The gates were open and people moved in and out carrying lumber, wagons of arrows, sacks of potatoes. From horseback, Voirrey waved at the lookout, the dark-haired boy who manned it looking in her direction. He climbed down from his roost as the women dismounted. Lilwenn gathered the reins, taking the horses, while Voirrey and Inry stepped forward to meet the lad.

"Hello!" he called, his gait stiff as he negotiated the passing folk to meet them.

"Greetings," Voirrey returned, waving.

His worried frown remained despite his smile of welcome. "Is all well at the Skalens' House?"

"Yes, preparations are proceeding as planned," she assured him, and then lowering her voice continued. "We have come to seek audience with Maeryn, if we may pass."

He glanced uncomfortably at Skalen Inry, fearing as others did that she might not be a fugitive after all, but some kind of spy sent to destroy Avishae's only advantage in the coming conflict: having an Intercessor of their own.

"Wait here," he said, holding out his hand as if that might stop them from proceeding.

"Of course," Voirrey said, lowering her eyes.

After he had gone, Voirrey caught Inry's uncertain gaze. "Maeryn is a true friend and someone I trust. She is not one to keep stock of old debts." She paused. "And even if you can't forget those debts, there are more important matters at hand."

Inry's face tightened a little, a reflex against tears.

The young man returned then, gesturing for them to follow him inside.

"That far hut, over there," he said, pointing to a squat thatched hut at the edge of a dirt square.

Voirrey thanked him and they made their approach, Lilwenn's eyes darting nervously as the crowd turned to watch them.

Walking confidently ahead, Voirrey went and rapped on the door. When the Greslets arrived beside her, she whispered. "We are welcome here, everything will be fine."

She knocked once more. "Hello, Maeryn, it's Voirrey."

Inside came a shuffling sound, and the catch clicked open.

The old woman appeared in the doorway. "Come in, friends," Maeryn said.

The three of them huddled into the small space, the Greslet women removing their veils.

"Sit down, sit down. I'll brew some tea," she said.

Voirrey noticed that Maeryn had changed her style of dress from modest robes and over-cloaks that hid her round figure to something approximating the local dress. She looked for all the world an unassuming woodlander, her brown tunic embroidered at the edge with tiny flowers. She wore a bright loose-weave scarf that brought colour to her cheeks. There was power in her, formidable as a wolf dressed in the skin of a lamb.

They sat. Maeryn's teapot steamed quietly between them.

"A hard journey you have had," Maeryn said, addressing them as one. "I sense that you have come here together, but each of you for different reasons."

Voirrey would not interrupt her, knowing that the Intercessor could sense the tides in the room much more keenly than she.

"We have great trials before us, great trials. But I do believe that we will survive them." The old woman laid her palm face up on the table. "Forgiveness may not be mine to give, but in me, you will find the sanctuary of Intercession. If you want it."

Voirrey found herself sweating, her palms growing hot of their own accord.

For the first time, Maeryn raised her eyes, settling her attention on Inry. "Would you like me to take away some of your pain?"

The Skalen's dark eyes marbled with tears. Her neck was so tight the tendons stood out and Voirrey watched as her throat wrestled with itself, wanting and not wanting. She let out a shaky breath.

Maeryn poured out the tea, each cup seeming to take a long while to fill.

"If you wish it, simply lay your hand in mine," the Intercessor said.

Lilwenn's curious and slightly horrified gaze fixed on the side of her mother's face as her delicate hand abandoned the teacup to hover over Maeryn's.

Inry's reddening face contorted with emotion even before their hands touched. "You won't make me relive it?" Her gleaming eyes now streamed with tears.

Maeryn slowly shook her head.

Inry's hand fell into the Intercessor's warm palm and Lilwenn watched her mother's face in rigid fascination.

Within moments, Inry's brow relaxed, her cheeks softening. The tears continued their course, tracing her fine jaw and long neck. Her nose ran clear onto her upper lip but she was somewhere else now and did not wipe it. Voirrey felt her own worries lift the longer she looked at the woman. The peace that had settled upon her was so profound, her head listed, gently upturned as if to the sun.

Lilwenn's eyes shifted to Voirrey.

"We can go outside if you like," Voirrey said, knowing that Inry was deep enough now not to be disturbed.

Lilwenn shook her head protectively.

"You can stay," Voirrey said. "But she will be alright if you want to go."

The girl would not go, which was to be expected.

Voirrey picked up her tea, a blend of chicory and spices that she savoured, feeling good about things. She had got them here, and now they would be okay.

Out the window, a tree branch swayed, its leaves flickering dark and silver.

The process took almost an hour and when it was ended, Inry embraced the Intercessor, squeezing the old woman so she rocked from side to side. Inry glowed. She was almost unrecognisable as the tortured wretch that Voirrey had met in Maglore.

Maeryn returned her smile but Voirrey could see that she, by comparison, had been left drained. Her eyes looked sickly, her cheeks almost grey, and there was a taint to her, bitter in the air for someone who knew her.

"I must attend to some things now," Maeryn said. "But will be happy to see your daughter soon, should she wish it."

Inry grasped Lilwenn's hand. "Thank you, Maeryn. Thank you." She looked at her daughter with joy and surprise and laughed.

Maeryn took her shadows outside and wandered northward of the camp into the forest.

As Inry emerged into daylight, she exclaimed over the vegetable garden, the industrious children with their dark eyes, the *little society* that went on here. The flowers! She plucked two white daisies and set them in her hair.

Lilwenn hung back with Voirrey. "Will she stay like this?" the girl whispered.

Voirrey looked at her with sympathy. "Maeryn has the power to do this for you. To give you a new life."

She grit her teeth. "You tried and it didn't work," she said.

"If I could have healed you that night in Maglore, I would have done. I do not have a fraction of her power," Voirrey said.

Across the way, Inry had bent down beside the well and Voirrey wondered what the woman was doing.

"Oh Lily, come, I found a frog!" she called, and sure enough, Voirrey spied a green tree frog clinging to her forearm.

When Voirrey looked back, she saw something in Lilwenn's face. "She has not called me that in years," she said with trepidation. "Are you sure she hasn't lost her memories?"

Voirrey could see that this pained her, that she and her mother would be intolerably estranged without their shared suffering.

"The memories are there, but the feelings are not so strong. It is like a story that happened to someone else. If you bring your heart close you can cry, you can feel, but you don't have to."

Lilwenn's face darkened, anger mounting in her voice. "I will have to protect her now, as if she is a little child. How is she going to fight when they come? You heard what Illiam said, they could arrive any day now."

Her comment reminded Voirrey of the time, and she realised that Davina must have woken by now. Maeryn had gone off to cleanse herself before attempting Lilwenn's healing, was probably vomiting into the bracken as they spoke. Voirrey must find her, get this thing done, and return them to the Skalens' House.

"In peace time and in war, innocence must be protected," Voirrey said dismissively, knowing that Maeryn had done right by Inry. "You and your mother should hide, no matter what happens." Seeing that the girl looked unconvinced, she pressed the matter. "What skills do you possess to use in battle?" she demanded. *See yourself and know these limits before you begin*, she thought.

Lilwenn's chin jutted in defiance. "I can ride a horse. I can use a knife. I–"

"Can you kill with a knife?" Voirrey pressed. "Can you overpower a guardsman, fully armoured, with sword drawn? How many could you kill?"

Lilwenn bared her teeth. "I would kill them all. You have no idea what I am capable of."

Anger. So much anger. Voirrey would not convince her this way. She needed Lilwenn to be cleansed before the Magloreans came. The blinding stone shelter was the only place that would be truly safe, and she was sure that Inry would go there willingly now. If Lilwenn could be soothed of her fears, they could both hide themselves until the fighting was done.

Just then, Voirrey heard a tinkling sound, musical in the distance.

Everyone froze where they stood–with wheelbarrows in hand, sacks half-filled with dirt-stained carrots, blades hovering above their whetstones–all looking to the lad in the watch tower signalling with wide eyes. He pointed, shouting to a man by the fence. Then, with great violence, camp bell began to ring.

61

AVISHAE

Zohar awoke, disoriented, to the clanging of bells.

On the bed, the little girl, Davina, watched her. She did not look sleepy at all.

Shaking herself from her dream, Zohar finally recognised with cold dread what the bell meant. Maglore. The invasion had begun.

Running to the window she looked out, seeing guardsmen streaming down the hill, and many more mounting their horses.

Illiam. Where was Illiam?

She wanted to run and find him but could not leave the girl.

"Davina, come here and I'll carry you. We need to hide," she said, whisking her up into her arms.

The girl's frightened eyes measured her but she clung on as Zohar fled the room, thundering down the Attendant's stair as fast as she could. Elspeth, coming up the stair, nearly collided with her.

"Take her to the shelter," Zohar said, attempting to pass Davina into her Attendant's arms.

The girl clung to her and Zohar felt a sudden and powerful urge to remain with the child. "You must hide in the shelter," she tried to explain, disentangling the girl's legs from her waist. "You will be safe with Elspeth, I promise," Zohar left them, feeling awful.

Voirrey and the others had not returned. This was not good.

Zohar ran, gasping now, turning the corner to find a window onto the valley. She peered out, the diamond panes fogging with her breath which she scrubbed furiously with her sleeve. More Avishaen forces came down the hill. Some from Baden Forest. Others rushing up the Skalens' Road to seek shelter. She scanned the periphery but could not yet see the Magloreans.

Wait... Smoke coiled upward from Haydentown. They were here, alright.

Though her parents had strictly forbidden it, Zohar removed her Meridian, fixed her inner sense on Illiam. The pungent whiff of sweat, of horses and ready men. *The stables.*

Zohar ran, re-buckling her Meridian as she went, shoving past countless people once she reached the courtyard.

She saw him. "Illiam!"

He peered at her through passing heads, gestured for her to come.

The people were like a rip-tide, and she felt the same fear that had gripped her when she was young, of swimming with Ambrose and not being able to reach him.

Finally, she was in his arms. "I'm shaking Illiam. How can I be shaking?" She was supposed to lead those fleeing the town to safety. She and Illiam were to decide who entered the blinding stone shelter, and who remained within the Skalens' House Gates should the fight reach them. They were, in desperation, to take their people to the cliffside where a rope ladder had been hung to get them to the boats.

Now that the bell had rung, people were simply running in.

She looked up, saw her parents on horseback: both of them in plate armour and helmets so she barely recognised them.

"Zohar, to the gate!" her mother called.

"Take command of the gate!" her father seconded and then they were off at full gallop, charging down the hill.

Illiam grabbed her hand, lending her strength and they hurried to their post.

"If we are calm, they will be calm," he said.

They stood either side of the gate and Zohar managed a quivering smile as a young mother arrived with her baby. "Come inside to the shelter," she said.

The woman nodded breathlessly and went on.

Regaining her senses, Zohar tried to estimate how many must already be inside. Fifty, maybe?

Guardsmen were still filing out but some would remain behind.

When she took a moment to turn, she was relieved to find Guardsman Elis standing there along with twelve or so others.

Noticing a group of men pushing a wagon load of children, she bid the guards help so the men could return to the valley. Seeing how frightened they were, she told Elis to take her place so she could escort them downstairs.

Instructing the older children to lead the younger, she picked up a sniffling, skinny boy who was inconsolably upset. Looking into his red-rimmed eyes she smiled. "Look at you, lucky last. I will carry you down."

His mouth fell open, realising who she was.

The other children gazed at her, too.

She took them down to the lower floors, where it was cool and dim but where there were many more faces than she was used to seeing in this place. She had expected chaos. A rushing crowd of people: crying, bickering, fearful. But this was the beauty of blinding stone. Those who sat leaning against the walls seemed listlessly calm, and the children lay their heads upon their protector's laps. Some in the centre of the room were in full meditative posture–silent and still.

The new arrivals walked shyly inside, the little boy looking up at Zohar one last time before taking after his fellows.

She searched the sea of heads for Davina, seeing many who were not her.

Green eyes. A pulse of recognition like an electric shock. The girl stared at her across the room and Zohar bowed so she would know that she had not forgotten her. There was something uncanny about the girl. Zohar felt a tumult of feeling where she should have none. It was because of Sybilla, she thought. Because she was Sybilla's child.

Zohar went back up to join Illiam, passing children, the crippled and elderly couples limping to their destination. Through the crowd she caught sight of Illiam's short curly hair, his hand gesturing. She pushed through the crowd and was almost at the gate when she felt it–the air thick with magnetism–and her legs turned to mud. *Illiam!* she cried.

He lurched toward her, liquid and streaming.

The people around her were waves that she swam through, her spirit surging forward to meet him, until, together, they crashed.

Blindly their waters raged, storming one another in desperate caress.

My mirror, my love.

62

AVISHAE

Maeryn spat into the dirt, pulling at her hair. *Disgusting. Disgusting.*

She felt vileness at the very centre of her being. *Caged.*

She paced and circled, scraped her wrists hard against the bark of a great oak tree. *Out, out, get out!*

She screamed as if vomiting demons from her mouth.

This is what she needed; she must not spend it. She stoppered herself, let the filth boil up into her eyes so it yellowed her vision. She would sweat poison like a toad.

Touch me, come and touch me and seek your death.

The stone was hot in her hand. Not so far away, she could feel the Maglorean guard sweeping their oars, leathers creaking as they readied themselves for slaughter.

And slaughter it would be.

Maeryn ran down the slope like a woman half her age, re-entering the camp.

At the sight of her, Voirrey grew pale.

Maeryn released her grip on the stone, repressed the poison–just a bit.

"Landyn, ready my horse!" Her voice was harsh and deep, threatening even to her own ears.

Edith came running over, ready with her bow.

Maeryn snatched her arm. "Not you. Stay here, I order it."

Edith staggered back and stared in confusion. Maeryn trudged away, leaving her where she stood. All of them were in her way, now, and she had no time to explain.

Landyn brought the horse out from behind the huts, and as Maeryn hurried forward, she saw Lilwenn standing there, pale as a ghost. Her gaze locked on the girl and she squinted as if dust had blown into her eyes. In her vivid state, Maeryn recognised a certain commonality between the poison she had swallowed and the deep reservoir that the girl possessed.

Redness. Such redness. Pulsing, like coals beneath dry ash.

A dark thrill ran through her. *Daughter of Maglore*, she called into the girl's mind. *If you want to bring down death upon them, come with me.*

A wave of heat coursed off her, making her sweat.

Lilwenn held the Intercessor's unwavering gaze and gave the barest nod, her face pinched with intent.

Inry watched slack-jawed and Voirrey put her arm around her, both of them stupefied as they watched the Intercessor steal Lilwenn away.

They rode hard, Maeryn in her peasant's smock and Lilwenn holding her waist, both of them completely unarmed.

When they reached the ridge where the Skalens' Road cupped the valley, Maeryn called to a contingent of guardsmen and bid them to follow. A great circle of horsed guards gathered about them, their faces expressionless and calm as they held their spirits in Hiatus.

Maeryn could hear fighting in the distance and brought Lilwenn into the sphere of her protection. Touching the stone with her thumb, she tested her power on the men about her.

Good, she thought, as they advanced, unflinching, not a single one of them buckling in his saddle. *These are holy men, as in days of old, and here the imposters will see what good their weapons can do against us.*

She felt righteous and large, like the great and powerful kshidol. Before them, Haydentown roared with smoke and mingled cries.

This next part would be impossible on horseback and she signalled to keep formation as they dismounted. As their feet met the earth, Maeryn sensed the enemy sprinting toward them, though they made little sound. The Avishaens moved forward, readying their swords.

"Fall back, Intercessor, let us clear the way!" the guard commanded.

Maeryn ignored him, focused on the boiling filth beneath her skin.

"Hold my hand, girl, and have your revenge," she said, catching the girl's grey eyes.

Lilwenn looked at her hesitatingly, so small among the horses and guards.

She gave her hand and Maeryn fastened their spirits as one, creating a channel between them.

The child, deformed at the cusp of her womanhood, held her venom compressed in her hip bone, right there at the joint. Maeryn drew at the poison. Not in the usual way where she siphoned it off, but to animate it, setting it flowing between them in a figure of eight.

Lilwenn's eyes were wild and Maeryn saw her with her soul's eye, the protective urge turned to predation as it renewed its redness.

No longer did she have to speak now that their minds and wills were one. Lilwenn the rudder and Maeryn the guiding wind.

Take them, Maeryn bid. *Try your strength.*

A hot little flare, uncontrolled.

Maeryn helped her picture their faces, helped her to smell their flesh and feel their relentless progress through the grass. So close, now.

Lilwenn blazed and on that hot tide Maeryn felt them spasm, crying out as they lost their footing and the strength in their legs failed them. The Avishaens moved in, slashing with their swords, trampling the helpless men as they entered the town proper.

Through the swishing tails of the horses before them, Maeryn glimpsed the outer streets of Haydentown, saw flames rising from the bell tower. Though this was only a fraction of what she really saw.

With her inner eye she sensed them–pulsing hot–all sweat and sticky blood. Coarse hair, muscles and innards–pierced and piercing–teeth and sour sweat, piss and fear.

Maeryn drew herself into deep focus, thinking only of their shushing footsteps, their rhythms moving as one.

Are you ready, Lilwenn? she asked, her eyes greasy and sick.

With her soul's eye, she saw Lilwenn's skin peeling away so she walked naked and red. In response to Maeryn's call, her sweat rose fetid and sour, her little rabbit heart beating its song of death.

Maeryn exposed the stone, holding it hard against her bare forehead, walking on with eyes closed.

"Leave us!" she called to the guardsmen. "Go before us and kill as many as you can."

At her signal, the guardsmen fanned out, abandoning their horses to fight their way down the narrow streets. Steel clanged in every direction, uncomfortably close, and now that the Guard had moved out, she saw the mangled corpses, the half-dead and the horde that charged in their direction.

The thick feeling rose dark about her chest, merging swiftly with Lilwenn's will. It learned her song, joined primal voices to sing its harmony, so the men began to fall to their knees, dropping their swords as if the metal burned them.

Louder, stronger, replicating, expanding, Maeryn fed the black fire to a blazing pitch until the world around them dissolved and grew dim. Gone was the day, the blue sky, and thick-fleeced clouds, the dirt road beneath their feet, the trees that framed the valley. Maeryn saw with her deep sense, saw spirits dark and swirling, gusting red and giving off sparks, saw the weak points where they could be shattered.

Guardsmen ran from them now, staggering as they tried to escape the sickening tide. But still, they drew breath and might rise again.

With all the force of her gift she sparked the stone, its energies flooding out, dissolving boundaries, unifying substances so all became a medium for her to travel through.

Half-concussed, Maeryn and Lilwenn walked forward, walking

the cobblestones now, their hands ironbound. Lilwenn's hair lifted from her neck, her eyes grey vortexes girt by blood.

At Lilwenn's feet the Magloreans fell, desperate and screaming, some clutching their chests in a rictus of agony, some voiding their bowels in terror.

Breathless Avishaens armed with shovels and hammers backed away from the scene. They were, all of them, sickly pale, bathed in the stone's unholy charge. The men all leant upon one another in twos and threes, as if crippled by a blast.

Guardsman John saw them and knew what was needed. Like a statue upon his horse, he called: "Avishaens, go to the valley and put your hands upon the cairn. Or else find yourselves a shelter in the Bay of Knives. Blind yourselves, brothers." And on he led the Guard, deeper into Haydentown.

Maeryn and Lilwenn moved slowly, street by street, not bothering to avoid the fallen bodies as they walked. The bodies, real and unreal, like sacks of potatoes and spilt wine, like pig's carcasses and butcher's waste–things that once were living, now emptied. All about them, the spirits screamed, their forms yawning wide and splitting apart. Here, a hand, pale and unmoving. There, some bright fragment, glassy in the sunlight. They were in the thick of it, this business, this evil task, this cleansing that spanned so many bodies; it seemed the dead were all of one flesh.

These fragments, both feverish and spectral, were fathers and workers and laughing men. These were murderers, and children of Velspar. Such complexity, such mixture.

Separate! Maeryn bid the substances. Sifting the redness out of them until their chests grew silent.

Maeryn marvelled at the carnage, the curious sounds of the dying.

Lilwenn's fingernails dug into her arm, her teeth bared with the furious charge rushing through her.

We are using too much energy, Maeryn thought, directing this knowing into Lilwenn's awareness.

Their slow hypnotic step took them deeper into the warren of alleyways, past shops with shattered windows where swords were dropped like cutlery from a drunkard's table.

Men staggered in all directions, grievously injured, their haunted eyes piteous and round.

Maeryn directed Lilwenn's poison in throbbing gusts, and three of the nearest fell. Yet there were more. Too many. She could hear the Avishaen Guard hacking with their swords not far behind.

Lilwenn set her eyes upon the flaming bell tower, and Maeryn followed her thought. If they feared the fire, if they were made to insufferably thirst, they would flee to the river, and there, they could drown them.

Together, they drank the fire with their eyes, tasted smoke upon their tongues. Maeryn pictured the aperture of their throats and focused the fire there. So much muscle, so much brute strength, but here: a point of weakness.

One of the Magloreans was close enough to reach out and touch her, then, all of a sudden, he stopped. He clutched at his throat, his face reddening as if he'd swallowed a wasp. Others lost their swords, choking, falling to their knees, and for the first time Maeryn saw Lilwenn smile.

The guards who had moved to encircle them now fled in terror. Several ran in the direction of the valley, but the Avishaens came stalking from the alleyways, slicing and hacking the men who had forgotten how to do anything but raise their hands to their faces.

It was difficult to see through the smoke but Maeryn led Lilwenn steadily toward the docks, knowing that there they would spend their last. She could see masts and anchor posts like dead trees in mist. Lilwenn began to cough, and Maeryn watched her intently as men ran past them left and right, splashing into the water.

Maeryn called for the Avishaens to release the boats and soon they were drifting like flotsam, heading straight for the Bay of Knives.

Lilwenn's footing slowed and she leaned on Maeryn, looking faint. Knowing they had little time, Maeryn dragged the girl close enough so they could see the water below.

Hold them down, Maeryn bid her, and Lilwenn stared at their flailing forms. She watched them listlessly—*so many*—the Selbourne writing with face and limb. Maeryn set her entire being to the task, feeling the girl was spent. She stripped the redness from their arms, their legs, so they could not move. They screamed bubbles and breathed water, and fought her all the way to the bottom.

The thrashing called up memories of incense and prayers, as if the siatka had come home to feed.

The thought shook her, stealing her focus, and for a moment she came clear.

Oh, Siatka, Great Mother, what have I done?

The Intercessor's hand loosened, and Lilwenn turned, the connection fracturing. Lilwenn let out a terrified sob, and suddenly the stone's pulse seemed profoundly evil. She let it go. Looking behind her, she saw the ruin of the town, the Avishaen guards dispatching stragglers.

Guardsman John, profoundly pale in his shining helmet, nodded. "We have the rest. It is done."

Maeryn exhaled, stumbling in the haze of the stone. She fumbled with the case, lodged it halfway in and grabbed Lilwenn's hand.

She must get her away from here before the girl fainted.

They wandered numbly and without sense of their bodies. Maeryn felt an irritation, like a splinter, stuck in her periphery where Lilwenn was. As she focused on the feeling, it grew clearer. Inside, Lilwenn still held the fiery shard of her torture. A sliver of glass in which smiled the dead face of Degore.

He is dead, you saw him die, she whispered into the girl's mind as if to remind herself that she was still an Intercessor. She would still help the girl.

Lilwenn turned to her, uncertain and afraid. She tried to let him go, but all was numbness and confusion and Maeryn could not tell if it had worked.

Their shoes squelched with blood. The sound accompanied their passage as they tried to escape the maze of streets, stepping over bodies with empty eyes.

Once they reached the valley, they left their shoes behind, with a great buzzing in their ears that drowned out the day. Maeryn let go of

Lilwenn's hand, and now she felt a shame so profound it made her sick to remain within her own skin.

Weakly, she called on the stone.

Leech us of this poison. She cried, her tears like blood.

The old woman screamed–a sound wide and ragged. Lilwenn joined her, and Maeryn howled again. The coarse air of their lungs that must scour them from the inside out.

She set her hands upon the spinning earth. *Take this from us, Velspar, wash us in the Stream and flow it far from us*. Knowing she did not deserve to be healed, but trying, for Lilwenn's sake.

As the heaviness began to lift, Maeryn heard other voices–kind voices, holy voices–whispers of Intercession enfolding her. The Temple's hollow throat began to chant the song of healing as she cloaked herself in memory. Her body, raised up on a cloud of Alma smoke; her body leaden on the damp grass.

She reached for the girl's hand. Grey eyes tried to find her. The red corona spreading round the grey iris, like a solar eclipse. *Close your eyes, child*, she whispered, for she was fading and could not help her anymore.

The song of the stone suffused her, voices darting through her wards. A chorus of placatory hands, combing through her, all familiar and fond. She was in their realm now, and she felt the will to toss herself to the wind. To be inconstant and shifting and abandon the world of forms. The world of slow labour and fixed patterns where there must be spaces in between. Severed parts. Little sparks caught in flesh. Some dim, some bright, then endless and undifferentiated, in the Great and glittering Stream.

Her awareness meandered farther than it should. Her essence became a word repeated so often, that it lost its meaning. Right now, in this time and place, children lay curled in their shelter, as men's spirits burst with sensations that sent them floating like fox fur on the wind. Horses thundered up the hill and people shivered in the undergrowth. Trees creaked in the breeze, waves crashed about the faces of the slain, and in some obscure treetop she spied the kshidol's nest. Winds drifted through her, all flavoured with the lives of others, beautiful and bright, humble as the scent of home. Too many to know or understand. A curious melange of which she was part. She did not need to be anything else. Maeryn had saved them and soon she would allow that name to slip away.

Then, straight into her heart, the sharp beak of a sparrow pierced her. With the impact it fell, and kept falling. Without knowing why, she needed Voirrey to catch that bird. Voirrey. She knew that name. A spirit tied to many threads.

63

***

AVISHAE

Edith was ready. All week she had been fletching arrows, parrying with the sword, and not sleeping at all. That was before the sightings on the coast. Since then, three separate runners had come to the Raeburn camp with the news: Head Guardsman Rayhmer was here.

She could almost feel the bruises about her eyes, the dryness of her mouth that could not be quenched with water, her heart racing in erratic bursts at the slightest noise. She had been ready, had done everything, had retraced Maeryn's instruction about how to use the stone but could do nothing more than imagine the havoc it might wreak. She could not fight these men with her mind alone. It was beyond absurdity.

She fingered her knife hilt.

The town bell was ringing and Rowan locked eyes with hers across the way. She stared as he ran to the camp gate, ringing the bell so forcefully and so loud she had to cover her ears. He just kept ringing it–though surely the entire camp had got the message– ringing it as if he were beating a man with the bell hammer.

Maeryn ran past her looking half-mad. "Landyn, ready my horse!" she growled.

Edith, breaking from her fugue, went to follow Maeryn.

The Intercessor met her with a savage look that felt like a punch to the guts. "Not you. Stay here, I order it."

Edith watched Maeryn with the Greslet girl in paralysed confusion. There was a force on her, she could feel it. She stared at them, watching their mouths move but could not hear a word of what was said.

It was only after they had gone that she regained herself. One minute, she was standing there, poised to follow Maeryn. The next, Landyn and Voirrey were at her side, the sound of the bell an echo in her mind.

They all looked at one another feeling that their plan had already been turned on its head.

Landyn spoke through gritted teeth, looking old and haggard, white stubble on his leathered skin. "She means us to defend the camp. Rayhmer has slipped our sights again and it is likely he will try to establish a stronghold here before attacking the Skalens' House." He struggled with the words and rubbed his face.

Inry Greslet still sat with her back to the well, her knees drawn up, face buried in her palms. The task Maeryn had set her was impossible. How was she to protect the Greslets now? *She does not even fight*, Edith thought, *she does not even fight for her own daughter.* She exhaled sharply, scanning the trees, feeling hopelessly exposed.

Landyn spoke slowly, in low tones. "We must not lose our heads. Remember the plan. We know the formations, the shapes we must form to defend our people. Maeryn will explain herself when she returns."

Voirrey nodded. "I understand your strategy and am prepared to fight but I will serve you better as a healer today."

He shot her a glance, suspecting cowardice, but Edith knew far more of Voirrey from Maeryn's stories and shook her head at him. "She does not deceive you. Ma Bet can choose helpers for her and the two of them can be in charge of the injured."

There was no one he trusted more than Ma Bet. She was old and slow, fierce with her words but not with a weapon. Whatever he suspected of Voirrey, Ma Bet would be safest this way.

"And you?" Landyn said, fixing Edith with his sharpening stare.

"I am ready for this," she said. "But I don't play well with others. You keep your formations, I'll cover the cracks."

He smirked, seeing the fire in her eyes. Trusting her on this and liking that he would not have her underfoot to upset his command.

Landyn nodded, appraising her. "Velspar's blessings upon you, then."

Edith gave him a grim half-smile, hoping she'd see the old man again. "And on you."

64

___

AVISHAE

REBEKAH AND ULRIC waited on the ridge, surveying the northern mountains for signs of movement. They headed up a contingent of villagers, who looked capable of killing a man, but not easily or well. Much like their Skalens. Since the clan wars in the days of the First Diviner, no Skalen had been required to shed blood with their own hand. Sword lessons were an art, a dance of their station, a communion between Skalen and Guard–strike and parry, parry and strike– we command you and respect your dance, we know what it is we ask. But did they?

Skalens once ruled with Intercessors at their left hand and Guards at their right. Now they fought with one arm bound, this imbalance prompting endless adjustments until they were all just people wrestling in blood, fighting for their lives. And here, the right arm of Avishae must hack off the Maglorean's right, for it was rotten and must be purged.

Rebekah sweated hot about her neck and armpits, her armour heavy and horribly cold. She could not quite see, and yet she feared to remove her helm now that they could hear screaming in the distance. She glanced at Ulric, fearful of what was happening there. The nightmarish sensation of the stone crept about them in unseen tendrils.

The aperture through which her son had disappeared was opening.

Ulric turned his horse about, addressed the villagers.

"When the Magloreans come, you must use your knowledge of the forest to your advantage. The men who came here recently were scouts, I have no doubt in my mind about that. They will have mapped the Raeburn camp, the ways that lead to the Skalens' House, but they will not know these mountains as you do. They found one track, and if they have described it to their men, they will have given them landmarks to look for. Think of the places in the North where the Temple can be seen. Think of shelters and glades."

Many of those gathered cast their minds in thought, looking away from their Skalens to consider the path they would take.

Ulric continued. "Be not deterred by their livery. They wear the Guardsman's Star but they are villagers just like you. They have been trained only to kill, not to master themselves or to act with honour. If you find yourself outmatched, you must separate and confuse them. Long has the mainland underestimated Avishae, and we will not abide this act of conquest."

"Aye!" chorused the villagers.

Rebekah watched her husband, his grey beard visible inside the shining silver of his helm. His bloodshot eyes caught hers. He could feel it too. The stone and its death-tide.

Rebekah brought up her horse beside him.

"Protect one another," she said. "And leave no Avishaen free of their Meridian."

Gravely, some of the men nodded, glancing in the direction of Haydentown.

Ulric saw their trepidation. "You must trust our holy protector. Intercessor Maeryn knows you from the invaders. She is wise and will not do you harm. If you do lose your Meridian, it will not be death you face. Her magic will only harm those who harbour red thoughts. Hold fast to your faith and her spell will not touch you."

Rebekah knew at this point there was little more to say. All of them scented smoke and could hear screaming from the town.

Rebekah held her husband's gaze as they prepared themselves. *I love you Ulric*, she thought, her heart surging. *We do this together and yet we do this alone.*

"With me!" Ulric called, leading his group further up the hill.

Rebekah gestured for her contingent to hide themselves but to remain nearby where she had a good line of sight.

They waited like this for what might have been half an hour. Ulric was too far away for her to make out, but now and then she caught the gleam of his armour. Across the valley's expanse, the town still smoked, though without any signs of visible flame. She could sense a weakening of the stone, an absence of nausea that left her able to hear and see quite clearly. The Guard had not emerged, which could mean anything: victory or utter defeat.

Behind her, she heard a crash followed by a gurgling sound and turned in horror to find one of her group run through by an Maglorean sword. She charged at him, knocking the man off-balance and striking the air with her sword. Moments later, Clara, the dairy maid, rounded on him with her pitchfork, the girl's father knifing him in the throat as he staggered back.

The sound of her breath was overloud in her helm, sucking in and out.

The guard was dead, but where were the others?

"Down there, in the trees!" Patrick Milwain pointed and started off, his sons and nephews charging after.

Rebekah heard the clang of swords up where Ulric's group had gone but could not see anything. They had not come from the town. They came like a swarm from up river.

"Forget the town, they're in the woods!" she hissed.

"Tom!" she called. "Bring the Avishaen Guard, any they can spare."

The freckle-faced boy nodded and ran streaking toward the town.

As she turned, Magloreans burst from the trees.

She slashed at them, running her horse in circles, completely out of her depth. Her sword met flesh and came back bloody. Everywhere, murderers writhed on the ground, injured and groaning, some staggering to their feet. Not many dead.

She couldn't see with this thing on her head. They were too fast, behind her, around her.

Rebekah charged through them, getting clear just long enough to remove her helm.

Patrick's boys rejoined them, coming back through the trees, dispatching the injured Magloreans in brutal and systematic fashion, like cattle at reaping time. Clara was clutching her side, bleeding, trying to edge herself behind a tree.

There was movement on the ridge. Three men moved with great purpose, seemingly ignoring the skirmishes in their wake. She rode for them and at the thunder of hooves they turned. Within seconds, one had aimed his bow and before she could register what was happening, she slammed into the earth, her horse screaming. Dizzied, she scrambled backwards, away from the horse, feeling its massive writhing weight ready to crush her.

In the blur, she saw Ulric, gleaming silver, his vigorous horse, heard the smash of swords quick and deadly. She coughed blood but could not understand her injuries. The tortured face of her horse thrashed in her line of vision so she could not see what was happening.

More horses, dark horses, thundered across the valley. They streaked past her–Avishaen guardsmen–more than she could count. She came up on her knees and managed to stand. Her horse was dead now, lying still in the grass, an arrow in its breast.

"Skalen!" Guardsman Elis called, riding over to her. "Skalen," he panted, "we have won the town. Can you walk?"

Rebekah nodded, feeling battered and unsteady.

"I'll send someone back down for you and the Intercessor. She and the girl are down there, across the valley." At this he rode off.

She watched him go, seeing the last of the Avishaen guard disappear into the trees. Ulric must have gone with them. *Velspar protect him*, she prayed. Peering into the sun, she trudged through the heather to find Maeryn. As she went, she wondered: *The girl? What girl?*

The grass and bobbing flowers were high about her knees, still wet from yesterday's rain. In the bright distance, she could see the public cairn. She had imagined her people down there wailing, trying to bury themselves in blinding stone to be free of the Intercessor's unholy magics, but there were few there about the mound.

More than once, she turned to the hill near the Skalens' House to check the Guard still kept their vigil. A rotation of seven sentinels watched her son, and she saw that they remained in place, beneath the shady tree.

Rebekah could not see where Maeryn had fallen but somehow, she knew. Dark tides wafted toward her, both familiar and alien. She felt Ambrose there, intermixed with a pleroma of ancestral voices: her own parents, her grandparents, ancient faces she did not know. They were like a draught coming from outside with the perfume of snow, seeping from another place, making it so she barely saw the fields in which she walked.

Ambrose! Her mind narrowed, seeking the restlessness of him, the way he'd sit there biting his nails and frowning at his plate. She thought of the last time she'd seen him, the grazes on his skin, the last time she'd seen him...

But the other voices were a swarm flying at her face and she lost him. All of them said, *Yes, Mother, I am your son.* All of them came to her, curious and wild, wanting to tell her things. She was alive, they must tell her. Bright and living, listening and alive. *Kindred, hear me, hear my story above all others, my story and me and mine, all that I have loved and lost, all the unfinished things that I need you to do. Kindred!*

Abruptly, she pulled herself back–all the way in–making herself cold, silent and still. Some of them diverted as if she had turned out the lantern and they could no longer find her.

Moths, they are like moths, she thought, *finding what is bright.* Her cantering heart slowed as she reasoned, and though part of her still screamed for her son, another part held fast, growing stronger, clearing her mind.

She touched the tips of the grass, felt her toes and boots wet, made herself look upon the smoke that trailed from Haydentown and in time she found them. Two bodies upon the grass, unconscious and blood-smudged, yet breathing. In the old woman's hand, she saw the exposed sliver of the stone.

Rebekah crouched. Through waves of nausea and terrible weeping desire, she pushed it back in and sealed it.

She lay down beside them and closed her eyes.

65

AVISHAE

THEY WERE everywhere, bursting from the forest paths like rats.

THE MAGLOREAN HORDE converged on the camp, kicking down doors, finding the place empty. Edith watched them from above. Big men, and lots of them. Her bow creaked as she levelled it, but they moved too quickly and she would waste her arrows if she loosed them now.

In seconds, it seemed, they discovered the first band of Raeburn fighters. Figures ran from their hiding places, screaming, thrashing, barking commands. She watched for a tall man with dark hair and pockmarked skin–as if killing Rayhmer would make the others stop.

They all looked the same.

Together the little figures clashed in a fever of death. Her people, and the devils of Maglore. Suddenly, the stone seemed useful after all–but could she trust herself? If she killed, would she kill them all? In dissolving their redness, might she weaken the sword arm of her kin?

No magic. No powers beyond her wits and the bow in her hand.

Badly, she wanted to run down and join them, but she was there for the stragglers, the unseen column advancing from an unexpected angle. At least, for now, they had not located the tent behind the camp where Voirrey and Ma Bet were to see to the wounded. If they went that way, she would have to pursue them.

She tried to calm herself, her entire being white-hot and burning itself into incandescence before she had a chance to do anything. *Keep it together, you fool.*

Suddenly, there were horses riding into the camp, and to her dizzying relief she recognised Skalen Ulric at the head of a sizeable troop of Avishaen guards. Without warning, they charged into the fray, horses screaming, such a terrible force that surely the Magloreans would be outnumbered.

Edith shifted in her crouch as she noticed figures fleeing on the right-hand side, running up the hill. This was her cue. She drew her arrow, aimed, and loosed, striking one in the shoulder. The man fell, but his fellows quickly identified her position and set off after her.

Below, Avishaens, too, were fleeing from the melee. Shocked and tattered, covered in blood, they scrambled up the incline. She turned back to the Magloreans–drew and loosed–striking another in the leg, barely slowing him as he bellowed in rage. There were four or five of them pursuing her and none of them looked to be bowmen.

They would have to catch her first, and she would not make it easy.

Edith darted through the brush, knowing the way–ducking, shifting–her breath rasping cold in her throat.

Distantly, she heard a voice. "Edith!" Rowan's voice.

With a sinking feeling, she turned, but in the chaos of foliage she felt blind, her blood moving too fast for her to focus.

"Edith!" he called, desperate, as though he wanted her to wait for him. To *wait up*, as if this were a running race. His voice tore at her heart but more than that she was angry that he might risk her life so stupidly. Slowing her down at a time like this just to wait for him. *Dammit!*

She kept going, and soon she emerged in the high clearing where her stone altar stood. She did not know if it would work but knew she had to try.

Edith stood upon the stone and set the pendant Maeryn had

given her in her palm. Quickly, before she could change her mind, she tore off her Meridian and unsheathed the stone.

From the centre of her being she called: *Swift feather. Traveller. Blood-beaked, Kshidol! Hear my call.*

Time seemed to lengthen and expand, and she called the Kshidol not simply from their nests but from their source, the eternal place of emanation.

Rowan appeared, stopping before her wide-eyed. He looked above her and by his look she knew. She could smell the musk of their feathers, glorious on the breeze, though they kept themselves high.

Rowan spun about, his back to her and sword drawn against the Magloreans who crashed through the clearing. Three of them now.

Two went straight for Rowan—one stocky blonde, one tall and dark. He thrashed wildly with his sword and was just barely keeping them off. Edith drew her bow and shot the skinny guard coming at her. He fell, but as the blonde guard advanced on Rowan, the tall one marked her and strode forward with measured ease.

She aimed her bow at him but faltered as her eyes were drawn to something far more terrifying. A sword protruded bright and red from Rowan's back. She screamed. He arched with a terrible shudder like that time she'd pulled a shard of glass from his foot when they were children.

"Rowan!" Edith screamed but he was slumped in the dirt, blood drooling from his open mouth.

She was about to loose an arrow at the Maglorean when she noticed how close the blonde guard had come. She pointed the arrow at him now.

"Stop," she commanded, standing taller than them on her rock as long as they remained where they were.

The dark, craggy-faced man smiled at her. "One arrow left. Who will it be? Or might we catch you first?" He lunged at her jokingly and drew back, testing her reflexes.

The blonde stared above, expression agog. "Rayhmer! Bloody kshidol. Shit! Get down!"

Her stomach flipped–*this was Rayhmer*. She took his measure, feeling the likelihood of her survival shrink to a hair's breadth.

Edith heard the beat of wings.

This time, she did not hesitate. Just as his eyes went up, she loosed. Rayhmer dodged, but still, the arrow caught him in the side of the throat. For a moment he stumbled, dropping his sword, then, with blazing eyes he lunged at her. The blonde came in too, but before he could get himself up on the rock, the kshidol swooped. She saw him in her periphery, thrashing at the sky as the winged ones came down, deft in their feints despite their size.

Rayhmer yanked her legs and pulled her off the rock, her head smacking the hard earth. If she had not braced herself, her skull would have cracked on the edge of the rock. She tried to pull herself back, but he was too strong. Anger seared her, extending like a lightning flash.

Great wings beat down, and Rayhmer grunted as the kshidol tore at him with their talons. His fists sought them and missed. He still had her legs, though. Had pinned her with his chest, and was reaching for his sword, little more than an arm's length away. She could hear the other guard's harried cries as he fled. This was her chance, her only chance.

As the kshidol swarmed him, she slid the knife from her belt, gripped it tight. He was reaching in the other direction, his eyes on his sword as she rammed the knife up under his ear.

He let out a choking sound, of pain that had no air behind it, his brown eyes wide with shock. And as his teeth spread pink with blood, his mighty fist came down.

Edith sensed blackness and pain, swollen burning pain. Through the ringing in her ears, she tried to wake herself. She could smell him, the oil of his hair, the blood, the sourness of his rotten breath. Finally, her eyes opened, though one of them remained shut. Her blinded eye would not abide her touch and her hair was sticky at the back.

Rayhmer was still on top of her, his head in her lap. He must be dead. Her clothes were soaked in his blood. Still, she was afraid to move in case she woke him.

Desperate tears came to her eyes that stung so horribly she willed herself to stop. She could see them, the kshidol, one up there above her on the altar watching her with its reddened beak, its all-seeing eye.

Like cloaked shadows, the kshidol bobbed about, investigating the dead. One of them bent with its broad back to her, its snaking neck twisted down, licking or eating, she could not tell.

Again, she checked Rayhmer's body for movement and began shifting out from under him. How could a man be so heavy? She heaved him upward with her thighs and rolled to the side, her numbed legs now free.

From this new angle, she could see Rowan, his eyes closed, his dark brows all free of concern.

The kshidol licked blood from his wound. She wanted to shoo them away, to hold him, but she just stared numbly, unable to move.

Other kshidol came loitering around Rayhmer's corpse, nudging with their beaks.

"No, not him!" she cried, not wanting them to ingest the redness in the guardsman's flesh.

She kicked at them and they hopped backwards.

She turned back to Rowan, knowing it would kill her to watch them do it but this might be the only opportunity he would have to be taken whole into the blessed Stream.

"Take this one, he is good," she managed, trying to focus, to use the stone as she had before but she felt entirely disconnected from her body.

The kshidol did not heed her and went on licking at the blood, whatever blood they could find. They did not tear at the flesh as this was not their way. Sky burial required careful preparation and time for decomposition. It was a small consolation. This was her altar, the only altar left in all the Seven Lands and it had been defiled. It had witnessed Rowan's murder!

Edith felt faint and out of control and it was not until Guardsman John was within a few paces of her that she saw the contingent emerge into the clearing. With expressions of shock, they took in the scene.

She fell to her knees. "John! Rowan is dead...Rowan–"

John crouched and put an arm around her. His gaze lingered on Rayhmer's face and he grew very still. All the guards had grown still. At that moment she knew their transgression. By their hand, the Holy Ones had perished in the hundreds and here they were, resurrections outside of ritual, in a place where they should not be. They were awed, and they were fearful too.

John bowed to the kshidol, solemnly and with trembling hands. "Father Kshidol, we honour you."

The other guards also bowed but did not dare speak.

When he stood, he collected Edith in his arms like a child.

"Bring him," John said, gesturing to Rayhmer's corpse. "The head, and his surcoat."

66

AVISHAE

THE TENT WAS stifling hot and smelt awful.

Voirrey leaned closer, fighting the urge to push a stray hair from her face as she made the second incision in the man's thigh. As expected, he cried out, pulling hard on the ropes that bound him.

"Hold him fast!" she glared at Inry as sweat dripped into her eyes.

Inry nodded and pulled the ropes as hard as she could.

Voirrey had run out of Alma oil and was not used to working under such conditions. She took a sharp breath and peered into the opened wound. The arrowhead was near the surface and she was quite confident she could get it out, if only the man could lay still.

"Are you going to let me do it?" she demanded.

He nodded, closing his eyes in anguish as he tried not to look.

It was well that he was not looking. Voirrey drew out a thin, metal scoop and steadied her hand on his thigh. Carefully, she inserted the tip, using the incision she had made to get the tool behind the barbs of the arrow.

The man breathed hard through his teeth and Inry braced the rope. He began to tremble and Voirrey could tell he was about to lose his hold on the pain.

"Okay, I've got it under the barb on the first side," Voirrey assured him. "Now we do the second."

The man nodded fiercely, sweat coursing his chest.

"I need you to hold this," she nodded for Inry to take the protruding metal handle. "Delicately now, or we will have to start the whole thing again."

Inry released the rope hesitatingly and came to support the handle. The poor woman had been kicked in the face by the last patient when his pain reflex had got the better of him. There was no time to tie this one properly, so they would just have to chance it.

"The skin is going to tighten when I insert the other one and we don't want it to pop out. I may need to make another incision. You just hold it and keep out of my light."

Voirrey moved carefully to the other side of the cot.

The wound was bloody, the swelling flesh threatening to hide the barb once more. She inserted the second scoop and blood oozed out, obscuring the dark shape lodged beneath. Biting her lip, she slid the scoop deeper, feeling her way as she stared fixedly at the billowing tent flap.

Inry was breathing fast, watching Voirrey for instruction.

Feeling the scoop firmly anchored beneath the arrowhead, she knew she had it. She eased the instrument from Inry's hand. The woman backed away, hugging her stomach.

With eyes set in concentration, Voirrey worked her tools like a knife and fork trying to exhume some stubborn bone from dinner's meat.

"Quick, get me some rags!" she called. A gush of fresh blood coursed the man's shivering leg as the arrow head came free, flicking upwards and thunking into the dirt.

Inry ran forward, pressing boiled rags awkwardly into the wound.

Voirrey plunged her hands into a bowl of salt water and reached for the urn.

"Okay, ready?"

Inry removed the rags so Voirrey could cleanse the wound.

Patting the area dry, Voirrey took up one of the last remaining poultices, dipping it in honey. She pressed it into the mangled hole and held out her hand for bandages.

Inry passed her a small roll and she started wrapping. "More,

more, over there, pass them to me," Voirrey instructed. The blood was coming faster than she hoped. She almost swore, her hands shaking as the man writhed on the cot.

Just then, a body fell into the side of the tent, almost collapsing the structure. Men shouted, and Voirrey held her bloodied implements aloft in a defensive crouch. Inry ran to her side, leaving the man helpless where he lay.

Moments later a panting Avishaen stuck his head in. "Sorry, one nearly got past us. The perimeter has been secured." Then, seeing the man and his bandage. "You done with him? Got a bad one in the queue."

Voirrey nodded, beyond exhausted.

As the tent flap opened and the guards took their comrade out, Voirrey glimpsed the task before her. Wailing bodies, an endless, cowering line of them.

Somehow, in her concentration she had blocked out their cries but now she heard them all. The guards tasked with the protection of the wounded darted up and down the line, doing what they could. Ma Bet was directing them, keeping things in order, but it was not enough.

She and Inry locked eyes, each knowing what the other was thinking. *If we survive this day it will be a miracle...*

Her work was growing sloppy and there were too many of them. Too many!

The next patient was half-way through the opening, a woman with a dire head wound, when an urgent cry rang out.

"Quick, get him to the front, now!"

"Get him through!"

67

AVISHAE

Zohar sat silently with the others in the crowded room. Davina was in her lap and Illiam beside her. Each of them receded to the merest sliver of self, like a cat's eye in the sun, leaving abundant space for coolness and serenity. A place where they might wait in infinite patience for the hours to pass.

For the Maglorean storm to end its rain of blood and drift on out to sea.

Illiam squeezed her hand.

She returned the gesture. *I am still here*, she said in her mind, though she knew he could not sense her so clearly now.

When she smiled, the tear tracks on her cheeks felt tight with salt, but that emotion had since subsided.

Everything was going well at the Main Gate until Maeryn had started with the stone. One minute, Zohar and Illiam were among the crowd, the next they were staring into each other's eyes, the dark wind erasing everything. They gusted together as if made of vapour, as if plunged into a dream. Into each other they flowed, just as they had done on that fateful night on the hill. And with Illiam's spiritual caress, Zohar attained that bone-deep knowledge of him. Felt herself expand into him, oblivious of the world and its goings on. The desire to intermix with him was so insatiable, so blindly intense, that, if anything, it was stronger than the first time. Now, the horror of her brother's death was not the only force that connected them, drawing and repelling them in turn. This time, his soul became a shelter and she felt herself filled up. There was nothing beyond–no sense, no time, no reason to fight or flee or save. No need for anything.

The guards told her afterwards that they had stopped mid-sentence, staggered toward one another and had fallen into a tight embrace. When they did not respond and would not let each other go, the guards had lifted them, stuck together like conjoined twins. They had been taken to the shelter, as planned, and Elspeth had stroked their skin with blinding stone, gently separating their bodies until they returned to themselves.

Maeryn suspected something like this would happen, and that was why they were not permitted to join the fight. It was well that she was here with Davina. It felt good to comfort her, and to see the other children–the old men and women of Avishae, the infirm and the weak of arm–all here with her, under her wing. She smiled quietly to herself, amazed that such feelings were accessible to her at a time like this.

Illiam met her smile and kissed the side of her head.

We will wait, and when that door opens, it will be our time to give what we can.

The door opened with a clunk, and many of those sleeping awoke with a start. Zohar sensed the redness of the outside leaking in, stirring their senses. She stood, looked at Illiam and took his hand. They must be the first to emerge.

Guardsman Elis stood in the doorway, bloodstained and filthy, the tight expression he wore visibly relaxing as he crossed the threshold to meet them.

"Tell us," Zohar managed, feeling waves of sickness from the breach in the shelter.

"We have beat back the Magloreans and victory is assured," he exhaled, staring past her with longing, distracted by the calmness in the room.

Zohar knew what she was expected to do next but had difficulty working against her natural inclination to remain in the shelter.

"It is safe above? In the Skalens' House and in the village?" she asked, feeling Davina grasp her skirt.

"Aye, it is. There may be stragglers north of the mountains but they are in retreat. Rayhmer is dead and they will not persist without him," he said.

"Good," Zohar said, the wonder of this news leaving her somewhat lost for words. She needed to show her usefulness now but was finding it difficult to rouse her sense of urgency. "Illiam and I will clear the shelter and make room for those who need it."

"Your father sent me ahead of him. Do not be alarmed, Zohar. He received a wound but our best healers are up at the camp with him. Your mother is alive, down in the valley, with Maeryn and the Greslet girl. There are many more to be accounted for, but we will commence the tally when the dust has settled."

"Very good, Elis," she said, not daring to ask about Voirrey in front of Davina.

Elis nodded and went out.

Elspeth, who had been waiting outside the door, looked ragged and tense, as did the group of assembled guards stationed there. Zohar caught Elspeth's concerned gaze as her eyes darted between her and Illiam.

Zohar raised her voice up. "Victory has been won. And now we must return to our homes, thankful to those who fought for us. We who sheltered here must devote ourselves to the care of those who shed blood in our name. It is our duty from this day forward, and for the rest of our lives. Give thanks to Velspar that this is your gift to give."

A chorus of soft voices praised Velspar and the clean uninjured came shuffling out, all in a line.

Zohar escorted them up the stair, their quiet procession gathering guilt as it emerged, the true devastation of the day growing apparent.

A crowd of men and women, filthy grunting with pain, filed past, making their way into the cool chamber they had just left.

Both processions averted their eyes and kept a solemn distance.

Davina would not leave her, and Zohar held the girl to her chest to stave off the judgement of the returning townsfolk. When her arms grew tired, Illiam held her, and between them, they arranged the population of the shelter into groups on the hillside. Those who could walk, those who needed a cart, those who could wait, and those who could help others now that the danger had passed.

Now and then, Zohar glanced over at the smoking bell tower, finding it difficult to believe that it was safe to return.

There seemed a steady stream of injured emerging from Baden Forest and she still had not received a full report of activities there. Her father was injured, but she did not see his face among the hobbling wounded. It would be safer not to move him, she reasoned. But why had her mother not come?

Zohar scanned the faces distractedly, looking for people she knew.

She could see figures gathering about the public cairn in the distance and realised she had stopped moving.

Illiam came up beside her. "I just heard from one of the men that your mother is down there. She wants the bodies of the dead to be brought down to the valley." He rubbed her shoulder. "I think she is okay. You should go to the Raeburn camp to see your father, I can manage things here."

She felt relief at being allowed to go, but an equal desire to remain close to Illiam, to never be apart from him.

"I feel what you feel," he said meaningfully. "It will hurt less as the power of the stone subsides. I will be here when you return."

Zohar nodded and as she left him; Davina's eyes followed her.

She forced herself onward, approaching the nearest guard to get her a horse. She rode blindly, the wind stinging her cheeks, running against the current and off the main track as the wounded kept coming with their makeshift slings and bloodstains.

When she made it to the camp, the true horror of the attack struck her. Rowan's watchtower lay smashed on the ground, the perimeter fence in tatters. Doors and roofs were hacked apart, belongings strewn about, and everywhere, the injured.

Slowing her mount, she stared at a series of injured men who did not have anyone attending to them. In shock, she realised that they were dead and looked away before she could recognise them.

Just then, she caught sight of Guardsman John, flush-faced, carrying a bloody sack. There were guardsmen everywhere, and she had to struggle through the darting bodies to get to him.

"John!" she called, but he didn't hear, distracted as he was by the business of tying the sack to the saddle of his restless stead.

A faint voice caught her hearing. "Cousin." And again, she heard it. A voice like Edith's but so toneless that Zohar feared to turn around.

Through the milling crowd she saw Edith sitting utterly still atop a pile of logs. Edith held up her palm in greeting, moving slow, her face ashen and unsmiling.

Zohar ran to her. "Edith, what happened here? Are you hurt?" There was a bandage covering her eye and dark blood all over her.

Edith shook her head.

Zohar reached out and touched her knee, which was the closest part of her within reach, holding her hand there.

Edith's face cracked, her good eye swelling with tears. "Rowan!" she wailed, looking in the direction of his watch post. She clutched her hand to her chest as if to staunch the pain.

Zohar released her palm from her knee, watching sorrow break on Edith's face, her pain so consuming that there was no room for words.

Climbing up the side of the wood pile, she sat beside Edith, hanging her head.

When Edith's tears subsided, she sniffed, wiping her blotched face with her sleeve.

"Your father is here," she said, finally, meeting Zohar's gaze. "I'm sorry. I should have told you that from the first."

Zohar started shaking her head but Edith had already started down the side of the wood pile.

"I'll take you," she said. "He was set upon just outside the camp and was brought here soon after. Landyn told me to shoo everyone off but now they have guards helping with that. Voirrey's been in and out, and Skalen Inry has been helping her with the injured."

Zohar followed Edith to her grandfather's hut, terrified at what she would find.

Now that she looked properly, she could see the ring of guards stationed there.

At the sight of her, the guardsmen parted, and Edith hung back, the small abode already crowded with helpers. With more than a little trepidation, Zohar entered the dim room with its confusion of smells and memories.

Her father's waxen face and bared chest seemed to glow against the dark bedhead. It was exceedingly strange to see him there in her grandfather's bed, a patchwork blanket on his knees.

Voirrey dabbed at small cuts on his arms and Zohar felt herself relax thinking that it was only a couple of flesh wounds. That was until he saw her and tried to speak. He doubled over in pain and gasped for air, the movement causing a spreading stain to form on his bandages.

"Father!" she whispered and rushed to his side.

Patiently, Voirrey helped him into a position where he could breathe and be still, though his eyes remained on Zohar, his dry hand grasping hers.

Zohar could not ask Voirrey or the others how bad it was. Not in front of him.

"I'm here, Father. I'm here. Mother is alive." She glanced at Voirrey. "And Davina is safe with Illiam."

His eyes fluttered closed in thanks.

Zohar knew her father appreciated those around him but had never been comfortable with her grandfather, who presently stood in the corner, a harried frown creasing his face. She had not yet seen Ma Bet...

"Voirrey, could I have a moment alone with my father?" Zohar asked in low tones.

"Of course," she said, and began ushering people out.

The last to depart, Voirrey fixed Zohar with a look of sympathy that sent ice through her stomach.

The door clunked shut, and she was alone with her father, the noises from outside muffled and remote.

She smiled to hide the tear glistening upon her cheek.

His vulnerability scared her. And for the first time in her life, he could not walk away–he could not go up into his tower, or ride off to the village, or go to the Guard's barracks. All he could do was lie there and meet her with his eyes.

She examined his bare shoulder and bandaged side. Someone who loved him must witness this.

His blue-green eyes, always so distant, were constellations gathered about her. Her heart beat strangely to be seen so directly. His eyes seemed to say: *At least you and your mother are safe. I protected you, at least.*

She nodded and removed her Meridian, pushing wisps of hair from her face.

When his hands came up to unbuckle his own, she helped him, easing it from the back of his head.

She caught the smoky scent of his hair, a smell unique to him that she did not realise she treasured until this moment. His head pressed warmly against her temple and she could hear the clicking sobs starting up in his throat. This was all she had ever wanted from him, this closeness that he held back from his children for no good reason at all.

She squeezed his hand, fearing the tears would make him cough and then the bleeding would worsen. Still, she felt his wishes exuding bright from his heart. He was telling her that he was proud of her, and that he loved her, that she grew more beautiful each day.

Pain seared away the details, contracting time, making everything urgent and simple. The dirty blade that had pierced him as thin as death's narrow way. It came from nowhere, just as he was turning, the shock so deep that some part of him had already ceased, had already given itself over to the glare of the pain, the asphyxiating noise of it that continued to shake the very fibre of his being.

With some effort, he mastered his breath, keeping it shallow, making it creep in and out. His spirit trespassed in this body now, this body that leaked blood and would not follow his command.

She must get her mother, she must get her here now.

Her father grunted and began to cough, not so hard as before, but Zohar saw the wetness revive at the centre of the bandage and knew they had little time.

"Voirrey!" Zohar called, her voice overloud after so much silence.

Moments later, Voirrey appeared, slipping quietly in and closing the door behind her. Her mouth was a grim line and she went directly to Ulric's bedside, inspecting the bandage and administering Alma oil beneath the tongue.

Zohar smiled so as not to alarm her father. "Thank you so much, Voirrey. I would appreciate it if you could send a messenger to fetch my mother."

Voirrey put a hand on her shoulder and met her father's eyes. "It is already done. She will be here soon, Ulric."

Zohar thanked her and sat back down. She and her father remained side by side in grim but companionable silence. The water of his spirit moved against her. *I always loved you and Ambrose. I remember the day you were born. I remember Bethany who was taken from us because of what we did. I did my best. I wish I had done more. I wish, I want...*

...I want to live.

She listened, and it was like the ocean crashing against the foundations of the Skalens' House, lifting up its spray. *Ambrose is out there,* she thought, *my brother is out there. Somewhere.*

(*He is where you are going*). That thought she silenced, hiding it from him.

(*When you die, I will know that you are with Ambrose and that will be some comfort*). *Do not think,* she commanded herself, *be here with him.*

Her thoughts branched out, showing her father too much, showing him the depth of her love but so much more that might hurt him.

"I love you, Father," she said, to distract him from thoughts of the Great Stream, of the stone, of Ambrose and Intercessors and the dangers that lay ahead for Zohar and her mother. "Everything will be well," she said, as if shushing a baby. "Mother will be here soon."

He turned his head so she was forced to look at him. The pained look on his face was so naked, so shocking, she did not know what to do. Slowly, he moved a trembling hand to his forehead and seemed to relax.

Holding her gaze, he mouthed the words, "Forgive me."

She frowned, shaking her head as if it was a silly thing to say.

He did not smile. "Forgive me," he said, this time with a whisper of air that caught in the back of his throat.

Slowly she nodded, understanding that he was not talking about her. He was talking about the Purge, the killing of the Intercessors, of the siatka and kshidol. He was talking about Ambrose and the terrible guilt he could not release.

She grasped his hands to her forehead and whispered. "You are forgiven." She paused, knowing he needed more. "I will make Avishae all that you wished it to be."

He placed his other hand on the crown of her head, its warmth seeping through her, making her spirit quake at the thought that he might leave her.

She heard voices close outside the door, and recognising her mother's, she sat up. Her father looked expectantly, almost fearfully, at the door. In a quick movement it opened and her mother appeared, her braided hair haloed with frizz.

Zohar stood back as her mother rushed in.

"Ulric! Ulric, no..." She touched his face, her eyes roving his body–finding the dark stain, reading his face, noticing the hitching of his chest, the dark stain that hid its secrets deep in his body. She sensed the forces of mortality that did not care if she was his wife.

Zohar moved outside, into the chaos of the day and closed the door behind her.

Everywhere she looked, things were broken and disordered. Her eyes settling on the row of bodies outside the perimeter fence. Dully, she wandered toward them.

I must see them, I must know their names. They will be recorded and remembered. Their names must be recognised in the Skalens' Tally.

She saw them: the Milwain boys–Cam and Benji–and Rowan, and Guardsman Timothy, and Ma Bet. Looking at them did not help.

The Maglorean dead were there too, piled at a distance, their bodies hastily dumped. All this had happened while she hid in the shelter. This violence, this horror had pierced her father's side and had started his journey away from her. She could feel the Stream tugging at him with its dark and creeping tide. *Don't take him*, she prayed, her eyes lingering on that stubborn old woman who had teased her and made her laugh, at the young man whose vigil had ever been a ward against danger. Cold and still, unblinking. Gone.

Don't take my father. Don't take him. Please.

68

AVISHAE

HER FATHER WAS asleep when she left him, tucked up in his own bed in the Skalens' House. The sheets were crisp white, his tired face taking on a bluish tint. Dimly, she noted that the new year had begun, but time seemed to have fled this place and there would be no Festival this year.

Zohar had spent the morning with him and had removed herself to her parents' solar across the hall. She could hear Voirrey giving the Attendants instructions, Elspeth among them, for none would wish to fall short on the task of caring for the dying Skalen. These details, along with the fact that Voirrey was leaving, could not register in her mind. She could not conceive of what life would be in the home of her birth with her father gone, and with a child in her care. Davina was to stay with them for the foreseeable future, until Voirrey could make her return.

Illiam was good with children, Zohar had discovered, and that morning he had taken Davina to the Kinnon farm to play with others her own age. The Kinnon's had lost their boy Tom and had taken two orphans into their care. Zohar had to remind herself daily that there was not a person in Avishae who did not hurt as she did. Everyone had lost more than they could bear.

It seemed like a terrible dream.

She walked over to the window and looked out upon the valley where bodies lay piled like so many effigies. From here, they were as patches of mould poisoning the velvet grass. Her mother was down there with Maeryn and she had set herself the task of caring for her father. For the first week, she watched him while he slept, alert to changes in his breathing, but soon she realised that he did not need her. His malady was predictable, persistent, and capably managed by the Attendants.

As for herself, the task of watching him only made her sleepless, irritable, and vague. She spent herself on worry and that did not help anyone. She looked back at his face, wanting to warm him in the bonfire's glow. Wanting all of Avishae to stand together, bathed in gusts of sweet Alma, to burn these horrors away.

Father was asleep and did not need her, she told herself, and before she could think any further, she walked herself out of the building, past the main gate and out into the field to find her mother.

There, the insects still buzzed, the flowers still showed their gay faces to the sun, heedless of death's miasma and the deeds that had been done. Down there, countless bodies were piled about the public cairn. Dragged from the forest on wooden rafts. Pulled dripping from the Selbourne. Set on wagons and bound with ropes so they could be hauled together in groups. Already, Zohar was finding it hard to breathe.

Her Meridian helped to dull the sensations but not well enough.

Among the bodies, villagers and guardsmen worked, their faces wrapped with cloth. Guardsman Elis saw her and waved. Zohar gestured for him to come to her.

Obliging, he came nearer. "Miss Zohar," he said, looking at her with some concern. "Is all well?"

"Thank you, Elis, my father is sleeping. He is as well as can be expected." Feeling a wave of nausea, Zohar covered her mouth, and when the moment passed, she continued. "I want to do something to help, Elis. I can't just sit around and do nothing."

Elis nodded. "This work is about the worst you could choose but I will not talk you out of it. Although I think you should speak to your mother first. She and Maeryn have been arguing about what to do with the Maglorean dead. It is a problem that needs resolving." Elis looked about and after spotting her mother, pointed Zohar in her direction.

Zohar walked cautiously around the bodies, their faces all covered.

Her mother came to meet her, pinched and apprehensive.

"Father is asleep," Zohar said quickly, to put her mind at rest.

"Oh, good," her mother said, wiping her palms on her dirty apron. She looked tired. Her face was ruddy with exertion, her hands trembling from lack of sustenance. Zohar had barely seen her eat this past week. In fact, she'd barely seen her at all.

"Mother, let me help. Whatever needs doing. You've got to let me help," Zohar said. Things needed to be put right.

Her mother bit her tongue and sighed, then pulled her into a firm embrace.

"This is the horror I wanted to save you from," she whispered fiercely into her hair. "All of this. It is too much like the Purge. I can't do it again, not without your father."

Zohar didn't say anything. The stench of the bodies, the fact that the dead lay all around her, these realities kept pushing themselves into her core, making her want to run, and yet she had chosen to come here and here she must remain.

With her head over her mother's shoulder, Zohar saw Maeryn coming towards them. "Maeryn comes," Zohar whispered, and felt her mother's body tense.

They stood apart to greet the Intercessor, and Zohar felt an unexpected jolt of fear as she came close. Something in her eyes. Wild and black, and barely controlled.

Zohar acknowledged her with a wave of her hand. In the midst of such carnage, this was no place for smiles.

Maeryn reached them damp with perspiration, her breath laboured.

"It is good to see you here, Zohar," Maeryn said, glancing at her mother. "There is something both of you need to see."

Her mother stared at Maeryn. Weary, disbelieving, the skin of their last argument near to peeling itself away.

"I can't walk back down, my knees won't have it," Maeryn said, choosing to ignore the tension in the air. "It is a historic moment. One that you should share."

Her mother grabbed Zohar's hand, barely nodding at Maeryn, and the two of them started off in the direction of the Bay.

They were not walking terribly fast but as they rushed down the grass corridor that separated the Maglorean dead from the Avishaens, Zohar felt each rigid limb, each cloth-masked face, as a witnessing crowd.

The spirits lingered, and Zohar wondered if this had been the root of their disagreement.

"Where are we going?" Zohar panted, following her mother's mincing tread as she negotiated the narrow strip.

Her mother didn't answer, and as they reached the end of the line, Zohar felt a sudden freedom, a fresh gust of salt air that wanted to make her clean. She gasped, gulping the air, but it could not erase the fetid stink. The smell persisted, defiling her homeland, fouling it with violence.

Her mother trudged on through the long grass, making her way to the outcrop where she and Ambrose used to visit, just for the view. It was the highest point along the coast aside from the Skalens' House itself.

There, her mother stopped, her body and whipping hair silhouetted against a glare of afternoon sun.

Zohar blinked, trying to make her eyes adjust to the harsh light that shone from the water below.

There were figures down there: guardsmen, fisher folk, a few hovering on their rafts between the bladed rocks. The two remaining Sherburn brothers, probably, and their father.

"What's going on?" Zohar said, trying to crack her mother's impenetrable expression.

Her eyes were like golden stones, shafted with shadow, her eyes fixed on the water–the far water–not where the men were.

Zohar followed her line of vision, seeing nothing.

But then she did see. Her hands shot up, covering her mouth.

Snaking. Black. It breached–her eyes straining to see, to register what was happening–the black length of it gleaming as it plunged back down.

In her periphery, her mother stood like a gilt statue.

After a breathless moment, the head reappeared, slipped beneath, moved into an area obscured by the great stone shards that littered the Bay.

When Zohar could not find it again, her eyes went scanning the shore. They were tracking it, these men.

"Siatka," Zohar whispered, disembodied with fear.

Her mother turned, eyes opalescent with tears, her face a ruin. She set her back to the sea, put her arm around Zohar's shoulder. She looked past the bodies, her anguished face upturned.

Zohar's eyes rested there, too. The Temple, white and still among the dusky pines, standing vigil. Watching dark shapes gather in sea and sky.

Velspar's servants coming home.

69

AVISHAE

Edith chewed her thumbnail as she listened, her cheeks red from the fire, though the night about them was cold.

"The siatka come for the dead. It is their purpose. Their nature," Maeryn explained. She reached for the bowl of roasted nuts that sat at her feet. She popped a handful in her mouth and chewed slowly.

Rebekah looked agitated, even more so than usual. "We have seen but three these past days, and our dead are in the hundreds. It will not work Maeryn. There is no way it can be done! Don't you understand? Everything has changed. Everything. There is no going back."

The others around the fire–Zohar, Illiam and Landyn–all kept their silence. Edith watched Landyn, feeling kinship with his pain, knowing the hollow that Ma Bet had left in his life, just as Rowan had been carved out of her, like a vital organ. He had stopped listening, she could tell. What did any of it matter now? He was an old man. He had played his role, the steadfast patriarch of the Raeburn clan, stubborn to the last, never bending to the new order, never relinquishing. Despite all that he had done, Ma Bet had been relinquished of him.

The camp was in tatters. All of Avishae was in disrepair. All were grieving and there seemed no point to any of it. They had to fight to protect themselves, but where would it end? They all waited for news of the attack to make its way to the mainland Skalens and the factions

377

of the Guard. They had either ended the Maglorean threat, or they had started a war they could not hope to survive. And so, these days were precious.

We survive. We live another day and must be grateful for it.

Edith heard Illiam mention her name. "Edith has been tending the kshidol for years without the proper rites. Things may never go back to the way they were, but does this mean we should not try? These miracles have happened in Avishae for a reason." He spoke to her with sympathy and warmth. A little too candidly, Edith thought.

Zohar was holding Illiam's hand, and as he finished, Edith saw Zohar's approval and thanks for saying what she could not.

Rebekah's expression was made yet harsher by the light of the fire, accentuating the furrow of her brow, the dark circles of sleepless-ness beneath her eyes. She mustered her patience before giving her reply. "People cannot live with uncertainty. They trust me to guide them with a superior wisdom." Her voice cracked a little in the confession that, right now, she ruled alone. "I do not know what the siatka will do. If people find their offerings washed up upon the beach they will see it as a bad omen." She dared to meet Maeryn's eyes, then, she went on, "Illiam, your generation have only childhood recollections of the Holy Ones. The rest of us have an entirely different experience. We cannot have half-rituals and failed attempts. Blood Call has a certain form that is right and complete in itself. Sea burial and sky burial, the same. To perform these rituals badly is worse than not performing them at all. And the simple fact remains that the siatka and kshidol that have returned to us cannot stomach the fruit of this battle."

Edith's irritation sparked, compelling her to speak. "With respect, Skalen, you asked the Raeburns to foster this bond with the remaining kshidol." Her pulse rose, and though she was angry, she did not dare speak more directly.

Rebekah regarded her for a long moment, the exchange finally rousing Landyn from his fugue.

"You are right, Edith," Rebekah said. "You have done good work here. All of you have done good work." She looked at her father. "All these years, you have been steadfast..."

The old man had tears in his eyes. He swallowed thickly and nodded. Edith had never known him to favour silence in circumstances like this, and it scared her. For a weightless moment, she saw herself, saw Illiam and Zohar as they would one day be. Old, and heavy with responsibility, trying and failing to explain themselves to the young.

Rebekah sighed, and not looking at her, addressed the Intercessor. "Maeryn...You do not speak. Do you understand my concerns here, or does your position remain unchanged?"

Edith watched Maeryn, her teacher and confidant, this old woman who had slaughtered the Maglorean horde and had broken Lilwenn in the process. The pendant still hung about her neck, its darkness sheathed, for now.

Maeryn stared into the fire. "I will speak," she said. "But would you have me speak here as an Intercessor to her Skalen, or as a friend?"

Rebekah covered her face with her hands, pressing her cheeks to cool her skin. "If you speak as an Intercessor, your counsel will be for the good of Velspar, and I have lost too much in my life to think of Velspar now. Speak to me as a friend, thinking of my people, my family. I will not have Avishae sacrifice anything more for the good of the mainland, or for prophecies–I need to protect my own now."

Maeryn's presence seemed to expand, and now all eyes turned to her.

"Once, all seemed lost. But now Avishae holds Siatka and Kshidol, the Mother and the Father, one in each hand. This is not something to take for granted. An old friend once spoke to me of prophecy, and at that time I asked him to imagine what the First Diviner must have felt, the moment before his holy vision. What of the moment after, when Velspar bid him to do what had never been done? To write the ritual from the beginning, to sound the first heartbeat that all must mirror in an unbroken succession... This time that we live in is one such sacred pause, and our actions now will have great consequences. We live as the First Diviner once lived, and we must mirror his faith and daring. I grant you, things cannot return to the way they were. We have discovered much in these dark years to reveal a new path for Velspar."

She paused, narrowing her focus on Rebekah.

"You worry about your son," she said, almost whispering. "You worry about those who died without the proper rites, and those who have been raised without Intercession and the certainty of Blood Call."

Edith felt a coldness about her mirrored in Rebekah's anguished face, feelings that circled and could find no release. It was the fear that despite her efforts, it had not been enough, that their souls would not be drawn back into Velspar's embrace. That Ulric was on the verge of death and that he, too, would be lost to her.

"My friend," Maeryn continued. "I have seen your son. As I have seen Rowan." Her glance pierced Edith to the core. "And dear Ma Bet..." She gave a brief smile, meeting Landyn's expectant eyes. "I have seen my brethren, and old friends from across the sea. This will come as a shock, but there are others I have seen. Do you want to know?"

The fire crackled in the charged silence.

Rebekah made a gesture of resignation, bidding her to go on.

"Domhnall, and Edlin Greslet are now one with the Stream. ...as is Sybilla." While her tone was careful, there was no emotion in it. The flatness in her eyes made the message seem false.

Landyn leaned toward her, his tone sharp now. "Do not give us riddles, Intercessor."

"I do not give you riddles, I assure you," Maeryn shot back. "The stone has shown me and the further I extend myself into its blackness, the more it imparts." She paused. "When I was young, and my brethren spoke of their visions, I thought I had seen into the darkness. I thought I had wisdom to share. I believed that no soul is too tarnished, that it is possible to draw the redness out and make all of them clean again. This truth wed me to the living." She broke off, her expression fierce. "Don't interrupt me, Rebekah. I have suffered for this vision and you will hear it. You will hear it as my Skalen, and Landyn, you will record these words. You three," she pointed to

Edith, Zohar, and Illiam in turn, "will harbour this wisdom and keep it aflame unto your dying breath."

Edith felt her heart thumping in her ears. Silence burned like the crest of a wave carrying the Intercessor's voice from somewhere far off and alien. She watched as Maeryn's eyes closed, her face and chest illuminated, her hands half there, half-submerged in shadow. It was as if the entire world had dropped away–their campfire a sun, and those gathered, suspended in darkness with nothing but the old woman's face to harken to.

"Velspar is a totality of spirit. In the maelstrom, like attracts like, and fragments form. They gather, and dance. It is just as the First Diviner described. There are tides and there are points like whirlpools where the fragments are drawn ever to the centre. In life, in a living body, this essence becomes trapped. It distils and refines. It repeats itself, grows consistent and is given a name. And yet, Velspar is always moving and seeks to be as it was in its original state. It seeks to combine and intermingle. This is the substrate that allows Intercession and sympathy. This substrate is like air because it moves gently and its tides are never stronger than the flesh. The flesh keeps anchor and does not relinquish itself."

Edith felt the terrifying familiarity of what Maeryn described. It was as if these truths tugged at her inner essence, drawing it to the surface of her skin where it might escape into the night. She thought she knew where Maeryn was going, that she would reveal the presence of Rowan's spirit, right here, pressing against her skin from the outside.

She found herself praying. *I am Edith, keep my anchor. I am Edith. Edith.*

Maeryn looked at her then, gentleness softening her gaze. "The flesh is strong. Its magnetism is greater than the other tides. But when the flesh relinquishes its hold, the spirit learns once more to dance. It divides, losing its centre. Some pieces are inward-looking and form strong tides that still speak the name they were given in life. Other pieces move elsewhere, drawn to the light of love or vengeance. I saw this in my vision and know it to be true. Redness is when we burn bright, for good or ill, and this redness is a beacon. It is the beacon of conception, without which there would be no fleshly life."

Maeryn paused. "All these years I thought I understood the nature of redness, and the reason it must be dispersed. It must be dispersed because Velspar will flow where the light shines, and there is nothing but our fragile morality to keep it from flowing ever into evil. Those fragmentary spirits that make up the Great Stream do not remember the morality of the body. They are curious and strange, their names smoothed away like pebbles on the shore. It is only in living flesh–in a spirit's life-time–that this essence can remain focused and enter into an awakened state. Those who are awake must record their visions to keep wisdom alive in the waking realm, before we disassemble and return to Velspar."

Maeryn looked around the group. "Ask me your questions and give honour to that which is awake in you."

Edith felt the air of ceremony in this moment, felt called, as the others were, as if Maeryn truly was the centre of the whirlpool around which all of them spun.

Landyn began, and it felt right that he should speak first, being the eldest among them. "You say that you saw your brethren in the Stream. You saw High Intercessor Camis, and those of the Temples of the Seven Lands. Is that right? Did you see those who died in the Purge?"

Maeryn answered. "I felt the multitude and recognised aspects of people I have known in life. I saw Intercessor Rankin of Vaelnyr like a fish beneath the shining surface. I saw Camis as if he were an autumn leaf caught on the wind. And I know what you mean to ask: what do they say now of the prophecy of the Eighth Gate? To answer this, I can say only what I suspect. I believe now that my brethren chose eternal communion with Velspar, believing it a superior state to that of fleshly life. I believe they sought to tip the balance and to bring about a new world that did not require rebirth."

Landyn frowned. "Camis told me the very opposite, that the Inter-cessors would return. That their revolution was to be won by 'flooding the many wombs,' to create a generation of Intercessors that would outnumber the ungifted."

Maeryn looked thoughtful, then spoke as if to herself. "I have sent them a different kind of flood. One they may not have anticipated." She returned her attention to Landyn. "I cannot answer your question. Either they have lost their mission along with their names, or they are waiting."

"What would they wait for?" Landyn asked.

"Brightness," Maeryn returned, and her answer landed like a stone.

"Redness," Landyn said.

And Maeryn nodded, all of them aware of the blood spilt in recent days.

Rebekah watched her father's face. "Does this mean that we have changed the course of things through this battle?"

Maeryn shook her head. "It is impossible to know."

Rebekah sighed. "Now that you have told me what is behind your thinking, tell me again what you think it means that the siatka have returned."

Maeryn took a sip from her water skin before answering. "The siatka and kshidol are not exactly like us, but they can sense the light of Velspar. They are attracted to our blood and to the scent of the Alma. But are they the only passage through which a soul may travel to reach the Great Stream? I think the true answer to that question is, no. Still, there is value in our dedication to the Holy Ones. Our rites, of yearly Blood Call and our gifting of the dead to these spiritual guides, teaches a deeper message: that we are a part of Velspar and at the moment of death we must strive to that centre for fear of the dark expanse at our back. We cling to Mother Siatka, to Father Kshidol. Those gathered to send us off are focused on this journey. These living beings create a raft for the dead with their wishes and their fears. We focus the spirit in this way. The spirit takes this journey with our help, and, when reunited with Velspar, they are plunged into the shivering dark of the Stream. They follow the light of our sorrow, the flaring of our spirits as we mourn the dead, and that is how they return to us."

Rebekah's expression was attentive, her gaze deep in imaginings as she pictured what Maeryn described.

The Intercessor continued. "You are right when you speak of the instinct we feel about the death rites of old. We must find a way to speak the hidden truth through new rites. If we are careful, and if we keep this truth foremost in our minds, we will find a way. And part of that involves forgiveness of the dead. Whatever our dedication to the Holy Ones, we must overcome this separation of the Maglorean from the Avishaen. Velspar will not be divided."

For the first time, Rebekah listened to Maeryn's plea without anger. "You are sure?"

Maeryn nodded. "The Stream cannot be polluted. Don't you understand? All return to Velspar, because it is their nature. If we curse the dead and burn them, that is us rejecting what is hateful, but Velspar will not allow the spark in them to die. No matter how small it has become in these faithless men of Maglore, Velspar will take back its gift."

Rebekah sighed and rubbed her tired face. "I will heed your counsel on this, but we must talk on it in the morning. I need to contemplate. I think we all need some time to understand what you have said. To take in what this means for those that we have lost and... forgive me, I cannot bring myself to simply accept what you have said about Sybilla and Domhnall, and Inry's son. What do you know of this? Can you honestly stand before Voirrey and little Davina and tell them that Sybilla is gone? Voirrey awaits a ship from Nothelm to bring an army to save her. What could I say to Inry after all she has suffered here?"

Maeryn tapped the sheathed pendant in her palm. "I know what I know, Rebekah. It is all I can give you. But I do not blame you for your doubts or for seeking reasonable evidence that what I say is true."

It was some small consolation.

Rebekah looked to the sky. The glittering vastness beheld all and said nothing.

"Edith," she said, startling her. "I want you to be a part of this. You alone have kept the kshidol close."

Edith felt a surge of injustice. "Ma Bet, too. I couldn't have done it without her."

Rebekah's face softened. "Ma Bet was dear to me, too. Believe me. To you it must seem that I have always been in the Skalens' House, but I grew up with Ma Bet. No doubt she is the one that convinced me to do what I thought was right–no matter the rules. You might think that I am the great destroyer of the old ways but I kept what I could from the flames. I really did."

Edith swallowed. It was true that she had never felt much kinship with Rebekah, that she had mimicked the anger of her elders without questioning its source. And suddenly, without Ma Bet around and Landyn's cunning dulled by grief, it was as if all Raeburns had become orphans, now answerable to Skalens and the blows of fate.

Maeryn answered on her behalf. "Edith does not fear the siatka. She does not fear the rites themselves but the preparation of the bodies."

A flush of recognition filled Edith's chest. She had not thought about it in such terms but Maeryn had cut to the root of it.

"Ah," Rebekah said. "It is a matter that I will discuss with Maeryn in private and we will come to an agreement about what is best. But be assured that Guardsman John has committed his men to whatever task is required. If you are to lead the Call, you will be taken out from shore on a sturdy raft to the great rock. You will have assistants who will pass the Alma wine to draw the siatka close, and you will be given a bowl of prepared offerings to toss into the sea."

Edith pictured it, feeling the elation of her gift, though her mouth ran dry at the thought of what she must do. As a child, in innocence and wonder, she had called the kshidol down. She had been too young to understand that she communed with the last survivors of what had once been a vast flock. The dark wings that had long patterned the sky, shot down in blood by the very guardsmen once sworn to their glory. The Skalens had given them new orders and so they must follow them. She had not understood the moment of forgiveness as a child, but now she must extend the hand of Avishae to the wounded siatka. She must do this, fully aware of what she asked. Forgive us and serve us once more. Guide our spirits home. And what could she offer in return? The dance of honour, the commitment of her soul, the majestic fluid that drew them near, the

Alma, that spoke of their bond, that connected them beyond rite and reason.

"When must I go down?" Edith asked.

Rebekah looked at Maeryn. "Three days, I think."

The Intercessor gave her a look of confirmation.

"Very well," Rebekah said. "Now, the night grows late, and Father I thank you for preparing beds for us in the camp. I think we should speak further in the morning when we have all had a chance to consider how best to approach Maeryn's intuitions about Maglore."

Maeryn gave her a wry look at this choice of words. Rebekah had conceded, in principle at least, to the Intercessor's wishes, but she would not accept this other knowledge so easily. Even Edith found it difficult to accept that Maeryn could identify the voices in the Stream when to her they seemed a wild cacophony.

"Bless us, Velspar, and keep us," Rebekah said.

"Bless us, Velspar," they all intoned.

Edith wearily arose, taking Zohar and Illiam to Bon and Meddy's cabin, a vacant place now where anyone could sleep. Opening the latch, she swung the door, lantern light showing the familiar place stripped of its usual knick-knacks, though some of the old smell remained. The smell of milk dripped on the floor that the old couple could not bend down to wipe away. Of Bon's pipe that he took to smoking of an evening. Of rosemary charms that Meddy used to keep the moths from eating holes in their clothes.

Edith shook herself of these thoughts, ushering Zohar and Illiam inside. Again, she was struck by their uncanny "twinness," the way Illiam clouded Zohar, making Edith feel it was impossible to ever have a private conversation with her friend.

"Goodnight," she must have said, as she closed the door to return to her own place of rest. The fire they had gathered around glowed dimly just outside the camp, her footsteps pattering in the cold dark.

She was tired. So tired. As she flopped down into her bed, she felt the static whisper of the stone. Maeryn's gift was hidden up in the rafters, as far from her body as she could place it. Only now that she was alone did she sense it clearly, though it was always there. The stone cut through spirit, and once it made its perforation, it would always have a channel through which to flow. She must remain vigilant, keep herself together, stop herself from leaking away into the black chaos of the Stream. Maeryn's words lingered in her mind, full of terrible truth. She felt them, the stone-touched, clinging to the shore of life. Maeryn had waded deep in the tide, so subsumed in spiritual blood, that less of her remained among the living. And yet her message spoke from the living part of her that endured.

Hold fast, my children. Do not let go.

70

AVISHAE

ZOHAR HELD HER mother's hand. They stood at the cliff's edge, with all the people of Avishae behind them. The presence at their back was palpable and made her neck tingle, and wish for Illiam's protection, though he was not so far away.

Below, on the shore, the Guardsmen walked in a slow procession, the dusk-coloured flag of Avishae with its Skalens' Star fluttering in the wind.

My father's spirit hovers there. My father's flesh, my father's blood in that bowl. My father's sacrifice.

Zohar felt her mother's whole body shudder.

An unearthly wind gathered about them. She had felt it coming all day. They were here, the dead, an unseen storm raining down. Zohar tried to focus only on the bowl, held by Guardsman John as Robert Sherburn cast the raft off from shore. Edith waited on the rock, hardly recognisable in her white robe.

Velspar receive him, receive my father, Skalen of Avishae, she prayed.

The wind intensified, turning her skirt into a sail, making her mother's hair whip into her eyes. Down below, Edith raised her arms and began the Call. Moments later, Guardsman John placed the bowl at her feet and the raft retreated.

He rejoined the crescent of guardsmen and turned to his Skalen, palms at his forehead as he bowed. Zohar and her mother returned the gesture and behind them, the crowd rustled with movement, released a babble of whispered prayers.

An Attendant passed Edith the Alma wine. Holding it aloft, she poured it into the sea.

Zohar fixed her gaze upon the hazy water, the flickering movement of the waves setting her heart thrumming.

Forgive my father, please. Accept him, Velspar.

Zohar's mind moved beneath the waves, to the places her brother longed to take her. To the edge of knowledge and beyond. She felt him distinctly, like a fragrance on her tongue. Her attention fixed itself to his brightness, the flash among the waves, dark and snaking, like the curls of his hair.

The thread within her that knew its way into the eternal sparked with recognition. The deep movement beneath things that was Siatka, the presence she had felt before when it had come for Sybilla's soul.

Zohar heard her mother cry out in astonishment and grief. A choking cry, "She comes!"

Zohar raised her arm in victory.

A roar went up, "Bless us, Siatka!"

The ache within her chest exploded in exultation. Smiling so hard her cheeks hurt, she felt the rightness of it. Her brother knew this wilderness and would carry her father home. He flowed in the deep water, primal as Siatka, shape shifting, unmoored and endless. A creature borne on dark wings, a creature of the Stream.

Her mother fell to her knees, and Zohar came down with her to lay her forehead to the earth in prayer.

When she arose she turned to find a sea of faces, tear-stained and wild, right there with her in this moment. She shivered.

"My father is home!" she called, for she knew they could not see with their own eyes.

A chorus in his name, their voices, so many voices, holding him aloft, drawing him up.

A Skalen she was at that moment.

One who guides the way.

71

AVISHAE

MAERYN WATCHED Ulric's funerary rite from the Temple window.

All in Avishae was aligned and this pattern would flow, interlocking like feather and scale, the length of the mainland.

The stone had changed her and these changes were irrevocable. It was just as she had warned Waldemar, and now she must become a hypocrite in his eyes.

She controlled the stone. She had mastered it, but even she could see the grim lines that etched her face, the harshness in her that made her indifferent to human suffering. Only in this state did she understand the unwavering calm of the High Intercessors.

She had risen to this position now and felt herself literally above human concerns. Though some part of her fought the prophecy of the Eighth Gate, her soul gripping the thread that bound her to the cause of the living, and she would not relinquish it.

She saw the seething crowd, felt the hot shiver that came off them like steam from a pot. The sensation was pleasurable, though her mind was elsewhere. Unlike the people of Avishae, Maeryn felt the threat of the mainland, insistent and undiminished. She had told Rebekah that she must go to Maglore with Inry and Lilwenn to secure power there, that Voirrey must achieve her mission regardless of the cost.

It was a cruel thing to seek Rebekah's sanction on the day of Ulric's death, and yet she knew that she must.

"Yes, of course," Rebekah had nodded, bleary eyed.

Please, take the Greslets from me, I cannot bear any more grief. Were the words that sounded in her heart.

"And yes, we will care for Davina until Voirrey returns," she had said. "Will you tell Voirrey that Sybilla is dead?"

"Yes," Maeryn had said. Though she had not made any promises as to when.

None of them would confront the child with knowledge of her mother's death on the basis of a vision. And no one but herself knew what Sybilla meant to Voirrey. She would fight tooth and nail to save her and this was what was needed to raise an army. Voirrey was the kind of woman who would temper her revenge, would turn it inward and grow bitter with it. No, now was not the time to tell her. Get her to Nothelm. Let her take up the reins and turn Guardsman Edric to her cause.

With Maeryn in the South and Voirrey in the North, they would bring their restoration.

Maeryn thought she heard someone on the stair below but as she descended, she saw it was only a bird that had got in. At the sight of her, it flew up, battering itself against the marble. This went on for a time, but finally, the dazed creature fell to the floor. It was breathing rapidly, its head submerged in the thick feathers of its neck as she came up behind it. Its nervous little eye searched for her, and then her palms came down. She grasped the quivering thing against her chest, making her way to the ground level and out into the daylight. She set the bird down at the foot of a great pine tree. It remained still and she set her attention elsewhere, thinking practicalities and travel plans.

The bird burst up into the sky, streaking out of sight.

She felt its need to escape, felt the smallness of Avishae like an overcrowded hut.

Once Voirrey goes, we shall follow, Maeryn thought. *I must prepare the way.*

72

PASSAGE TO NOTHELM

SWALLOWS CHITTERED along the riverbank, darting across the gleaming water. Voirrey held Davina close. "I will come back, I promise." There were tears in her eyes, a bright, desperate feeling in her chest that numbed her somehow.

The ship was waiting, a handsome vessel of polished wood with forest green sails. A Braedal boat sent by her parents to follow their letter. They had heard of the Maglorean invasion of Avishae and of Sybilla's disappearance. They knew of Voirrey's presence in Avishae. It was time she came home, after the miracle of their victory, to rid neighbouring Vaelnyr of the Maglorean influence and restore order in Velspar.

Davina had been angry with her all morning, doing her best to refuse anything Voirrey suggested. After tripping and cutting her knee, she had burst into a fit of crying that had gone on for close to an hour. Now, she said nothing. She did not fight or beg her to stay. Voirrey was holding her small body but the girl's arms had already gone slack. She had heard Voirrey say it, and now it would be true. She would stay in Avishae with Zohar in the Skalens' House. She would stay until her mother was released from Maglore. Then everything would be good again.

Voirrey kissed the girl's forehead. "Goodbye, Vina." She stood back, cupped her face in her hand. "Wave to me when I'm on deck?"

Davina nodded once and Voirrey let go.

One last time, Voirrey turned and waved at those gathered. Maeryn and Inry, Rebekah, Zohar and Illiam. Zohar grasped her mother's elbow with fierce resolve trying not to cry. Rebekah stood blankly, the shell of her body doing what it must while her spirit roved, pursuing Ulric's fading form.

Edith was back at the camp tending to Lilwenn as Voirrey had taught her. She gave tonics for the tremors, and vapours to wake her when she looked as though she would sleep for days.

Voirrey had left instructions with half the inhabitants of the Raeburn camp who tended their own wounds or those of others. And if they had none, they were to go down to the farms and the town and do what they could there.

All of them, she must leave behind. Why did she feel the pull to stay when Sybilla desperately needed her? She had abandoned her. It seemed unforgivable now.

The great green sail flapped in the breeze and finally she turned to the guardsman waiting in the small boat to take her across. Stepping into the boat, she kept her back to her friends as the man beside her rowed.

She took this journey to make Velspar safe for Davina, and to crush the Maglorean threat into oblivion. She and Sybilla would do what they had always dreamed. They would rule the North together and put all this horror behind them.

Voirrey climbed the rope ladder and when she made the deck, she waved. Tiny figures on the shore waved back. They were so small.

The deck smelt of men. Palm sweat on the ropes, and piss buckets that never rinsed clean. There were only a handful of women among the crew.

The day was not cold, but her wet shoes and splashed ankles brought an unwelcome chill to her bones. If she remained with the people below, she would simply dry her shoes in the sun. She would wiggle her toes and make Davina laugh.

But here, among the guard of her homeland she must embody all that she would one day become: a Skalen strong enough to rule without a consort, a ruler wise enough to follow unto death.

She turned, catching the furtive eyes of a new recruit staring at her. Voirrey smiled, though her look was remote, and instinctively, it seemed, she imitated her mother.

"Guardsman," she said. "Show me to the captain."

The lad bowed, then took her down below.

In the dimness, foreign odours met her, but it seemed a clean and well-kept ship, all in all.

The lad rapped at the captain's door and Voirrey prepared herself. The door creaked open and Voirrey came face-to-face with Guardsman Rosmere. Not Edric, then.

"Miss Voirrey," he grumbled, eyeing the lad with mild irritation.

"Guardsman Rosmere, I wanted to thank you for coming to my aid. How was your journey?"

He waved the young guard away. "Good, good. Fine winds. And it should be a fair journey home." He smiled, revealing a missing tooth.

They went together into the captain's quarters and sat either side of a wooden table. She prompted him for news of Maglore, of the Regencies of Brivia and Lindesal, of the latest from Vaelnyr and Seltsland. In the lantern light beneath the decks, the shores of Avishae slipped away.

For hours, they talked, and exhausted and reeling from all that she had learned, she went up to gaze upon the star-drenched sky. Seltsland was a problem. A far larger problem than she had anticipated. Maglore had an ally, after all.

Her mind ticked, now doubting if her parents would spare forces as far south as Maglore if the Askier were causing trouble on their doorstep.

But surely, she could argue for Sybilla's rescue to stabilise the North. It was not enough to have Head Guards and Regents. There must be Skalens. Yes. On that count they could not disagree. On that count, they must end the unlawful imprisonment of Sybilla Ladain in the lands of Maglore.

Voirrey watched the inky shore, trying to penetrate its darkness. And at some point near morning, she saw the lights of the Maglorean docks. Her mind scrambled for reasons she might give to bring them to land. *Sybilla!* How real her torment seemed now. How could she glide past like this?

She gripped the timber rail, her heart abraded by every passing moment, by the lights that shone there and the people ashore who must not see them.

I will come back for you, Sybilla. I will come back with a mighty force. Voirrey's prayers surged from her heart, invisible and silent, the twinkling lights like candle flames gathered in vigil.

She thought of the dead men that clotted the river Selbourne, and the many injuries Maglore had suffered.

Please, despite all this, let her be safe.

And for the first time in months, she opened herself to Sybilla's spirit. Meridian clutched in her hand, she sent her awareness out across the water, past the shore, and into the deep of the Skalens' House.

She searched for the scorching pain of injury, for the heat of anger, for the accusation of betrayal. She let those old memories arise in her mind, of the first time she had met Sybilla and the state of her suffering. Pregnant and half-mad with grief. Such pain about her and the tender heart that beat deep within.

As memories, they burned. Artefacts unchanging.

And out there, a horrible absence she could not fathom.

Do not even think it, Voirrey, she told herself, and weeping, seemed to feel Sybilla's hands on her shoulders. The scent of dark roses and ash, the dark of her eyes, her serious look. The dust of death that Voirrey had cleaned away, if only for a time.

Do not even think it. Voirrey grit her teeth.

If Maeryn could not know Amand's fate, then Voirrey could not pretend to know Sybilla's. *It is impossible to know,* she told herself.

In life and in death, she would love her, and with this thought came another hot surge of tears.

Stop it. Do not even think it. Do not even think.

She rubbed her eyes dry on the sleeve of her shirt. She set her Meridian in place, and watched those little lights die.

73

MAGLORE

MAERYN CAUGHT Lilwenn's eye. The girl was lying in the back of the cart, swathed in cloth. Her face was dim in the shade but the Intercessor saw the gleam of recognition there.

"This is the border. Right here," Maeryn said. She turned to Inry, who sat beside her. "Your land. As we pass this threshold, I want you to feel the truth of your inheritance. We do not return to the past and we do not return to misbegotten rule. Whatever we find when we enter your House, it will be yours to remake."

Inry smiled a little and nodded, squinting in the sun.

Maeryn passed her the reins. "Your turn to take charge," she said with a smirk.

Uncertainly, Inry took them into her hands and urged the horse into motion. Maeryn knew how she must feel. Once a proud Skalen of limitless power, beautiful and admired, reduced to driving a peasant's cart with her addled daughter lying silent and shrouded, the embalmed head of Guardsman Rayhmer by her feet.

The horse moved slowly, the reins loose in Inry's hands. "I can bear almost anything but I fear what has become of my husband and son. It is a terrible feeling. And whatever I do, I can't quite believe that Sybilla will have survived this. I told Voirrey...she just doesn't understand–" Inry broke off.

Maeryn put a hand on Inry's forearm, the touch making her start.

"We will rebuild, whatever we find," she said.

A tear slipped down Inry's cheek, making the fine lines around her eyes glisten.

"You thought you would find Waldemar in Brivia, but you didn't," Inry said, a note of challenge in her voice. "We could be taken by marauders at any moment and never reach the Skalens' House. We are not equipped to fight." And there was the fear again, Inry's eyes scanning the countryside.

"Skalen, I will not say that I know all. But you must put your faith somewhere and you could do worse than to have faith in me. Between us, we must have trust."

Inry glanced at her, a look of unguarded emotion that acknowledged all that they had shared.

Maeryn went on, "Both of us are guilty of red thoughts and red deeds. Both of us have failed those we were sworn to protect...and yet we carry on. I am not done with this life and neither should you be." At this point, the Intercessor turned to find Lilwenn's eyes fixed on her, and somewhere deep within, the girl was listening.

Inry exhaled a great breath and closed her eyes.

"And if anyone is fool enough to threaten us, we'll show them the head," Maeryn said with a twinkle in her eye.

Inry let out a choking laugh, caught off-guard by Maeryn's remark.

Maeryn chuckled and, when their laughter died, found herself fiddling with the pendant about her neck.

"You need not fear, my Skalen, so long as I am with you. There is no guard, nor even a hundred who could stand against me." She knew the grim truth of it.

Indeed, Maeryn had been using her subtle craft for hours now, turning wandering guards around on their heel before they reached the road, making farmhands and vagrants hurry off, searching for lost items in the brush. There were no curious children, no errands run, no messages passed from hand to hand that day.

There must be no obstacles in their path.

And so, the Intercessor, the Skalen, and the girl who decimated an army, went on to Maglore to build their world anew.

Inry remained silent, her curls jostling with the movement of the cart, her look far away. But Maeryn could see how these words steadied her, her posture growing a little taller, her bearing almost imperious, as she must have been once upon a time.

ABOUT THE AUTHOR

Sarah K. Balstrup is an Australian author of dark fantasy with a background in Religion Studies.

If you enjoyed this novel, please consider leaving a review on Goodreads or elsewhere online. Your support helps keep the words flowing and the wind in this author's sails.